Life in November

To anyone who has ever lost a friend to life, or to death.
...and to Gary and Elaine who rescued me on my own paddle board. I
hope I spelled your names right.

Life in November

Author's Note

Dear Reader,

Thank you so much for picking up Life in November.

This story is so special to me for so many reasons, and I'm so happy you're here. But before you start reading, there's a few things I think you should know about this book.

Yes—it's a romance. It's a story with a meet cute of epic proportions, about two people who were truly, in this giant, vast world, meant to find one another. But it's also a story about love and loss. It's about one of the worst kinds of loss we can ever experience, actually. The loss of a best friend.

I think there are so many ways to lose a friend—to life, or in November's case, to death. But it's this unique sort of way to become unmoored from reality, when you lose the person who loved you more than you loved yourself. Who you thought would stand with you when you achieved all the milestones important to you—whether that was beside you on your wedding day, clapping for you when you walked across a graduation stage, the person who would show up at your door in the middle of the night if you needed them, or the first person you'd want to hold your brand new baby.

A best friend can be all of those wonderful, supportive things. But they're also the person who can forgive you of anything—your self-destruction, your poor decision making, your fallibility and your utter humanness. They're the one who would pick you up off a proverbial or literal floor after you fell so, so short of the standards you hold yourself to. That's what this book is about. Falling so unbelievably short, and feeling like there's no one left to catch you.

In so many ways, that kind of loss feels like the death of being misunderstood.

This book explores death in so many facets—both with the professional neutrality of someone who deals in bones and forensics like November, but examines what it means for someone to die twice: when they stopped breathing, and then this second kind of death that can happen when you realize that, maybe, they weren't who you thought they were at all.

It deals with loss, both personal and professional, drug use, explores the lived experience of an eating disorder and related behaviours, and includes frank discussions of suicidal ideation.

But even though it's a story of grief so big it spans countries, it's a story of falling in love, finding someone who loves you in all the ways you can love a person, and finding forgiveness for yourself and for the people who've left you.

As much as I would love you to read this book, you matter more.

Take care of yourself, always.

Haley

Life in November

Chapter One

I've already met the love of my life, and she's dead.

I'm sure there are different kinds of love. Some might mean more than others. Some might be deeper, more life-altering. I'm sure you can quantify them differently. But I've had one great love. My best love.

My best friend in the entire world. We used to give each other Brazilian waxes with shitty drug store wax strips. We fought over the best nacho on the plate. She used to feed me. She would always laugh when she brought me these elaborate Greek dishes, ready to fill me up when I was crying, when I was sad. I would ask her what it was that I did for her. She said I fed her soul. It would have been easier if I was in love with her, or her with me, I think. But it wasn't like that with us. Somehow, she was my whole world just the same.

She had that effect on people, you know? People were in awe of her, probably a bit scared of her; they gravitated toward her, pulled in by whatever magnetism she possessed. I was just lucky to be along for the ride. At least that's what I thought. I loved her, I did. Don't get me wrong. But I am decidedly fucked off that she crashed into a cliff face paragliding in Thailand and died on me.

It was so typically her—so Arna—that I almost laughed when her brother Sebastian called to tell me. Actually, I did laugh. For a moment. Just a moment, before overwhelming, all-consuming grief shattered me. Shredded my heart like paper.

And now, six months later, I'm floating on a paddleboard with no paddle in the middle of the Philippine Sea. It sounds like a metaphor, but I'm serious. My paddle literally drifted away. Now the clouds are rolling in, and I'm lying on my back in a dumb black string bikini watching lightning flash across the sky.

Cue the voiceover of the main character of a show quipping, "Now you might be wondering how I got here…" But I'm not the main character of a show; I would be the side character in a show starring Arna. Somehow, I'm left with all the carnage.

Arna and Sebastian Pavlides were the heirs to their family's shipping business. Sounds made up, but it's not. I remember a time when Greek shipping tycoons were all the rage in the tabloids, becoming a part of mainstream Hollywood celebrities, for some reason. Arna and I used to pour over them and imagine her or Sebastian on the arm of someone famous. Their parents died in a car crash when we were in higher secondary at boarding school just outside of Toronto. Their mother grew up in Canada and insisted they attend school there, because she felt they would be less entitled than if they went to an international boarding school. The car crash may or may not have been an accident. Again, it sounds made up, but it's not. I remember the day they received the summons to return to Greece and continue life there with their grandfather. It came in the form of an honest to God's telegram when we were sitting at breakfast in the dining hall. Arna knocked her head back, a derisive sort of cackle came from her, and she ripped it up, proceeding to dunk the scraps in her morning coffee. I remember her looking at me, in the way she only looked at me and her brother, and reached out her hand to whisper that there was no way she would be leaving me.

We met on the first day of junior school (fifth grade, for anyone who didn't go to boarding school and exists in a weird microcosm of mostly unwanted children). I was standing to the side of the reception desk in one of the main buildings, suitcases piled around me and flipping through a book on the history of surgery for children. Arna popped her head over my shoulder, nose slightly in the air like it always was, her brown hair pushed back with a pompous Burberry headband, and she asked what I was reading.

Me being at boarding school really had nothing to do with being rich. I didn't even know how my parents afforded it. They were firmly Canadian middle class, but they never wanted me. I was sort of an accident they were stuck with, because my mom didn't realize she was pregnant until it was too late for an abortion, and it was actually a reprieve for the three of us when they sent me away each year. Sometimes I caught myself jealous, in a twisted way, of Arna and Sebastian's status as orphans. At least then I would have a tangible excuse for why I never went home over the holidays. The first Thanksgiving break, I stayed on campus, supervised by the junior school matrons. When Arna flew back in from Greece and realized I was there all alone, even though I didn't really mind, she insisted I spend holidays in Greece with her family or wherever they jetted or yachted off to. My parents were fine, don't get me wrong. They weren't abusive or cruel. They just had their own lives that I never really fit into. They still called me on my birthday and always extended an obligatory invite to whatever country they were visiting during the holidays. I would go sometimes when I was younger, and then for a brief period when I entered adulthood, but it was just so awkward, and I usually spent my time wandering the streets alone, texting Arna for recommendations, because there weren't many countries she hadn't been to. So, we became a few-phone-calls-a-year family, and that was fine for all of us. I was practically a Pavlides, anyway. At least in all the ways that mattered.

The day Arna died, at least in my world, was a Wednesday. November 5th. It's not what ended up being reflected on her death certificate because of the time change, but that's when she left me. I was in my tiny office at the dental practice where I worked. Cut vegetables were arranged just so in front of me, not touching, perfectly sectioned into thin slices and in the order they would be consumed, when my phone rang. Sebastian Pavlides' face appeared under his name, his head tipped against the forehead of his partner, Jace. Where Sebastian was like Arna, all dark hair, brooding features and olive skin, Jace was eyes that put the blue tiles in Santorini to shame, and golden blond hair that was straight from a shampoo commercial. I didn't really hear from Sebastian much, certainly not by phone. And in retrospect, I should have known something was off—an intuition like a tingle in my spine, but I was too focused on the fact that a seed was stuck to the inside of one of my peppers. I was so sure I washed them all off. Things like that had been following me around my whole life, since I was a little kid, way too little to be concerned about the shape and size of my food, the caloric intake, the texture, and the fat in it. Our boarding school nurse sent me to an outpatient recovery clinic when I was fifteen. Arna came with me every day and waited outside my sessions, flipping through Vogue

Greece—shipped in from her grandfather, a formidable man they called Pappous—or doing homework until I graduated in the spring. But my food rituals had never really left.

But when I picked up that phone, when Sebastian told me she was dead, smashed into and then ultimately scraped off a cliff face somewhere in Thailand, the thought of the seed sticking to my food, encroaching where it didn't belong, was instantly washed away by the tsunami of grief. For the first time in my life, I wasn't staring at the order of my vegetables, inspecting them with my fingers and eyes before I ate them, ever so conscious of the band of my scrubs against my stomach, or the brush of the fabric against my thighs. My mind, my world went quiet. And I was pretty sure it would never be loud, or lively, or joyful, again.

The last time I would ever see her, Arna somehow looked like a doll. The entire flight to Athens, I couldn't stop picturing her exposed mandible, constant rumination on the fact that if she went face first into the cliff, she might have actually scraped all her skin off. And because of my line of work, I knew exactly what a mandible looked like. But she didn't. She looked like a perfectly made-up version of who she was in life. I wouldn't have been surprised if Sebastian, or their grandfather, paid for post-mortem reconstructive surgery. Arna would have approved. She was really fucking vain.

The Pavlides family were traditional, and the wake was held in their family home in Ekali, a suburb in North Athens. Her coffin was in the incredibly grandiose front entranceway, facing the door, surrounded by dripping taper candles. People were expressing their grief in a way that would never feel normal to me, an inhabitant of a home with emotional distance so vast it could stretch longer than the Mariana Trench. Sobs and sounds of utter despair echoed through the hall, with people leaning down to kiss her one last time. I sort of just stared through blurred vision, reaching out to touch her face and then snatching my hand back at the last second. I was worried if I touched her, I might disrupt whatever wax was surely covering her exposed jaw. I didn't remember much of the funeral that followed. As her best friend, Sebastian demanded I participate and carry her to the church—just that I trailed beside her casket, one hand draped across the crossbar on the side. I didn't really lift anything at all, because there were nine more members of her family, all male cousins, doing all the work. I felt awkward, uncomfortable standing there, trying my best to blend into the cultural display of reverence in grief and death happening around me.

The rest of the service passed, surrounded by slowly dimming candlelight and wisps of smoke as the white tapers melted away. There was kneeling and singing, praying and grief reverberating against the thick stone walls of the church. I should have paid attention, held my gaze on her body for as long as I could, and taken in every moment she existed above ground. But I didn't.

And then I was back home, sitting in the dental practice I worked at, scraping plaque off teeth, and using the tiniest tools to fix the imperfections people were either born with or gave themselves. My world continued to be quiet, desolate, even. I still cut my food just so, followed all my carefully cultivated rituals that were safe and comfortable for me. I still went to my spin class at five every morning before a day full of those tiny tools, the whirring of small drills, and the sound of suctioning more saliva than most people would be comfortable with.

In a bitter twist of irony, or fate maybe, Arna's face was splashed all over tabloids and entertainment magazines, some even going as far to suggest that perhaps it wasn't an accident but some poorly executed attempt to extort billions from her family. If there was any noise at all, any silent whir of the cogs starting again in my brain, it was beaten to death with a hammer as soon as I saw those magazines anywhere, much like I imagined Arna's face to have been by the cliff. But the most silence, the heaviest silence, came when I was walking up the steps to my townhouse one night after work. I was still wearing my scrubs, with a nasty spurt of blood down my chest from a root canal that went wrong, when I saw it. A box I recognized and knew like the back of my hand or the map of a mouth. I could describe all parts of it, even the torn left corner, like I could tell you the steps of removing the mandibular second molar, as it sat on my front porch.

A card was placed on the top, and there was my name, my dumb name, written in Arna's handwriting. *November.* For a child they didn't want, my parents had given me what you might think was a deep, meaningful or sentimental name. Turns out, it was just weird.

I jolted to a stop, gripping the pillar of the front porch with my hand, doubling over, and clutching my stomach with the other. I couldn't hear a thing. Nothing at all. Which was, of course, physically impossible. But here it was happening to me. The city stopped making noise. Toronto stopped sounding like anything. There was just the pain in my chest that made it hard to breathe, and Arna's calligraphy-esque handwriting forming the lilting letters of my stupid name, sitting on top of the box she used to store all her secrets as a teenager. At the time, those were things like condoms, marijuana, cigarettes or almost empty bottles of alcohol. The box sat on her standard issue, boarding school oak dresser. All her secrets sat under family photos and various trinkets she claimed reminded her of home. I dropped to my knees in front of it, the silence still squeezing my eardrums. I couldn't even hear the pounding of my own heart as I sloppily tore open the envelope, fingers trembling in a way that would surely stab one of my patients with a periodontal scaler.

Dear Nova,

If you're reading this, I guess I'm dead. How did I die??? I wish you could tell me. Maybe get a Ouija board and try to contact me from beyond. I hope it was magnificent. Did I go out in flames? Get killed by a rogue firework on the Niarchos yacht? I hope you're not mad at me. I would never leave you on purpose, Nov. The rest of the world, maybe. But never you.

The idea to do this came to me one night when I was in Mauritius with Pappous. I thought about you, about me, about all the living we've done together, and how all I want is for you to get everything you want in life. Unbidden. No more worries about the size and shape of your food, if the texture will be weird. I want you to be able to go to a restaurant without looking at the menu first. Maybe this is me foisting upon you what I think living is, but I worry about you. I worry about you sitting hunched over in a dental chair fixing other people's teeth because you destroyed yours.

So, I have a proposition for you. I'm assuming if this letter made it to you, I had no kids and I wasn't married. Even if I was married, I would have wanted you to have it all, anyway. You were my first love, and I'm certain, even though ours is a purely platonic love, yours would far surpass anyone who shackled themselves to me, anyway. I would be content to spend the rest of my life with you. So, if I am married, so sorry to my unfortunate spouse—everything is going to you.

All my shares in Palvides Inc., whatever is left in my trust (because God only knows how much I've spent of it by now), and anything else I own is yours. This will probably come as a surprise to Sebastian and Pappous. Seb will understand. Pappous, who knows. I suggest you ignore his calls for a while until he settles down. But not to worry—when all is said and done, you can go back to your dental chair, extract and perform root canals, and identify dental records to your heart's content. You don't have to take up the mantle of my oh-so-important position in Palvides Inc. You can sell your shares back to the family when it's all over, you can give back the trust if you don't want it, but you have to do what I've planned for you. Can you go sit on that unfortunate couch of yours and do a drum roll for me on the ancient coffee table? It's time for my big reveal...

Inside this box (my secrets' box, if you recall), there are twelve envelopes. Each envelope is marked with a country, and inside there are itineraries with everything you'll need—all my favorite places, things to see, and things to eat in each country. And no, I've only listed the foods in their local names, and you CANNOT GOOGLE THEM, OR I SWEAR TO GOD I WILL HAUNT YOU. There's another envelope in there with all the boring shit: info on your new trust, the deeds to any properties currently in my possession, how to access your shares and what to do with them blah, blah, blah. I can picture your face right now, Novie, and I know you don't want to do this. But this was actually really annoying to set up with my lawyer to make sure it was executed properly in advance.

You have to do this for me, because I'm dead. I will forever have the trump card over you now, November. You can't play the "my parents didn't love me" card, and I can't play the orphan card. The "I'm dead" card reigns supreme. So, do this for me, please? I hate the thought of leaving you in this world alone. I knew you when you didn't love yourself. The thought of that happening again breaks my heart. Happy Reading.

Love eternally,

Arna

"Is this *P.S. I Love You* for best friends?" I shrieked, throwing the box against my front door.

I was alone, entirely alone in the universe now that Arna was gone, but I hoped if there was such a thing as heaven or hell, she was watching me and knew how mad I was at her. I made a point to wave both up and down as I stormed through the rooms of my townhome, throwing things in between earth shattering sobs. I couldn't be sure where she would have ended up. She hadn't been the best person in life, but she had been mine.

That's the other thing. I'm not going to pretend Arna lit up a room with her smile, was generous and charitable with her time and money. People *did* gravitate toward her, at least for a moment in time, pulled into her orbit, because they wanted to be on her good side. She was kind of a bitch, if I was being totally honest, morally gray down to her core. I was the exception to her rule.

When my first boyfriend cheated on me, she started a rumor that he had sex with someone he just met by an overflowing garbage bin under the overpass by the lake. There would have been nothing really wrong with that, but it was a less than desirable location and she really embellished the whole thing. We were teenagers, so she picked something she thought she could do the most possible damage with and ran with it. He ended up leaving school at the end of the semester, transferred to a boarding school in Vancouver. There were probably quite a few people who saw the headline about her sudden death and thought to themselves: *What a bitch*.

It's what I was thinking as lightning cracked across the sky and thunder rolled in. The paddleboard was starting to rock back and forth on the waves in a way that had me gripping the sides of it. The water sloshed over the side, biting at my fingers, and I couldn't help but think maybe I would be joining Arna wherever she was in the afterlife before long. Maybe that had been her plan all along. She always hated being alone. It would be exactly like her to try and get me killed so she could drag my soul along with her. No one even knew where I was. The storm was going to wash me out to sea, my body would start to decompose, and eventually all that would be left of me were bones. Maybe someone would be tasked with identifying me based on dental records alone, which really was the epitome of irony, because I happened to be one of the go-to people in North America for matching dental records. But I wasn't in North America, and I wouldn't be alive to match my own teeth.

Chapter Two

"Oi!"

I jerk upward, immediately regretting it as a giant splash of water washes over my legs. My grip tenses, and despite the thick rain, I've floated into some sort of little resort cove.

Those overwater bungalows you see in magazines dot the shoreline, and I'm about to crash into one, judging by the swift change of the current and the rocking of my paddleboard. Each has a beautiful deck extending from them, complete with some sort of miniature infinity pool and even a hammock suspended over the water. I imagine it would be a really nice place to lay in solitude and read the International Journal of Oral Science or catch up on any special issues on forensic odontology. But the closest bungalow looks like it's seconds from being swallowed up, alongside me and my shitty paddleboard, by the ocean. And there's a shirtless man standing on the deck, peering down at me.

"You right there?" he calls, his voice thick with a British accent I can hear, even over the wind.

He's kind of hard to make out, looking somewhat like a shapeless blob holding a beer bottle with what looks to be soaking wet, dark hair matted to his forehead.

I grip the sides of the board, my wet knuckles stark white, and I push myself up to rest on my calves. "I don't have a paddle," I offer uselessly, raising my voice to cut across the sounds of the storm. "I, uh, lost it. I don't really know what to do. I'm kind of stuck."

"Bit of a bind, then." He crouches down, propping up his arms on top of his knees, beer bottle still hanging casually from his fingertips.

I'm close enough now to see that a tattoo takes up one of his shoulders, moving down his bicep and stops just short of his forearm, but I can't see what it is through the rain. "Lay down and paddle with your hands this way. I'll lift you up."

Hesitating to let go of the sides of the board, lest I be knocked off by a rogue wave and become nothing but a mandible in the silt of the Philippine Sea, I float aimlessly for a moment, doing nothing before he whistles for my attention.

My eyes snap up, irritated. I don't want to be summoned like a dog, no matter my current predicament of being at the mercy of the sea and his desire to be a good Samaritan. "I'm not a dog!" I shout as thunder ominously cracks overhead.

He cocks his head, grinning and revealing perfect straight, white teeth. Most people wouldn't be able to tell. Not from so far away, but I can. There isn't even any mild crowding of his incisors. I feel myself leaning forward to get a better look. No fucking way there wasn't at least one anterior tooth that was slightly turned. But he brings the beer to his mouth, obscuring my view and taking a long sip. "Funny because you're going to need to lay down and paddle like one. Can't reach you from here." He extends his arm, hand grabbing at nothing.

Seething, I carefully pry my fingers off the edges and lay my palms flat before dropping my chest down to the board. If she wasn't already dead, I would have killed Arna. This felt like it was decidedly her fault. If it wasn't for her, I would be at home, using those tiny precise tools I loved so much to fix teeth. Or, maybe I would be in court matching a bite mark to a dental impression, or taking cranial measurements in an autopsy suite, where everything was quiet, and I was the best. I was not good at talking to strangers, and I certainly wasn't good at doggy-paddling against a raging sea. The water is frigid, biting at my fingertips as I sweep my hands ineffectually.

"Good girl." His voice sounds closer as I begrudgingly keep paddling, noticing the supports of the bungalow looks like they're drawing nearer.

I should take a moment to refute the patronization, but I want off this board and out of this water, and then I'm going right back to Toronto. Fuck this and fuck Arna's dumb quest, but his hand extends in front of my face. There are numbers tattooed below each of his knuckles, covered by a tiny dusting of dark hair. Some are clearly older than others, having bled or faded slightly into his skin. Except for the one on his pinky finger. It's new, still raised off the skin just a bit. The number twenty-two. Craning my neck, I peer upward at him.

I can see his teeth clearly now, despite the rain pelting us. They're perfect to the naked eye, but I can tell one of his incisors is an implant. It's very well done. Those teeth that look like they belong on one of the models you practice on in dental school are framed by two full lips. The top one has a scar just above it on the left side. A square, angular jaw covered in what I would say is uneven, unkempt stubble that borders uncared for. Startling gray eyes look down at me, and early lines of age wrinkle at the corners. He twirls the now empty beer bottle between his fingers, that hand dangling casually by his side while the other is still extended in front of me. He looks bored, like some dumbass in a string bikini who's seconds from drowning because she lost her best friend and then subsequently her paddle isn't at all that entertaining to him.

He snaps his fingers impatiently, waiting for me to grab his hand. I place my shaking hand in his, the frozen water and high-wind combination not ideal and likely sending me down a path to hypothermia. He pulls forward roughly, his hand engulfs mine, and my board collides with the ladder that descends from the deck into the water. I drop his hand quickly, exchanging it for the wet iron of the ladder.

That's another thing—I really, really didn't like to be touched. Arna was very loving, affectionate. Her whole family was overly touchy. Constantly hugging, kissing cheeks and expressing their love in what I considered to be too much, too open. My parents aren't affectionate with me, and they never have been. They weren't terribly affectionate with one another, at least not in front of me. Arna told me I was damaged, frigid even. And she was probably right. My developing brain formed connections at a time in my life when physical affection wasn't withheld; it simply didn't exist.

My feet slip a bit on the ladder, and he's still leaning much too close to me, in my personal space. He casually rolls the empty bottle between his fingers, still crouched down, forearms resting on his knees. I haul myself onto the deck, very aware of the lack of material covering my body. The cord is still wrapped around my ankle, connecting me to the godforsaken paddleboard. But I don't care. I wasn't going to die and have my cartilage consumed by fish and my teeth slowly sink into the silty bottom.

The ironic part, aside from the fact that I would probably be needed to identify my own teeth, was that no one would miss me. Not now. No one even knows where I am. Sebastian knows I'm on a trip, some sort of Hansel and Gretel-style adventure set by his sister, but he doesn't know where I am, or where else I'm going. The only one who would have missed me was Arna.

I drop to my elbows, legs still dangling over the ladder, not caring that my ankle is being tugged violently by the cord and the paddleboard that is seemingly being knocked into the supports of the bungalow. My hair hangs in cold clumps against my neck, and lightning cracks across the sky. I flick my middle finger upward, salty lips moving to mouth the words *fuck you* to the sky. But again, there was no guarantee that's where Arna ended up.

I jerk upward, the feeling of an overly large hand wrapping around my ankle. Mr. Perfect Teeth abandons his empty bottle and pulls at the wrap securing me to the board from around my ankle. My thigh muscle twitches at the contact, but his hand was already moving on, deftly wrapping the cord around his palm and hauling the board up.

He looks like something straight out of a movie—impossibly broad shoulders tapering down to reveal muscles I didn't even know could exist in your back. I can name all the muscles in your face and neck without even having to think twice, their names roll through my mind on a steady mantra, and I'm pretty comfortable with gross anatomy in general, but those have to be brand new, undiscovered muscles, because no one looks like that. The rain literally looks like it's being repelled by the stacks of taut back muscle, just ricocheting off him.

The paddleboard drops to the deck, and he towers over me, that same tattooed hand extending to me. He jerks his chin toward the board. "I'll drive you back to wherever you came from when the storm passes."

I have no idea where I am now, or how far I drifted after I lost my paddle.

I was too busy re-reading the second letter from Arna in my mind. Because I had sat in my own bungalow, not dissimilar to this one, eyes tracking words that were somehow familiar and foreign all at the same time. Reading and re-reading obsessively until the edges of her stupid monogrammed stationery were soft and worn. I was thinking about what she said, the fact that she was just gone, and then I remembered what food she instructed me to eat. My breathing started to get shallow and difficult, and when I dropped to my knees on the board to try and regulate it, I dropped the paddle, too. And then I just sat there. The hard fiberglass biting at my knees, and I wondered what the hell Kare-Kare was, and how many other things I didn't know about Arna.

My baby Nov,

Welcome to letter number one! Or, number two, if we're counting the other one. I like to consider that one as more of a prologue, a prequel even.

Has the initial shock about my death worn off? I'm assuming yes and no. Yes, because you're stoic, cold and unfeeling to anyone but me, so your exterior is back to normal and you're flossing teeth by day, identifying bodies by night. And no, because you're stoic, cold and unfeeling to anyone but me. I hate that I'm dead. I'm sure wherever I am, heaven or hell, my shock hasn't worn off, either.

I deserved better. You deserved better. I want you to live the life you deserve, Novie. Not some desolate sad one where you count almonds and spend way too much time in people's mouths.

Which brings me to stop number one. The Philippines. I stayed at the place I've picked for you, you know. It was beautiful. Do you remember the summer after second year? I told you that I was interning in the mailroom at Palvides Inc. You were in some sort of weirdo biology summer school. I'm not sure you ever bought that lie. I wouldn't have been caught dead in the mailroom. But I was actually there, where you will be. Living in the Philippines. With this girl and guy I met there before my internship was supposed to start. The three of us were together, a relationship of sorts, that summer while we worked as paddleboard guides for rich tourists.

Don't be mad I never told you. I wasn't worried about you judging me. I just didn't think you would understand why I left the mailroom to sit on a beach. You were always too smart for this world. Oh, and you need to try Kare-Kare.

I'd say don't kill me, but I'm already dead.

Yours in life (and death),

Arna

Fingers snap in my face. My upper lip pulls back, revealing my own teeth. They're only straight like his because of braces that my parents paid for in a weird fit of gallantry when I was in junior school.

"Anyone in there?" he asks, voice dry. "Waves knock you a little hard?"

"I'm fine," I answer, pushing myself up and pointedly ignoring his hand.

"I've got towels inside." He tips his chin again, this time toward the open door of the bungalow. His gaze drops, raking over me, one eyebrow rising on his forehead.

I try to cover up and fail, my folded arms doing nothing to shield my exposed skin, save for my practically non-existent cleavage. The string bikini isn't doing much for me either, my stomach and legs on display. It's not even something I would usually wear, but it's all I had.

My teeth start to chatter. Without waiting for an answer, he snatches the empty bottle from the deck and leaves me behind to continue to be pelted by rain and gale force winds. I hesitate for a moment before following.

Chapter Three

I've spent enough time around murder victims to pause and wonder if I'm going to end up dead after all—teeth and face smashed in beyond any possible recognition. It happens. I've seen it. But I walk through the open door behind him anyway.

His bungalow *would* have been nice. Definitely more than I could have afforded before Arna foisted her money on me.

There's even one of those glass floors in the living room. A giant, marble table sits atop it. Which is also probably nice on a good day. But this clearly isn't a good day. It's littered with empty beer bottles, labels peeling at the edges, like he's been worrying at them with those tattooed thumbs. The counter in the kitchen isn't any better, and beyond that, through open glass doors, I can see that the bedding on the giant king bed is twisted into a ball, rumpled and unmade.

"It looks like a frat house threw up in here," I say, trying to sound like I'm feeling something other than what I am, which is entirely unmoored. But my teeth keep chattering, and the whole thing comes out punctuated and stilted.

He turns, one hand extended into a closet door in the long hallway, lips pulling back into an incredulous smile. "You could start with thank you." He looks at me, the grin turning wry when he cocks his head. I stand there, resolute and shivering as he pulls out two huge white towels before continuing. "No? The insult will have to do then."

I watch in abject horror as he starts toweling off, not a care in the world that a stranger stands feet away. It turns out there aren't just muscles on his back, either. They're everywhere. His entire torso tenses and pulls as he dries off his head before shaking his hair like a dog, slinging the towel around his shoulders. He had been imposing out on the deck, staring down at me, framed by the storm and my own runaway thoughts, but nothing compares to here. Where he stalks toward me, one tattooed hand casually holding the second towel out to me, head still cocked, and gray eyes bordering on predatory. It's like being alone in a room with the kind of guy your parents warned you about, if you had parents that cared about that sort of thing.

I uncross my arms, one tentative hand reaching out. "Thank you," I offer flatly, winding the towel around my body as quickly as possible.

"Are you going to tell me your name?" he asks, still grinning before taking a measured step back, reaching into the sink where I hear the telltale clink of ice.

My lips pull back as I watch him bring the unopened beer bottle to his mouth and twist the cap between his teeth. "Don't—you shouldn't do that." I can practically hear the scrape against his teeth—the sharp edges of the cap cutting up his enamel. "People think teeth are bone, but they're a mix of soft and hard tissue. Enamel is the hardest substance in the human body, but it's a dead one. Your teeth aren't living, and they can't repair themselves once the damage is done. Don't do that."

Cocking his head again, he holds the neck of the bottle loosely, and I watch him roll the cap around his mouth with his tongue before he bites down on it with those perfect front teeth that he clearly doesn't deserve before spitting it in the sink. "You a dentist or something?"

"Yes, and I probably would have refused your help if I knew you treated your teeth with such blatant disregard."

That wasn't true at all.

I spent a lot of my weekends doing free dental work around the city, mostly in shelters and on mobile public health units. I loved giving people their smiles back. I didn't care if they pulled their teeth out themselves. There was nothing—and I repeat—nothing, like watching someone's face light up when they smiled at themselves in the mirror and liked what they saw.

"Only mental cases are dentists," he offers, both his eyebrows rising. I watch while he takes what seems to be the longest sip in the history of the world. "Ethan, by the way. When you paddle home to whoever's waiting for you, you can tell them the name of the man who saved you from certain death."

There was no one waiting for me, and there never would be again.

"November." I smile, but it probably looks more like a grimace. Arna always told me I was very off-putting, and that's why I never had many friends.

"November?" he asks, the bottle pulled back just before his lips. "The tenth month?"

"Eleven. The eleventh month." I raise my eyebrows, correcting his math while tugging the towel that's now a dress tighter around me.

His lips quirk, and he tips his head again, leaning against the counter. His eyes narrow for a moment, like he's counting the months out in his head. His lower lip juts out, and he nods thoughtfully before continuing. "Guess I've been on the lash for a while. Your parents big G&R fans?"

I know he means Guns and Roses. November Rain is one of the most titular songs of all time. There isn't a single joke I haven't heard about my name. The truth is that my parents never cared about me, not really, and I never bothered to ask them where the name came from. I was born in September. And they never bothered to enlighten me. Arna and I used to joke about it. It was the source of her many nicknames for me. I had been Nov, Novie, Baby Nov, and Nova for as long as I can remember. After I graduated dental school, she took to calling me the most esteemed Dr. Morris. Most of the nicknames were mocking, pedestrian. But Nova. Nova had been special to us both. Nova meant new. Whenever I was Nova, I could be someone else. Anyone else.

But I don't say any of that. Instead, I shrug, indifferently. "I don't know what G&R means."

Ethan eyes me, eyebrows knit and gray eyes curious. "Pint?"

I open my mouth to say no, to ask for anything else, because I know approximately how many calories and carbs are in a dark brown bottle like that.

Beer is one thing that has a chokehold on me; I can never really get over it, no matter how hard I try. But I can hear Arna whispering in my ear, feeling her fingers pressing into my shoulders while she speaks to me, the way she had spoken to me for years and years. How she used to shove cups of lukewarm, foamy beer into my hands at parties, half the liquid slopping over and making my fingers sticky. She would tell me it was fine, it was okay, and if I drank all those carbs, all those calories, I was safe with her. She would still love me in the morning, even when I didn't love myself.

But Arna isn't here. Not really. But this is her dumb adventure I had set out upon. So, I smile tightly while my middle finger twitches against my palm, ready to be waved around at her ghost again. "Sure. That'd be great, thanks."

His lips quirk to the side, and he raises his eyebrows at me. "Doesn't sound like you think it's great, but I'll try not to be insulted." The tattooed hand emerges from the sink, droplets of water sliding down it, and those fingers wrap around the neck of a wet beer bottle, label soaked and peeling. Pushing off the counter, Ethan steps forward and invades my space, albeit unhurriedly. He doesn't seem like the type to do anything quickly, but his slow meander toward me has me taking a measured step backward. He cocks his head, grinning at me again before tipping his chin toward a knife block on the marble counter. "You want to hold one of those? Might make you feel safer."

"Listen. I watch a lot of true crime. Is this some sort of disarming technique? I'm supposed to fall for whatever this is? The boyish charm and attitude? Next thing I know, you're burning off my fingerprints," I snap, grabbing the towel tighter.

This. This was why Arna said people didn't like me. When I was nervous, I said the weirdest shit. Whatever popped into my brain first. I could usually see it in people's eyes, their pupils would dilate ever so slightly, and the set of their jaw would shift, and I could tell they were forcing themselves to smile politely, but inside they were probably thinking this girl is so fucking strange. And I was. I was strange. I was okay with that; Arna had been okay with that. But most other people weren't.

Ethan considers me, fingers loose on the neck of the beer bottle extended toward me. "Oh, a woman who watches true crime. Shocker. No, sweetheart. I'm not going to burn your fingerprints off. Not a terribly big fan of blood."

My fingers twitch in hesitancy as I reach out for the bottle. One hand clamps firmly on my towel dress, the other extends in space, refusing not to take the drink, because all I can hear is Arna in my ear. "Burning doesn't make you bleed like that," I say, for some unknown reason, snatching the bottle from him. I don't know why I said things like this, but I could never seem to stop.

"Maybe I should be the one who's worried. Why does a dentist know so much about murder?" he asks through a grin.

"I'm a forensic odontologist," I mutter, fingers feathering against the bottle nervously. I bring it to my lips, once, twice, three times before exhaling firmly through my nose and taking a sip.

"Don't know what that is." He shrugs, taking a lengthy sip of his own that only highlights the muscles in his neck. He has nice-looking longitudinal pharyngeal muscles. At least from the outside. Ethan raises his eyebrows at me one more time before moving into his disaster of a living room and dropping to the couch. "Might as well make yourself comfortable. Storm's not going anywhere."

I don't move. I'm uncomfortable. I'm uncomfortable most of the time. In social situations, in my own mind, and certainly in my own skin. The taste of beer is sour in my mouth, not because I don't like the flavor. Whatever it is, it's nice, actually. But it burns like acid on the way down, because I can't remember the last time I drank a colored liquid that wasn't black coffee, and I could feel Arna's hands on my shoulders and her voice thick in my ear, that she's proud of me. To take another sip. That's what this had all been about. Living. Living life in all the moments I existed in. Not just the ones that were innately comfortable for me.

Becoming a forensic odontologist takes you down a weird, winding path. There's lots of additional coursework, hours in the field, certification exams, and generally, a longer time spent with bones and dead bodies than most people are comfortable with. But I liked the silence. The stillness. It made my mind stop, and I was never wondering what the bodies in front of me were thinking about, looking at when they looked at me. Because they weren't seeing.

Arna spent a disproportionate amount of time in therapy, mainly because she thought it was what someone like her should do. An heiress. Richer than God. Someone like that should surely have endless problems. But I think she mostly used the time to talk about me. Because she knew I would never go, even though a therapist can't diagnose someone they've never met. She went anyway. So she told me things, tried to make me understand myself. See me in the way only she saw me. That I wasn't weird, my child brain had just formed weird connections, because it was starved for love.

It's why I found comfort in people who weren't alive to show me anything different, she claimed. Why I liked to spend my time in people's mouths, because they couldn't talk back, couldn't hurt me, and neither could the dead. It was why I liked giving people their smiles back, why I liked doing identification work. I liked giving people back to their families, their loved ones. It was an entirely different kind of fulfilling—to be the person responsible for the reason that two parents know what had happened to their child. Watching a display of love I would never, ever receive. It filled that part of me. Or, so Arna and her cabal of therapists said.

"You alright?" Ethan's voice sounds, not disdainful, concerned maybe. Weirded out, more likely than not. It's a nice voice. Deep, kind of rough. More pronounced by the accent.

But as I look at him, gray eyes clouded over and eyebrows knit, tattooed fingers rolling the neck of the beer bottle with expert grace, I shrug. Because even though it was a surface question, I'm not alright.

I would never be alright again. So, I say exactly that. "I'm not alright. Because I'm weird and awkward and have no filter, and no one will ever love me again."

To his credit, he doesn't balk, and he doesn't get the usual forced smile of politeness or awkwardness when things like that pop from my mouth. It twitches instead. "Look, I didn't mean to make you uncomfortable. I'll get you back to wherever you need to be as soon as the storm clears."

I say nothing but tighten my grip. I was usually the one making people uncomfortable. I can't think of anything else to do, so I took another sip.

"What were you doing out there?" He runs a hand through the still-damp curls. "You uh...said you'd never be alright again. Add that with the scene out there; I'm just wondering..."

"If I was trying to kill myself?" I ask plainly. One bare foot rises, pointing forward, testing the possible move to sit on the couch opposite him. "No. I meant it. I lost my paddle. I got distracted, thinking about my best friend."

Whether or not he believes me, he nods, like this is a perfectly normal thing that happens to people. "They waiting for you back at wherever it is you came from?"

"She's dead," I offer, voice flat, blunt and void of anything. Because if I can do one thing, it is to assess death neutrally.

My toes finally brave the floor to propel me to the couch. When I say things like this, people get a look of pity in their gaze that I can't stand, or they try to tell me they understand. But he doesn't. He just keeps staring at me.

"When'd she die?"

"In November," I start, watching his lips pull apart, like he couldn't believe that. "I know. The irony isn't lost on me."

"How'd she die?" This is the most anyone has asked me about Arna since I went back to the dental practice. I tip my head, pausing at his bluntness. Most people would have been put off by that, in the way they were put off by me. But I feel some of the tension ease out of my shoulders. It's a question I'm comfortable with.

"Paragliding in Thailand. Completely fucked up by a cliff face. Like most things in her life, it sounds made up, but it's not."

His eyes widen a fraction, distracting me from what I should have known was going to follow, because Arna's death had been front page news.

But I'm busy thinking back to freshman biology, picturing Arna openly asleep in the lecture hall beside me when we talked about recessive genes, before we started talking about eyeballs. People with gray eyes have little-to-no melanin in their irises, but they have more collagen in the stroma than all other eye colors. This was a fact that I found endlessly fascinating, so much so, that I elbowed Arna awake. She hissed at me, pinching my hand before dramatically throwing up the hood of her sweater and settling back in for another nap. She didn't even need to take the class. She was a business major.

I'm distracted—by the memory, by the lack of melanin but surplus of collagen in his eyes—to realize. He's British. Arna's death took over European tabloids for weeks.

"The shipping heiress?" His lips pull back in disbelief to reveal those perfect teeth before he continues speaking. "Pavlides something. The brother...he's with that other famous bloke. Talk Show host."

"Arna." Her name tumbles from my lips, warm against them as it always is. "Her brother's name is Sebastian, and his partner's name is Jace."

He nods, full lower lip jutting out before he tips the almost-empty bottle back into his mouth. "That was all over the tabloids. Bit of a reprieve for me when she died."

"Excuse me?" I jerk back in disbelief. Arna's death is anything but a reprieve for me.

Ethan's already making his way to the kitchen. I eye the already amassed number of empties. Apparently, it's set to be ever-growing. He levels me with a look before grabbing another beer from the sink. "I didn't mean it like that. I, uh, tore my Achilles. Failed a drug test, and uh, lost my contract—"

"I don't see what any of that has to do with Arna's death being a *bit of a reprieve for you.*" My voice takes on a poor imitation of his accent when I speak. "Nor do I see why anyone in the general population would give a shit about your torn Achilles. What are you, some sort of professional athlete?"

"Yes," he answers pointedly, twisting the cap off with his hands this time. "Football."

"There's no football team over there." My features contort in rage, because I don't care who he was, and what he said about Arna, the only person who ever mattered and would ever matter to me, grates against my brain and sounds like a fucking bone saw.

Those gray eyes practically roll to the back of his head, and Ethan tips the bottle back, a generous swallow illuminating those annoying muscles in his neck. "You Americans call it soccer."

"I'm Canadian." For lack of anything better to do, and because I want to be anywhere else, be anyone else but the person without their only friend, their soulmate, the love of their life, I drain the rest of the warm beer.

"Same thing." He shrugs, eyeing me as I slam the empty bottle down on the table. It teeters slightly, bumping against another dark amber bottle with a label that's long since peeled off, rolling around along the bottom before righting itself. Disaster averted. Line of beer dominoes did not fall. "Almost knocked over my display."

"Are you proud of this display? Probably shouldn't be drinking since you just failed a drug test," I say, arching a brow. I'm being off-putting. The exact way Arna told me time and time again not to be. I should be thankful to him, this stranger who saved me from certain doom. But I'm not.

Thunder crashes overhead, followed by lightning that throws everything in the room into sharp contrast. The lights hanging overhead flicker ominously. Ethan raises his eyebrows, ignoring me and looking up at the light momentarily. "Like I said, not going anywhere for a while. I'll get you some clothes. You can get changed, yeah?"

Ethan drains the last of his beer, dropping the empty bottle on the table. He pushes off his knees, leaving me sitting there, in nothing but a now-wet towel and bathing suit, stuck in a good-looking stranger's luxury overwater bungalow in the Philippines for the foreseeable future.

Even though I know she wouldn't have predicted this, it's exactly the type of thing Arna would have loved. She would have shrieked with delight over it, thought it was the epitome of living, what life was truly about.

Maybe that's what makes me lean back against the couch and smile when I flip my middle finger up toward the ceiling, illuminated by the steady flashes of lightning.

I look like a drowned rat. My dyed blonde hair is hardly recognizable, but at least it blends with my darker roots now, because I forgot to get them done before I left. Arna always liked when I let my roots grow in. I've been dyeing my hair for as long as I can remember. But she said it looked boho-chic, like it was intentional, and I didn't have a care in the world when it grew in.

I tuck the still-damp strands behind my ears and look at myself in the bathroom mirror. I wring my hair out a few times and use the towel Ethan gave me to try and dry it. The black sweater he tossed me hangs off me, alongside the much-too-big shorts, but it's better than the bathing suit and towel.

I blink at my reflection—hazel eyes that trick people into thinking they're green, high cheekbones and pillowy cheeks with an angular jaw. Desirable bone structure, and one of the only things to thank my parents for, according to Arna.

The bathroom is much neater than the rest of the bungalow. A large, stone tub sits in the middle of the room, with a towering matte black faucet over the middle of it. The marble countertop is bare, save for a brandless, black toiletry bag that sits zipped up toward the left side of the sink. But there's one beer bottle, sitting empty in the garbage beside the vanity.

I blink once more before turning away and sliding open the bathroom door.

The sound of screaming fills my ears, and I look up, eyebrows knit. Someone's being stabbed on the television. I walk across the stone floor, coming to stand behind the couch where Ethan's draped across with a fresh beer.

Ethan looks back at me, one arm slung over the back of the couch. Alarm dots his features, and he hastily reaches for the remote across the table. "Ah, sorry about that. Texas Chainsaw Massacre. It's just what's on. I'll change it—"

"It doesn't bother me," I say, and it's the truth.

I walk around the couch as someone starts to get their arm hacked off.

"Not a bit...off to you...that some bloke you just met is watching horror movies in the middle of a storm while you're trapped in his overwater bungalow?" Ethan asks, voice dry.

"No," I shake my head, dropping down one cushion over and folding my legs underneath me. "I mean, it probably should be."

Ethan laughs, and it's sort of a bark that catches me off guard. The sound seems unused, like maybe he hasn't had anything to laugh about in a long time. "You're a bit weird, yeah?"

"So I've heard." I smile at him, and I can hear Arna in my head—barging into my room in college and turning off my television because she didn't want to hear screams coming from my room anymore, and that I should watch something else. "Are you on vacation or something?"

He looks at me, grinning, but it doesn't meet his eyes. "Exile. Like I said…bit of a pariah back home. I, uh, didn't mean anything about your friend. I just meant the tabloids. I got injured and acted like a right prat, got caught, lost my contract. Just got sick of seeing my own face everywhere, that's all."

"It's okay," I say quietly. And it is okay.

Ethan looks like I think I look. Someone who is entirely lost and has no fucking idea what to do or where to go next.

"You can use my phone, yeah? Call whoever you need to call…let them know you're okay?" Ethan's lips turn down, and I notice his tattooed thumb taps against the glass bottle, while his left leg starts to bounce up and down, restlessly. There's a raised scar there along the back of his calf, still red and angry. It can't be very old.

"There's no one to call," I say softly, shrugging like it's nothing. But he looks at me, like he knows I'm lying. "Can I have another beer?"

Surprise lights his features, but Ethan nods, pushing off the couch. I hear the sounds of the ice in the sink moments before he's back, holding out a freshly opened bottle, label peeling and water-logged. I smile at him briefly, taking it and gripping it with both hands for a moment.

"That body would be really hard to identify by traditional means," I say more to myself, but I tip my elbow toward the television as I take a sip of the beer.

"Oh, yeah? Tell me more," Ethan says, dropping back down at the other end of the couch. He rolls his neck to look at me, curiosity radiating from him.

So, I do.

Chapter Four

It seems typical that this was Arna's first destination for me, and it took me forever to decide to actually go on her quest, that I landed myself here during one of the worst storms in months, according to Ethan's Google search. But the sky is clear this morning. My feet swing back and forth over the edge of the deck, my legs bare from the knees down, because Ethan's shorts are huge. I fell asleep on the couch at some point, still wearing the giant black sweater he gave me that had some form of crest on the front. It wasn't until this morning, when I was splashing cold water on my face in the washroom, hoping that this—all of this, my life without Arna is some sort of fever dream—when I noticed there was a name across the back and a number. Barclay. Eight. Ethan Barclay. Former number eight of whatever professional "football" team he previously belonged to.

There's a dull thump behind both of my eyeballs, blood vessels surely constricted because of his shitty warm beer. But the evening hadn't been unpleasant, not entirely. Ethan spoke most of the time, asking me questions about my favorite horror movies, offering his own dry commentary on the movies while the table grew evermore cluttered with empties. And when I did speak, I said things that I would usually have only said to Arna. How you might have identified the remains of the characters after the killer or the ghost or the demon, or the whatever was done with them, things about cases I had worked on that were similar. But he just nodded along. Sometimes his eyebrows rose a fraction, but he gave nothing else away. I'm not sure when I fell asleep, but I woke up with a blanket thrown over me, and the door to the equally messy bedroom was firmly closed this morning.

The paddleboard from my ill-fated voyage sits beside me on the bungalow deck, sunlight reflecting off the too-vibrant turquoise and purple coloring. No sign of my near stranding and death to be found on the surface. It just sits here, inanimate and shining in the sunlight to mock me.

"Thinking of taking it out for another spin?"

I look over my shoulder. Ethan leans against the now open door of the bungalow, no shirt again, but I suppose if I looked like that, I wouldn't wear one much, either. His hair is messy, curls poking every which way, and his eyes look sleepy. His voice, though—it's sort of scratchy. I realized I liked his voice, his accent, last night. It's nice. But it's nothing compared to this.

"No. I'm contemplating my retirement from all water sports." I turn back, staring out at the seemingly endless expanse of ocean.

"Shame." His voice is closer now, just behind me, and I watch the muscles in his calves, followed by the ones in his thighs flex and stretch as he swings his legs out to dangle off the deck beside me. "You sleep alright?"

"You're quite concerned with how hospitable I consider you," I say with a shrug, "I slept fine. Thank you for coming to my rescue. I am forever in your debt."

"English manners," Ethan says. "I can take you back to your resort. You know where you're staying?"

I nod. "I don't think it's far from here. I couldn't have drifted that fucking far."

"Never know," Ethan shrugs, running a hand through his hair. "Contemplating the vastness of the universe can take you many a place."

"Big philosopher when you're hungover?" I ask, glancing at him sideways. His profile is striking in the light of day.

Ethan grins but stares out at the water for a moment longer, running a hand through disheveled, sleep-tousled hair. "Who says I'm rough?"

I brush my hands along the borrowed shorts, fingers running absentmindedly along the stitching of the number eight. "All the empties on the table."

"Ey," Ethan turns to me, his grin growing crooked. "Some of those were yours, yeah?"

"Maybe some of them." I smile softly at him, swinging my feet and looking back out onto the ocean.

It's sparkling endlessly under the morning sunlight, entirely serene and not at all like it was almost the scene of my untimely demise less than twenty-four hours ago.

I can see Ethan palm his jaw, scrub at his face for a moment before he pushes against the edge of the deck to stand. "Fancy a brew? Then, I'll run you back?"

I turn, incredulous, raising a hand to shield my eyes from the sun. "A brew? No, I don't need another beer, and I'm not sure you do, either."

Ethan scoffs, swinging his arms across his chest to stretch them, clearly not bothered that he's shirtless. It just highlights the various stacks of muscles and veins that are so prominent he looks like he must be dehydrated, which judging by the coffee table—he is. "You North Americans are so titchy. Brew. Warm beverage, like coffee or tea, yeah?"

"Wouldn't put it past you. No rules in exile," I say, quoting his words from the previous night.

Ethan Barclay, former soccer star, now rotting away in self-imposed exile in Boracay.

He shakes his head, eyes rolling before he starts walking backward toward the still open door. "Let me guess. No milk, no cream, no sugar. Black?"

I nod, and Ethan turns, disappearing back into the bungalow. Swinging my legs again where they hang above the water, I look back out, and I kind of want to laugh. There's a thinly veiled metaphor here. Me, without my soulmate, chasing something I'll never get back. Entirely adrift.

I don't feel like I ever got off the paddleboard.

Raindrops shimmer on the palmed awning of the bungalow. I can see them through the window of the jeep as Ethan wheels it up to the front entrance. There isn't really a road through the resort so much as a worn-down dirt path that ended up being wide enough for the jeep.

It should be weird, sitting here in some sort of vehicle that wouldn't look out of place in Jurassic Park with a complete stranger after having been stranded in his bungalow. But it's not. It doesn't seem to bother him that I haven't said much. He hasn't said much either, seemingly content to drum his fingers against the worn leather of the steering wheel, tongue occasionally poking into his cheek, taking away from the permanent, almost severe set of his jaw. He's got the type of lines people love to photograph. There's a whole area of study that focuses on lifestyle and how it impacts the human jawbone, and it makes me wonder what kind of life he's lived.

Those tattooed hands leave the steering wheel to put the jeep in park before turning the key and killing the engine. He raises his eyebrows at me. "This you, yeah?"

I nod, unsure of what either of us are supposed to do now. Things like this don't happen in real life. But, then again, neither does your best friend smashing into a cliff and leaving you a set of instructions from beyond the grave. "This is me. Thank you for driving me back and for making sure I didn't end up nothing more than a maxilla with a few incisors left in the sea beneath your bungalow."

Ethan tips his head, and his eyebrows crease. "Don't really have the fucking faintest what that means, Ten."

"Ten? What the hell is that supposed to mean?" I ask, eyes narrowing in on him.

"Ten. November. The Tenth Month, yeah?"

I feel my lip curl upward and my nose wrinkle. "Don't tell me you're one of those men who gives everyone a nickname or calls them sweetheart, and you think it's endearing because you have an accent?"

"You're a real piece of work, yeah?" Ethan shakes his head, a rueful sort of grin stretching across his face. "Thought you might find it funny. What would you rather me call you?"

"How about my name?" I raise my eyebrows at him before unbuckling the seatbelt. A white, stitched number eight catches my eye on the corner of the too-large black shorts covering most of my thighs. I'm still wearing his clothes. "If you want to come in, I'll get changed, and I can give these back to you?"

"Nowhere better to be," he says, like it's a nothing statement.

But I watch him roll his shoulders from the corner of my eye and see the way a muscle in his neck jumps, and I know it's not nothing. It feels like it might just be everything.

I push open the door and step down, still without shoes. My sandals, ancient worn flip-flops, are sitting on the deck just beyond my bungalow. I close the door and hear Ethan follow a moment later. Large palm trees, impossibly green from the unseasonal rain, hang over the winding path toward the front door. Ethan gestures for me to walk ahead of him but not before his eyes track down my legs to my bare feet. He raises his eyebrows, and I wait for him to make some stupid remark about carrying me in, but he doesn't.

We walk down the short path, Ethan behind me, and I realize I'm keenly aware of his presence just over my shoulder. The worn wooden door comes into view as we step out from under the last oversized palm; waxy green leaves still sparkle with raindrops. The keypad beside the door is such a juxtaposition that a scoff rises in my throat. I'm tempted to tip my head back and scream, yell at Arna for getting me into this stupid fucking position. I'm lucky that whoever is in charge of security at the resort decided to upgrade to electronics instead of regular keys, because if they hadn't, I would be completely fucked.

I'm a lot of things. I'm abrasive, off-putting, and so introverted it borders on anti-social. But I'm never unprepared. Ending up stuck on a paddleboard in the middle of the sea with no shoes, no phone, and no keys is not something that would happen to me. It's something that would happen to Arna, but she wouldn't have ended up with some washed-up soccer player who may or may not have had a drug problem. She would have found her way to the yacht of some arms dealer and proceeded to have a weekend of wild sex and regaled me with tales of her many orgasms when she finally landed herself back in the real world.

But Arna also wouldn't have remembered the code for the door. I feel like tipping my nose up in the air, the way she always would, and setting my shoulders back haughtily as I punch in the numbers.

The keypad illuminates under my fingertips, glowing green and mollifying me, because I might be many things, but I'm not forgetful.

I can feel Ethan behind me as I shoulder into the bungalow, cool air rushing out to meet the thick, borderline oppressive humidity we're standing in now. It's odd to me that I can feel him like that.

I know he's behind me, because I didn't hear him run off back to the jeep, forsaking his sweater and shorts to avoid following the stranger who commented on how to identify bones all night. But, the feeling is more innate than that. I roll my shoulders as I step into the long hallway that leads to the center of the space. I don't like it. I don't really believe in that sort of thing. That was always more Arna. Along with her cabal of therapists, she had a whole list of psychics and tarot card readers on speed dial. She was very much one for feelings, for intuition, for seeking out signs and offerings from the universe. She said it was no different than following your heart. I never bought that fully, when her heart conveniently took her in whatever direction that aligned with what her horoscope had said earlier that day.

"Ey, no table full of empty pints?"

I peer over my shoulder to see Ethan, leaning against the wall, lips pulled to the side, and one eyebrow raised. The cotton of his gray t-shirt strains against his chest, and it's almost the same gray as his eyes. The same eyes that are now sweeping all around my bungalow, appraising everything.

He was right, the coffee table is without empty beer bottles, but otherwise, it's like a low-rent version of his without the glass flooring. Ethan's bungalow is all marble and modern finishings. But this one—this one—Arna chose for me. She always said I liked things crunchy, earthy, my style and preferences bordering on Bohemian. Exposed brick, teakwood, I've always loved things like that. I think I just like things the way they are. No fancy flourishes. This place is all natural woods and bright colors with worn stone walls and flooring.

There's no infinity pool off the deck into the water, just a stretch of wood with two cushioned lounge chairs, and a regular ladder that disappeared off the edge so you could climb into the water of the bay.

And instead of an unmade king-size bed with sheets rolled into a ball that indicated someone was restless, even in sleep, there's a queen bed with a worn wooden frame and white sheets tucked into the corners that sit across from floor-to-ceiling windows with thin, gauzy curtains moving in a breeze I can't feel.

"No empties," I finally say, and Ethan's eyes swing back to me.

The coffee table is almost empty, save for one piece of paper. The first letter, so worn now from my hands that the edges furl away from the wood of the table, like those words she whispered into that paper are just trying to get somewhere.

No empty beer bottles, but one of the final pieces of my best friend.

"You have any beer? I can start your collection for you, yeah?" Ethan's voice is dry, and for some reason, I have the distinct impression he doesn't want to go back to his sad, messy bungalow. His fingers twitch, feathering over his biceps where his arms are crossed.

I glance back at the letter, and I don't want to be alone, either.

"Did you want to go grab some food with me? It's the least I can do. You did save me from certain doom, after all." I don't know why I asked. The words just spilled from my lips, my tongue articulating the syllables required to structure the sentence.

Ethan stares at me for a moment before jerking his head in a noncommittal sort of agreement. "Yeah, alright. Like I said, nowhere better to be."

"Let me just get changed, and we can go." I turn away from him before I can think better of it.

"Don't want to wear my number around all day? My name looks pretty good on you, Ten," he calls, as I pad across the stone floor and begin to pull the sliding door to the bedroom shut.

I've spent a lot of my life saying things I don't mean, or that I wish I didn't. This is one of those times. I look over my shoulder and say, "Former number."

I don't wait to see the inevitable hurt on his face, but just before I pull the door shut, I think I see surprise lighting up behind those eyes and a grin stretching across his face.

My bed might be made, but my suitcase is a fucking disaster. I've always been like that. I can't keep anything folded or orderly. All the clothes are just wrapped up in one big pile now, and I haphazardly pull out a worn pair of denim shorts, far too frayed at the edges. I'm rifling through the fabrics for a t-shirt when my finger catches and slices on something. I recoil, and I know what it is. There's only one thing in here that could hurt me.

All the other letters, more than a handful, with countries and numbers scrawled across the envelopes are there. Sitting in the bottom of my suitcase.

I don't want to look at them right now. It's supposed to be a gift she's given me; I know that. Who gets to hear from their best friend, or anyone really, one final time after they've left the earth? But, I'm looking at those letters, and it doesn't feel like much of anything. My heart just feels heavy.

It's still heavy when I pull on the oversized, white t-shirt. It might knock me over, the weight of my body entirely uneven because so much of it sits in my chest. When I bend over and gather the sweater and shorts, I wonder if I'll even be able to stand up straight. I bring the clothes to my chest, breathing for a moment, and if it were physiologically possible, I would think my heart has now snagged on one of my ribs. But I can stand up, so I cross the room, pulling the door back to find Ethan still leaning against the wall.

Before I can think better of it, I walk over to the coffee table and shove the letter in my pocket.

"You sure you can come for lunch? You weren't planning on adding to your beer bottle tower today?" I ask, crossing my arms.

The letter feels like it's growing heavier than paper should, where it's folded in my pocket. I bounce back and forth on my feet momentarily, like that might change the weight of it. But it's more than just a letter.

"Piece of work, like I said." But he grins at me. If I had that smile, even though my teeth are objectively fine, I would probably do it more often, too. He gestures behind him to the hallway. "Lead the way. Anywhere you want to go?"

I shake my head, handing him the clothes I'm still clutching. "Someone gave me a recommendation for a bar nearby. We can walk just down the beach that runs alongside the resort."

I'm not sure you can call it a recommendation from someone when it came in the form of a letter from my dead best friend, and she was just telling me to try some sort of food. Ethan falls into step beside me, and we move back out into the warm air, the door sealing with a mechanical click when I press the lock button on the keypad. He tosses the sweater and shorts into the backseat of the jeep.

We say nothing as I gesture to a winding path, shadowed with leafy palms falling over it in a sort of canopy.

The bar *is* just down the beach, one that doesn't look unlike either of our respective bungalows, with peeling wooden high-top tables and more tourists drinking beer, wearing nothing but their bathing suits, one of the many inlets of impossibly blue water and towering mountain formations as a backdrop. I walked down there two nights ago, before I decided to get on that paddleboard. And there was a menu sign. Across the top, in an untidy scrawl that would have made Arna and her dumb calligraphy shudder, was an endless list of meals. But there was one that stood out. Kare-Kare.

The beach appears ahead of us, water glittering and winking under the sunlight as the trees thin. We fall into step together, sandaled feet sinking into the sand. It feels like my left side, the pocket with the letter, is being pulled down, down, down. And maybe it is, Arna's manicured fingers wrapped around my left ankle and trying to tug me down through the world so she doesn't have to be alone.

Chapter Five

The steps up to the bar creak under my feet, and a cacophony of laughter and faint music play overhead, with speakers strung up along the rafters. Tables are scattered across the worn floor, littered with people and covered with drinks, empty bottles, and plates. A raised ledge lines the sides of the restaurant, barstools pushed against it, looking out onto the beach and the ocean. I weave through the tables toward one sitting right by the ledge, water still in sight.

Ethan reaches out ahead of me, pulling my chair back before dropping into his own. He raises one hand before I've even sat down, tips his chin, and holds up two fingers in what must be some sort of universal signal of disgraced professional athletes-in-hiding, because moments later, two amber bottles are set down in front of us by a server.

I arch an eyebrow as he slides a bottle across the table to me before taking his own. "You don't waste any time."

"How'd you end up here?" Ethan tips back in his chair, one hand raising to rub the back of his neck.

His shirt strains against his chest, and I can clearly see the whirls of ink on the inside of his bicep. The right one. His left arm is entirely devoid of ink, save for the numbers on his knuckles. The part of the sleeve on the front of his arm is all seemingly mismatched things—a bridge stretching over water, trees, and a clock face stretching across his shoulder peeks out from the arm of his shirt—like most sleeves seem to me. But on his inner bicep, there's a hand, outstretched, reaching into nothingness, the space beside it entirely empty.

I blink. It feels private, for some reason, to see that tattoo tucked away there. I look away and fix my gaze back to his face. His features are impassive, and he brings his beer to his mouth and cocks an eyebrow, waiting.

"In the proverbial sense of the word? Or, the literal?" I ask, taking a sip of my own beer. It's growing on me.

"Best mate dies, you almost drown on a paddleboard, crash into my bungalow..." Ethan shrugs, lips pulling down. "Don't tell me you did her wrong and you're in a self-imposed exile like yours truly."

I puff out my cheeks, almost laughing, and shake my head. "No. She left me these letters. Some sort of self-guided tour around the world. This was stop number one."

I'm not sure why I do it, because it's impossibly private, some of her last words, her final thoughts, but I pull out the folded, worn letter and toss it across the scratched up table toward him. Ethan glances down and then looks back up at me. I offer a tiny nod of permission.

He tips back in his chair again, taking one more swig of beer before reaching forward and unfolding the letter.

I study him as his eyes move along, crinkling at the corners occasionally. It might be impossible for someone who didn't know us, who didn't know our friendship, to make even the slightest bit of sense of it. But he tips his head, occasionally nodding almost indiscernibly, taking another sip of beer, before he looks up at me.

"The trump card? What's that when it's at home?" Ethan asks, setting the letter down between us. My lips part, eyes widening, and I start to shake my head when Ethan grins, clarifying. "What does that mean?"

"That's a ridiculous saying." I find myself smiling for a moment, before it falters, and I start trying to explain to a stranger what it means to find your soulmate when you are ten. "I was weird, and she was normal. At least in elementary and high school terms." Ethan's eyebrows crease, but he waits for me to continue. "I stayed in voluntarily to read or watch shark attack movies. She was the star athlete at our boarding school, and I had no interest in organized sports. She was president of the student council, and I don't think I owned a single item with our school's crest, aside from the ones I was mandated to have."

My thumb starts to worry at the already-peeling label on my beer before I glance out at the beach, where more than one group of girls sit in a semi-circle or stand side-by-side, taking photos. I clear my throat before continuing.

"But we had this thing, you know? I mean the whole friendship was a thing, I guess. But when it was between what either of us wanted to do, we started competing for trump cards. It could have been something like I got called on in AP Chem and didn't know the answers, or I forgot my gym uniform and had to wear something from the lost and found. But it always escalated, and whoever had the worst card won. My biggest one was always that my parents didn't want me, or they don't love me. That won a lot and was always an absolute. When her parents died in a car crash, hers became *"Mine are dead,"* or *"I'm an orphan."*

Which, arguably, trumps not being loved. But if it was something I really wanted to do...she never played the card. She would concede at "*I missed a pop quiz in physics.*" It was all dramatic flourishes and the back of her hand to her forehead, but then she would come to the cadaver exhibit at the museum downtown just the same, peer with her nose up in the air through the glass, staring at all the preserved bodies, never even mentioning the fact that she wanted to be at the hockey party. She was just content to be with me."

"And were you content to be with her?" Ethan asks, skating by all the other information, still rocking back on his chair, and there's a tone to his voice that makes me hope for a second he tips over backward.

"Pardon me?" I narrow my eyes at him.

Ethan takes a sip of his beer but gestures widely with his hand while doing so. "That whole spiel—you say it like she was just donating her time to charity, November."

I open my mouth, indignant and fucking annoyed. "Hey—I don't know you, and you don't know me. You don't get to pass judgment on me for something you know nothing about."

"You're right. I'm sorry, Ten." He grins a bit when I roll my eyes. I'm about to tell him again that it isn't my name, and November has never been the tenth month, that he just can't count, when he keeps talking. "Tell me something about you, then. Can't really say we're strangers when you've slept in my clothes."

"I like looking at the sea, or the ocean, whatever body of water is closest." I tip my beer bottle, pointing with the neck toward the bay. Tourists are splayed out on the sand, some wading around in the shallow water, and a group of kids kick a soccer ball up and down the sprawling beach. "The lake in Toronto leaves something to be desired."

Ethan smirks at me from behind his bottle, eyes only leaving me when a server comes along and drops two frayed, stained menus down between us. He shoves one of the menus toward me, holding the other, while his eyes track across the meager list of available food. "You really dug deep with that one, yeah? Do you want to know something about me?"

I don't need to look at the menu. My order has been pre-determined for me, but I pick it up out of habit, eyes roving across the options before flicking back up to Ethan. "I'm sure you'll tell me anyway."

"I was on track to be the top scorer in the league last year, before I tore my Achilles and pissed it all away on a bag of shitty coke," Ethan offers blandly, like he's delivering me a weather report.

I raise my eyebrows. "You shouldn't do cocaine. It'll eat away at your sinus cavity."

"You don't say?" Ethan asks wryly, holding up the menu over his shoulder, another secret universal sign, and the server nods to him across the restaurant and starts weaving through the tables. "That's what you took from that? You're not going to take the piss out of me for being full of myself? Bragging about my prowess?"

"It's not bragging if it's true," I shrug, lips pulling to the side ruefully. "Why'd you do it? It's pretty common knowledge that professional athletes aren't supposed to take drugs, recreational or otherwise."

Ethan's nostrils flare, and he looks out at the water for a moment before looking back at me. He shakes his head, lips pulling down, and he looks like he's thinking, trying maybe to find an answer for me but for himself, too. "Not a fucking clue. I was on injury reserve, and the surgeon said I might not be the same. It just felt pretty fucking bleak. My parents live in the countryside...bit uppity. Was easier for them, maybe a bit easier for everybody if I just disappeared for a while. Like I said, got sick of seeing my own face and failed dreams splashed everywhere. And here we are now."

He extends his arm, beer bottle dangling loosely and waiting for mine. It might be the most pathetic cheers in the world, but I find myself bringing my own bottle to meet his; and when he smiles back at me, perfect teeth and tiny scar stretching across his lip, I don't feel so alone.

Chapter Six

I had about five bites of my Kare-Kare before the anxiety took over, because I don't know what's in it. So, I just focused on eating the white rice that accompanied it with sauce from the stew. I liked the flavor, so I asked to take it home, because I thought I might try more when I'm alone, when Ethan isn't across the table, eating chicken adobo, which looked much more my speed. He stared at me while I kept wiping my palms across the denim of my shorts, blinking rapidly, because I wanted to know what was in the dish as badly as I wanted to be able to just eat it, entirely carefree, the way Arna intended.

We walked down the steps of the restaurant together that spilled out onto the beach, and the soccer ball the kids had been kicking all throughout our meal rolled to Ethan's feet. He kicked the ball up with his toe, holding his calf out to the side and catching it on the inside of his foot, bouncing it up a few times before kicking it higher and bouncing it back and forth between his knees. Before he could kick it back to them, the four kids swarmed him, shrieking and grabbing at his elbows and forearms, asking if he would play with them.

I watch as Ethan bounces the soccer ball on each knee, sending it higher into the air and letting it drop in the sand between him and the four children he's been kicking it back and forth with.

I tip my head, hand raised to shield my eyes from the sunlight. I wish I had brought my sunglasses, so I could see better. There's something special about getting to see someone do something they love—something they were born to do.

Ethan kicks the ball back to them before he bends down, gesturing to the ball and the inner side of their shoes. I watch him smile at them, all those sharp edges softening, and he claps the tallest boy on the shoulder. I have the full view of the back of his calves as he stands. The scar stretches across the back of his left one, raised, still red, and looking like the skin is still tight and uncomfortable, the way incisions are when they're healing. He rubs at it absentmindedly before he's upright again, towering over the kids who are holding out their hands for expectant high fives.

He doesn't seem like the high-fiving type, but he's still smiling when he moves through the tiny circle of children, bouncing back and forth on their feet in barely contained excitement. Ethan watches for a moment as the tallest one hurriedly grabs the ball, and they all sprint down the beach toward the flatter, wet sand closest to the water.

He tugs at the hair curling against the nape of his neck before he turns back, hiking back up the beach to where I'm sitting.

I peer up at him as he approaches, his shadow stretching out and blocking the sunlight. Dropping my hand, I laugh softly as I look up at him. "Quite the fan club you've got there. What were you showing them? When you were pointing to the inside of their feet?"

Ethan cracks a grin, dropping beside me, coming to rest his elbows on his knees. "How to kick a ball. They were kicking with their toes."

"That's not correct?" I arch an eyebrow, turning to face him.

The sun is much lower in the sky than it was earlier, and it's throwing all his features into an even sharper contrast, emphasizing the dark shadow of stubble growing along his jawline.

He glances at me sideways, lips pulling back. "No, Ten, that's not correct."

His voice is indignant, incredulous even, and a laugh tumbles from my lips.

"You didn't look so bad out there. You hardly look like someone who went through a career-altering surgery," I offer quietly. I pull my legs close to my chest and wrap my arms around them.

"Wasn't trying that hard." Ethan rubs his palm across his jaw before offering me a rueful smile.

"Don't tell them that." I gesture to the kids, now running the length of the beach, trying to keep the ball away from one another, their screams and shrieks of joy echoing all the way up to us.

Ethan says nothing, but his nostrils flare as he exhales. It's deep; so low it's like he's letting go of all the air in his lungs. He stares out ahead of him, seemingly at the endless expanse of the water in front of us. A muscle ticks in his jaw, and I feel my hand twitch. I don't like to touch people, let alone strangers, but I feel like reaching out and touching him, seeing if I could rub away the hurt with a few brushes of my thumb.

I drop the side of my head to my knees so I can properly see how the reds and pinks from the slowly setting sun look on him. "Did you know sunsets or sunrises seem faster depending on the time of the year? The tilt of the Earth's axis changes."

Ethan finally turns to me, but he's smiling now, and I think the heaviness in my heart lightens just a fraction. "No macabre fact about bones or death for me?"

My lips pull upward, and I shake my head lightly. "I know lots of things. My knowledge isn't limited to teeth and bones."

"Noted." Ethan's voice drops, and I watch him bite down on the inside of his cheek for a moment.

I'm about to tell him not to do that, because the skin on the inside of your mouth is soft and easily damaged, but he glances back out at the water once before pushing to stand up. He's blocking the last of the sunlight, and when I look up at him, he's holding his hand out to me. "I'll walk you home, yeah?"

"Sure, yeah." I nod, offering him a smile.

I take his hand and start to push up from the sand, grabbing my takeout container. Ethan's other hand comes out, grabbing my elbow like he's trying to keep me steady. His left hand and all those numbered fingers engulf mine, and I glance at his other hand, the one gripping my elbow. His thumb twitches against my arm for a moment, and I look up at him. It's hard to see his face, but the way he's looking at me, it feels sort of like he sees me, and I'm not sure I like it. I think my body must be having some sort of serotonin-induced physiological response, one brought on solely from lack of contact—the natural kind you have when someone touches you and causes your endorphins to release, because my heart stumbles over itself.

Taking a measured step back, I extract my hand from his and roll my arm so his grip on my elbow drops. His hand stays there, extended in space for a moment. Ethan clears his throat, gesturing for me to start down the beach before dropping his hands into his pockets.

My feet sink into the sand beside his as we start walking, and I fold my arms over my chest against a non-existent chill. The kids are still running down the beach, silhouetted against the setting sun. Groups of friends are still laying out, coolers full of beer flipped open. All the vibrant colors of the water, the towering mountains are muted.

"It's beautiful," I murmur. "I can see why she stayed here for a summer."

"No better place to go into exile," Ethan says, voice light.

"That too." I glance over at him. The set of his jaw is harsh, and I see it pop back and forth. His words are light, but I think he's anything but.

We're silent as we walk farther down the beach, up toward the tiny path with the draping palms that leads back up to the resort. It feels weird because objectively, at the end of this tiny dirt road, we're going to part ways.

We might have spent almost twenty-four hours together, he might have provided me a safe place to land for a night—shared his slice of exile with me—and I might have shared some of the things most precious to me in this world with him—memories and my best friend's last words. But we're just strangers.

Ethan steps ahead of me, pushing back the lowest hanging palm, and I duck under it, stepping out onto the crumbling pavement path right beside my bungalow. The jeep is where he left it, shadows stretching across the front of the property, and the tiny lights hung in all the trees across the resort have flickered on.

I rock back and forth on my feet, not sure what to say when Ethan steps out from the path. There's only about two feet between us, but it feels endless—like he's standing on his deck and I'm standing on mine—and we're each staring across the bay because we think we can see something in the distance that we'll never be able to reach.

"I'll see you around, Ten." Ethan's lips quirk to the side, and he extends a hand to me.

His tattooed hand. All those numbers that mean something to him. I think I'll remember them for the rest of my life.

Eight, seventeen, nineteen, twenty, twenty-two.

I think I might remember him for the rest of my life, too.

"Ethan," I whisper, reaching out to shake his hand. "If I ever make another friend, you'll be the party story I tell. Hey, did you know—disgraced professional soccer player, almost the top scorer of the league, Ethan Barclay, rescued me on a paddleboard in Boracay once?"

"If I see you again, I'll hold you to that, yeah?" Ethan's grin stretches across his face, and his thumb brushes against the back of my hand before he drops it. He raises his eyebrows at me and walks toward the jeep.

He turns around, walking backward for a moment, and we stare at each other until he walks around the side, but he pauses at the driver's side door.

Ethan looks at me, leaning forward and arms reaching out to grip the bars of the jeep. I can see him swallow—that same muscle from earlier feathering in his jaw. I raise my hand, clutching my takeout box closer to me, in some sort of farewell wave I'm not sure I really want to be making, when his gaze flicks up.

"Ah, fuck. The paddleboard." Ethan hangs his head between his outstretched arms momentarily.

My lips part, and I look up to the empty roof racks on the jeep. It's still sitting on the deck back at his bungalow.

"Oh, I can see if someone from the resort can—" I start, but he raises his head, and the shadows that I think live in his eyes seem to have come alive.

"You fancy giving it another shot?" Ethan tips his head, and his fingers drum against the bars of the jeep. "I'll bring it back over tomorrow, and we can take it out for another spin. Stay in the bay this time so you don't get swept out to sea."

I tilt my head, lips tugging upward, and my heart unsnags from my rib cage. "You want to go paddleboarding with me? The girl who lost her paddle and almost died in a storm?"

Ethan leans forward, lips pulling up into a grin. "Yeah, I think I do."

I see it in his eyes, and I feel it in my heart. Neither of us want to be alone.

"Fine. Ten o'clock. Should be easy for you to remember because you think it's my name." I tip my chin up, and we stare at each other for a moment before I raise my eyebrows and turn on my heel toward the path leading to my door.

"I'll wait till I see you get in the door, yeah? 'Case Leatherface is waiting in the palm fronds over there." His voice follows me up the path, and a laugh catches in my throat.

I look over my shoulder, and my cheeks burn a bit from my smile, the muscles unused for so long. "Goodnight, Ethan."

Chapter Seven

I hear the jeep when I'm stretched out on the lounge chair, the latest letter from Arna furling in my lap. It already looks dog-eared, the ink smudged from my fingertips and tears splashed across the page, making her painstaking, carefully curated handwriting bleed. It felt fitting, because I wondered if I was bleeding a bit, too.

Blinking down at the letter for a moment, my eyes start to burn again behind my sunglasses. I smooth out the letter against my leg, trying to curl down the edges, because I know it would bother her that it didn't look perfect, still curated exactly the way she intended before I carefully fold it into a tiny square and shove it in the back of my shorts.

I can hear the engine cut and the door close from out here. There's no noise—it's entirely serene, save for the occasional lap of the gentle current against the supports of the bungalow. I left the door unlocked for Ethan, fairly certain he would be more than happy to let himself in. When I hear a rap on the glass behind me, my lips twitch a bit, because I was right.

Craning my neck and leaning over the back of the chair, I see him standing there, tattooed hand raised and ready to knock against the glass again. My paddleboard, all bright colors and bearing no signs it almost went down with me and my proverbial ship, is tucked under his arm. There's another one, just simple black and white blocks of color that's leaning up against the door beside him.

Swinging my legs off the chair, I smooth out the front of my shorts and move to pull open the door for Ethan. I'm wearing the same bathing suit top that I got stranded in. It might be a bad omen, but I didn't think I would be participating in so many water activities, and I only brought one. I'm usually a better packer than this—it was always Arna who would end up places with an entirely climate inappropriate wardrobe. I think she did it on purpose, honestly. So she could buy an entirely new one and claim it was some sort of serendipitous, lost-luggage-type of scenario that left her greatly inconvenienced and stranded and tell anyone who would listen where she got her shirt.

"Hi." I look up at him as I pull back the sliding door.

Ethan grins lazily at me, eyes hidden behind a pair of Ray Bans. "Ten. Alright?"

"You're on time," I say, tipping my chin up. "I was worried you'd still be sleeping off last night's bender."

"Someone nicked all my pints the other night. Kept me in line." He passes the paddleboard through the open doorway to me, and I stumble a bit when I try to shove it under my arm, to hold it as effortlessly as he was.

I give up and drop it to the deck, shoving against it with my foot toward the edge while Ethan effortlessly lifts the second board through the door alongside two paddles. He drops his beside mine, tossing one of the paddles on top of it.

"Brought you a new paddle. Rest in peace to your former one, yeah?" Ethan holds the other paddle up before starting to spin it around in his palm with a shocking amount of control and impressive dexterity.

"It's not a fucking lightsaber." I duck backward, afraid the flat edge might send me flying off the deck.

Ethan grins then stops spinning it, closing his fingers over the shaft of the paddle. "How would you know? Can't even keep a hold of one when it gets a bit windy."

"Oh, I'm sorry. I didn't realize I was not only in the presence of a soccer superstar but a paddleboard aficionado."

Rolling my eyes, I watch as Ethan shrugs a bag off his shoulders, rolling them a few times before he reaches over his head to fist the neck of his shirt. It's pulled off in the next second, and every part of him tenses before he rolls his shoulders again.

He's always moving, and I don't think he was meant to be still.

He looks back at me, and the same lazy smile stretches across his face. "Don't worry, you're safe with me. You ready?"

I don't dignify him with an answer because it wouldn't be a simple one. Instead, I step out of my shorts, folding them between my hands and moving to set them down on the lounge chair.

"There's a couple spots down the bay, thought we could paddle there for a drink." Ethan rips open the drawstrings of a plastic bag, holding out his hand for my folded up shorts. "It's a dry bag, yeah?"

I hesitate for a moment, because the letter is still in my pocket. And even though it's already worn, my eyes having tracked every single line and slash and loop of the words, I'm not done reading it, because I'm not sure I understand it yet.

"It seals, Ten. Nothing'll get wet. I use one all the time at home for surfing." Ethan lifts his eyes before gesturing for me to drop the shorts into the bag.

My lips purse, and I bend down, carefully placing the shorts in the bag. Ethan drops his previously discarded shirt, sunglasses, and his phone unceremoniously on top of them and pulls the drawstrings, sealing them in together. I watch as he rolls the top of the bag over itself before clipping it shut.

He raises his eyes to mine, still narrowed and staring shrewdly at the bag. He grips the clipped handle for a moment before a small smirk pulls on his lips, and he pushes up to stand, tossing the bag off the deck.

I lurch forward, fingers scrambling against the wood of the deck, gripping the edges, ready to throw myself into the water to try and salvage her words. But the bag bobs against the surface of the impossibly blue, impossibly transparent water, floating back and forth in the practically non-existent current of the bay.

I look up at Ethan, not really caring that I'm on all fours in nothing but the same bathing suit I was stranded in. His lips twitch as he looks down at me.

"Wouldn't ruin your shorts on purpose." He reaches down, grabbing my ill-fated paddleboard with one hand, muscles in his forearm tensing momentarily as he tosses it down alongside the bag.

It's not just shorts, but I don't correct him.

He grabs the next board, the one he brought with him, and shoves it off the deck. It claps against the water. "You climb down the ladder, and I'll hand you the cord."

Ethan hoists the two paddles up, tossing those off the deck without a care before he raises his eyebrows at me. I don't have a chance to answer because he turns, rolling his shoulders and the edges of the clock face stretching across his shoulder wink at me in the sunlight for a moment before he arches his back and dives off the deck, too.

I watch him disappear under the water for a brief moment, outline obscure because of the splash, but then he's there, treading water, one hand pushing the dark curls off his face and shaking his head out quickly. The whirls of ink across his shoulder and down his arm blur under the surface of the water.

He floats aimlessly between the two boards for a moment, tips his head back and closes his eyes against the sun, the paddles bobbing alongside him. It's a trick of the light, some sort of refraction and reflection because of the way the sun's shining down on him. It's just how the cones and rods in my eyes absorb it and send information back to my brain. Because when he opens them back up and looks at me, I think his eyes might match the clear sky, like nothing bad has ever happened to him.

Ethan jerks his chin toward the ladder, and I swing my feet off the deck and start to climb down. I can hear his body slice through the water as he grabs my paddleboard and pushes it toward me, one hand holding the cord and extending for my foot as I reach the water.

His hand deftly wraps the band around my ankle. Ethan tugs on the cord and looks up at me. There's one curl matted to his forehead, a sheen of water across his shoulders, and the part of his chest above the water. "All good?"

I look at him for a moment longer. "All good."

The stretched skin of the scar running along Ethan's calf looks stark against his tanned skin. The sunlight almost makes it look like it's shining, but that feels wrong to me. I don't think anything that could make someone hurt like that, could steal from them like that, deserves a positive descriptor.

But I can't think of anything else, another word to describe the vertical slash that looks like an intruder. Logically, I know it's just fresh skin. New growth over a wound that's just a part of his body now. I watched him, when he finally stood on his own board after waiting with me, floating beside me in the water until I was upright, paddle so securely gripped in hand it wasn't going anywhere. The water rolled off him, as he pushed up onto his own board, fingers flexing and gripping the sides, and right after he let go, before he stood, they carved over the scar, the expanse of raised skin across the back of his calf, like he was checking to see if it was still there.

It might be a part of his physiology, his body, but I don't think it will ever be a part of *him*.

"I read there aren't many turtles out here anymore," I tell Ethan as he paddles just ahead of me. "Too much disruption to their habitats. I think that's kind of sad."

The bay is quiet, but it's dotted with resorts not unlike mine, and probably not as nice as the one Ethan was at; tiny beach bars with their patrons spilling out onto the sand, and sprawling estates peeking from the trees on the rolling mountains of the island behind us.

"You like animals?" Ethan looks back over his shoulder at me as the paddle slices through the still water.

"Yeah. Before I dreamed about being a dentist, I dreamed about being a marine biologist, believe it or not." My own paddling pales in comparison to Ethan's longer strokes.

"What stopped you? Seem like the type who could have been anything in this life." His voice carries back to me.

"Arna, actually. I would have gone to school on a different coast, and it just felt weird to do that part of life without her. And only children want to be marine biologists."

I look away from Ethan, peering over my own board. The occasional school of fish dart by, just a flash of silver and hardly discernible against the white sand at the bottom of the bay.

"Told you only mental cases want to be dentists," Ethan tosses over his shoulder, barely sparing me a glance, but I think I see him smile.

"And only little kids dream about being professional athletes." I roll my eyes, legs wobbling slightly as I try to stay upright. "Did you ever dream about being anything else?"

"Not for a single second." Ethan's paddle stops mid-stroke, and in a motion that's so annoyingly swift, it looks like he's spent his professional life paddleboarding instead of kicking a ball around a field, he drops to his knees, setting the paddle down across the board, too. "You regret it? Not following that dream?"

"No. There are a lot of things that wouldn't have happened in life otherwise," I tell him, and it's true.

"Yeah?" he prompts, dropping to sit back on the board, legs swinging out and over, into the water.

"Yeah." I push backward in the water to slow the board down near Ethan, unsure how to get down when he holds his hand out to steady my board. "Work things, mostly. But other things. Memories I wouldn't trade. Jake."

"Jake?" Ethan questions, hand still holding my board steady as I drop down, with significantly less finesse than he did.

I nod, gently setting my paddle on the board before swinging my legs into the water. It's cool against my skin, and I study my legs, all warped and misshapen under the surface. "Jake. Five-year relationship, as shocking as that might be. Two years older than me. Investment banker who never really understood me."

"Ah, Ten. What a cliché." He glances at me, gray eyes glinting.

A small laugh falls from my lips as I nod. We fall silent for a moment, the boards rocking softly underneath us against the current. I can see Ethan drumming his fingers against the edges of the board, just the tips of them in the water. Turning my head, I study him for a moment. The curls of his hair are poking every which way, even wilder from the saltwater, and a shadow across his jaw from stubble already poking through his skin, sharp cheekbones, and even sharper eyes.

I kick up my foot, sending a tiny spray of water toward him. "What about you? Anyone in your life shackled to you for five years?"

Ethan looks down where his hands rest on his knees, drops of water now peppering them. The muscles in his left contracting for a moment before he shrugs, all casual indifference. "Nothing that stuck. I was always pretty easy to leave."

"That can't be true," I whisper, and I mean it. According to my dead best friend, I'm cold, distant and unfeeling. If anyone would find someone easy to leave, it would be me.

Ethan turns to look at me, rolling his shoulders briefly. "Ah well, they all moved on pretty fucking sharpish."

I can't think of anything else to do, so I kick up my foot sending another tiny spray of water across his chest.

Ethan widens his eyes for a moment and then angles his head. There's a predatory set to his mouth, full lips peeling back in feral delight. "You a child, Ten?"

I raise my eyebrows at him, and my lips curl upward. Before I can even lift my leg, to even pretend to send another splash of water over him, Ethan's hands grip the front of my paddleboard, and he sends it toppling over.

I've never shrieked in my life, water sputtering against my lips as I break through the surface of the bay. My lips part, and all I can taste is salt. I blink at Ethan, where he's still sitting on his board, watching me splashing around like I've never been in water before. But he's smiling now, perfect teeth and scar just visible underneath the stubble.

"You won't be able to tip me, Ten. Got excellent balance," Ethan offers, leaning forward. "I'll do you a favor."

I think he's still smiling when he jumps in after me.

Chapter Eight

Sand sticks to the bottom of my feet and my legs, and there's still a dusting of it across Ethan's arms from where he dragged our paddleboards up the beach towards one of the many bars dotting it. We're sitting across from one another now, at a table not unlike the one we sat at yesterday. The scratched wood stretches between us, two perspiring bottles clutched in our respective hands.

My skin itches from the saltwater and feels tight against my bones. My cheeks are warm from the sun, and my hair curls off my face, still damp against my neck in a hastily gathered ponytail. Ethan's looks the same, curls poking every which way against his head, curling around his ears and the nape of his neck. His skin is still damp, shirt sticking to him.

We haven't said anything in a bit, but silence with Ethan Barclay isn't uncomfortable. He's looking out at the water, the seemingly endless stretch of the winking surface. When he looks back at me, his head tips slightly, and it's like he's studying me, wondering about something.

"What was he?" Ethan questions, rolling the beer bottle back and forth on the table, leaving perspiration rings in its wake.

"What was Jake?" I clarify, even though there's no need for it. Even if we hadn't talked about him, he's the only person who has ever come even close to occupying a space in me, and he still wasn't even within spitting distance of my best friend. "He was many things. But he was never everything, and that wasn't enough for him."

Ethan narrows his eyes, like those words don't sit right. "Isn't that what people should want? Not to be everything…just to be something."

"That's a nice sentiment," I consider.

And it is nice, but it's flawed and entirely obvious Ethan has never loved anyone with his whole heart, because how could you settle for less after understanding what it was like—to have your once in a lifetime love.

"Did you love him?"

"Did I love him?" I repeat the words, considering them for a moment.

I tip my head to the side, and my ponytail falls forward over my collarbone.

Ethan's eyes move with it before snapping back up to my face. He nods, bringing the bottle of beer to his lips.

"In a way. My own way. But not as much as I loved her." I offer him the truth with a small shrug.

It's the only truth I have. I did love Jake, or I thought I did. I was my own version of devastated when he finally called it. I just never needed him for the things that you're supposed to need a partner for. It grated on him, over time. He was never the first to know anything. Never the first person I would call about anything, good or bad. Never the shoulder I cried on, never the person who made me laugh the most. We never spent time with my parents, a damning point of contention in our relationship, but he hadn't grown up with me, so he never understood that they just didn't love me the way a parent was meant to love a child. He thought it somehow meant I didn't value him or didn't see a future with him, so eventually, he stopped seeing one with me.

"Were you in love with her?" Ethan asks. The words are plain as they come out of his mouth.

His eyebrows crease a bit, and I think for a second the idea bothers him; that I was hopelessly in love with her, and she was in love with me this whole time, and now we were both alone. It would be a horribly sad story if it were true. I think the reality is even sadder. I've had my one love, and she's gone.

"No." I shake my head. It's the truth. "You've never had a best friend...someone who was more yourself than you were?"

"No." He shakes his head, one strand of hair falls onto his forehead.

"Then I feel sorry for you." I shrug, taking a sip of my own beer.

There are a lot of things in my life right now I wouldn't have predicted: the notable and forever absence of my best friend and the hole she tore in my heart, my soul, the fiber of my being when she took her last breath, the man with tattooed hands and sad eyes sitting across from me in this restaurant in Boracay, and my sudden affinity for beer. The last one feels the most surprising somehow. But I imagine Arna, just beyond the veil, or wherever it is we go, watching with a knowing glint in her eye because her plan was working. Only a few days in the Philippines, and here I am, with a stranger, and a new beverage in my rotation.

"Don't think I have many mates left if I'm being honest. Self-imposed exile does that, I suppose. Calls stopped coming after a few weeks. Only one who still rings is my agent once every few days to make sure I'm still alive." Ethan looks troubled for a moment, full lips turning down before he raises his eyebrows and drains the rest of his bottle. With more finesse than I would ever manage, he reaches forward, grabs another from the perspiring steel bucket between us, and brings the neck of the bottle to the side of the table. His hand comes down, and the cap of the bottle falls into the sand below our feet. He looks up at me, lips quirking to the side. "I'll pick it up, yeah? You don't look much for littering."

I feel myself smile at him. "I'm not. But thank you for not using your teeth."

Ethan grins, turning the bottle between his fingers. I catch glimpses of the numbers—eight, seventeen, nineteen, twenty, twenty-two. I haven't asked what they mean. But I assume they're important. "Any more dental hygiene tips?"

"I'll assess your brushing and flossing technique for free. Consider it a payment for saving me from the sea." I raise my eyebrows at him before pushing some of the curling hair off my forehead. I can feel my ponytail expanding the longer we sit here. Ethan's waves and curls somehow look unmarred, drying perfectly. If my hair was down, it would expand into a triangle around my head until the waves were nothing more than frizz. "How come your agent still calls you?"

His pupils expand, just a fraction, and then he offers me a shrug like it's no big deal that he had it all and lost it. "I, uh, skipped out on rehab...all the physical therapy I was supposed to do after the surgery when I lost my contract. He's invested a lot in me, so he's probably crossing his fingers for some sort of resurrection if he can shop me around with the promise of improvement."

"Is that what you want?" I survey Ethan, watching as he leans back, one arm coming to rest over the back of his worn chair. He tips backward, rocking on the legs back and forth. Everything around him glitters endlessly under the relentless sun—the bay stretching out beside us and the towering mountains interspersed with impossibly green jungle climbing up beyond.

His eyes cut back to me, and he runs a palm over his jaw before shrugging. "I don't know what I want. I just know I fancied being alone. Needed to get away for a bit."

"And then some dumbass with a death wish crashes into your frat boy bungalow, disrupting whatever sense of peace you found." I try the attempt at humor because I don't like how sad he looks—like a little lost boy, endlessly searching for what he used to have.

I can see it in his eyes, and I know he's lying. The endless yearning. Regret. He knows exactly what he wants.

It falls flat, though, because Ethan cuts me a look, cheekbones somehow looking sharper, and shakes his head. "You're not a dumbass. Reckon that brain of yours is pretty weird. Smartest one in most rooms."

I arch an eyebrow and start to pick at the label of my own beer before taking a sip. His unwarranted, innate defense of me settles against my skin. It's something Arna would have done. When my own mind whispered cruel, calculated things meant to slowly tear me down, peg by peg, she was ready to counteract them all. She did think I was weird—so fucking weird—in her words, but she loved me just the same.

Ethan smiles at me, and the corners of his eyes crease slightly. "What do you want?"

He's just returning the question; it's how polite conversation works. But my heart hurts, infinitely heavy in my chest, because I just want things to be the way they were. We're the same in that way, Ethan and me. Endless pining for a life that left us behind, that was never meant to be ours forever.

"Something I can never have," I answer truthfully, showing him a small, wistful smile.

Textbooks and any therapist would tell you that's what I should feel by now—wistful. It's been six months. I should be able to smile about her now, think about her fondly. Every memory shouldn't feel like my organs are being sliced open and skewered; my heart shouldn't feel leaden. Grief is normal, a standard part of the human experience. We're meant to move through it. It's not meant to stop us in our tracks entirely; to fester the way it is in me.

"Don't you have any other mates? No other friends to fill the void?" Ethan asks, lips pulling to the side.

He swirls his beer, fingers drumming against the peeling label, and I see flashes of those numbers, probably the most important things to him.

I tip my head and gesture to his hand. "The same reason you don't get those lasered off. I'll never expect anyone who hasn't lost the best parts of themselves, the other half of them, their best friend, to understand. Losing a friend, to life or to death…I can't explain it. I think it might be the worst kind of grief in the world." Ethan's full lower lip juts past the top for a moment, and then he nods. I watch him flex his hand, studying the numbers there before I continue. "I was one half of a whole. I have been since I was ten years old. I was smart, I excelled at school, I was top of my class, and I'm good at my job. Those things filled me. It fills me now, gives me purpose, to give people back their children, their loved ones, to solve those mysteries for them. To give people their smiles back. But the thing I was most proud of was being a best friend, having someone like that…I don't know how to be me without her. I think a big part of me died when she did, and I can't explain it better than that."

My voice is kind of sad and quiet, echoing forever against a world that feels empty because she's not in it.

Ethan shrugs again, but I notice his eyes flick down to his fingers. "Seems kind of cracked...unwise, maybe, to love someone like that. Especially when it's not for any greater romantic purpose."

"Love doesn't only look one way, Ethan." I debate telling him that it often doesn't even look the way we think it should.

My parents are a perfect example. Their love for one another knows no bounds. They're what people write stories about. What people sing about and what they yearn for. They love each other more than anything in the entire world, the universe. So much that it was all dried up—nothing left for me when I came along. I had to find that fulfillment elsewhere.

Ethan grins wryly before leaning forward, gray eyes intent on me. "What's next then? Can't imagine all these letters are leading you to one place."

They're not.

I opened the third last night after Ethan left. And I read it again, and again, and again. And then again this morning when I was waiting to see if he would show.

It's still in my pocket now, still dry because his ridiculous bag did its job.

"Bali," I answer, pulling the folded paper from my pocket—something Arna would consider sacrilege—seeing how much effort she put into her stupid handwriting.

I set it gingerly in the middle of the table, careful to avoid any condensation or perspiration from our bottles that pools on the wood. I push it toward Ethan in invitation. I shouldn't want to share these last words with anyone, but maybe I'm just hoping for someone to understand.

Ethan tips back again briefly before leaning forward, and something in my heart swells when I see how gingerly, carefully, almost reverently his fingers are as they pick up the paper and slowly unfold it.

I could watch him, study as his eyes track her words, her instructions, her secrets—but I have the letter memorized now. I know what parts will cause his pupils to expand, his eyebrows to raise, maybe even when his lower lip would jut out in disbelief. So I look away, hand clutched around the sweating, still cold beer.

I'm watching the people on the beach, spilled out across the sand with unbuttoned denim shorts, skin bronzed and freckled by the sun, tipping their heads back as they tilt the necks of their beer back. Laughter spills from their lips and echoes out there across the sea, just like Arna's letter echoes in my head.

Novie Novie Novie,

I miss you. Wherever I am, wherever you are, I miss you.

Did you do what I asked? I guess I'll never know. Unless I'm really sitting up there on fluffy endlessly soft clouds, looking down at you in outrage. Or, maybe I'm lounging on a throne of flames, and I'm looking up at you.

Was there a bone in the oxtail of your Kare-Kare? You should be used to bones. That's why I suggested it. Did you like it? I hope you did. But if you didn't, I hope you felt it. The excitement that comes when you're trying something new. How magical, how beautiful it can be, when you're waiting and something you've never tried before is set down in front of you—and all around you, the world is beautiful, you know?

I hope you tried it. And I hope you're not mad at me.

I knew everything about you, and now you know one more thing about me. I wasn't keeping secrets from you, not really.

It was just a little time on the beach.

There are a lot of things you didn't know about me, if I'm being honest. And I might as well because what do I have to lose?

Just never forget—never ever—that I loved you. To infinity and beyond.

Thoughts from my throne of flames (because let's be honest, if there's a Hell, I'm burning in it),

Arna

P.S.: Open the next letter when you get to Bali.

To infinity and beyond.

Arna never met my parents, which seems almost impossible, but they never came to pick me up or visit me at school like regular parents would. I never invited her to stay at my house over summer break. But over Easter break in year six, in an entirely uncharacteristic move, they decided not to leave me behind. I had spent the previous Thanksgiving and Christmas break with the Pavlides family. Once with Arna, Sebastian, and their parents in Palm Springs, and then Arna had demanded to stay behind, Sebastian following suit, because they had never seen snow. So, it was just the three of us and a handful of other unwanted children, traipsing across the snow-covered campus, noses running, and warming our hands on the cups of hot chocolate the matrons made us after they dragged us back inside.

But that Easter—I remember it. My mom called the office and left a message that I would be picked up alongside everyone else to go home. Arna and Sebastian weren't going back to Greece. Not because their parents wouldn't have sent for them, but because they celebrated at the Orthodox, which was a few weeks later. I had been thrilled, in the way that children are thrilled. The small seed of mollification and hope, approval even, budding and blooming in me to create a childlike excitement in the days leading up to it.

I hadn't been home since the summer, not that my parents were great company, but it was my home, and I missed my books and my room. That was my refuge. Where I would read and learn and pretend.

They changed their minds the day of because they decided to go to Morocco. Amazing, can't miss flights, if my eleven-year-old self could understand that. The office received the message too late, and no one pulled me aside until I was ready with my bag.

It wasn't a surprise, even to me as a child. I remember it—nodding along and sloughing it off because it was no big deal—but I think those blooms in me died forever. Maybe that was where it all started—why I would go on to prefer the company of dead people over living ones.

But I was ushered to one of the lower school common rooms, and when I poked my head in, I saw the matrons had all the left behind, lonely children watching Toy Story. Every single student left behind was probably too old for that movie, but it didn't seem to matter. The cartoon splayed out across the screen that stretched across the room, and students lounged around, out of their uniforms—not a shade of plaid to be found.

Save for the telltale patten of a Burberry headband, pushing back chestnut hair toward the back of the room. Arna and Sebastian were sitting there; the latter looking perpetually bored and flipping through a cellphone that probably had no internet capability, but he was a haughty Year Eight, much too cool for this room and this movie.

Arna was flipping through a copy of Teen Vogue—decidedly too old for her—not paying the slightest bit of attention to the movie. I wove my way to the back of the room, keeping my head down. Even though it wasn't surprising, in retrospect, our teachers probably dealt with shades of this all the time, children being discarded and entirely unwanted. I didn't want to look anyone in the eye and have them know that I had been promised something else and ended up left behind entirely.

I dropped beside Arna, saying nothing, but her eyes snapped up and she folded her magazine, setting it to the side with a grace that belonged to a Finishing School graduate, not a child, and she tipped her head to survey me, hazel eyes shrewd. Sebastian leaned around her next, disregarding his phone momentarily. He smiled at me, softly. He was the softer version of his sister. Everything about him, significantly less sharp—cheekbones, jaw, eyes, words. But their eyes, even though they were almost exactly the same—down to the last stroma fiber—they just held different things behind them.

Arna didn't pick up the magazine again, pushing Sebastian to sit backward and gesturing to the screen. She flipped both her palms up; one for me, and one for him. I hesitated for a moment, physical affection still foreign to me, having never received any myself. But I interlaced our fingers anyway before her brother grabbed hers, as easy as breathing. She rolled her shoulders back, settling against the wall and making room for my head on the crook of her neck.

I dropped it there, eyes burning and throat hurting because I felt so alone, all alone in the universe, when she squeezed my hand for a brief moment before whispering words that were just for me, for her, for her brother: *To infinity and beyond.*

I can hear her, those same words, echoing in her tiny voice alongside Ethan's as he repeats them. My head snaps over, away from where I was staring vacantly out at the beach. He's holding the letter, but he's looking at me now.

"To infinity and beyond?" he repeats, this time there's a question there.

I give him a small smile and shrug again. He'll never understand. No one will. "It's just something we used to say to each other."

Ethan quirks his lips like he doesn't really believe me, and he shouldn't; I'm lying to him. It's not just something. It's that tattoo that branded our hearts together as unwanted and left behind children who found a family somewhere else. I watch again as he folds up the paper, gently, careful not to snag any of the worn edges, and he holds it out between two tattooed fingers.

It shouldn't mean anything—the fact that he's treating a piece of paper, a letter that doesn't belong to him with such reverence, but it does. It means everything.

"Bali, huh? You ever been to Indonesia?" Ethan leans forward, folding his arms against the table. He keeps talking as I shake my head, carefully securing the letter back in the pocket of my shorts. "I haven't been, either, but a lot of mates I played with, they'd go on holidays there and whatnot. Looks nice."

It does look nice, and I remember thinking the same thing when Arna was there, allegedly on some sort of wellness retreat where she was going to do her yoga teacher training the summer before our last year of school. But all the photos she sent me were of her in precarious positions, hanging off some stranger she just met and something that looked suspiciously like a fishbowl cocktail secured to her other hand.

That was what she thought living was—always onto new experiences, new people, new things. I couldn't recall the last time she stayed in one place for longer than a month in her adult life. When we were kids and then teenagers accompanying her parents, and then her grandfather on their vacations, it was always her arranging the rendezvous location point and time for the three of us to sneak out of whatever vacation home or resort we were staying at, long after we were supposed to be asleep.

I liked doing those things with her, with Sebastian. But they never energized me, gave me life, the way they seemed to for her. I was always too nervous, too anxious, too worried there would be nothing for me to eat, and I'd spiral. Arna was always off, beguiling strangers, spending weekends that would turn into weeks or longer with them.

I look over at Ethan, who's still looking at me. Full lips are pulled back in a sort of half-smile, with that tiny scar there on his upper lip, dark stubble peppering his jaw, and tattoos all the way up his right arm with only those numbers on his left hand. He's practically a stranger to me, albeit one I've now shared more than one bizarre experience with and who I've shown parts of me, parts of my best friend that I wouldn't give to anyone else. It's not just the presence of a different body, someone new to me. It's the mountains behind him and the sea that glitters and winks at me, open, inviting, friendly even. It's the condensation on my fingertips from the amber bottle I'm holding. All new experiences, new things, even a new person.

He's a stranger, and I tip my head, studying the objectively sharp edges and off-putting aura he has emitting from him, cheekbones that are meant to enthrall and then rip out the heart of young girls, ominous-looking, seemingly meaningless swirls of ink and sad eyes.

He's a stranger, but he doesn't look like one. He looks like me. A little lost boy who's been unmoored from the thing he needed most in the world. In his case, it's his career—the once-in-a-lifetime talent that sits in those ligaments and fibers that make up the muscles spanning his body. In my case, it's the death of one-half of my heart.

So, I say something that would make Arna proud. Something she would call living. "Do you want to come with me?"

Chapter Nine

Denpasar is approximately a four-hour flight from Manila. We had to take a short regional flight from Boracay this morning. Ethan picked me up, shockingly on time, because he's given me no indication he's a punctual human being. He strikes me as the opposite, actually. I waited outside by the door, suitcase packed, and letters tucked safely away in one of my sweaters, when he wheeled the jeep in. Waiting outside wouldn't have changed anything if Ethan didn't show up. But he did, only tipping his head before surveying me, one curl falling on his forehead, and his mouth splitting into a grin—agreeing when I said I must have had a brain hemorrhage when I asked him to come with me.

But he was on time. He left his rental at the airport in Boracay and got on that short flight, and now he's sitting beside me. The only seats left were in what they call *club class*. There wasn't first class on the flight because it wasn't big enough, and no business section, either. Just four rows of two seats at the front of the plane.

He gave me the window seat, and I can see him from the corner of my eye, rubbing his palm across his jaw, and his left leg bouncing up and down.

I glance at him. "Are you a nervous flier?"

Ethan shakes his head, palm leaving his jaw and running through his hair quickly, before settling on our shared armrest. His left hand. The one with the numbers.

"Just restless when I have to sit still these days." He arches an eyebrow at me and tries to give me a wry grin, but it falls flat like his eyes are. He doesn't like where his mind goes when he has nothing to distract him. I don't either. But at least I have the benefit of an intact career.

My eyes flick down to the numbers that rise and fall as he drums his fingers against the armrest. Eight on the thumb, followed by seventeen as he raises his index finger, nineteen on the middle, twenty for his ring finger, and the smallest one of all on his pinky finger: twenty-two. I can guess what they mean. Eight was his jersey number; I know that from the sweater he lent me. The rest are probably significant years in his career. We haven't talked about it much, save for what he told me when we met, and the fact that it was the only dream he's ever had. He tore his Achilles. He had surgery and thought his career was over, snorted a line of coke, and failed a drug test he didn't think would apply to him. I googled it, quickly, because I had to look away. I didn't want to look at his failed dreams. He was right. The tabloids ran away with it until Arna died. He had a nickname and everything: Party Boy Barclay.

My lips part, and I'm going to ask him about them, the numbers and what they mean to him, because I genuinely want to know when he speaks again.

"So, if this plane crashed, they'd call in someone like you to identify the remains?" Ethan drops his head against the seat and rolls his neck to look at me.

He's looking at me like he's actually interested. This would be the point that Arna would slap her hands over her ears, or Sebastian, if he was with us, would tell me not to say things like that out loud.

"In all likelihood, yes. It's what's called a mass casualty accident." I cross my legs on my seat and turn to face Ethan. "There's an established protocol to be followed. It does vary from country to country, but it's similar enough. It would usually be a team that was dispatched, for something like a plane this big."

He nods, lips twitching at the corners, like he's amused. "Have you ever had to? For a plane crash?"

It's morbid, macabre, and probably in poor taste for us to be talking about this in the airplane cabin, but Ethan doesn't seem bothered. "Yes, once for a plane two years ago. It wasn't this big. There were thirty-five passengers. It was in Northern British Columbia. One of the engines failed, and it went down in the mountains. They didn't find it for a while."

"You were a bit young for that, to be considered an expert, yeah?" Ethan asks, and his features are softer, like it makes him sad somehow. I don't know why it would, though.

It's sinister, gruesome to most people, but not to me, because they don't see what I see. When parents fall to the ground, sobbing in relief because it wasn't their kid found buried, or when shoulders sag, weary with relief because they know where their loved one was after all this time.

"I am...I was. Young, I mean. I'm just good at it, I guess." I shrug and smile softly.

His thumb twitches, and he exhales, head still rolled to face me, raising his eyebrows. "Who grows up wanting to be a dentist? And then takes it even further, to be a special kind of dentist who identifies bodies and bones?"

"I do a lot of free work. In mobile public health units, in shelters and rehabs. Drugs ruin your teeth pretty quickly, especially if you don't have access to regular dental care. Giving someone their smile back, when they were too embarrassed to use it when their teeth were bad or gone, or when society told them they didn't deserve one because maybe they ruined it themselves...or being the reason a parent knows where their child has been all this time because I was able to extract the pulp from a tooth someone found in a creek bed? I can't think of a more worthwhile existence." I pause, nostrils flaring, and a bit of embarrassment flaming across my cheeks because he asked me a rhetorical question, meant to be a joke, and I gave him a soliloquy.

But a muscle in Ethan's cheek twitches, and he knits his eyebrows, attention rapt.

"And you know, no one ruins their teeth like a young girl who spends hours throwing up, because she just doesn't feel like she's enough. I work with a few local eating disorder inpatient and outpatient rehabs—"

"That one sounds important," Ethan interrupts.

"It is. I had an eating...thing. Some issues, when I was younger. It turns out stomach acid is hard on your molars," I say with a forced levity. I look up at him, lips pulling to the side. "We can't all be soccer stars, Ethan."

"Football," he corrects immediately, but he's smiling.

"Okay." I roll my eyes, pushing his arm over so I can use the armrest too, before settling back in my seat.

I hear him laugh beside me, and I can see his head roll back. He fishes his phone out of the pocket of his khaki shorts. I watch from the corner of my eye as he opens a book, and I want to lean over and ask what he's reading, but his legs and fingers aren't jumping anymore, and everything about him feels quiet, so I stay quiet too.

I booked the homestay written on the back of the envelope by Arna—somewhere she stayed when she came to Bali one summer on a whim, saying she was going to become a certified yoga teacher and open a studio for rich, shipping wives in Athens. It lasted about two weeks, as far as I remember, but she stayed for a month or two longer than that.

It didn't occur to me to call and ask.

Ethan pulls back the sliding glass door. The room is on the second floor, a wraparound balcony with two chairs and a table just in front overlooking the ground-level bungalows surrounding the plunge pool. The property is beautiful—all Balinese architecture with swirling adornments of red and gold, leafy palms, and greenery I can't even begin to name lining the property.

But I can hear Arna laughing maniacally in my ear at this twist of fate. I asked a stranger to accompany me, a beautiful one, and there's only one bed.

Ethan steps into the bedroom, and I follow, colliding with his back.

One bed. Albeit, a nice one. Crisp white sheets are tucked tightly into the corners of the chestnut bed frame, an intricate red and gold runner that mirrors the architecture outside stretches along the foot. A long sideboard that matches the same wood grain as the bed is pushed against the side wall with shelves for both of our suitcases. A TV is mounted to the wall right across from the bed and beside it sits a desk with an ornate mirror with chipped gold-painted molding surrounding it.

My lips part, and a sort of abject horror fills me. I feel my fingers curling upward, the middle one pointing toward the sky, because even though I know she didn't plan this, it feels decidedly like something she would—me, a stranger, and one bed.

Ethan looks at me over his shoulder, lips splitting into a wry grin. His oversized backpack hits the floor when he shrugs it off his shoulders. It looks like it's one of those giant 70L ones that backpackers take for months at a time, and it makes me think he was planning on being in self-imposed exile for a long time.

"You trying to get me in bed, Ten?" he asks, peeling my hand off the handle of my suitcase and hauling it over the tiny step to get into the room.

I narrow my eyes at him, pushing past him into the room. "You have a rather inflated sense of self, Ethan."

"What? You never shared a bed with a stranger before?" Ethan brings my suitcase over to the sideboard, shoving it onto the top shelf.

"Yes. But it's typically been because of an invitation, not a surprise foisted upon me because I didn't think to ask when I called to book the room." I fold my arms across my chest, out of habit more than anything. I started doing it after Arna died.

It's apparently a turn of phrase, a figure of speech—that your heart breaks. But just ask anyone who's grieving, and they might tell you otherwise. It hurt a little less when I did that, added a physical barrier to keep my heart from tumbling out of my chest, made the dull ache seem a little more distant.

I move past Ethan, where his tattooed hands are tugging on the bed runner, inspecting the gold threads as he peers into the bathroom.

It's simple. An open shower, nothing but a drain on the floor and a head hanging from the ceiling, a toilet, sink, and mirror. Close quarters for me and a man I hardly know.

I lean against the wooden doorway, arms still folded. It's warm in here, the frayed edges of my ancient denim shorts sticking to my thighs. My hair in desperate need of a touch-up, curls around my face.

Ethan raises his eyebrows at me, lips quirking up to the side, and nodding slowly at my answer. He's splayed out on the bed now, the right side, closest to the door. His right hand is behind his head, revealing the tattoo on his inner bicep.

I tip my elbow up toward the ink of that hand, seemingly reaching for nothing. It's a small expanse of skin, but it seems endless. "What's that one mean?"

He peers down at it briefly before his lower lip juts out, and he shakes his head. "Nothing really."

"So, what? They're all just meaningless whirls of ink?" I ask, and it's a bit more sardonic than I mean for it to be.

I watch him lift his left hand from where it sits on his thigh, the one with all those numbers on it, and bring it to the front of his face. He rolls his fingers briefly before making a fist, and his gaze flicks up to mine. "Pretty much."

I open my mouth to apologize. I don't know what they mean, but I know they're important.

But his hand is resting on his thigh again, one smooth motion, muscles twitching so quickly I hardly see it, and his head angles to the side as he asks, "What's next?"

The next letter, marked number four with this very address scrawled across the back sits unopened atop all my clothes in my suitcase.

I raise my eyebrows at him, holding tighter around my chest, because my heart hurts extra at the thought of it, and with a bravado I don't feel, I cross the room and open my suitcase quickly, ignoring the mess of haphazardly folded clothes, and grab the letter. My breath sticks in my throat, and I carefully tear open the envelope. "Let's see."

Baby Nov,

Welcome to Bali—the world of lost little privileged girls like me.

It's beautiful there. I was there that fall after you spent the summer in Spetses with Sebastian and me. Remember, the clinic you worked at had a flood, and you were left with unexpected time off? You were doing your first courses on forensic dentistry after you graduated. We would go to the beach all morning and then come back for you to take your classes online when they started back in the Eastern Time zone.

Sebastian and I would lounge by the pool, you would sit in the shade, under the awning of the house, textbooks all spread around you, with those noise-canceling headphones you bought because you said our laughs were too loud. But you would always sneak a glass of wine when Seb and I drank Ouzu. I loved that summer.

You left, back to Toronto, back to the practice when it opened back up, and I had decided the corporate shipping life was not for me, so I left, too.

I said I was going to do my yoga teacher training, and I was. I took one teacher training class, and when I was waiting for a smoothie at the bar afterward, I met this guy. His name isn't worth mentioning, and he's not really worth remembering, save for the fact that it turned out he was running some sort of wannabe international drug smuggling ring—getting party drugs into the hands of kids with too much money and no sense of self-preservation because nothing bad had ever happened to them.

I said I would do it once because he was incredible in bed (the only redeeming quality about him), and I thought I owed him at least that for the orgasms. But it turned out I was good at it, and I kind of liked it. So I did it a few more times.

Maybe I did it because I knew that any trouble I got in would never stick. For the thrill. Who knows. But I did it, and then I got bored one day and was onto the next thing.

I wouldn't recommend you follow in my exact footsteps, Nov. You would be a horrible drug mule. But I did take more than one cooking class. I loved Balinese cooking. Don't ferry the drugs—but learn how to make satay.

Love,

Arna

I blink, once, twice, three times—entirely unsure of what the hell I just read. It wasn't surprising; it was sort of typical of her actually. It was the type of outlandish thing she would do and get away with, the kind of story she would have in her back pocket to pull out at the opportune moment to shock and awe. She was full of stories like that, and she had a particular knack for telling them at exactly the right moment, using them to pull people into her orbit.

What surprises me is that she didn't tell me. I didn't know about the random party boy with his drugs or his affinity for serving orgasms, I didn't know about her relationship on the beach, I didn't know that she worked as a paddleboard guide all summer and lied about it. Maybe there were lots of things I didn't know about her.

I press my palm into my chest briefly, waiting for the ache to stop, and it does, sort of. It feels like a dull thud—the occasional spurt of blood from a limb that's already been hacked off and has been bleeding out for a while now. "I guess that explains why she never got her certification."

I feel like shoving the letter back into my suitcase, not giving a shit if it folds and creases, if her perfectly curated and illustrated swooping g's and annoyingly loopy l's were destroyed. But I don't do that. I fold it up and tuck it in the pocket of my jean shorts.

"What's that?" Ethan asks, and I look over my shoulder. He's still lying on the bed, one hand behind his head, but his eyebrows are pulled together.

I smile, a dumb bland smile of someone whose stomach was slowly being eaten away with dread. It shouldn't be a big deal—two little white lies between best friends. And to most people it wouldn't be. But most best friends weren't me and Arna. "Nevermind."

His lips turn down, and he looks at me appraisingly, probably because I'm a shitty liar and always have been. "So, what's next?"

"Cooking class," I say through the still-forced smile.

"Nothing tonight then? I'm fucking starved, so we can grab dinner, yeah?" Ethan sits up, contraction of his abdominal muscles annoyingly obvious through the thin t-shirt.

I narrow my eyes at him. "You ate on the plane, less than an hour ago."

Ethan grins, shaking his head before pushing off the bed and stretching his arms across his chest. "Professional athlete. Very hungry most of the time."

"Former," I say quietly, a tiny smile pulling at my lips. He's a stranger, but I think he's laughed more at my jokes than most people I know in real life.

Cocking his head, he studies me for a moment before his smile stretches even wider. "Told you that you were a piece of work. Next time you mention your best friend, you want me to add the *former* addendum?"

My smile falls briefly because it doesn't feel funny for a moment, doesn't feel like something I can laugh about right now, not when there were actually secrets between us. Former is too close to *liar* in my head.

I nod softly instead and tip my chin toward the door.

Ethan raises his eyebrows before shoving both of his hands in his pockets and stepping in front of me for a moment. He's imposing—all broad shoulders and entirely too moody. His lips quirk to the side, and my breath catches in my throat.

I'm still clutching my heart through my chest, and I can feel it—the moment the rhythm changes. My eyes widen, and he must know, must possess some preternatural awareness of what happens when someone who looks like him stares at anyone because he winks at me.

It's entirely possible I imagined it, the grief and little lies all intermingling in my brain and making my neurons misfire, because he leaves my space, my breath leaves my throat, and he's across the room.

Ethan pulls open the sliding door for me, and I watch that hand on his bicep stretch into the abyss.

I look up at him and smile in thanks, and I step out onto the balcony that surrounds our room, like I know my best friend moonlit as a drug mule, and pretend that there are still no secrets between us.

Chapter Ten

He might be perfect. Genetically, I mean. He's clearly got a penchant for bad choices if that line of coke that cost him his career was any indication—an example of a grown-up man with too much money's version of a temper tantrum when something didn't go his way. And he's kind of abrasive. Ethan isn't outright rude. He's polite and follows all normal conventions of conversation and social interaction. He makes eye contact when people speak to him, and he says please and thank you. But I've noticed he doesn't smile at others much, and there's a harsh, unfriendly set of his features when he's talking to anyone but me.

But he's sitting across from me, the scratched wooden table stretching between us. The restaurant is down the road from our homestay, the walkway to where we're sitting now is bordered by palm fronds, tiny sparkling lights, and a chalkboard with a hastily written menu. But it says *beer*, and that's good enough for Ethan. He tipped his chin and pushed back some of the leaves in a fit of gallantry when we walked in. It's oppressively humid, especially on the short walk over, the denim of my shorts sticking to my thighs uncomfortably.

I can picture Arna, nose wrinkled in displeasure that I didn't bring a cute linen matching set like the ones she favored every summer in Greece. She would have told me I packed all wrong, and she would probably be right. She evidently knew more about packing than even I knew because apparently she was lugging drugs all over this country and never got caught.

Dim lights are strewn above us, anchored on poles that are randomly stuck into the floor across the restaurant. Colored bean bag chairs that look like they've seen better days are scattered around, interspersed between long wooden picnic tables like the one we're at.

In the light of day, he's striking. But under the dim light? I think that's what he was made for. It's throwing shadows across his jaw that make the bone structure more impressive somehow. His hair, dark brown in the daylight, borders black now, all iridescent while the lights swing over it, and I think his eyes see right through me.

"Do you ever drink water?" I ask as he raises a bottle to his mouth.

He pauses, pulling it back and studying it for a moment before taking a sip. "No." His response is clipped and dry, but his eyes light up for a moment.

My thumb worries at the peeling plastic, covering the restaurant menu that was dropped at our table before we sat down. I have a hard time going to restaurants without looking at the menu first. Food, the actual composition of it, the idea of it, doesn't really bother me as much anymore. I was able to work through most of that during my outpatient program. Arna had diligently and faithfully planted herself in the poorly lit waiting room, back ramrod straight in the shitty, plastic yellow chair while she flipped through Cosmopolitan or Vogue instead of doing her homework.

It's more about the social situations now, the things I worked to protect myself against, so the inevitable sweating of my palms and tightening of my throat wouldn't start, so I wouldn't start counting the calories, the composition and the nutrients of the food. I needed to know what was on the menu everywhere I went, what might be served for dinner, how the food might have been prepared. Arna didn't think that was living. She said she hated it, for me, that I couldn't swing by a restaurant or a bar on impulse, that I needed to pick out all my meals ahead of time. She never quite understood that if I had to choose—a war with myself so fucking horrible that even looking in a mirror felt insurmountable most days, or the inability to go somewhere now without looking at the menu—I would always pick the latter.

But I was trying, for her. Because she was dead and gone, and one of us needed to live now.

I was trying so hard when the server came to take our order, I pointed to the first thing I saw on the menu, and now I'm too scared to look to see what's in it when it comes out. Ethan didn't seem to care what he ordered, either, randomly picking three dishes and seeming more interested in their beer selection.

I look up at him, smiling tightly. It probably looks fake, because it is.

He shrewdly eyes me for a moment before he slides his beer across the table to me. It knocks against my plastic green cup of water. Sharing his beer is probably the Ethan Barclay equivalent of a hug.

My smile turns soft because it seems as much of a consoling gesture as he could possibly make. The glass is cold against my fingers, a welcome reprieve, and I bring it to my mouth, taking a small sip before pushing it back across the table.

"Are you going to tell me what was in that last letter?" Ethan asks, tattooed fingers wrapping against the glass again. I don't think it's ever occurred to me how big his hands are. He'd make a terrible dentist. Under the light, the edges of those numbers on his fingers look like they're bleeding into his skin.

I can feel the letter in my pocket, and my hand drops to it subconsciously. I don't want to talk about the letter. I tip my chin toward his hand, all those numbers. "Are you going to tell me what those mean?"

His hand tenses for a moment, and he lets go of the bottle, opening his hand and studying his fingers. Ethan stays silent for a moment, tongue poking into his left cheek, and when he looks up at me, there's a sort of resignation about his features and the ghost of a tiny, wistful smile.

He sticks up his thumb, turning it toward me, so I can see the number eight. "My number, as you well know, Ten. Since I could kick a ball. Always been mine. Looked pretty good on your back." He touches his thumb against his palm, his index finger facing me now. "Seventeen years old. Playing for the academy and got called up. Signed my contract but rode the bench for half a year." His index finger goes down, and his middle finger goes up. My lips part, but he grins at me. *Nineteen.* "Not a fuck you, but the year we were league champions, and I scored the final goal." His middle finger goes down, and his ring finger goes up. *Twenty.* "My first Euro Cup." His pinky finger, still bigger than any of my own, is the last to go up. *Twenty-two.* "World Cup. We played like fucking shit, and I lost a tooth."

I smile, noticing his mouth move in a way that tells me his tongue is running along his incisor. "Your implant is impeccable. Whoever did it, did excellent work."

"If I'm ever out of exile, I'll tell them you said so." Ethan smiles, but it feels forced, and I notice his eyes stray to his right hand, all the knuckles empty and ready to be painted with other numbers, with meaning. "Think I should get one on this hand that says 23? The year I lost it all and became Great Britain's biggest fuck up?"

I watch him for a moment, and I have a hard time believing he couldn't get it all back if wanted to, if he tried to. Instead he's here with me.

"Why'd you come with me, Ethan?" I ask softly, tipping my head, and my loose braid falls to the side. I think I know why. I'm not stupid; I'm the opposite, actually. Highly logical to a fault. But it feels important to hear him say it, for some reason.

I hear him exhale through his nostrils, and his eyes go back down to his tattoos one more time. He looks back up at me, and I think I see something shatter behind them. "Nothing else to do. And besides, bit of a reprieve to spend time with someone who doesn't look at me like I'm England's biggest failure."

I'm about to say something, to make what Arna would call one of my off-putting jokes, but Ethan seems to like my humor when our plates are dropped in between us.

I don't see what Ethan ordered because I only see what's set in front of me. I see bone, covered in a sticky, thick-looking sauce. Pork. I have the hardest time with meat. It takes me hours to pick out cuts of meat at the grocery store because it needs to be just right—look exactly like I need it to look. The only person in the world I trusted to pick something like that out for me is dead. It's terribly ironic really, that the sight of an animal bone would make my eyes burn and my palms go clammy, my fingers to feather uselessly in space, because I don't think I can grab one of these, even though I know I'd probably like the taste. That the sight of this bone would make me want to cry.

I squint, half-tempted to rub my hands against my eyes, like I can make it go away and pretend I'm not a thirty-year-old woman, haunted by the ghosts of food that used to control her life. And then I see those numbers—eight, seventeen, nineteen, twenty, twenty-two. Ethan grabs my plate, dragging it over to his side of the table, the other hand pushing one of his in front of me.

This dish, I recognize. I've had it before. Mi Goreng. Vegetarian. Onion. Bok Choy. Shallot. Cabbage. One somehow perfectly cooked fried egg on top.

"Why'd you do that?" I look up, lips parted, everything about me feeling so fucking heavy, but my lungs feel fuller because I like the looks of this dish. It's something I would have picked for myself.

Ethan shrugs, grabbing a rib with his bare hands and looking beyond me at the TV hanging over the bar. "Yours looks better."

I can tell he's lying. I feel like crying for an entirely different reason, but I just smile at him. All the sharp edges that make up this stranger, who sits across from me eating my food because I couldn't, feel soft against my skin and my heart. I reach forward and grab his beer, bringing it to my lips before grabbing the chopsticks from the center of the table and looking down at my own plate.

The corners of Ethan's lips twitch, and he raises his hand to the bartender for another drink.

The night air is still warm, but a breeze picks up as Ethan and I leave the restaurant. He ate all the accidentally ordered ribs, griped when I finished his beer but ordered me another. He didn't mention the letter or Arna again, save for briefly mentioning he's never attended a cooking class, and for the first time in his adult life, he's free to eat whatever he wants whenever he wants because he doesn't need to put away a certain amount of calories to sustain his body when he's on a "Day Two, Day Six" schedule, whatever that means.

I didn't ask anything more about his failed dreams and general state of possibly permanent exile. It's easy to fill a night with him, and whenever silence fell, it wasn't uncomfortable.

I sort of forgot about the one bed, the forced trope of a romance novel I'm certainly not living in, until he pulls open the sliding glass door of the room, one hand holding a six-pack he stopped at a tiny market for on the four-minute walk back, and there it is—one bed.

He set the six-pack on the nightstand, and I avoid the looming single mattress and change into my pajamas, which only match because Arna gifted them to me. It was some sort of set that made me look like I was wearing a tuxedo.

"I won't make a pass at you, Ten. You're safe with me, yeah?" Ethan flops down on the bed, and now I'm standing here awkwardly by the bathroom door, shifting back and forth on the balls of my feet. Getting changed for Ethan only consisted of him ditching his shirt and changing into a pair of sweat shorts; the same ones I slept in when I met him, the letter eight stitched along the bottom on the left leg.

His forehead creases, and he sits up, running a palm across his face. "Oi—if the bed makes you uncomfortable, I'll ring down and see if they have a cot or something, yeah? If not, I'll sleep on the floor?"

"It's fine, Ethan." I force a smile.

Sharing a bed with a stranger is something I usually reserve for sex. I've had plenty of casual sex, which might be a surprising fact for many reasons, for the amount of time I've spent at war with the body I live in. And there was a time it was a physical impossibility for me, and sometimes it still was, but recovery taught me my war, my personal siege, the one I waged and the trenches I dug and fought in, was more with myself than it ever was the flesh and bones that made up my body. It always surprised Arna because she maintained the thought of me being a cold and unfeeling person, distant and void, because my parents never loved me, and therefore likely incapable of a loving relationship. It never even bothered me when they stayed the night.

I'm not about to have casual sex with him, a travel companion I've collected while I chase my dead best friend's ghost. He's beautiful, entirely unworldly, and physically perfect. But I think I might be a bit worried Ethan's like a scared deer—one wrong movement, and he'll dart away into the bushes of the next country to continue his exile, when he sort of feels like a buoy. A lifeboat of sorts who rescued me from the literal and proverbial stormy sea. It feels easier to follow around Arna's ghost when I'm not alone.

"If you say so." He eyes me for a moment before pulling two bottles from the six-pack sitting on the nightstand beside him.

I've seen him shirtless—multiple times now, actually. But this feels more intimate. The way a person undresses in private, it's entirely different than how you might take off a sweater, remove a shirt covering up a bathing suit in public. Entirely safe, guard down, no walls up when you're undressing in your home. That's what this feels like.

As I drop down onto the bed beside him, pushing up to sit against the headboard, and taking the now open bottle of beer, it's like I've been invited into his home, and he's been invited into mine.

I pick up my phone from where I left it on the nightstand—no text messages, shocker. But I start to go through my emails as Ethan turns on the TV and flicks through the channels.

I'm on an extended leave from my practice, but I left myself open to consultation appointments I have with different police departments and medical examiners. It's not usually just one forensic odontologist on appointment or on consultation. There's usually a list of us, but I said I could make myself available for anything that required an opinion from a distance. It strikes me as being kind of pathetic. I'm doing the exact opposite of living my life in the moment, so I start looking for cooking classes in Ubud we can go to instead, when there's a loud, shrill noise, like a scream coming from the TV.

I glance up, and there *are* screams coming from behind the opening credits of some horror movie or another.

Ethan rolls his head against the headboard, eyes glinting. "Picked this one for you."

I roll my eyes at him but point toward the TV, with the opening scene playing now. A group of friends open the door to a lakeside cabin rental, and one of the brunettes is the first to walk through, shrieking and throwing her arms open and spinning around in a wide circle. "She gets killed first."

"How do you know?" Ethan scoffs, pausing mid-sip, fingers poised on the neck of the bottle. "Seen this before?"

"No." I shake my head. "It's just a fact. She's the effervescent one, the center of attention, and will probably do something reckless. The first one to jump into the lake, blah blah. The killer will find her first and dismember her in a very memorable death scene."

She's like Arna—kind of a bitch, but somehow magnetic in all the right ways. Arna was many things, but she definitely would have been killed first in a horror film.

"You're pretty weird, yeah?" Ethan says, head still rolled to face me. But he's smiling when he says it, like it's endearing somehow. "Is this some sort of...pick me thing? Your commitment to weirdness, stuff that makes most people uncomfortable?"

My lips pull down, and I shake my head at him again, blinking a few times. "No. You've never just...said something and had the rest of the room wonder what the fuck it is you're talking about?"

"No," Ethan answers, running a hand through his hair and taking a swig of beer.

"Oh. Well, how lucky for you." I turn back to my phone, clicking on the first link to a multi-course traditional Balinese cooking class.

"You can say whatever you want to me, Ten. I don't mind," Ethan offers, bringing a hand to rest behind his head.

I can see his obliques tense and stretch from the corner of my eye, and the pop of his tricep. It's annoying and distracting, so I narrow my eyes on the phone screen.

Jake was in good shape. He worked out every morning before he went into the office, and I think most of that was for posterity more than anything, just making sure he looked the part. But you can tell Ethan has spent a lifetime like this. It's just the natural state of his body now, what he's genetically destined for.

"How charitable of you," I murmur, scrolling through the photos of the cooking class. It looks nice, hosted in the home of the instructors and moving through five courses. The kitchen looks beautiful, huge and stretching out across an open air space, set against sprawling fields. "Does this class look okay to you?"

Ethan peers over my shoulder. He's entirely in my space, taking up all the oxygen, and the stacked muscles of his shoulders are much too close to my mouth. He's disarming. It's entirely scientific, what someone like him does to your body. You get a spike of serotonin when someone who looks like he looks is close to you, and right now it's making it hard to breathe. He nods, a curl falling against the top of his right ear. "Looks alright."

He leans back, some of the air goes back into my lungs, and I stare determinedly away from him for a moment before looking back at my phone.

"It doesn't say what they're making," I mutter, more to myself. Eyes narrowed on the screen, my thumb swipes furiously to try and find the menu when Ethan grips my wrist for a moment.

I turn my head, and he lets go quickly, swallowing, like he's embarrassed, and he thinks he overstepped. But he hasn't. I'm not sure why. I don't usually like to be touched; Arna and the occasional hug from her brother had been the only exceptions. But I don't mind the feeling of Ethan's fingers on my skin.

"It'll be alright, Ten," he whispers before tipping his chin back toward the TV, where that girl from the start of the movie is currently getting hacked apart because the killer found her in her shitty hiding spot. "You called it, yeah?"

I offer him a smile and toss my phone down between us, the bedding puffing up around it. I finally take the first sip of my own beer, shoulders relaxing ever so slightly. "I guess I did."

Chapter Eleven

We both fell asleep at some point, the sound of screams and the hacking of body parts clearly not deterring either of us. Sharing a bed wasn't uncomfortable. But we were each pushed to the absolute opposite ends this morning, careful not to stray or fall too close to the middle.

We skipped the complimentary morning breakfast because our cooking class was meeting in a nearby food market. Buying the day's ingredients was part of the class, apparently. I'm not sure if that made me more comfortable or less, the idea of getting to pick out everything individually to my specifications.

We're trailing behind the host, Made, who is much more exuberant than I am in general, and certainly Ethan, who keeps yawning widely and stretching his arms up, making his white t-shirt rise up on his abdomen. I elbowed him the first time, because it seemed rude, and now his sunglasses are over his eyes, and he keeps covering his mouth with a closed fist, swallowing yawns that are anything but subtle.

Craning my neck, I say nothing as Made walks everyone else in the group through the market, gesturing to various spices and vegetables, landing us at a butcher's counter. There's a slab of chicken sitting on a butcher's block, and it's a bit hard to hear the specifics back here amongst all the other noises.

It's an open air market, just off one of the main roads in Ubud, only a ten-minute walk from our homestay. I'm running my hand along the back of my neck, gathering some of the hairs curling there, and attempting in futility to slick them back into the knot at the back of my head, when I feel fingers brush against the sides of my ribs, just under my arm, tugging slightly at the linen of my loose tank top. I pull back, swatting his hand away, and look over to see Ethan's sunglasses are pushed down his nose, his eyes narrowed on my skin. I feel the linen brush back against the spot, but I can still feel his gaze there.

He cocks his head, lips parting in a sort of feral smile. A low whistle sounds from his throat, and he arches one eyebrow at me, gray eyes glinting mischievously. "And you say my tattoos are meaningless whirls of ink, Ten. Didn't notice that before."

"Pay attention," I whisper, widening my eyes at him and tipping my chin toward the front of the group.

"No, I wanna see your tattoo." Ethan's tone is goading, and he forms a fist before flexing out his fingers.

I turn my back to him and cross my arms, fingers coming within reach of the tattoo he's so intent on seeing, just beyond the thin material of my shirt. "And I want to learn. We don't all get what we want, apparently."

"Don't tell me you were the one who shushed everyone in class when they were having a good time?" Ethan bends down so his mouth is level with my ear.

I can feel him behind me. My breath catches, and I straighten my spine and neck, tipping my chin up and continuing to look pointedly forward where Made holds up various cuts of meat.

"Yes. I liked learning then, and I like learning now." My words are steady, but I can feel his breath on my ear. My lips part involuntarily, and I swallow before closing them, biting down on the bottom one. "You're disarming. Leave me alone."

His palm finds my ribcage, fingers whispering over the seam of my top. His voice drops and so does my heart. "Show me."

I narrow my eyes at him, even though he can't see me, and try to swat his hand away from where his fingers are now rubbing the material of my tank top back and forth, yanking down the already loose side. The ink is unobscured because of my thin bralette, with only a tiny strap that wraps around my ribcage.

He doesn't touch the inked letter, the thick block that makes up the serif font of the letter "A" that's bled a bit over the years. Arna had a matching one, an N on the opposite side. He doesn't touch it, but his fingers get close, and I can feel them as they trace the air above it.

I drop my hand and let the linen cover it once again. "And the matching one for me doesn't exist on this earth anymore because her body is well and through the active decay process, six feet under the ground in a cemetery in Athens. Happy?"

I can see Ethan pull his hand back, and it flutters uselessly in space for a moment before he takes his sunglasses off, hanging them on the neckline of his t-shirt. His thumb scores a line, barely there, down my shoulder before he shoves his hands in his pockets. "No, Ten. That doesn't make me happy. Tell me about it."

The group starts shuffling forward as Made moves to the next stall, all cut fruits and freshly squeezed juices. She picks up something that looks like a dragon fruit and holds it out to an old man, who looks like he's going to be annoying, and his wife. They're both wearing matching t-shirts that have a map of Bali printed on them.

Ethan presses a knuckle into my back gently, and we move to the periphery of the semi-circle the group has formed.

My nostrils flare and lips press together before I speak. "We got them when we were eighteen. You know we went to school together from the time we were ten until we graduated college at twenty-two. It was her idea, something about how we'd never be parted. What is it you want to know? That we were constantly laughing at things only we found funny? That we were entirely different but somehow the same? That we could spend hours in silence, and it was just as comfortable as spending hours talking? She pretended to be philosophical but really she just hopped onto any trend she thought was in vogue—mediums, tarot, energy healing. That no one was ever as proud of one of us as the other? That we watched the same TV shows religiously over years and liked the same music? That she would stand in the grocery aisle for hours until she found the exact food she knew I would want, that—"

I suck in a breath and cut myself off, shaking my head. The group has moved on to the next stall, all woven baskets of what look to be different herbs. "She was my best friend," I whisper uselessly, my eyes prickling. I blink rapidly, wiping my fingers along my lash line.

Ethan's head is tipped toward me, his mouth still dangerously close to my ear. I feel his hands behind my back, moving between my shoulder blades, and I'm about to ask him what he's doing when he holds his sunglasses out to me. A strangled laugh catches in my throat, and I take them, sliding them over my eyes, even though we're sort of inside. "Thank you."

Ethan smiles at me, and it's an entirely different smile. It's soft, and the edges of his lips twitch. He looks boyish, but just for a minute, and then he's all sharp edges again. "Anytime, Ten."

He walks ahead of me, stopping at the stall everyone was just at. I stand back, seemingly rooted into the ground through the bottoms of my too-thin sandals. Tears well behind the sunglasses, and I blink for a moment longer, as Ethan nods at the vendor, pulling his wallet from his pocket and tugging out Rupiah, Indonesia's currency, to trade it for some sort of light pink juice.

His hand wraps around the whole thing, and he jerks his head at me, like he's beckoning me.

A tiny smile pulls at my lips. "I'm not a dog."

Ethan grins at me, holding the already perspiring cup out, as I finally step forward, breaking whatever roots and vines that snuck up through the Earth along with the memory of my best friend, keeping me there, trapped in time.

I'm still smiling softly at him when I take it because it reminds me of something Arna would have done. Plied me with food, drink, anything to feed me, because she said it was the way to heal the soul, to heal my heart. It's cold against my fingertips, and without thinking, I press it to my chest for a moment before tipping my neck. I close my eyes and smile again, bringing the straw to my lips.

His pupils widen a fraction, tracing the drops of liquid the perspiration left across my collarbone and the column of my neck. His jaw twitches, and I watch him swallow.

Swallowing involves about twenty muscles. I had always thought they were interesting from a purely scientific perspective—what those tiny little ligaments and tendons can do, how they support an essential function for your body to survive. But on him, the cords of muscle that taper down his neck—he makes it look beautiful. Watching him, those fascinating small muscles at work, it makes me feel for just a moment like maybe I can survive, too.

"Thank you, Ethan," I whisper as I walk toward the entrance of the market where the rest of the group is headed, back to the parked van.

He falls into step beside me, and I take another sip before handing it to him. I notice he's careful to keep his fingers from touching mine when he takes it.

"How are you fucking doing that so neatly?" Ethan mutters, fingers fumbling over the rice paper in front of him. All the ingredients he's supposed to be wrapping in the Balinese lumpia spill out onto the tiny leaf-shaped plate he's working over.

I glance over at him, tucking the rice paper in tightly around the vermicelli noodles, bean sprouts, and everything else chopped up in there. "Excellent dexterity. Yours should be better, professional athlete."

Ethan shoves the plate away from him, taking a swig of the beer sitting beside him. He levels me with a look, leaning back in his chair, and tossing one arm over the back of it. The arm of his shirt pulls up, and there's that hand again, stretching across his bicep. We stare for just for a moment, and Ethan looks like he's going to say something when we're interrupted.

"Did you say professional athlete? I thought you looked familiar." The older man, who *is* exceedingly annoying, asks from where he sits across from me.

"No. I don't." Ethan barely spares him a glance, lip curling in distaste before gesturing to my plate. "Give me yours then, yeah?"

He reaches for it, reflexes still practically subhuman given the fact that the most physical activity I've seen him do is open beer bottles.

I jerk it back, fingers wrapping around the porcelain stem on my own leaf-shaped plate. "I'm not giving you my lumpia. Children don't get rewarded for being rude and neither will you."

"November." Ethan's voice is low, a mocking sort of warning in it as his eyes flash. He starts forward, raising his eyebrows at me. "You have extra."

Pushing my plate farther out of his reach, I lean forward and grab his. It's a mess of sticky rice paper that he used too much oil on and half-smashed noodles. "I'll see if I can salvage any of this...wreckage."

"How do you two know each other?" the older woman asks, smiling blandly at us while sloppily folding her own paper around its poorly packaged contents.

Ire fills Ethan's eyes, and he rolls his neck, deigning to look over at the two of them. His fingers twist on the neck of his beer before he speaks. "Ten and I go way back."

"Ten?" the old man asks, voice perking up like he senses some sort of quirky story, when really Ethan is just fucking bad at math. "Why do you call her Ten? I thought you said your name was November?"

"Just look at her." Ethan offers with a shrug, taking a sip of his beer.

The roll slips from my hand, and everything I was working on spills across the plate. I flick my eyes up to Ethan, ready to tell him to fuck off—that it's entirely crossing the line to make fun of me. But any angry retort dies in my mouth when I see the way he's looking at me. I don't think anyone has ever looked at me like that.

His full lips are in their usual harsh line, jaw set as always. But it's in his eyes. Dark and endlessly fascinating, and usually the exact color of an ominous cloud—no light to get down to earth—they look lighter. Like I've made him lighter. I'm about to tell him he can't look at me like that. I'm not in the business of making anyone lighter, and it's a mistake if he thinks I'm some grand solution to his pain when I'm drowning in my own; lungs constantly on the verge of an awful death rattle, when clapping starts behind us.

Ethan jerks his head, and whatever was living in the stroma fibers of his eyes is gone now, and I blink rapidly, because I think I miss it already.

Turning my head to see Made now holding a tray, beautifully painted and inlaid with reds and golds that match her open-air kitchen, but it's host to matte black bowls, and I don't know what's in them.

I can't hear her, either. I look down at my hands, spreading my fingers and trying to ignore the gnawing of my heart against my ribcage. I don't know what's in those bowls, and I didn't prepare for this. I blink, trying to ignore the other voice in my head, the one that's sobbing and pleading, a desperate wish to be a normal person who could just try a food without being set back a decade, who could be like Arna, who could be what they're trying to be.

The edges of my vision blur, and I duck my head, wiping at my eyes because I don't want to eat it. But I wish so badly I was normal and could.

I can't really tell what it is when the bowl is set in front of me, but I think it's some sort of seafood soup. There's a tiny ladle set down beside me.

I don't want to be rude, and I want to be anyone but the person I am, so I pick it up, fingers slipping against the smooth porcelain. There's a scrape of a chair moving across the floor, and a tattooed hand grabs my wrist. I turn my head, blinking rapidly, but it does nothing to stop the tears. I feel one fall down my cheek.

Ethan's there beside me, fingers warm as he takes the spoon with his other hand and sets it down. "You don't need to eat it, November."

"Arna would have," I whisper uselessly, my features sort of collapsing and a sob sneaking up my throat.

"Why are you doing this? Why would she want you to do this? It seems cruel." The usual biting, arrogant tone found in Ethan's voice is gone. It's soft now, and I think his thumb brushes across the sensitive skin of my inner wrist.

I gesture to the bowl, shaking my head. He'll never understand. No one will. She was with me when my life was utterly gone, entirely consumed by food. "Food—it was all part of living for her. She just wants me to live."

He tips his head to the side, leaning forward so I know the words are just meant for me. Not for anyone else in this room, and certainly not for the ghost with manicured hands that's been following me around. "Maybe she should have thought about what living meant to you."

"Please don't start," I say, my voice small and utterly pathetic.

I want to throw the bowl across the room, to watch it smash against the brocade wall, and I want to tip my head back and scream.

But most of all I want to know why the universe would be so cruel, to leave me alone without the only person who ever understood me.

Ethan looks like he wants to argue, but his lips pull up to the side, a sort of resigned grin, as he tips his chin to the bowl in front of me. "Just give me whatever you don't want, yeah?"

There's a room full of people, but I think it's just us here.

Chapter Twelve

The gate to the homestay property creaks as Ethan pushes it open, revealing the cracked stone that paves the way past the front entrance desk. They wind down around the pool, and the surrounding ground floor bungalows, all the way to the steps at the end that lead up to the second floor where our room is.

It's quiet, seemingly empty. The only sounds are coming from the pool, and the lights strung all around the property in and amongst the plant life and greenery twinkle at us as the sun fades.

His back is against the gate as I step past him and offer a smile as he keeps it open for me. Earlier, he did as promised, dragging his chair around the table so close to mine that our thighs could touch, occasionally helping himself to things sitting on my plate or waiting until I folded my hands. Then, he'd drag my picked-at-dishes over to his side, eating whatever was left.

I was all thrown off—the sudden appearance of something I hadn't planned for sending all my synapses firing in the wrong directions. I might as well have been fifteen. Maybe Arna had a point about living, what it really meant. I was failing spectacularly at what I was supposed to be doing, eating without looking, her equivalent of biking without safety wheels. I was supposed to go into it all without a clue, entirely unknown. It was the point of her saying she would leave me these obscure dishes to try.

But Ethan's words, that maybe living didn't mean the same thing to everyone, were sitting there, just under my skin, heavy on my chest and heart, alongside the death of my best friend.

Ethan raises his brows at me, eyes as impassive as they've been all afternoon, and gently closes the gate behind us. It clicks, and I feel like we're effectively closed in, just us in here, and nothing out there. It's a beautiful property, truly. All swirling, ornately carved wood surrounding the buildings, some of the paint chipping here and there to reveal the teak color behind.

I cross my arms, not moving down the path that would take us back to our room, the cookbook we all left the class with sticking to the skin under my arm.

I'm not sure what to do next exactly. I haven't read the next letter marked Bali #2. And I'm entirely unsure what to expect. It would be so like her, for each secret to become wilder and wilder, all grandiose flourishes and finishes to her writing until her grand finale. Maybe she moved on from drug smuggling to partaking in the wild animal trade. Who fucking knows. She was always pushing boundaries, trying out this or that, nothing sticking or fitting. It had been like that since we were children. Arna went from playing with toys that were off limits, staying out later than curfew and sneaking into dorm rooms she wasn't supposed to be in, to smuggling drugs in exchange for orgasms, apparently. She once told me it was a common affliction, according to her therapist du jour, for children who had everything to focus on trying to find something they could want for.

"Fancy a swim?" Ethan's voice is low, breaking my reverie, and I jerk my head over. He surveys me, head tipped to the side, both hands in his pockets, alongside the makeshift cookbook he promptly folded up and shoved in his pocket.

"Sure," I nod softly.

But instead of turning toward the room, Ethan walks directly down the pathway that leads to the pool.

I'm about to tell him we should go get changed, when one hand reaches behind his head, grabs the neck of his shirt, and begins to tug it off. One whirl of ink extends over his deltoid and stops just short of his trapezius, the tail end of the clock that stretches across his shoulder. The broad stretch of his shoulders tapers down, and every other muscle seems unfairly prominent, flexing ever so slightly as he walks along the edge of the path. He balls up his shirt, tossing it on an empty cushioned lounge chair that lines the tiny pool.

Ethan kicks off his shoes, dipping one foot into the water, and looks over his shoulder at me. "It's nice."

"It'd be nicer in swimsuits," I answer, walking behind him and setting my cookbook and purse alongside his shirt on the chair.

He kicks off another shoe, turning toward me and arching an eyebrow. He's staring at me, a grin starting to form on his face as he pulls off his shorts. The muscles in his thighs flex beneath a thin layer of dark hair against tanned skin. As he stands up straight, his calves stretch when he kicks the shorts to the side. Ethan extends a tattooed hand, beckoning through the few feet between us. But my eyes go immediately to the stitched number eight, along the left side of the material of his underwear that clings to the muscles of his thigh.

"I'm sorry, do your underwear have your number on them?" I ask, an incredulous laugh rising in my throat and a smile stretching across my face.

Ethan looks confused for a second before he drops his gaze, catching on the white stitching. He looks back up, grinning widely at me, eyes glinting. "Did some modeling for the brand when they were a sponsor for the last Euro Cup. Problem?"

"You were an underwear model?" I ask, my voice deadpan.

The thought of it *is* funny. Ethan is so fucking grouchy he would never have managed to smile for the camera, but I'm sure the photos were stunning.

"The whole team did it." He shrugs, like it's nothing, not a big deal at all, that he was special enough to be included in something like that. Ethan flexes his hand, still outstretched, and gestures to the pool. "Don't make me throw you in, Ten."

"You might think it's appropriate to be some sort of exhibitionist...but, I, on the other hand, can go get changed." I tip my chin toward the balcony surrounding the property where you can faintly see the door to our room.

He starts toward me, and a tiny sort of shriek comes out of my mouth as I step backward. Ethan's eyes track over my neck, where hair curls against the nape.

A shiver runs across my shoulders and under the thin straps of my oversized linen tank top. I push back and forth on the balls of my feet, the hem of my black linen shorts brushing against my mid-thigh.

"Where's the fun in that?" Ethan raises his eyebrows before stretching each arm across his broad chest, like he's preparing for some sort of Olympic freestyle. "Come for a swim with me, Ten."

It's certainly not the fact that Ethan feels a bit like a friend, kind of like looking in the mirror in the hallway of your home. Like our two lost souls recognize one another, that they like wandering beside one another, or because he gets my sense of humor and likes it, makes me laugh, and I make him laugh. It's certainly not the fact that my heart feels inexplicably lighter when he looks at me. These are none of the reasons that have me saying yes.

It's probably because he was genetically built to be disarming, to make people all over the world lose their minds when he's standing in front of them, practically naked save for underwear that doesn't leave much to the imagination. It's probably the low lighting that frames his face better than any other time of day, or the spike of serotonin a human being gets when someone like him smiles at you and invites you to do something—anything—with them.

I say it softly, and something lights up behind his eyes. I like the way it looks, I realize, to see him happy. He doesn't have a terribly high opinion of himself, and I think it should be higher. No one notices someone else the way he seems to notice me and is actually as careless and sharp as he pretends to be. He's shown me more care, more attention today than I think anyone else in my life has, save for someone who no longer breathes.

Ethan smiles, one of those rarer, softer smiles, and winks at me before turning away and moving toward the stone steps that lead into the pool. Lights flick on, illuminating the water from below.

I watch him as I grab the edges of my top and pull it over my head. He's obscured for just a moment in time, wading down the steps, twisting back and forth in the water.

I inhale when I drop the shirt behind me, the warm air whispering past my exposed skin. It's just the thin bralette covering me, and I wait for Ethan to turn around, but his back stays turned to me, like he's giving me privacy, even though anyone could walk out of a room or down the pathway at any time. It's sweet. Another thing he does that's entirely at odds with whoever he pretends to be when he's talking to anyone but me. Unbuttoning my shorts, I step carefully out of them, leaving them there. I shift back and forth for a moment, my thighs bare now, except for the lace boyshorts. I fold my arms across my chest before running across the stone on the balls of my feet, pretending it's not just us out here in our underwear. It's no different than being in a bathing suit, not really. But it feels different, feels like something that should make me nervous, anxious even, but it doesn't because it's just me and him.

I don't test the water with my toes first and practically run down the steps after Ethan.

The water pools around his waist, leaving the tapered muscles that lead up his back exposed. He's taller than me, so it lands around my ribcage. It's warm, not at all uncomfortable but a reprieve from the night air.

There's a ledge running just underneath the surface around the pool to sit on, and I wade across to it, the water rippling and lights underneath distorting with the movement. I turn, dropping to sit on the worn stone, the water sloshing against my skin and moving around my collarbone.

Ethan says nothing but drops himself below the surface of the water for a moment; his body and features are distorted by the refraction of the light before he pops back up and flips his head back, an entire cascade of water droplets flying behind him. He runs his hand over his face, brushing away the droplets before pushing his sopping hair back.

I watch him for a moment longer, leaning forward and gripping the underside of the ledge. He looks up at me, and it's just us here. It doesn't feel like anyone could walk by at any moment.

"Thank you, for today. For helping...with the food," I murmur.

I would usually be embarrassed, would usually feel flames across my cheek—the usual sense of dread churning in my stomach if someone else was privy to the inner workings of my brain. But the feelings never come.

Ethan wades toward me, one thumb running across his mouth before dropping to a crouch in front of me. "On the plane...you said that you had an eating issue—"

"I had an eating disorder growing up," I say, cutting him off, offering a shrug and dry smile. "They say you recover, but I don't know. Do you? Sometimes I feel like I've had two constant companions in my life...Arna and my eating disorder. It's not restricting or vomiting anymore, but I still have these...they're called behaviors. When I was diagnosed, the nurse at our boarding school sent me to an outpatient program. Back then they called it EDNOS, Eating Disorder Not Otherwise Specified, because I didn't neatly fall into one of the two diagnostic categories they had at the time. It has a different name now. But Arna...she came with me to every appointment, multiple times a week, and she would just wait for me."

"You're beautiful." Ethan drops his voice, and his lips turn down.

He palms his jaw, and I can see the muscles in his shoulders and neck tense. It bothers him. But I can tell he's not just saying it to say it. His eyes are earnest, and they move across my collarbone, across the droplets of water, up the curve of my neck, over my jaw and over my lips, and then up to look right at me.

"Can you tell fifteen-year-old November that?" I laugh, raising my hand and watching the water run over the back of my hand, droplets running down my arm. "Thank you, Ethan. But it wasn't really about that, at least that's what I spent all those hours in therapy to try and understand. For me, it was just this...constant need to feel enough. I'm okay now though, mostly. What would have possibly happened to me today if you had somewhere else to be?"

I'm teasing when I say it because I am thankful, endlessly thankful, eternally grateful that he's here with me, and I'm not alone in this.

But his smile doesn't reach his eyes, and they look sad again.

"Do you miss it?" I ask, starting to swing my feet back and forth, the water rushing around them. One of my toes accidentally grazes Ethan's thigh where he's still crouched in front of me, but he doesn't move.

"Every minute, of every fucking day. It was my dream, you know? How many people get to live out their dreams? Not just any bloke on the street, and I pissed mine away." His voice is harsh, bordering on bitter. "It was the only thing I ever wanted, the thing I was best at. Once in a lifetime kind of talent, and Party Boy Barclay wasted it all."

I tilt my head, swinging my feet once more before coming to rest one on the top of his thigh. I don't know why I do it. Ethan glances down briefly, and one of his hands grips my ankle. "Did you do that often? Party?"

A snort escapes him, and he shakes his head. "Nah, that was just a name with a hook the gossip rags came up with. I was regimented. Hardly drank during the season, hadn't touched a bag since I was too young to know any better. I was just fucking lost. Thought I'd never get it back, rehab seemed impossible, couldn't see the forest through the trees, all that bullshit."

"Well, aren't we a pair? No career and no friends?" I laugh again, and I mean it. It feels serendipitous that he and I would find one another. Two lost souls left to wander together.

"I'll be your friend." His voice shifts entirely, eyes flick down to my mouth, and his own lips part. The tiny scar is illuminated, and I have this urge—I want to reach out my other leg, to wrap them both around his waist.

But then I feel a manicured hand brush past the hair curling at my neck, tapping on my shoulder. It's probably exactly what she would want for me—to fall into bed and fuck this man who looks like he was made in a lab, professional athlete who seems like he would know exactly what he's doing, whether he's disgraced and hated by the entire United Kingdom or not. But sex won't bring back my best friend, won't start to sew the holes in my wrecked heart back together. Nothing will. So, I push back, shoulder blades jutting into the edge of the pool. "I should go. I have a letter to read."

Ethan says nothing, but nods, releasing my foot and scrubbing his jaw briefly before turning away from me to do laps in the tiny pool.

I push up, practically scrambling out of the pool and grabbing my clothes as I follow the path back to our room.

The sounds of Ethan's body slicing through the water follows me all the way back to the room.

Chapter Thirteen

Ethan's silhouette ripples just past the white, gauzy curtains pulled across the sliding glass door of our room. I look out at his shadow, a towel wrapped around my freshly washed hair, and my pajamas sticking intermittently to my still damp skin. I can see as he tips the neck of a beer bottle back, one hand resting on his outstretched leg, foot propped up on the balcony railing as he rocks back and forth in one of the tiny chairs that sits in front of our room. He must have come back up when I was in the shower.

I came up here, still in my soaking wet bra and underwear from our little clandestine swim, and ripped the next letter out of my suitcase, barely breathing and damp fingers smudging the edges, blinking eyes skimmed across her lilting words.

I think I wish I hadn't read it, wishing I could have scrubbed it from my skin while I tried and failed to scrub off the feeling of the pool water in the shower, because I didn't understand this letter, either.

Novie,

Do you remember our college house? The one with the great view of the sunrise from the roof?

Your window was easier to get out of, but mine had the better view. Remember, we would climb out there after a night out and wait? I'd make you drag your duvet from your room because it was softer than mine, and we would lay down and watch as the sky changed. The stars would disappear, and the sky would start to glow.

These are some of my best memories, my favorite memories. If I close my eyes, I can hear us. Laughing and cackling about how stupid our fucking friends were, how Hina and Sam finally, finally banged, how Layla fell asleep at the bar, and Michaela took too much E.

There's a beautiful sunrise near you on Mount Batur. You climb straight up the volcano for about two hours in the dark, but when you get to the top, there are benches everywhere, and you can sit there and wait. The sun rises behind a neighboring volcano. The mist clears, and it's hard to describe. You know me, I was hardly ever speechless in life, and I'm not even speechless in death. But I remember sitting there, every time, and wishing you were with me. I used to do the hike to pass the drugs off to one of the buyers at the top. But don't let that deter you. Even drug mules can recognize a beautiful view when they see one.

Do the hike, Nov. And come back and have Balinese banana pancakes afterward.

I have all kinds of memories that I'll be fortunate enough to leave the Earth with, but I loved being in college with you. Boarding school was fun—the quintessential experience you would imagine. But college. When it came time to apply, I couldn't imagine going anywhere without you. You were always the smarter one, and I remember being so scared I wouldn't get in. So, I did what any good little shipping heiress would do and had Pappous buy my way in.

I would have bought your way in, too, but I had zero doubts you would get in everywhere. And you did. You always made me so proud.

I almost didn't graduate, but money fixed that, too. There was no way I wasn't going to walk across that stage with you. Maybe that's why I never told you. I didn't want you to have a reason not to be proud of me.

After you've climbed the mountain—after you've seen it—I think you should go to Vietnam.

Happy sunrise November,

Arna

I had screamed a bit in frustration in the stream of the water. It mixed in with the tears tracking down my cheeks and into my open mouth. My sobs were great, sputtering, rasping things.

It didn't make sense to me; why she would have kept those things from me. I didn't care who she fucked, who she spent her time with, and I wouldn't have given a shit if she didn't get into the same college as me, or if she dropped out. She rarely ever opened a textbook. She would have only had herself to blame. She wasn't stupid, far from it. She'd been shrewd and calculating, significantly smarter than the general population, but it just made people more malleable to her. Except for me, the alleged exception to her rule.

They might be white lies to some people, innocuous, inconsequential and almost innocent, because who was she hurting with them?

But I felt my ribs crack open a bit, shrapnel in the form of bone fragments embedding into my lungs, all the oxygen leaking out of my body, and into my heart where I think I might have started to bleed out.

It would be a slow death, I think, to learn that maybe the person I loved more than I loved myself wasn't who I thought she was at all.

It's what makes me cross the room, take one of Ethan's beers from the tiny fridge, and pull open the sliding door to join him on the balcony, even though I think I upset him in the pool.

He glances sideways at me as I step out, freeing my hair from the towel, and laying it over the side of the balcony railing to dry. The night air is still sticky, cloying to my damp skin. But it's quiet out here, just us and the vague hum of the lights that line the property. He holds his hand out for me, gesturing for me to give him the beer bottle.

My lips part and a tiny scoff escapes them. "I'm sorry, are you not going to share with me?"

Ethan levels me with a look before setting his own bottle down at the tiny table and leaning forward to snatch mine from me. I'm about to take it back, in some sort of childlike battle of wills, when he palms the cap. "It's a twist-off. Like to see you try with those tiny little hands."

My mouth pops open, and I hold both my hands up, like it somehow refutes the fact. "Hey—I extract adult molars with these hands."

Ethan raises one eyebrow, twisting his hand and holding up the cap in proof before tossing it into an empty ashtray on the table beside him. He tips the bottle toward me. "That supposed to prove something to me? They're miniscule, Ten."

"I'll have you know my hands are normal size. Maybe yours are abnormally large. Maybe you aren't as evolved as me. Our hands grew smaller as we split from our relatives, the chimpanzees." I snatch the bottle from him and sit in the chair across from him, folding my legs underneath me.

He leans back in his chair, grinning now. He's still wearing the shorts he swam in, but a towel is slung around his neck. "That true?"

"No." I wrinkle my nose and smile at him, taking a sip of the beer, but I start to make a so-so gesture with my hand as I swallow. "Well, sort of. It has a lot more to do with hand proportions than actual size as we both diverged from our last common ancestor."

Ethan nods, tongue poking into his cheek before he palms his jaw. "I didn't mean to—ah, did I make you uncomfortable in the pool?"

"No," I answer plainly. And it's true. He didn't make me uncomfortable. He hasn't made me uncomfortable for a single second, actually. "I thought we were already friends. Besides, I'm usually the off-putting one, making people uncomfortable."

"You don't make me uncomfortable," Ethan says, pausing his bottle against his lips, eyes cutting to me before he takes a sip. "How was the letter?"

"I didn't really understand it. She wrote some stuff about college and told me to do a sunrise hike and eat some banana pancakes." It's a half-truth.

I understand the pancakes. I understand the hike, I understand why she would have loved it. She lived for moments like that—anything that might have made her feel alive. I even understand why she would have used it as a route to lug her drugs around. I'm sure the hike is chalked full of tourists. But I don't understand why she lied.

I turn in my seat, one hand rubbing absentmindedly across my chest. "You'll do the hike with me?"

Ethan leans forward, elbows coming to rest on his knees, beer bottle hanging loosely from his fingertips. He angles his head toward me, and it's a real smile he gives me. "What else are friends for?"

Chapter Fourteen

The sky is all mottled hues of pink and orange, white clouds stretching across it, and the morning sun is breaking through. I watch it from the balcony, hands wrapped around a chipped white mug that was sitting here, along with a waiting carafe of coffee, on the tiny table outside of our room.

I look for a moment longer as the clouds tumble along the sky, before I fold my legs underneath me and sit back in the chair. There's a soft ringing somewhere in the distance, the twisted boughs of the trees scattered across the property sag under heavy green leaves. I can faintly hear the water in the pool, lapping against the stone sides, and the fountain bubbling behind it.

It's peaceful. It's the type of place I would usually love to sit out, entirely alone—reading, doing work. Whatever I feel like. It's the type of place I would usually enjoy, unequivocally. But exhaustion tugs at my eyes, and my bones hurt.

I was up long after Ethan fell asleep, propped up on one arm, and the other slung out over his pillow, pushed to the opposite side of the bed.

I watched as the shadows stretched across his back and illuminated the clock face on his shoulder. The hands of the clock never moved, and I felt like they were mocking me.

I finally fell asleep after combing through Instagram for hours, until I found a photo of Arna on her page, posing on top of a stretched out mat in an open air pavilion, backing onto sprawling rice fields. Yoga House, only a twenty-minute walk from here.

The door slides open, and Ethan steps out, shirtless, rolling his neck back and forth before he reaches up under his jaw and cracks it. It's loud—resounding through the former silence. He offers me a grin and flops down into the chair across from me.

He's radiant when he's still half-asleep, I think. Waves are a mess, haphazard and poking out in too many directions to count, severe lines of his cheekbones and jaw more prominent, peppered with stubble, and eyes that look like the first light of dawn.

"Ey. You sleep alright?" Ethan stifles a yawn, flipping up a chipped mug that matches mine with his tattooed hand, and pours himself coffee.

I nod.

It's funny how you can lie without saying anything.

Ethan leans back, right arm coming up to rub at the back of his head absentmindedly, and there's that hand, outstretched and reaching on his inner bicep. He brings the mug to his mouth, about to take a sip when his phone starts ringing in his pocket. His eyebrows narrow, and he sets the mug down on the table, coffee splashing up over the side, fishing the phone out of his pocket. He hardly glances at the screen before his thumb, and the number eight, press down to silence it. Ethan throws the phone down on the table with a clatter, face down, before picking his coffee back up.

"Do you need to take that?" I ask quietly.

His jaw pops back and forth for a moment before his lower lip juts out a bit, and he shakes his head. "Nah. Just my agent."

"Maybe you should—"

"No." Ethan cuts in, words flat with no room for discussion, so I just nod and take another small sip of my coffee. He changes the subject. "Anything you want to do today?"

We found a guide to take us on the sunrise hike last night, sitting out here together as the table gathered empty bottles. But they aren't picking us up until two a.m., so we'll have enough time to hike up the mountain for sunrise tomorrow morning at five-thirty.

Last night, we were sitting in the same spots we are now, Ethan articulating grand hand gestures, gray eyes growing hazy, my cheeks growing warmer, hair curling around my face, and my laugh stretching longer and louder each time, when one of the desk attendants—Gede—came up the stairs and asked us if we wanted breakfast for this morning.

He had a paper menu with little spots to tick off your selection, and a similar one would be left for us each afternoon if we wanted to order something for the next day.

There were banana pancakes, but I couldn't really look at them. I couldn't really look at the menu at all, but I picked an omelet. I usually would have asked what was in it, how it was prepared, just so I would know, so there would be no surprises when it was dropped in front of me in the morning. But I didn't have the energy. I shoved the menu at Ethan instead, looking away and blinking rapidly.

I could feel him staring at me, eyes boring into the back of my head, when he started asking questions. What was in the omelet, how were the vegetables prepared, how many eggs were used, what were the sides. He picked something else in the end, but not before he asked about every single other dish.

Gede appears now at the end of the balcony, holding a tray with two massive plates in the center of it.

Ethan stands, taking the plates, and exchanging more pleasantries than I would have thought he was capable of.

I smile blandly, fingers starting to shake a bit against my mug as my breathing picks up.

Ethan's eyes are on me as he pushes my food toward me across the tiny table.

"There's a yoga class I want to check out," I tell him, eyes finally flicking down to my plate.

It looks exactly as I would have pictured it from all the questions Ethan asked last night, all the ways he helped me prepare. But the omelet is huge, and some of the fruit has seeds still in it. I breathe in and out for a moment before looking back up at him.

"Didn't peg you for one of those." Ethan eyes me for a moment, utensils poised above his plate. "Omelet okay?"

"I'm not really." I shrug and slice down the middle of the omelet. "It's fine, but it's too big. Will you share this with me?"

Ethan nods. "Put half on my plate then, yeah?"

"And take some of this fruit?"

He pushes all of his food to the side to make room for mine.

I recognize the pavilion the second we round the corner of the winding, stone path we've been following since we saw the sign for the studio alongside the road. It's a simple structure—palm fronds thatched together to make a roof and no walls. Just a concrete slab on the ground in the middle of the property.

Entirely ordinary. But it's not, because my best friend once stood here.

I stared at that photo of Arna, posing not even twenty feet from where I stand now, for so long I think it's seared into the back of my retinas. I'd seen it before, but it was of no consequence to me then. It feels monumental now because it was like looking at someone I'm not sure I recognized. There she is—chestnut hair braided off her face, the haughty set to her features and shrewd eyes.

I blink, and she's gone. It's just her ghost in this world now.

Turning to Ethan, I gesture to his sweat shorts and the black shirt he's wearing. It's that sweat-wicking material, and there's a faded crest stamped over his heart. "You didn't have to take the class with me. You could have done something else."

Ethan shakes his head, a tiny scoff escapes his throat. "Please, Ten. This is probably the longest I've gone without exercise since I could kick a ball."

"Will your leg be okay?" I gesture to his left calf, to the angry stretch of pink skin there.

Ethan shoots me a look. "I know how to stretch properly. Been doing it for years."

Holding up my hands, I smile at him. "Far be it from me to question a superstar."

"Former," Ethan adds dryly.

He pauses at the stone steps leading up to the pavilion, where mats are laid out across the floor, and gestures for me to go first.

Adjusting my bag on my shoulder, some ancient canvas that Arna bought me at a market somewhere, I step past him. It used to be all vibrant colors, but it's faded now. My wallet, and her last two letters are in there. I'm not sure why I brought them; they weren't missing pieces to some puzzle that would finally click into place when they were in the same place where their author had once lived, had once breathed.

I weave through the mats, some already occupied, until I stop at two in the corner, near the back of the class.

"Didn't strike me as the type of person who sits in the back of the class," Ethan says from behind me, voice low and teasing. I like it when it's like that. All gravelly and rough.

I look over my shoulder at Ethan, offering him a smile. "Don't need to sit in the front to be the smartest one in the room."

His eyes light up—a clear sky—and a grin splits across his face. The scar across his top lip has grown more prominent the longer he spends in the sun, a thin white slash against tanned skin. But it suits him.

Ethan stops at the mat beside me, reaching up to stretch his neck.

I drop my bag, toe off my sandals, and pull down the spandex that's riding up my legs. The bike shorts are covered by an oversized, faded t-shirt that reads: University of Toronto, Faculty of Dentistry on it. My hair is tied into a messy knot on the top of my head, but wisps are already escaping and curling around my face from the humidity.

I fold down onto my mat, stretching my legs out ahead of me. I try to avoid staring at the space in the center of the room where Arna once stood. Instead, I look out at the stretching, impossibly green rice fields and the tall grass that sways in a practically nonexistent breeze.

I'm still staring when a loud laugh, followed by a sharp shushing noise has me looking back across the room.

"I think they like you," I whisper, widening my eyes and tipping my chin just beyond our mats.

Three girls, probably around my age or younger, are clustered in the opposite corner. They're spread out across their mats, shiny hair slicked back in perfect knots or ponytails, and wearing the same matching set in various shades of neon. Heads are tipped together, and lips are pulled back in coy little smiles as their eyes dart over toward Ethan on his mat.

He's been stretching like he's training for a triathlon since we sat down, with far more flexibility than I would have thought possible. It's impressive, actually. But I don't think they're looking at how far he can push his tendons.

Ethan pushes against his thigh, stretching beyond the point of comfort for most regular people, his other leg out beside him, inner thigh practically touching the mat. He glances over his shoulder before looking back at me laughing through his nose. "Everyone likes me."

I wrinkle my nose and shake my head before bringing my arm to stretch behind my back. "That's simply not true."

"Jesus Ten, your range of motion is for shit." Ethan's head pulls back, and his lip curls up a bit, like the fact that I can hardly reach behind me offends him.

"My back's a mess, actually." I tip my head up at him, turning slightly to show him just how poor my range of motion is and wiggle my fingers where they barely skim my shoulder blade. "It's from being hunched over bodies, both living and dead, so often."

Ethan pushes off his leg, coming to stretch each one out on the side, almost in a split before he starts walking his feet back inward to stand. He jerks his chin toward my mat. "Lay down on your stomach. I'll stretch it for you, yeah?"

I blink at him for a moment, but he widens his eyes again, looking pointedly at the mat. My cheeks heat, but I swing my legs out from underneath me to lay down on the mat, bringing my head to rest down on my hands.

"Arms at your sides," Ethan instructs, and as I move them to lay flat beside me, I feel his knees drop on either side of my hips, his inner thighs brushing against my sides. He grips my wrists, tugging slightly as he pulls my arms for a moment. "Roll your shoulders back and lift your chest up."

I do what he says, my shoulder blades stretching to meet, but it feels like an impossible distance because of all the knots of muscle. Ethan's hands are gentle on my wrists, and I might be imagining it, but I think his thumb might be scoring a line across the sensitive skin on purpose. He says nothing else as he pulls lightly on my arms, and I can feel the stretch across my shoulders, down my lateral muscles. His own muscles tense when he starts to move my arms side to side. It pulls, but it's kind of relaxing.

But his thighs on either side of me—Ethan and all that he is suspended above me—that's anything but relaxing. I feel him, the edges of his muscles against me, and my broken heart beats a bit harder than it should be able to.

"That better?" He clears his throat and drops my hands unceremoniously. It's jarring.

The presence of his thighs, and the entirety of him hovering above me, is suddenly absent, and when I drop my chest and rest my head on my hands again, I can see he's back on his own mat.

His lips twitch, and I feel like sitting up, leaning forward and running my tongue along the thin scar that runs through the top one. But instead, I blink and whisper, "Thank you."

"Anytime, Ten." He swallows, and his eyes are on me for just a moment longer before they swing to the front of the room where the instructor is now setting up her mat.

I think I can still feel his hands on my wrists, his thighs against my sides, and him all around me when I push to stand up and start the class.

Chapter Fifteen

It turned out that Ethan made concentrating difficult. Not because I was so distracted by his presence like the three girls in the corner of the class who couldn't stop looking at him, finding any way to crane their necks to peer beyond their arms or their legs to glance in our general direction, but because he's significantly more flexible than I am, constantly extending his legs or his arms within my general vicinity.

I thought for a moment he somehow might have been a pinnacle athlete with zero sense of spatial awareness, but when his arm found its way to my mat for the fifth time, followed by poor attempts to knock me off balance, I realized he was doing it on purpose.

"Look too serious Ten," he whispered when he glanced over at me during some variation of a cobra pose, voice rough through intentionally measured breathing. He grinned at me for a moment longer, all perfect teeth, before winking and turning back to his own mat.

He's moving through some series of post-workout stretching now as the class files out.

I'm cross-legged on my mat, watching as he sits in what looks like an extended lunge. My lips peel back. "You just did a solid forty-five minutes of stretching. I don't think this is necessary."

"Just making sure nothing locks up," Ethan breathes.

I watch him inhale all the way through his diaphragm, the proper way to fill up your lungs, before a measured exhale leaves his nostrils.

He stretches his leg back to meet the other one and moves into a plank before he jumps up to standing position. Ethan scrubs a hand across his face quickly and snakes it back through his hair. But then he turns to me, his usual lazy grin in place while extending his hand to help me up.

"Why are soccer players so flexible?" I ask, grabbing his hand and letting him pull me up.

Ethan shakes his head, lips pulling back in a tight line, correcting me. "Football players."

I roll my eyes, pulling my hand from his because my skin is starting to feel too warm, and we fall into step beside one another, weaving through the mats and the people still lying on them. "Football players then. What's the flexibility for?"

"It's preventative. The sport's pretty repetitive, yeah? Puts your muscles at greater risk for injury if they're tight. Didn't do fuck all for me in the end." He shrugs, and I notice he brushes his thumb across his nose absentmindedly. "Depending on your position, it can help you maximize what you can do with the ball...more power behind a longer kick."

I nod. "What position did you play?"

Ethan flinches, like the past tense of the word settles uncomfortably in his skin. "Striker."

I don't say anything else because we're the same in that sense. I never thought much about the tense of a word, how the weight of it changes when something, or someone, becomes a *was* instead of an *is*.

We're walking down the stone steps, and his eyes are shielded behind sunglasses now, but I catch the way his neck tightens when he steps down with his left leg. He cocks his head as I continue to stare at him, arms folded across my chest, because I think my heart might be starting to hurt for an altogether different reason.

He gives me another sidelong glance. "I'm alright, Ten. No need to worry about me."

I nod softly at him, and we follow the winding path through the overgrown palms and blooming flowers, all vibrant colors and top-heavy, so they fall across the path intermittently. A wooden sign is stuck into the ground a few feet ahead, haphazardly leaning to one side. Scratched across it in swirling loops of chalk is an arrow with the words "Smoothie Bar" under it.

My heart beats a bit too fast, and I think it snags on my ribs again because I look down at the cracking stone path, the edges of my sandals blurring as my eyes sting. It's the same way she would have walked. Down from her yoga class where she was supposed to be learning, feet padding across the worn stone like we are, all the way down to that smoothie bar. I don't really care about the drugs. It was typical of her. I can't reconcile the fact that she kept it from me.

Maybe it started the day that picture was taken. I'll never know, and she's not here to tell me.

I look over at Ethan, and I point my chin toward the sign. "Can we go?"

His eyebrows slant downward, and I can tell he's thinking behind those sunglasses, even though I can't see his eyes, but he nods and turns left. There's only a few feet before the path abruptly ends, giving way to packed dirt and a hidden garden. Trees, boughs cracked and twisted, run along the edge of the hidden semi-circle. Picnic tables are scattered throughout with faded bean bag chairs pushed up under some of the larger trees. People in various states of athletic wear are littered across the opening, and there's a small, constructed bar in the center. It looks like it's made of bamboo, with thatched palms covering it and a chalkboard menu in front of it.

We weave through the tables and the people, some even lying down on mats, staring straight up at the sky that peaks through the canopy of leaves. I study the menu for a few moments before ordering something with mango.

We're silent as we wait, and I can feel Ethan's eyes on me while I look around. I'm not even sure why I wanted to come down here. Just to see it, I guess. I wonder if it looked the same when she was here, where she was holding court when she somehow got herself wrapped up in a drug ring. I snort softly and shake my head. It's the type of thing that would happen to her. The exact type of story she would want to collect for her arsenal.

Ethan grabs my smoothie and his, his hands so large they can each comfortably carry the carved out coconuts they're housed in. He inclines his head toward an empty picnic table, and I follow behind him before dropping down across from him. Ethan pushes my smoothie across the table, and the smile he throws me is one of those rarer, softer ones.

It makes me smile, too.

"Had a girlfriend who did a lot of yoga," Ethan offers, filling the silence, voice flat as he looks around. "Pretty much all she did, actually."

I press my lips together, considering him. "It's hard to picture you with a girlfriend."

Ethan throws me a look, lips pulling up to the side. His voice is dry when he speaks. "Same could be said for you. Investment Banker Jake?"

Objectively, it's a fair point. But Jake and I worked, until we didn't. At least I thought we did. He was quick to point out how flawed we were—how flawed I was—when it was all said and done. He was right. Ethan continues, all his features set in casual indifference. "Didn't last anyway."

"Who was she?" I ask.

I'm not sure I really want to know. The idea of Ethan existing with someone else seems odd, foreign to me somehow. There's only this version of him in my mind—broody and exiled, and maybe sort of mine.

"Tal." Ethan clears his throat, and he swirls the coconut in his hands, eyes narrowing in on the smoothie, like he wishes he was holding a beer bottle. "Talia. Probably would have married her. Thank fuck I didn't."

"Are any of those for her?" I gesture with my smoothie, straw pointing to the tattoos on his arm.

"No, and thank fuck for that, too," Ethan mutters, stretching his arm out to study the whirls of ink. They're starker, more vibrant the more tanned his skin gets.

I tip my head, studying him. "Did you love her?"

"Nah. Thought I might have for a moment there. Didn't stop it from hurting, though. When she picked someone else who still had it all." A muscle in his jaw jumps for a moment.

"What happened?"

"Left me when I lost my contract. She's with some chav she met on Instagram. Influencer type." Ethan's cheekbones sharpen for a moment. "Like I said, I'm easy to leave."

He's not.

"I bet her hands are huge. Very much below everyone else on the evolutionary food chain." I raise my eyebrows at him, straw pushed against my bottom lip.

A grin flashes across Ethan's face, and I think my chest splits open a fraction, too.

Before I can change my mind, I bend down and pull the last two letters out of the bag, sitting at my feet. I throw the letters, one folded much more neatly than the other, onto the table between us.

Ethan's eyebrows knit, and his eyes flick up to me. I nod and watch as he pulls them toward himself, unfolding the top one with the same care he showed the first letter I let him read, his eyes starting to move down the paper. One eyebrow raises, and his lips turn down. When he moves to the second one, he brushes his thumb across his jaw absentmindedly, but it pauses against his lips, and they peel backward for a second. He drops the letter, running a hand across his jaw before two fingers find his temple. Ethan looks up at me, lips parted and eyes wide. "What's the next one going to say? She was dealing in fucking ivory? Off to grab some elephant tusks in Africa, are we?"

My cracked open chest stretches even farther, my heart right there, beating outside of it, because he's made me smile.

I can't stop laughing, and neither can he.

Chapter Sixteen

Craning my neck, I peer upward at the shadow of the volcano behind us. The whole thing is shrouded in darkness. Only the strips of light from flashlights the guides are passing around at the base of the trail illuminate the winding path ahead. It starts out even, just a gradual incline that disappears into the mountainside. The air nips at my exposed cheeks. It's cold this early. Or this late, depending on how you look at it. I exhale, and you can see the puff of air suspended in front of me.

We're standing at the base of Mount Batur, other hikers milling around us, waiting for the signal from the guides that we can start the hike. Mount Agung still smokes behind us from a fairly recent explosion. It's still an active volcano and, apparently, one of the hardest hikes in Bali. Ethan seemed poised to switch hikes, eyebrows raising with interest when our guide told us on the drive here, but that wasn't the volcano my best friend used to lug drugs around.

"I think I'm fucking hung," Ethan mutters, scrubbing his jaw with his hands.

"You know that phrase has multiple meanings, right?" I raise my eyebrows.

Ethan gives me a flat look. "Rough. Hungover. Entirely incapacitated, yeah?"

I glance sideways at him, a tiny smile pulling at my lips. "Maybe you shouldn't have had so many beers."

Ethan lifts the hat he's wearing momentarily, tugging a hand through his hair before turning it backward. "Maybe we should have gone to sleep, yeah?"

My lips part. He looks good like this, tired and eyes all bleary. They're the same color as the sky right now; the dark before dawn. "You were the one who insisted on watching not one but two movies when you knew we were getting picked up at two a.m."

"I'm not the one who practically shot out of bed when they saw there was a Jaws marathon on."

Before I can answer, a line of light streaks across the sky from one of the guides at the start of the trail, signaling the beginning of the hike.

Ethan reaches out, grabbing the clasp on my backpack to clip it together so the two sides connect across my chest. He tugs it down slightly so it's not pulling on my sweater. "Better on your back if that's supported properly, yeah?"

"Sure." I nod, breath somehow entirely gone from my chest, and point toward the group ahead of us that's started walking.

His eyes sweep over me before he starts down the path.

The lights ahead of us bob up and down as other hikers follow the line of guides at the front, leading everyone up the mountain.

The occasional strip of light illuminates from behind, another set of guides trailing behind everyone so no one gets lost or left behind. It's still dark, and everything about Ethan is under shadow.

We don't say anything, but we move along the path carved into the mountainside. Tall grass sways in the breeze on either side of us. The footfalls of the other hikers echo around us, occasionally punctuated by laughter or muffled conversation.

The air is still cool against my skin, and I shiver occasionally under my sweater. Stars wink above us in the sky, still the milky gray of early morning. I try not to think of Arna, walking this path God knows how many times with God knows what in her backpack to pass off to God knows who at the top.

I've seen pictures of what the sunrise is supposed to look like, how there are benches scattered everywhere across the crest of the volcano where you can sit and watch the sunrise. There's even coffee and breakfast cooked for the hikers in the steam of the volcano, if the website is to be believed.

Ethan's breathing is barely labored as the incline shifts beneath our feet, moving from a flat path to a practically vertical one. He's a bit ahead of me, but he glances back over his shoulder. "You've not been right since you read those last letters. You can tell me what you're thinking, yeah?"

I don't think I've been right since she died, but I don't say that. Instead, I exhale a puff of air and watch the plume in front of me. "I just don't understand why she didn't tell me. Why she lied."

"Not really a lie if she just didn't tell you," Ethan offers, and I think I see his shoulders shrug underneath his sweater.

"A lie by omission then." I roll my eyes and inhale, the cold air cutting against my throat. It makes it all the way down to my lungs, but I don't really know if they're physiologically functioning properly anymore. I say nothing for a few more moments, focusing on my breathing and following behind the path Ethan's steps carve. "We told each other every-thing. From the time we were kids too young to know how to set a boundary. At least I thought we did."

The beak of Ethan's hat moves, and I think he's nodding along.

"Before I told you, she was the only other person who knew about my eating disorder," I whisper to him. "The only person who cared, other than our boarding school nurse, and she only did it out of legal obligation."

It's one of the sadder things in my life, I think. That there was only one person to care about fifteen-year-old November, and now she's dead. "But Arna, I told her everything...every dark, beyond fucked up thought. Like how I used to fantasize about cutting my taste buds out. Just...anything to make it stop. She never judged me for that. Why would I judge her for this?" I raise one hand, like she's all around us.

Ethan looks back over his shoulder, and I can tell his lips are pulled down, tension in his neck. "Your parents didn't notice anything?"

"That would require their attention, Ethan." I laugh, but it's bitter. "Couldn't she have just left me a watch like a fucking normal person?"

"Sometimes people aren't who we think they are." Ethan's voice car-ries back, but it lacks all the usual ire. It borders on gentle.

I scoff, concentrating on my feet as I follow behind him. "What does that make me?"

Ethan pauses, one hand flat against the winding rock face along the trail. He turns his head over his shoulder, but it's still dark and hard to tell what he might be thinking. "You're still you, Ten."

"And who is that exactly? A friendless, weird—"

"I don't think you're weird. You're just you." Ethan cuts me off, pushing off the rockface.

I blink, my own footsteps halting. I'm holding onto the straps of my backpack, and then he's in front of me, towering over me. I can see him more clearly now, the sky starting to fade to a gray that almost matches his eyes exactly. Most people would see gray as bland, bleak even. I'm starting to think it's one of the most hopeful colors.

He's looking down at me, and his features are set, sharp as usual, but he holds out a hand. One friend holding out their hand to another, helping them climb a literal and proverbial mountain.

My lips tug up, and even though I feel like taking his hand, feel like pressing it to my chest and seeing if it helps to piece together the broken shards of my heart, I laugh instead. "I may not be as athletically inclined as you, but I am fully capable of climbing up there before sunrise."

"Piece of fucking work." Ethan shakes his head, but he's grinning at me. He hauls me forward by the straps of my backpack, positioning me in front of him on the path. Bending down, his lips are level with my ear when his breath whispers past. "Go on then."

It's still dark, the sky different shades of gray while the stars give way to the sun, and the hints of a faint glow on the horizon stretch behind the neighboring volcano when we stepped out from between the two rock faces.

"Happy sunrise, Ten." Ethan's voice is low, bordering on soft.

I look over at him, and my breath catches because he's not looking at the sunrise, he's looking at me.

I don't know how many sunrises I've seen. How many I've been so lucky to watch, under a blanket and my hand in my best friend's. The person who knew me best in the entire world, who I thought I knew better than I even knew myself.

But I think this sunrise is my favorite. Mist hangs in the air, and I can feel it, cool against my skin. People are scattered around us, sitting shoulder to shoulder on sagging wooden benches, shoved up against the craggy backdrop of the volcano that stretches behind us. The chipped, tin coffee mug warms my palms, but it's his smile I feel in my chest, the tiny, almost iridescent spread of sunlight through my ribs to my heart.

I can faintly make out the scar hidden under the few days of stubble that dusts Ethan's face. Our shoulders press together because the bench is so tiny, and this close, I can see everything in his eyes. It's the hidden sorrow, anguish, and regret in the striations. It's the restlessness when he taps his fingers and thumbs incessantly against any surface, like he could will those special numbers that represent everything good in his life back out into the world. Or the way he brushes his thumb over his nose sometimes, how when he's sitting, his hand rubs the back of his leg out of habit, like he would take it all back if he could.

I thought there was only one person who understood me. Saw me. Knew all the sharp pieces of my edges and the way to soften them. But maybe they were never supposed to be soft. Maybe that's just who I am, and who I've always been. Maybe the sharp edges of me could fit within someone else's.

Warmth spreads across my cheeks, my chilled fingertips as the sun spills out from behind the neighboring volcano, and the mist evaporates like it was never there. It's just us and our edges now.

"Happy sunrise, Ethan."

"I can't believe that monkey stole my fucking chocolate bar," Ethan mutters, lips pulled into a thin line as he shakes his head.

"Ethan, you need to let it go," I turn, eyes wide and incredulous.

After the sun rose, we sat there, drinking the coffee and picking at the food the guides gave us when a monkey trundled along and helped itself to the chocolate bar Ethan had just peeled the foil back on. Ethan looked indignant for a single moment before I burst out laughing.

It started pouring rain right as we got out of the cab in front of our homestay afterward. We stood on the balcony, hanging forward, letting the rain soak through our clothes to watch the clouds roll in and the lightning fork across the sky.

Ethan looked lighter, positively alive with his sopping curls plastered to his forehead and a smile that seemed endless.

We stayed there until it started raining sideways, wind practically knocking us into the wall of the building.

The thunder was still cracking, the room illuminated by nothing but the lightning, when Ethan wrapped a towel around me, pulling it tight. We stared at one another for a moment longer, until he took a measured swallow, and I felt a manicured hand tapping on my shoulder, so I excused myself to take a shower.

He's lying beside me in bed now, set of his features decidedly grumpy.

I roll my head, looking at Ethan where he's propped up against the wall, pillows stacked behind him. "Did you know it's climbing season?"

"Huh?" He looks at me, still taller than me, and one hand runs through his hair. The other holds his phone loosely. He was reading—I can see the words on his phone, a book open.

"Everest. It's summit season. The window to summit the mountain. Look, they're all waiting in the death zone. It's the part of the mountain where the oxygen is lowest, but you need to pass through it to get to the top." I hold my own phone out, showing him the photo taken of the line of climbers waiting where there's practically no oxygen, just to get to the summit.

He doesn't take my phone from me; his hand wraps around my wrist. My breath catches in my throat because the number eight hovers in my vision line. It's not just a number to me now. It's infinite. Which is ironic because if you looked at the tattoo from the right angle, it would look endless.

But it's infinite, never-ending, for different reasons. Because there's a version of Ethan that plays out behind my eyes, and I think behind his, too—who he could have, would have, should have been. I think there's an infinite me somewhere there, too. One who still has a best friend, spends her days with teeth and bones but knows him, too.

I can't really imagine my life without him now. Arna's therapists always went on about trauma bonds. They said, according to her anyway, that was part of the reason she and I were so intertwined. Fused beyond repair or separation. Codependent down to the last syllable found in the definition of the word.

Ethan might be like that now.

He looks back at me, hand still gripping my wrist for a moment longer. "You want to enter the death zone, Ten?"

"I can't think of anyone else I'd rather try to summit a mountain with," I say. It's true. He's infinite, part of all the broken pieces left of me. I can't think of anyone else I would rather do most things with now.

"Ah, well, this one—" Ethan jabs his thumb toward my phone. "Is a bit harder to climb, yeah?"

He cocks his head, and his eyes light up for a moment when lightning flashes beyond the window. "But I'll make you a deal. You ever decide you want to climb that mountain, any mountain really, no matter where you are in the world—you call me, and I'll come, yeah?"

"Deal." I smile at him, but he's looking back at the phone again, eyebrows creased and face entirely quizzical.

He looks cute, sort of like a small child figuring something out. Ethan Barclay often looks many ways—almost always entirely too beautiful for this world—but I've never seen him look *cute*.

He turns back to me. "What would happen to a body up there anyway?"

"Literally nothing." I shake my head, laughing at the way his pupils widen. "Hardly any oxygen to start decomposition. They stay frozen, practically perfectly preserved. The mountain is covered with bodies, actually. World's tallest gravesite."

Ethan's lips pull back, and he pushes my phone away. "Who the fuck would want to climb that? I take it back, any mountain but that one."

"Alright. Deal amended." I try to nod solemnly at him, but my lips keep twitching.

Ethan leans back and looks at his phone, but his fingers drum against the screen for a moment before he looks back at me. His voice is rough. "Any mountains in Vietnam? That's next, yeah?"

"Do you want to come with me?" My voice is quiet, and I think it probably sounds hopeful. But that's what I feel. It might be what I've felt since I first saw him standing on that dock—entirely too moody and entirely too drunk. There's a tiny kernel in my chest, the thought of not being alone but being with him.

Ethan rolls his eyes, pushing my face away like a small child. "'Course I do. I'm in it now, Ten. Have to see how the story ends."

His hand stays pressed to my cheek for a moment, and it hangs between us, the hope. The promise of it, not being alone. I think it's what we both pretend we want, but maybe we're the exception to each other's rules. We stare at one another, like we're growing more and more prone to doing, a battle of wills to see who will break away first.

In this case, it's Ethan. "Just get a BnB with two beds. You hog the fucking covers, yeah?"

Chapter Seventeen

The cloying heat in Vietnam sticks to my skin, beyond oppressive and anything I felt in the Philippines or Indonesia.

Ethan's swearing, not at all under his breath, as he drags my suitcase across the cracked, uneven pavement. The streets are overcrowded, all the buildings of the Old Quarter practically on top of one another, foot traffic somehow blends seamlessly with scooters, and storefronts spill onto the street, with tiny plastic chairs scattered everywhere for vendors selling food or beer.

"It should be just up ahead," I call, looking down at my phone to see the instructions for the apartment again. "It's down the alleyway beside the textile shop."

"They're all textile shops." Ethan stops, a groan of frustration caught in his throat when he tries to rip my suitcase over a particularly large crack in the pavement. "We're ditching this and getting you a backpack, yeah?"

I wave my hands around before grabbing the braid that's draped across my shoulder and lifting it off my neck for a moment. "We are in the textile district. I'm sure we can find one if it's bothering you so much."

"It's not terribly practical." Ethan hauls it over the edge of the raised sidewalk.

"No one said you had to carry it for me." I look down at my phone again and back up at the numbers marking each building. "This is it."

Ethan stops in front of the alleyway, a textile shop to his right. A convenience store sits on the other side, illuminated signs in the window and peeling brand stickers all over the door. He rolls his shoulders, dropping his backpack unceremoniously to the ground beside my suitcase. He points to them and then looks up at me. "You watch these, yeah?"

"Where are you going?" I ask, dropping my hand to the handle of my suitcase, eyes narrowed up at him.

He jerks his tattooed thumb over his shoulder to the store. "To get a drink. I'm fucking boiling."

I watch, one eyebrow raised as Ethan runs a hand through his hair, the waves damp. He pulls the door and a small bell chimes.

There's a blast of cold air as he steps in, but when the door shuts, it effectively seals it off.

I don't even remember Arna coming here. I'm sure she did—there weren't many places she didn't go. But nothing of note sticks out to me as I survey the street. The Old Quarter is made up of thirty-six streets, each street reserved for a different craft, like textiles or jewelry, tucked away in the center of Hanoi. It's all Vietnamese architecture, cafés, shopfronts, and street food. Knotted branches and lush green draped leaves line either side of the road, despite the heat. Bike merchants weave in and out of traffic, and chipped signs list endless menus of Vietnamese food.

The bell chimes, and Ethan ducks out from the small door, an open bottle of beer perspiring in his hand. The other holds an open six-pack.

"You'll dehydrate at an alarming rate in this heat," I tell him, bending down to grab his backpack.

Ethan shrugs before tipping the bottle back. I watch the column of his neck as he swallows. There's a thin sheen of sweat clinging to his skin. He pauses, handing me the bottle. "This one's yours. Trade you."

He holds the bottle out, fingertips gripping it loosely until I grab it from him. It's cool to the touch, and I feel like rolling it across my neck. But Ethan shoulders his backpack and starts dragging my suitcase behind him, the other hand still holding the handle on his six-pack, so I follow him.

I watch him as he ducks under a hanging clothesline, and I take a sip of the beer. My lips press exactly where his were, touching the rim of the bottle where it met the scar across his mouth.

The alley is poorly lit, cut off almost entirely from the noises of the street not even five feet away. "It's the red door at the end," I call out to him.

I hear the creak of the door, sounding like it was practically thrown open, followed by Ethan swearing. I push aside another hanging sheet, and Ethan is shoving my suitcase through the door into the barely lit stairwell that leads to a set of practically vertical, peeling wood steps.

"This fucking thing—" Ethan's forearms tense as he lifts it to start pulling the suitcase up the staircase.

"Give it to me." I shove the open beer back in his direction, but he's already dragging it behind him, clearly not giving a shit that it hits each step with a resounding thud, because he refuses to put down the pack of beer.

It's only one floor up, albeit an entirely straight climb, full of Ethan's muttering and swearing and more bizarre British phrases whispered under his breath than I've ever heard in my life.

"What's the code again?" Ethan asks, practically kicking my suitcase to the side.

He waits for me to look back down at my phone, while his palm twists off the cap of one of the beer bottles.

"I told you on the plane. It's 1234." I push past him, thumbs moving across the keypad mounted to the door. The lock clicks open, and I glance over at him, tipping my chin up in triumph. "You should be able to remember that."

Ethan shakes his head, the beer bottle poised in front of his mouth. "Never been good with remembering random numbers. Sure you're fucking ace at math." His voice drips with sarcasm.

I purse my lips and look at him. "I am, actually. How much do you weigh?"

He eyes me behind the raised bottle "Why?"

I shrug, pushing my suitcase over the tiny bump in the floor and into the apartment. "I was just going to tell you how much lidocaine I would need to properly numb your mouth. But now you'll never know."

"Oh, shame." Ethan's voice is dry behind me.

A narrow hallway stretches out in front of the worn, stone flooring beneath our feet.

Ethan drops his backpack and gestures with his beer for me to start down the hall. I kick my sandals off, and the stone is cold under my feet, our footsteps silent as we clear the hallway.

A kitchen stretches across the wall, with a teak dining table in the middle of the open space. There's a worn cognac leather couch in the center of the living room, facing a TV that's mounted to the wall in the middle of wood paneling. There's another small hallway, just off the wall with the TV. I see two open bedroom doors along the side and a bathroom at the very end. Windows line the wall opposite us, framed by dark wood, with a folding door that leads out to the balcony.

I cross the floor, tugging open the heavy wooden doors to step out onto the balcony. It's narrow, with cracked tiles beneath my feet, two bamboo chairs, and a small table between them. Low lights framed by paper lanterns hang above us as I move to peer out over the railing and raise the beer to my lips.

We're up in the trees, all twisting branches and leaves blocking us in. I'd have to lean over the side entirely to see the street. And I do, watching for a moment at the scooters moving by below before falling to sit in one of the chairs.

Ethan's already sitting opposite me, legs splayed out when his phone starts ringing in his pocket, and his face falls flat. He doesn't even look at it as he pulls it out and silences it.

"Should you—" I start, but he cuts me off.

"No. I shouldn't." He pockets his phone and looks back up at me. "You going to tell me what's in the next letter?"

I press my lips together. I want to push, to pry. To tell him to answer the phone because maybe a second chance at his dream is waiting on the other end, but his eyes are entirely shuttered—storm clouds rolling in across a once clear sky. So I shrug, pulling the still sealed envelope out of the bag I dropped at my feet. "I haven't read it, yet."

"Why not? Figured you'd be busting to see what else she had to say." Ethan surveys me, leaning back, and lazily twirling the bottle between his fingers.

I run my fingers along the edges of the envelope, thumbs pressing down on the seal. "I'm nervous, I guess. About whatever else it is that she thinks she needs to tell me that I didn't know about."

Ethan leans forward, dropping his hands to his knees, and he offers me a grin. "Maybe she was working in PR for an illegal cockfighting ring. Who fucking knows, just open it, and we'll have a laugh, yeah?"

I'm still smiling at him when I tear open the envelope, my heart buoyed, floating above a raging sea, because he's smiling at me.

I read the letter, and not only is she dead, but I think I've died, too.

Chapter Eighteen

Nov,

Have you ever wondered how you impacted someone else? How you might have changed their trajectory? Shaped them in all the wrong ways?

You asked me once how much I weighed. We were young. It was when everything started with you. You had to keep your food separate on your plate, to eat it in a certain order. No stems, no seeds. Carefully planned out caloric intake. Small bites only. All those behaviors that turned into more.

I remember it like it was yesterday, and I think I'll remember it into the beyond. We were sitting in your dorm room in Year Ten. Do you remember it? We hung those tiny strands of twinkle lights along the stone wall behind your bed and stuck all those polaroids to the wall.

You came back from the washroom. I was sitting on your bed, post-volley-ball practice. I remember that because I was still wearing my spandex. You looked sad, kind of small even. I knew what was bothering you. I watched you pull at your shirt and shift back and forth on your feet uncomfortably. And you asked me. I remember looking down, Cosmopolitan in one hand, with some model on the cover, impossibly rake thin, and I didn't like the way my legs looked in the spandex at that moment pressed against the white bedding of yours. So, I lied. I told you I weighed a number that seemed like the number of pounds that were on that model on the cover of the magazine.

You started throwing up after that. You wore your teeth down with your own stomach acid. You cried when you did it. Sometimes I held your hand when I found you there on your knees in the stall, damp hair curling around your forehead.

And then it was too far gone, and we were too far down the road, so I lied about it forever.

You know how kids do that, don't you, Novie? They lie, and then they dig a hole. It felt like I was digging forever. I never wanted to set you back. I never wanted to hurt you. Maybe I was scared so much of what caused you pain had to do with me.

I tried to be better, to do better. I sat with you. I came with you to all of those outpatient appointments. I fed you. I picked out food, specifically for you. You know I would spend hours in the grocery store, picking through lettuce leaves and inspecting every inch of the tomato skin. I did those things. I did them for you because I think it's my fault.

I wanted you to stay alive, to live. One of my favorite dishes in the world can be found where you are now—Bún Chả Cá—when you have a bowl, think of it as me, spending eternity in the produce aisle making sure everything is just right for you.

You were always perfect the way you were,

Arna

The beer bottle slips from between my fingers and shatters on the tile floor, foam and liquid spraying up over my legs and sloshing over my feet.

I think Ethan speaks. I think I hear him say *Ten* and then say my name—*November, November, November.*

But I'm not listening.

I think I hear him open the door, and I think I hear glass crunch under his feet.

I drop the letter, and I don't care as it floats down on an invisible breeze, one corner landing in the liquid pooling there.

"No," I whisper, a sad little plea against an even crueler world.

I shake my head for a moment, and I still can't hear anything. It's like the day she died, like the day I found that box of letters on my porch. It's like all those things but infinitely worse.

I push off the chair, and I forget that I'm barefoot, but I don't feel the glass, not really, because I can't feel anything. Ethan's in the kitchen, grabbing a towel, and for the first time since we met, I'm not paying attention to Ethan Barclay. I don't even notice him as I walk to the front hallway and yank my suitcase onto the ground.

My fingers slip over the zipper, but I wrench it down, throwing open the top and tossing my clothes everywhere. The rest of the letters are sitting, safeguarded and wrapped in one of my sweaters—with more care than their author ever showed me—and I rip out the next one. It was on the top. I set it there, naively placing them all in order when I packed up.

The envelope shreds easily.

So does what's left of my heart.

November,

I hope you're reading this, that you haven't given up and left my letters to rot in some overflowing garbage can in the Old Quarter of Hanoi.

I fell in love once, you know.

It was all very Montague and Capulet of me, actually. It was the summer after you started dental school. Pappous made me stay home and try my hand at some sort of operational role in the company. We both know that didn't stick.

You had just met Jake. You called me. It was mid-morning for me and late night for you. I was in my office, and you were just getting home. In an uncharacteristic move, you went out with some of your classmates to celebrate finishing exams—on King West, of all places. You were sitting at a high-top, probably only drinking a vodka soda because you were still firmly in your no-colored-beverages era, and you made an American Psycho reference. Someone asked you what you were going to do this summer, and you said you had to return some videotapes.

Awkward silence and blank faces followed per usual when you would make one of those bizarre statements. But someone behind you laughed.

You turned around and there he was. All six-foot-one, fresh off his MBA and looking at you like the Toronto version of a Ken doll, because that's really what Jake was if we're being honest. Sandy brown hair and blue eyes, just enough muscle that it wasn't alarming. The kind of guy who pulled your chair out for you and never forgot to open the door. But he saw you, for that brief moment in time.

I met Levi thirty-five minutes after we hung up the phone. He was standing by the copier, of all things. Leaning over it and arms folded far too casually for the pearl gray Brunello Cucinelli suit he was wearing. My family was in negotiations to buy some arm of the shipping company his owned in Australia.

We didn't tell anyone because it would have been in poor taste, as my family was trying to swallow his empire, after all. But I loved him. I think I could have loved him, as wholly, completely as I loved you. He indulged me, thought I was funny. We spent the summer sneaking around, and I don't think that was part of it for me. But it turned out it was for him. Things went south with the deal, and even though we had made all these grand plans, he left me anyway.

I thought it was fate. That two would become four on the same day.

But yours stuck, and mine didn't.

Sometimes I wonder why I never encouraged you to put yourself out there. I thought you were so special. But I think I liked having you all to myself. Liked the way it made me feel that someone needed me when I was never needed by anyone my whole life. I think you could have been with Jake forever. Maybe it wouldn't have been a heart-stopping, earth-shattering love. But there was always a third person in that relationship.

Those trauma bonds will get you in the end.

I want you to go somewhere special now, November. Remember the Christmas break we spent in Costa Rica? Pappous rented that villa and then had to leave for some sort of emergency, and it was just me, you, and Sebastian.

Those were the best days. Please go there, and please don't forget them.

Forever,

Arna

She was a fucking liar, and none of it was ever real.

All a contrived manipulation. All of it. The care, the attention, the once-in-a-lifetime friendship with no boundaries, no secrets. The only love I ever really received.

I'm still carrying the letter, clenching it in my hand because I can't bring myself to care about her last words, her alleged great gift from the beyond, when I walk into the bathroom. I feel like ripping it, tearing it apart, and stomping on it. But I just let it fall to the ground, edges crumpled.

It's not on purpose, but it's terribly ironic. I fall to my knees, fingers slipping against the seat of the toilet and tears blurring my vision entirely—and I start throwing up.

I'm heaving, nothing at all left in my stomach, and sobs are sneaking up between them when a hand runs down my back. Tattooed fingers traverse the ridges of my spine, the sides of my ribcage.

I sob, one more empty heave to match my empty heart, before pushing back on shaking hands. Ethan's palm presses against my lower spine, the other gathers my hair and brings it to one side.

"Alright Ten?" His voice is low, soothing, and he stays upright on both knees, arms guiding me back to sit against the wall.

"I'm fine." I wipe my mouth on the back of my hand, tipping my head back against the wall. "It wasn't on purpose. I wasn't throwing up because of something I ate or drank."

Ethan reaches down and grabs the letter, smoothing out the wrinkled edges before setting it carefully back on the cold tile. "Never said it was."

He sits back against the wall, our shoulders brushing. I drop my head to his, and I feel his chin press against the crown of my hair. His hand finds mine, and he brings it to his lips, brushing them across it.

"Take as long as you need, November."

I inspect the bottom of my foot, eyeing the ribbons of shredded skin. There's no glass left in it from where I stomped across it, and no bloody footprints left in the stone hallway. Ethan cleaned them up while I took a shower and subsequently used a sanitized pair of tweezers from my bag to fish out the small fragments of glass before coming to the living room.

Leaning forward, I grab the open beer sitting on the coffee table. My fingers pull at the edges of the cut, nose wrinkling in discomfort while I take a sip. My hair, still soaking from the shower, is tied in a messy knot at the back of my head. And I'm wearing Ethan's sweater, the one with his name on the back, and the shorts with his number on them. They were laid out on my bed when I went to my room to change.

The door opens, and I look over my shoulder as Ethan moves down the hallway, two plastic bags weighed down in either hand. He drops them on the table before coming to sit beside me, peering at my foot for a moment before his lip curls back.

I hold the beer out to him, and he takes it, rolling his shoulders back before sinking into the couch. "That need stitches?"

"I mean, I'm a doctor of teeth." I glance at him, and he looks like he's about to interject, but I smile at him. "I don't think so. The skin on the bottom of your foot is so thin, anyway. It's not very deep. It just looks...ugly."

He nods, taking another swig of the beer before handing it back to me and pushing up off his knees. "Grabbed you some Band-Aids, more beer, and some phở. Just got you noodles and broth. That okay? I can go back out if—"

"It's fine, Ethan." I turn, resting my chin on the back of the couch. "Noodles and broth are okay."

"You'd tell me, yeah?" He pauses as he's tearing open the plastic bags, gray eyes cutting back to me, like he's nervous. "If I got you something that upset you—"

I dig my chin into the couch cushion. My cheeks hurt from crying, the skin rough from the salt in my tears. But I smile at him. "You haven't upset me."

Ethan pokes his tongue into his cheek, nodding as he continues to pull out the containers and bags. He grabs one of the paper bags, securing it between his teeth before his hands wrap around two of the containers.

"What, not going to tell me that's bad for my teeth?" Ethan says, all muffled because the paper is still in his mouth as he walks around the couch.

I reach out, grabbing the containers from him. They're warm against my hands as I set them down on the coffee table. Ethan tosses down two sets of chopsticks beside them before he grabs the paper bag and rips it open. Plastic bags of bean sprouts, cabbage, and other vegetables spill out across the table.

"It's just paper, and one of your teeth is fake." I look at him, smiling softly. "Don't worry, if you were doing anything that would compromise your oral health, I'd be the first to let you know."

Ethan tips his head, one curl falling across his forehead, and he throws me a grin before he lifts the lids off the containers and starts adding the noodles to the bowls of broth, steam rising off the top of them. "You can add your own vegetables, yeah? Whenever you feel ready."

My nostrils flare, and my eyes burn, but I nod anyway, accepting the steaming bowl and chopsticks from him. Ethan says nothing and grabs the remote, flipping through streaming services until he lands on Scream.

I look sideways at him, lips wanting desperately to tip upward, even though I'm so tired.

They're small gestures he makes. Just tiny little things he does to show me that he sees me.

Small, little things. Miniscule in the grand scheme of the universe, but they feel infinite.

He grabs the beer bottle he left sitting on the table before he went out, tipping the neck back to take a sip as he sits down beside me.

"That true?" He tips his head back, toward the table.

The two letters sit there, one with bleeding ink because the beer started to seep into the page before Ethan picked it up. I let him read it while we were still sitting on the floor.

I wish it wasn't.

I nod, swirling the noodles in my bowl, checking for any remnants of anything else. But I trust Ethan. I know he would have made sure it was just broth, just noodles. "Yes. I remember it. She told me a number lower than what I was seeing on the scale, and that was that. All those little things I was doing, things that were starting to make me uncomfortable like my food touching, daily caloric intake. They just became something so much bigger."

Ethan tips his head back, rolling it along the back of the couch. "But—"

"Logic didn't matter to my brain then, Ethan." I shake my head, offering him a shrug, but it's likely swallowed by his much larger clothing. "Eating disorders are one of the most illogical diseases there are. They often don't make sense to people who don't have them. You don't see logic, you don't even see what's really in the mirror. It's just you and a horribly distorted version of yourself. I know now that I had this insatiable desire to be enough, to feel worthy, to feel wanted, and I thought I could achieve that if I weighed less. But at the time, it all boiled down to what I was seeing when I looked at myself. She said the number, and that was that. My neurons fired, all the synapses clicked together, and the pathways were formed."

He nods, lips pulling to the side. "Would it have made a difference for you, if she told you the truth?"

My lips part, and a tiny breath escapes me. I twirl the chopsticks uselessly in my hands and worry at my bottom lip with my teeth. I know I shouldn't do that. There are too many reasons why—thin skin, the possibility of infection, external variables—but I do it because I don't think I have an answer. "I don't know. But it's changed everything all the same."

Ethan's looking at me, and I think he winces when I wipe at my eyes.

My breath shakes when I inhale and my teeth dig into my bottom lip. "She was the only one. The only one who took care of me...who loved me the way a fifteen-year-old deserves to be loved, and I thought it meant I was worthy, that maybe my brain was wrong. But she wasn't doing it from the goodness of her heart because she loved me. She was doing it to appease her conscience." Tears falling feely now, I whisper, "She was in love...she loved someone and didn't tell me. I would have...I would have taken care of her the way she always took care of me."

Ethan reaches forward, and I can see the number eight in the periphery of my vision. He wipes at my cheek, his thumb stroking back and forth for a few moments.

My eyelids feel heavy, and I press into his hand. "I'm sorry."

"For what?" he asks plainly.

I pull back, gesturing toward the windows. "Aren't you upset? We're in this new city, one of the food capitals of the world, and you grabbed take-out on our first night, and you're watching movies with me."

Ethan's lower lip comes out past the top one, and he shakes his head. "No, Ten, I'm not upset."

"Arna would have—"

"Don't really want to hear about Arna right now." Ethan tips his beer back to the screen. "Now shut up, eat your phở, and watch Scream. Strike me as the type who likes the scene where Billy's all covered in blood."

Chapter Nineteen

"Oi—" Ethan reaches out, smacking my shoulder with the back of his hand. "Did you know the freshest beer in the world is made here?"

I look over at him, stretched out in a chair across from me at some bar that spills onto the street.

Ethan's head lolls to the side, and everything about him looks decidedly lazy. He holds his phone out to me, and I take it, thumb brushing upward and reading the article.

He's right. Bia Hoi. Available right on the street only a few blocks away.

I look back over at him, the sunlight filtering down through the trees crowding the street.

His legs are pushed out in front of him, both hands stacked on top of his abdomen, and his head tipped back, messy hair, and what I'm beginning to suspect are the most beautiful eyes in the world hiding behind ancient, peeling Ray Bans.

We spent the day together. Just us, and a ghost that I did my best to shrug off. We walked aimlessly around the streets, stopping for drinks or food when Ethan was hungry, which was an amount that bordered on alarming.

He held my hand when we walked around Hoan Kiem Lake, and he left a Post-it Note on the wall of a café where we sat together drinking coffee. He drew a poor imitation of a heart, our initials scrawled in the middle.

EB + NM.

It was a joke, but we stared at one another for a bit too long afterward. Our hands probably brushed too often, but I think we kept trying to find reasons to touch one another. His hand on my shoulder when he was drawing my attention to something, my fingers wrapping around his forearm to point something out, and much too often, his hands on my heart.

He scares me, I think. Because I'll never be the me I am today—entirely unburdened, free of Arna. It's a temporary reprieve, granted to me by I don't know what, that allows me to forget, for just a moment—the truth.

That I've met the love of my life, and she's dead.

But I look at him now, and I think my earlier assessment might have been correct but flawed.

Genetically perfect, save for the implant. But entirely just right everywhere else, too.

I smile at him because I'm not sure how much longer it will last, this temporary freedom from loving my best friend and hating her at the same time, and slide the phone back across the tiny table. "Well, we came all this way."

Ethan looks comical under the lanterns that swing above us in a sort of non-existent breeze. He could never really look comical, not when he looks like he looks, but the tiny, plastic chairs that surround the tables sitting practically to the ground, lining the streets of the Old Quarter are so fucking small.

I raise my eyebrows as I watch Ethan across from me, nostrils flaring and arm muscles tense while he grips the sides of the yellow chair to shift it backward.

I wrinkle my nose as the plastic scrapes against the ground.

A noise caught between a groan and what might be a growl comes from his throat, and a snort escapes me. Ethan freezes, all those muscle fibers and ligaments stopping instantly with a sort of preternatural still-ness that could only belong to a prey animal, or someone who has spent their entire lifetime honing their body to move exactly the way they need it to. His eyes snap up to me, and his lips pull back, showing me all those perfect teeth.

"This funny, Ten?" Ethan raises an eyebrow before snatching his own plastic cup.

Foam sloshes over the rim and onto his hand, right over top of the last whirls of ink. I watch as he brings his hand to his mouth, his tongue running along the back quickly before taking a sip.

My lips part involuntarily, and a tiny breath catches in my throat.

I don't think I've ever seen Ethan's tongue. It's an important piece of anatomy, responsible for all sorts of things. Eight muscles. Four intrinsic muscles that help change the shape of your tongue and four extrinsic ones attached to bone that allow you to move it. Contrary to popular belief, it's not the strongest muscle in your body.

But it helps you speak, swallow, breath, and taste.

I've never seen Ethan's tongue, and I wonder what it would feel like against mine. Against my skin. Against me.

My cheeks heat, and I look up at him.

He stares back at me, still holding the cup to his mouth. The corners of his lips twitch, and those eyes bore into me as I watch his pupils dilate. His fingers tense, and he swallows, the column of his throat moving.

I drag my bottom lip between my teeth, Ethan shifts in his chair again, a much smaller movement this time, and we're still staring at one another.

But there it is. The spurt of blood from my already broken heart.

"I think your chair is too small, Ethan." I swallow, and I look away at the crowds of other people in chairs that are too small for almost everyone, sitting and drinking, their laughter spilling into the sky in the same way they spill onto the streets.

My cheeks feel hot, and I stare determinedly away from him.

I can feel Ethan still looking at me, heat everywhere those sharp eyes fall, and I think I can see his nostrils flare, something that almost borders a scoff escaping him.

He shakes his head, almost imperceptibly, and then drains the rest of his cup.

I'm still staring away, not really looking at anything besides all the different people, heads tipped back in laughter and arms gesticulating and waving around their own cups of beer, tiny little bits of foam splashing onto the worn lacquered tables. I'm not looking, but I can see Ethan in my periphery more clearly than I can see anything in front of me.

He reaches a hand up and jerks his chin before two fingers point down at the empty cup.

I think he's angry, and I don't know why.

Rude and brash, it's radiating off of him, and he looks exactly the way he's afraid everyone thinks he does.

My eyes flick back to him, and I bring my cup to my lips. My mouth dries, and my lips part when I see his cheek twitch.

His jaw pops back and forth, and I can tell he's grinding his teeth.

I feel myself cringe, and I'm going to tell him not to do that—not to grind his teeth, that he's wearing down his enamel as we speak, and if he ever dies, I'll have a harder time matching his teeth to records—but a server comes over and drops two more cups of the freshest beer in the world on the table.

Ethan snatches his, tattoos flashing briefly before I can't see them anymore as he tips his cup back quickly, and I can see the column of his throat as he swallows.

"Bloke over there keeps clocking you," he says before jerking his head across the street.

I feel myself turn, and I can see he's right. Two men, also too large for the yellow plastic chairs, sit directly across from us. And one of them smiles slightly when he sees me looking.

"So?" I ask, looking back at him.

Ethan shrugs. "You look titchy."

"So do you."

"Oi!" Ethan brings his arm up, waving his hand and gesturing for them to come join us. He nods his head, eyebrows raising and chin tipping.

I can hear the scrape of the chairs. The blond one who was looking at me and his friend are making their way across the tiny street full of spilled-out chairs to come sit with us.

I feel small, kind of insignificant at this moment. I'm not good at meeting new people, and I'm not usually comfortable around them. Strangers fill me with an inexplicable state of dread and a rolling stomach that only subsides when I pop an Ativan before I say something fucking off-putting, like the fact that I've seen more burned bodies than I've seen live ones. But I don't think it's because he's invited other people over to join us. It's because he's sitting across from me, impossibly spread out in that tiny fucking chair, arms stretched out, and broad chest and shoulders on display under the cotton of his shirt.

Tattooed fingers roll the empty cup, and he shrugs when I look at him.

I want to say something, anything. That I like when it's just us. That I don't care if this impossibly tall man looks like he walked off the pages of Vogue and is staring at me.

But Ethan speaks before I can. "Have it off, then. Been a stressful few days."

I blink—once, twice, three times—and Ethan jerks his chin toward the tiny chair beside me, as it's occupied with a man that is objectively so beautiful it should hurt to look at him—looks like he should be holding a surfboard under his arm, pushing wet hair off his face, and pulling a wetsuit down to show abs slicked with saltwater. His eyes are so blue that people would think they're full of color, but blue eyes don't actually have any pigment in the front layer. It's all scattered fibers and the absorption of light wavelengths. They're a trick.

Ethan isn't looking at me anymore. So, I don't look at him. I turn, and I smile in a way that would make Arna proud, even though I'm starting to think I might hate her.

"Hi," I offer, bringing my cup to cover my mouth because my smile is so fucking fake my cheeks feel like they're going to crack. "Who are you?"

A smile that would probably melt most people—but I'm not interested in it, because it isn't a full top lip bisected by a thin scar on the left, showing me the most perfect teeth in the world and a perfect implant—precedes an Australian accent. "Aiden, and you are?"

"November," I offer, reaching out my hand as it's engulfed in his much bigger one.

His thumb skates over the back of my hand for a brief moment before he drops it. But this thumb doesn't bear a number, so I don't care.

"November?" he repeats, and I know for certain I prefer the way my name sounds when it's said with a British accent. "That's a unique name. Must be other things unique about you, too?"

He leans forward, that average smile still stretching and those eyes endlessly blue, but they're fucking boring because they aren't gray, one tendril of blond hair flopping forward. He's looking at me like he's interested in me, so I start to answer and pretend I'm interested in him, too.

Chapter Twenty

I kick Aiden out of my bed and the apartment afterward. It wasn't that great, and I'm not even sure why I did it. Maybe it was the way Ethan looked at me, the set of his jaw, and the all-too-casual shrug of his shoulders when he suggested I take the *edge off* earlier. I didn't like that look on his face then, and I don't like replaying it now.

Or maybe I did it because my best friend is dead, and the only time I've felt anything in the last few months is when my name is on Ethan's lips. But I don't really want to think about that, so I throw back the crumpled white sheets that make my lip curl up.

In a different life, a different world, if I had a different heart, one that wasn't suddenly entirely occupied by tattooed hands and a voice that might overtake tiny dental drills for my favorite sound—it probably wouldn't have bothered me, sex with this stranger. I had sex when I wanted it or felt like I needed it. I haven't been in a lasting relationship since Jake left me because I was "emotionally unavailable," and I was looking back. I didn't really need him for anything, and it never bothered me when he worked until two a.m. doing whatever it is investment bankers do, and I never waited up for him. Maybe I should have. At that time in my life, I was sure I didn't really need anyone but Arna.

But in between these sheets, where our bodies moved, and I came, but it wasn't the body on top of mine that I was thinking about if I was honest with myself—I don't think there's anything more disgusting to me at this moment.

The tears start when I'm stripping the sheets, my movements all agitated and jilted. I can't get them off the bed fast enough. The sob sneaks up my throat when I'm grabbing them all in a ball. The ungodly noise moves past my teeth as I walk across the apartment. Shadows from the lights of the city crawl alongside me, and the sob finally escapes my lips when I throw open the small washing machine in the closet by the front door of the apartment.

My fingers slip as I pound against the buttons on the machine. The lettering surrounding them blurs, and I couldn't read it anyway because I can't read Vietnamese, and I don't care. I just want the water to wash away all the sins I feel like I just committed.

Ethan isn't home, and I want to text him and ask him to come back, but I don't know what to say. I'm done? All finished up over here, come on back?

My mouth goes dry because I wonder if he's gone out to do what he told me to do. His words ring in my ears, but they feel cruel as they reverberate against my eardrums. Another sob, this one wet and entirely guttural sneaks out of me when the washing machine finally whirs to life.

I'm crying more than I have since Arna died, since my world went quiet and not in a good way. I cry all the way to the bathroom and push the dial of the shower with more force than necessary, turning it all the way to hot, and I hope the water burns the ghosts of hands that don't belong to Ethan off my skin.

I'm still crying when I finally hear the door open. My chest opens a bit, too; the constriction and erratic hammering of my heart loosens and slows ever so slightly.

The dread is still there because I don't know where Ethan was, and I'm not sure I want to know. The thought of him doing what I was doing—his body moving over or under someone else, neck tensing and stacked muscles in his back shuddering when he thrusts—makes me want to vomit.

I don't know when it changed. I can't pinpoint it. It might have been the moment Ethan cocked his head, those eyebrows raised as he tipped the beer he was holding toward the bar, where Aiden was sitting and watching me intently from behind blue eyes I'm sure most people would crawl for. But they weren't the gray eyes that have been following me around—the ones branded on the inside of my heart now.

Maybe it was the moment our lips crashed together, and I found myself wanting to run my tongue over a scar that wasn't there; to kiss it better the way I wanted to kiss better all the scars on a heart that wasn't living in the body I was running my hands across.

Or maybe it was when I arched my back into his chest, nails digging into different muscles than the ones that were starting to feel like a map home, and closed my eyes and saw Ethan behind my eyelids.

I don't know when it changed; I just know that it did.

I wipe at my cheeks with my fingertips and push myself up to sit against the wall behind my bed. The clean sheets are wrapped around me now. They might be warm, entirely devoid of whatever we left on them, but they feel like they're chafing my skin. My wet hair is tied into some sort of sad replica of the messy knots Arna used to pull my hair into with just two simple flicks of her wrist. I left the door to my room open—the envelope of an invitation peeled back.

Ethan's footsteps are light in the hallway, like he doesn't know if I'm awake and isn't sure how softly to tread. Or maybe he doesn't know if I'm alone. The light from the hall stretches farther across the worn wood floor, reaching all the way to the rattan rug at the end of the bed. But I'm not looking in the doorway. I'm staring at the wooden shelving on the wall that's big enough to hold my suitcase. It's open, clothes thrown every which way because I practically tore it apart after my shower looking for clean pajamas.

I don't want to look at Ethan, I know he's in the doorway now, half-leaning into the room, because the entire chemical composition of air has changed. There's more oxygen for me to breathe, and I rub absentmindedly at my chest, still red from the shower. It feels easier to breathe now that he's here. But I don't want him to see what's written all over my face.

"Can't say I was a fan of that." Ethan's voice is dry. But it's not his usual irritation or irreverence. He's upset. I can hear it. His words are sharp.

It's what makes me turn to look at him, and I hastily wipe at my cheeks again. I can feel how red my eyes are, how tired my skin feels from crying.

He must see it, too, because his posture changes in an instant. The rigid lines of his neck down to his shoulders and across the tightened muscles in his forearms leading to clenched hands in his pockets that soften. Ethan starts forward but stops before fully leaving the doorway. I can't see his face clearly because it's dark, but I hope it's telling a similar story to mine.

"Me neither, as it turns out," I offer, shrugging my shoulders. I push myself farther to the opposite side of the bed, leaving room for Ethan. "Sheets are clean."

"You right? Did something happen, Nov?" Ethan's voice cracks, and I'm looking back at the shelves again because I don't want to see the concern or the pity on his face.

But I feel the bed shift under me as Ethan sits beside me.

I shake my head, puffing my cheeks out. Nothing happened, not really. Nothing I feel like sharing anyway. "I'm just sad."

And I was sad. For so many fucking reasons. I wished I could take it all back. I wanted to go back in time, tell Aiden to fuck off, that I wasn't interested because my heart was suddenly wholly, entirely occupied and reach across that tiny table and grab Ethan's hand, press those tattoos, those numbers, to my chest and feel them all the way down to my soul. And I missed my best friend. I missed Arna so much I could feel it in my teeth, in my bones, and I fucking hated myself for it at the same time because it felt like her fault. I had thought—for one brief, stupid moment—her letters were a gift, a part of her that she was leaving me. But they didn't feel like a gift. Not anymore. There was a growing sense of dread in me each time I opened one, whenever I could see them peeking out from under my clothes, wondering what she was going to reveal to me this time. It felt cruel, an unusual sort of punishment I wasn't sure I deserved. But it seemed like something she would do—one final trick, the final act in the play of her life that ensured she would never be forgotten, never to be upstaged.

But most of all, I was starting to wonder if I ever really knew her the way she knew me. Some of it had been innocuous, not of any real consequence in the story of our lives. It didn't really matter that she didn't tell me she lived on a beach in the Philippines once, or that she apparently moonlighted as a drug smuggler. When I juxtaposed those with the last two secrets, two that really, truly, hurt me, I was beginning to wonder if she was just setting the stage for her big reveal. It didn't seem like something that would leave any survivors.

"Sad? Do you not...uh...have it off very often?" Ethan palms his jaw before scrubbing his face quickly.

I stop crying and look at him flatly. "What the hell does that mean?"

"Boff. Shag. Sex, November. Do you not have sex...like that, very often?" Ethan rolls his eyes at me.

He tugs on his hair briefly before resting one arm on his propped-up knee. I can see the raised edge of his scar just under the too-pronounced calf muscle. The definition of his muscles, particularly in his legs, makes him look permanently dehydrated. He probably is, with the amount of beer he drinks, but I think he would look like this anyway.

"Casual sex you mean?" I arch an eyebrow at him. "I have. And I do, when I feel like it. I guess I just wasn't as into it as I thought I was."

Ethan nods, dropping his head back against the wall, and drums his fingers against his kneecap. "I'm sorry. Feel a bit rubbish about that. Like

I forced your hand. I just thought that you might enjoy it, and then I realized I didn't exactly love it, and uh, here we are."

"You didn't force me to do anything. I was a willing participant," I tell him, pulling my legs up and wrapping my arms around them.

My chin drops to my kneecap before I rest my cheek there instead, so I can finally look at Ethan.

He's looking at me. And there's something about it; the way the shadows are just making the edges of his jaw look that much sharper. His full lips are pressed together, and I can see his tongue poking at the inside of his cheek, how he rolls his shoulders against the wall, like he's trying to release tension. He looks like he's carrying some sort of inexplicable weight, like his chest is heavy, and I hope it's heavy with me, so I ask, "What didn't you love?"

"Didn't love seeing you leave a bar with someone who isn't me. I don't know, kind of feels like I'm the one who should be making sure you get home now," Ethan answers, but it feels more like an admittance. Instead of the casual indifference from earlier, there's a resignation about him.

I study him for a moment as he rolls his shoulders back before the feathering of his tattooed fingertips stops. He flips his palm up, and it stays there, open and waiting.

I don't let myself overthink or over-analyze, and I ignore all the warning bells ringing in my head that are trying to remind me that despite how he's existing in all its layers: endocardium, myocardium and epicardium, my heart is closed. I've already had one great love, and even though it was a platonic one, I'll never need or love anyone else the same.

I stretch my legs out, and I crawl across the minimal space between us. I watch Ethan's eyes darken and the muscles of his neck as he swallows when I'm on all fours, and a tiny smile pulls at my lips.

I grab his hand in mine, his fingers lacing through mine so easily it's like our hands know one another, like they're old familiar friends. I shuffle backward to sit beside him. My body is flush with his, and I stretch my legs out. He does the same and brings the back of my hand to his lips for an all-too-brief moment before he drops our joined hands into his lap. My eyes feel heavy, and I drop my head to his shoulder.

"I don't want you to go back to your room." I close my eyes as the words fall from my mouth.

I wait, breath caught in my lungs on the inhale. Breathing is easier around him, and I'm scared it'll start to hurt again if he leaves.

"Not going back to my room, Ten," he whispers.

I exhale.

Chapter Twenty-One

The spot beside me is empty when I wake up, but the sheets are tangled, and the crease is still there in the pillowcase. I reach across and run my fingers over it before letting my hand fall onto the sheets. They're softer than they were last night when I took them from the dryer, and that's enough for me. Evidence to prove that Ethan stayed with me all night, that I hadn't made it all up, that we hadn't stayed here—our backs eventually sliding from the concrete wall to being propped up on the pillows, heads turned to one another, and voices soft as we whispered.

We didn't talk about it, the fact that I had shared a bed with someone else, or the fact that it seemed like neither of us wanted me to, but we did talk about everything else. How old Ethan was when he kicked a ball for the first time, his favorite game ever (World Cup quarterfinals, three years ago, South Africa), and what it felt like to lose his dream. The thing he had worked for, yearned for, lived and breathed for.

He doesn't really like to ask me about Arna now because I don't think he's terribly fond of her, even though he never knew her. But I told him about her anyway. What it meant to love her and to lose her. How she was the only family I ever had, and the only one I really needed. People tend not to believe me or think there must be some nefarious reason I wasn't close with my parents. As if it would be so impossible they didn't love me, not the way a parent was supposed to love a child. Arna had just taken me into her world, her heart. She was the only family I needed.

Ethan just nodded, full lower lip coming out a bit past his top one when I told him again that my parents were really a non-factor in my life, well and truly just the people who had given me genetic materials. And that I was okay with that; I always have been. Because I had Arna. Now, I had no one.

His eyes had changed a bit at those words—clouds rolling in over an otherwise clear sky—but he just listened.

My eyelids grew heavy at one point, my fingers starting to twitch in his, but Ethan kept whispering to me, his words carrying more, sounding deeper because of the accent.

I've never minded sharing a bed, which seems like it would be directly at odds with who I am as a person, but it always made me feel less alone. I'm not much for touching someone, wrapping their body around mine. I've just always fallen asleep easier when someone else was there. Arna was kind of annoying to sleep with, but that was only because she kicked all over the place and had a habit of migrating toward the middle of the bed. I liked sleeping with Jake, but he took umbrage at the fact that I never woke up when he got home.

Maybe it was always more about safety than the actual person, but I liked the weight, the way Ethan's body sank a bit lower than mine, causing mine to curve around him. It was different from when we shared the bed in Bali. Because we chose it this time. It wasn't just another person here; it was someone who matters, someone I think my heart recognizes.

The bed might be empty, but my heart doesn't feel that way now. It's not quite full, either. It's been heavy in my chest for months now, like it might tumble through my pericardium and tissue keeping it in my chest cavity, but it still feels lighter than usual.

I should get up, shower maybe, but I don't quite feel the need to scrub another layer of my skin off. Instead, I stay here, breathing in and out while my hand still traces the invisible lines left in the bed by Ethan.

I wish Arna was here. Not physically here, with me and Ethan. Just in the more figurative sense of the word. I wish she was alive, breathing with a beating heart and on the other end of a cellphone where I could tell her I fucked someone, and I was thinking of someone else the whole time, something only a best friend could understand. I could tell her that I was trying with the food, but that I found someone who switched plates with me when he recognized the look on my face when I saw something I didn't like. That I think that was worth more to me than any first bite of a new food would ever be. Someone who sees me just as I am.

I could ask her why she lied.

I'm thinking about that, and I let myself wonder for a minute what it would be like for both of them to exist in my world. When it was me and Jake, it was never really just me and Jake. Never just us. And I never wanted it to be. I can't imagine Arna and Ethan existing in the same space. But they're all wrapped up in one another anyway because there would be no him without her.

I hear the front door open, and I push up in bed. Those are his footfalls in the hallway. I think I'd know them anywhere now. It's funny how that happens—someone forces their way into your life, then you can't imagine being without them, and nothing will ever be the same again.

The door creaks open, and Ethan steps in, leaning against the doorway. I can feel his eyes skate over my shoulders, trace my collarbone, and rest on my cheeks. I can tell my face is puffy, swollen even, from crying.

"Alright?" he asks, holding up his hands with two styrofoam cups of coffee. "Brought you that egg coffee. Noticed you kept looking at it on the menus...thought you might want to try it."

"Thank you," I answer, my voice raspy.

I pat the empty space beside me—forever the side of the bed he belongs on in my heart. The muscles in his thighs flex and contract as he crosses the stone floor. The skin on his thighs is bare, save for a light dusting of hair you can hardly see, because his skin is so dark from the sun. But I think a tattoo would look good there. "Would you ever get a tattoo on your thigh?"

Ethan looks down, lower lip jutting out past his top one, and cocks his head in consideration. "You want me to get a new tattoo, Ten? Thought you said they were all just meaningless whirls of ink?"

He holds out the coffee, and when I take it, I brush my thumb across the back of his, across the infinite number eight before looking up at him. "Not meaningless."

Ethan swallows and palms his jaw briefly before dropping down beside me. "You sleep okay?"

I nod and bring the coffee to my lips, pausing because I can smell how sweet it is already. My fingers tense against the cardboard cup, and like it's something he does every single day, has done for years, Ethan drops his hand to the top of the blankets covering my thigh. It's a tiny reassurance, but I feel it all the way down to my bones. I exhale through my nose and hesitate for a moment longer before taking a sip.

It's not as sweet as I thought—still too sweet for me, and it's thick but not unpleasant. I don't think I want any more. I know how I'll feel after drinking it. I'm worried I've regressed since reading that last letter. I've whispered to myself that it was inevitable. It would have happened anyway because that's how the synapses in my brain had been wired, probably from birth. There was a lot of interesting research on the genetic linkages for eating disorders. But all of that was irrelevant because she had lied. Lied to protect herself instead of protecting me the way she was supposed to. I think that particular revelation broke all the synapses I had worked so hard to rewire.

"You tried it." Ethan brings his hand up, palm open and waiting. I take one more tiny sip, a tiny victory, before depositing it in his hand. "I had a thought, Nov. You wanna get out of here? Me and you?"

I arch an eyebrow at him as he drops the coffee on the nightstand beside him. He looks back at me, and there's a sort of earnest expectation in his eyes that's so at odds with all the sharp angles of him. I open my palm and point toward my suitcase where it sits on the shelf lining the wall. "I can't remember what the letter said, there was something she mentioned about food, some meal—"

Ethan shakes his head, and his eyes go dark for a moment, like the suggestion of Arna and her letters has offended him, and it probably has. He leans forward, wrapping his hand around my wrist and bringing it back down to the bed. "No letters. Just me and you, yeah?"

I look away from the suitcase, from the buried letters, from what's left of the best friend I thought I knew but didn't, who I somehow still love with my whole heart, then look back at him. Ethan Barclay might be the most beautiful person on the planet. My eyes trace the sharp cheekbones and strong angle of his jaw, the dark stubble peppering it that I think I'd like to run my face along, and the thin scar on his lip. My breath catches in my throat, and I feel myself tug on my lower lip with my own teeth, wishing it was his. Wishing, not for the first time, he was the one touching me last night. I watch him swallow, the strong column of his throat moving before flicking my eyes up to his.

Beautiful, rare, gray eyes. People might just try to say they're light blue, but they would be wrong.

He's looking at me, and I'm looking at him. I think he might want to kiss me. I know I want to kiss him, so I lean forward, just a fraction, and I see a muscle jump in his jaw. But then I remember we aren't alone in this room, not in this life, and I'll always have a broken heart, because the only person who loved me lied to me, and then she left.

I look away quickly, and I catch him flaring his nostrils.

"Sure. Let me just shower and pack, and then I'll let you wow me with your great idea." I force a smile and look back at him, like there wasn't possibility on the other end of that moment hanging between us.

"Just me and you," he echoes, a reminder, like I'm somehow supposed to leave Arna behind, as if she isn't stitched into the fiber of who I am, like we didn't grow up together and find love and family together, when both of ours had abandoned us. But I can hear it. His voice sounds like it might be full of hope.

I feel that tiny flicker of something in my chest, too. Just me and him. I think I like the sound of that.

"I didn't know *just me and you* meant us and a boat full of other people." I narrow my eyes at Ethan where he stands at the bottom of the stairs exiting from the bus. "Or, a three-and-a-half hour bus ride from Hanoi, also full of other people."

Ethan tilts his head, gesturing for me to hand him my suitcase. "They're called junks, not boats, Ten."

I thrust the suitcase at him.

He grins at me, offering his hand for me to take as I step down from the bus.

I can feel wisps of hair curling around my face, and the cotton of my tank top sticks to my skin. Ethan's shirt sticks to him, too, but it's the furthest thing from unsightly, and all it does is highlight every carved inch of his muscles.

We packed up the apartment, still ours for a few more days, and I wove behind Ethan while he dragged my suitcase, his much more practical backpack strapped across him as he made his way through the crowded streets until we reached a sign, hanging from the thatched awning of the building that read: *Bai Travels*. A bus, way too large for the tiny, crowded streets pulled up ten minutes later, and we sat together at the back, each reading in a silence that had grown to be companionable, and as was typical, Ethan would bounce his left leg for a few minutes and reach down to grip the back of his calf periodically.

"You could get a second opinion, you know. It's probably not too late for rehab or physiotherapy," I whispered to him, peering at the tight lines of his clenched jaw from over my phone where I was reading an article about age estimation and dentin translucency.

"All good, Ten. Go back to reading about your bones." Ethan cracked a grin at me, but it didn't reach his eyes, and I wished with my whole heart I could fix it for him.

"Dentin, actually. Supports the enamel of your teeth." I smiled softly back at him, and he dropped his chin to my shoulder to read along with me, even though he had no idea what he was looking at, his own book discarded.

And now we're here, standing in a harbor that leads out to Halong Bay and Bai Tu Long Bay. It's host to endless wooden boats of varying sizes and colors, all with tall sails bearing their names in English and Vietnamese.

We follow our driver down a sloping road, my suitcase bumping along behind Ethan, whose lips pull into an irritated line each time it hits a crack.

I look up at Ethan, who looks like he's about to make a comment, to tell him not to be so stubborn, but then I feel his fingers tense, and his thumb moves over the tender skin of my wrist.

He never let go of my hand.

I study our joined hands, our interlaced fingers for a few moments before looking up at him again. He's looking down at me, and there's nothing particularly special about it, save for the usual: features that could probably cut stone if put to the test, full lips that look even better with the tiny scar—a tiny imperfection on a perfectly imperfect person—but it's in his eyes.

Your vision is all light, refraction, information transmitted from your retina to your photoreceptors where that light becomes electrical signals that travel all the way to your optic nerve. Your brain takes those signals and makes them images.

You don't really see anything with your eyes, all that aqueous humor and vitreous body.

But I think he sees me.

He raises his eyebrows for a brief moment before he winks at me.

Ethan pulls me along, nostrils flaring as my suitcase drags behind him, and we line up in front of a boat—all peeling white paint and intricate swirls of wood, black-framed windows, and three tall, brown sails stretching the full length, with the name *Treasure* painted on them.

"How much research did you do on this boat?" I tip my head up at Ethan as we shuffle forward through the slow-moving line.

Ethan shrugs, just one shoulder raised in derision, but his eyes glint with amusement. "Google. Why? Worried you'll go down with the ship, and no one will be left to identify the bodies?"

"No," I say, voice petulant. "I'm just wondering what kinds of activities there will be. Is this some sort of leisure cruise?"

"Yeah, Tai Chai at seven a.m followed by sunrise facials. I don't know, Ten. Read something about kayaking." Ethan gestures for me to step onto the gangplank before hoisting my suitcase up behind me.

I give him a pointed look over my shoulder. "You don't strike me as a particularly thorough researcher. It's a valid question."

Ethan raises his eyes, giving me a flat look. "Remind me whose recommendations you've been following?"

I pause for a moment as we reach the entrance to the boat, framed by thick planks of black wood. I shrug before I step inside. "A dead person's."

Ethan cracks a grin, and for some reason, I do, too.

Chapter Twenty-Two

The bay is beautiful. Flat turquoise water that breaks against rising limestone mountain formations scattered everywhere, covered in deep green foliage. Boats dot the horizon, but ours is traveling out farther into another part of the bay.

He did no research, but he found one of the only fourteen boats allowed to enter Bai Tu Long Bay, part of a responsible cruising commitment, and booked a two-night stay in the only available cabin.

The boat is beautiful, too. All dark, old wood lining it, chairs stretched out across the top deck with cream-cushioned loungers and lanterns for when the sun starts to set. Our cabin is small, with three port holes, and paneled walls stretching alongside the bed.

One bed.

But Ethan said nothing when he unlocked the door, a heavy brass key in an ornate lock, dropping our bags before winking at me, and holding out his hand so we could go back to the dining hall to start the tour of the boat.

I don't think about what it means—that I just slept with someone else but wished with my whole broken heart that it was him the entire time, that I'm not sure we'll ever sleep in separate beds again, and that I'm not sure I want to.

The warm air brushes against my cheeks, and everything beautiful and wonderful that stretches around me pales in comparison to Ethan.

This boy beside me on the top deck of the boat, right leg stretched out across the cushion of a lounge chair, looking entirely at ease for the first time, with one hand holding his phone, the other resting on his thigh and the pale pink, unbuttoned short-sleeve shirt revealing the expanse of muscle spanning his chest, and a pair of drawstring, linen shorts—this boy that looks like he could be on vacation anywhere in the world?

He might be the most beautiful thing out here.

"Oi, you ever been to Tahiti?" Ethan drops his head to the side to look at me.

I shake my head, turning to look at him.

He holds out his phone, and I squint as I peer down at the screen. It's a website for one of those resorts with bungalows like the ones in the Philippines. "No. Maybe we can go after Costa Rica."

The phone drops to the deck, a dull thud against the wood.

Ethan swings his legs up, all movements alarmingly quick, and then every part of him becomes utterly still. He fists the cushion and leans forward, one eyebrow raising above the rim of his sunglasses, and lips pulling back. "You must be fucking joking. You're not still going."

I purse my lips, shaking my head slowly. "Of course I'm still going. She was my best friend, Ethan. She—"

Ethan holds his arms wide, voice rising to a shout. "She was a fucking liar, Ten!"

I find myself yelling, my own voice raising, because the innate need in me to defend Arna is probably one of the only things that will forever remain unchanged. She might have been a liar, but she was mine. "She loved me when no one else did! When I didn't love myself! When I was weird, when I was—"

"Why was she always telling you that you were weird? You're not weird. Stop fucking saying that!" He's still shouting, not a care in the world that it's echoing against the water.

I blink, mouth opening uselessly, but Ethan stands, still holding his arms wide.

It would be comical: the former professional athlete, endless stacks of muscle, and too good-looking for his own good throwing a fit on the top of a boat in the middle of Southeast Asia.

It would be comical if it wasn't breaking my heart.

The muscles in his forearms tense, and he gestures widely. "What happens after you read the last letter, November? Just going to go home and live your life in the shadow of a dead person?"

"What do you care! You don't even know me! We're strangers, Ethan." I stand now, like I'm restoring the balance of power, but he still towers over me.

Ethan pulls back, eyes wide, and looking entirely like I just smacked him.

I didn't raise a single hand, but I can hear it. I hear the hurt reverberate, endless and stretching across the bay, before I see his heart break.

He shakes his head, like he can't believe me, and I'm not sure I believe me, either. Ethan turns, reaching down to snatch his phone from where it's still lying on the deck, and walks away from me.

The lanterns lining the deck are lit, tiny pools of light stretching across the dark wooden panels. It's quiet out here, just me and the occasional sound my bottle makes when it hits the table. I can see the lights from other boats in the distance, bobbing as the current of the bay shifts.

Ethan drops down in the chair across from me, his shirt buttoned now, save for the top few that are undone. His skin glows under the fading light. He tips his head, rolling a beer bottle between his fingers before speaking. "You're shitty at me."

We haven't spoken all afternoon. I don't know where he went after he walked away from me. He could have just been on the opposite side of the deck for all I knew. But I didn't want to go after him because I was scared he might be right.

I narrow my eyes at him, taking a small sip of my beer. "I don't know what that means, but, I guess I am. You yelled at me."

He pauses, the bottle poised at his lips—the glass touching that scar. "Well, you were being a right prat. Might say you deserved it, Ten."

It's the truth. He's not a stranger. Not even close. I should tell him that, tell him the whole truth—that he's taken up residence in my heart, living in the barely functioning left ventricle that sends out oxygenated blood to the body. But I don't. I tell a half-truth instead because Ethan Barclay helps me breathe, and there's nothing more terrifying than that. "You're not a stranger, Ethan. You're my friend." He's more than a friend, and we both know it.

Ethan looks at me, impassive features, before he speaks. "I know."

"Do you think people heard us?" I arch an eyebrow. It's a small boat, and all the rooms are booked.

Ethan arches a brow, too, and his lip curls back. He leans back in the seat, one arm slung over the back of his chair. "Do I look like I care?"

He doesn't. At all. I don't think Ethan Barclay cares about many things, but I think he cares about me.

"Are you ever going to tell me what that one means?" I point with my bottle toward his inner bicep, that outstretched hand.

Ethan tips back, eyes narrowing for a moment, and his lower lip extends past the top one. He lifts his arm, peering at his inner bicep. "Supposed to be about having faith."

I pull my head back. "You don't strike me as particularly religious."

He raises one eyebrow and shrugs. "I'm not. Used to mean that everything was in reach. That if I believed in myself, had enough faith in myself...that's what it felt like my whole life...that if I just worked hard enough...I don't know. Then, it didn't mean anything for a bit."

"What does it mean now?" I ask, tilting my head.

Ethan says nothing but leans back farther in his chair, eyes tracing the fading sun and all the limestone mountains dotting the surface of the water. His gaze flicks back to me, and his voice is quiet before he brings the bottle back to his lips. "To remember what's worth reaching for."

The waves lap against the hull of the boat. It's gentle, hardly even rocking me where I lay propped up on my side, peering out of one of the port holes. I wish I could still see all the other boats bobbing out there in the bay. It was soothing. But it's just us in the room now.

The room with one bed.

I can faintly hear the shower through the brocaded wall, and I know when Ethan comes out here, it's going to be different.

We've held hands. We've touched. We've almost kissed. We've chosen to share a bed.

He's beautiful. Genetically created to be entirely disarming, to give you a spike of serotonin and make you feel a certain way biologically. But it's not just that.

I want different, I want more, and I want it with him. But I can feel what's left of my heart where it hangs in tatters on my ribcage, forgotten strips of muscle tissue that only move when a perfunctory spurt of blood blows through. I don't think I know how to hold love in my heart for someone else—someone other than Arna.

The shower turns off, the silence abrupt, and I wince. I push up to sit against the headboard, pulling my legs up to my chest, waiting.

He steps out from the washroom, entirely thrown into shadow, and turns off the light. There's just one tiny lamp on the nightstand, and I can barely make out his features when he comes to stand at the end of the bed.

"Need to talk to you, yeah?" Ethan palms his jaw for a moment before he turns back and throws the towel from around his neck into the washroom.

Ethan borders on looking deranged, pacing back and forth in our tiny cabin.

I cock my head, wrapping my arms around my legs. I've told him I can do casual. I've had casual sex that he's known about, but I look at him, and I can feel him, even though he's not touching me. It wouldn't be casual. Not with him. Never with him.

His skin is still damp—all tanned with whirls of ink flashing by me as he walks back and forth at the foot of the bed. He's only wearing his underwear, a thin gray band wrapping around his obliques, and the black lycra clings to the ever-defined muscles of his thighs. His hair curls against his forehead and at the nape of his neck. He pauses, snaking one hand through his hair before rubbing his jaw again while his thumb brushes over the bridge of his nose.

Ethan turns to me, jaw popping back and forth, before both of his arms drop to the edge of the bed. He's still a few feet away, but he's effectively caging me in. It's not a big bed.

He waits a moment longer, features bordering on predatory—all sharp angles and ready to cut right into me. "You don't look at me like I'm England's biggest failure." His voice is rough, and his nostrils flare. "I can't go back there, Ten. It's why I don't answer any of those fucking calls—why I skipped out on all of it. Everyone was fucking looking at me like I was nothing because the only thing I ever was, was gone and if the rehab didn't work…if I couldn't play the way I used to, then it's true. I'm a fucking failure."

He swallows, and I study the muscles in his throat as they move downward.

I know the entire sequence of what connects to what—the signals sent from your brain to certain muscles to make you swallow. But I'm not thinking about that, because I'm thinking about him.

I blink, shaking my head. I wish he could see himself the way I see him. That if it were physiologically possible, I would lend him my vision, my sense of sight, so he could understand what it really means to look at someone like him, to see him. "You're not a failure, Ethan."

He shakes his head, leaning forward farther on his arms. His hands fist the bedding, cords and ropes of muscle tensing and stretching under his tanned skin. His arms are beautiful. He's beautiful. His thigh muscles strain against the edge of the bed for a moment, before he pulls himself up onto the bed. He's kneeling at the end, staring down at me.

I don't even realize I'm doing it, but I lower down onto the mattress, stretching out my own legs and head, finding the back of the pillow. His forearms come to rest on either side of my face, and it's just him, suspended above me, one thigh on either side of mine. It doesn't leave much to the imagination, and I can feel every hard ridge and edge of him just a whisper away from my skin. I wish it was just my skin out here for him, not covered in the cotton of my pajamas.

Ethan shakes his head, so close to me now that his nose brushes mine. "Not what I mean. You look at me, Ten. You look at me, and you don't see all that shit. You cock your head to the side, and you study me with that bloody fucking brilliant brain of yours, and those eyes see right through me. You tell me when I'm being a right fucking prat, and you make me laugh, and I think I make you laugh. No one knows—"

I interrupt. "I know who you are, Ethan. You're rude. You're impertinent and beyond full of yourself—"

Ethan interrupts me, thighs tensing on either side of mine. "And you're a piece of work."

"I wasn't done," I whisper. If I tip my chin, not even an inch, our lips would finally touch. But I can't. "You're all those things, but you're never those things with me. I like who you are with me. I like who I am with you. I like you, Ethan. I think I like everything. Even the fact that you threw a temper tantrum for the entire nation to see. It just means you were good enough at something to lose it. I like how your voice sounds in the mornings, and I like..."

A muscle twitches in Ethan's jaw, and I can see it before it happens. It's like a dam breaking open behind those eyes, in his heart. He's going to kiss me. He's going to kiss me, and I want him to so fucking badly, but we aren't alone in this room. I'm never alone, and I don't know if I ever will be again.

"I'm not ready," I whisper, my voice cracking in half. It wouldn't be just our bodies touching, moving together. I feel every inch of him against me, pressing into me, and it's entirely perfect. Not casual. Never with him. "I don't know how to explain it. I can't explain it. I know we weren't together, but she was the love of my life. She was—"

Ethan stops me, palm cupping my jaw, thumb stroking my cheekbone. "I hear you, Ten. I hear you."

I shake my head, and I blink because my eyes have started to burn. "It's not you. Please, please—if you hear anything. It's not you. It's me. It's me."

Ethan drops his lips to my forehead, and I feel them move as he speaks against my skin. It's on fire. "Whenever you're ready, November. I want you. I want *you*, yeah? In all the ways you can want a person."

He wants me, just me, as I am. The person who exists outside of someone else, their ghost, their shadow.

Ethan wants me without Arna. But I'm not sure there's a me without her.

He kisses my forehead, my nose, each of my cheeks, before his lips hover over mine for just a moment. He offers me a smile, one arm reaching out to turn off the lamp, before he pushes off me.

My skin feels entirely bare and exposed. I think I feel empty without him pressed against me. I can feel him, just out of reach on the other side of the bed, and I don't think that's enough.

I press my palm to my chest, and I feel it there—a tiny flicker of something. It's the hope that Ethan usually inspires, but I wonder if I'm hoping for something else now, too.

Chapter Twenty-Three

We left the next day, entirely disregarding the apartment that was still waiting for us back in the Old Quarter, the instruction in that letter from my dead best friend that broke my heart. I said I didn't care what she wanted me to eat, didn't care that it was meant to be some form of twisted apology—her showing me she loved me all along because she carefully curated this menu for me, that it was allegedly done with love.

But I did care. I thought about it the whole fucking flight and wished with my whole heart I was thinking of something else.

It took almost twenty-five hours and two plane changes to get from Hanoi to Liberia, Costa Rica. It was another three-hour drive from the airport to where we are now, a tiny town along the coast with too many bars with colorful chairs and more surf shops than you can count.

We found the rental, a small house set back on sprawling property ten minutes outside of town, when we were sitting on the deck of the boat.

"You ever been here?" Ethan asked me when we arrived, entirely bleary-eyed.

I had, and there was a sort of irony about Arna sending me here again. I did come here with her family, but it was ironic for another reason entirely. Jake loved Costa Rica, it was his preferred vacation destination, and I would never take the time off work to go with him. I lost count of the number of plane tickets he tried to surprise me with. Eventually he started buying cancellation insurance, and eventually he stopped asking entirely. Another way I didn't, couldn't, wouldn't, prioritize him. Another shovel of dirt overtop the coffin where our relationship would ultimately be laid to rest.

I didn't tell Ethan any of that, that this place was just another reminder of a life lived for someone else entirely, I just nodded, using the code left by the host in the instructions to unlock the gate. "Once, but it was years ago. My parents always found money to send me away with Arna, so they didn't have to deal with me. Most people don't believe me, you know. But it was more convenient for them that way. They never loved me."

An uneven stone path, lined with small lanterns stuck into the ground, revealed a stone plunge pool with a gurgling waterfall, covered in beautiful green leaves and hanging plants. Dark wood stretched out around it, with two cushioned lounge chairs sitting in front of the sliding glass doors of the house.

Ethan made a noise, a disagreement from the back of his throat, before he grabbed my suitcase from me, lifting it up the steps to the deck. "Just don't see how anyone couldn't love you."

We've spent two days here now, all sprawling beaches and sunsets. They're only beat by Ethan's laugh as he sits next to me—shirt open and moving in a breeze off the water, arms propped up on his knees and a beer dangling from lazy fingers as everything turns hues of pink, orange, and red until the stars are twinkling in the sky.

Two days where I loved being in this tiny town with him. Two days where our hands touched often, bodies constantly finding excuses to draw ever closer to one another. Two days where our breathing intermingled across a shared mattress. Two days where I acted like there wasn't another letter waiting for me. Two more days where I tried to pretend my best friend was still who I thought she was.

I should have known something was horribly, colossally wrong when I finally read the next letter.

Nova,

Welcome back to Costa Rica. The last time I was here was with you, actually. You and Sebastian. Do you remember? We were sixteen, and he was eighteen.

It felt fitting. To send you back somewhere, to a time and place where you knew with absolute certainty that I loved you more than anything. Remember that, okay?

I suppose in some ways this letter isn't as much about asking you to live, to throw caution to the wind and dig your fork in, as much as it is about appeasing my conscience.

I did something. Well, lots of somethings, I suppose.

But this one—I'm not sure why I did it. I just wanted to know—needed to know, even—what it was like for you.

Sometimes I think you and me, we were more each other than we were ourselves. You know what I mean by that. There was nothing you could have done to scare me. Nothing I wouldn't have wanted to know about you.

Remember all this, okay?

Time to rip off the proverbial Band-Aid.

I slept with Jake. First it was just once, and then it was twice. And then it just...was. It was after. If you believe anything, believe that.

He left you, and you were so sad, and I was so angry. Then, one night when I was visiting—you took that call for a mass casualty accident a few hours away, and you were gone. And I saw him in the city, and I just...needed to understand what could have been so special you kept him for so long and why you were so broken.

I never loved anyone like I loved you, because Levi left me, and sometimes it felt like you could have loved Jake more than me.

And then it became a habit.

You and I shared everything, and maybe I just thought we should share this, too.

Never forget that I loved you more than anything, Nova.

Yours in life, death, and eternity.

Arna

The letter flutters uselessly to the ground, Arna's lilting handwriting and pretty stationary now taking up residence on the worn stone floor, along with the dirt and the dust. Just like her body, moldering away underground somewhere in Athens.

This is a feeling I can't quite describe, and I think it's been coming on for a while. Each envelope, each looping letter, each secret, watered these seeds of grief and despair. They were full grown flowers now but an invasive species of flower. An evil vine, maybe. One that grew something beautiful, something otherworldly to attract you—to suck you in—before it poisoned you, made you blind, suffocated you. Killed you. Whatever invasive, evil species it is, it started by growing around all of my bones, feeding on all the things I thought I knew deep down in them. The things I held true about life and love and acceptance. But like most things that corrupt, they had grown over them entirely, my marrow just a host to feed their takeover. My bones are made of Arna's lies now. That's all I am, and all I ever would be again.

I want to be mad. I should be mad. She slept with my boyfriend. The only person I ever came close to loving as much as I loved her. To see what it was like for me. To be with someone the way I was. She lied to me pretty much all the time, if her stupid fucking death letters were any indication. I should be spitting on her grave. But I still fucking love her, and she was still my best friend in the entire world, and the only thing that made me was angry. But not at her. At myself for being so friendless and so pathetic that my soulmate came in the form of someone who clearly cared very little for me when all was said and done.

I'm staring at the letter, edges of vision flickering in and out. My blood pressure has surely plummeted. I don't hear him coming. And that's saying something because I'm keenly aware of Ethan's presence every second of every minute.

Ethan drops in front of me, tipping his head to the side. He cracks his tattooed knuckles before he crouches down and rests his hands on his knees. One curl has gone its own way, pointing entirely in the opposite direction of the rest, but that seems fitting. Not for Ethan but for me, my life, and its sudden downward spiral. Gray eyes are narrowed on me, cloudy with concern.

Tipping my chin toward the discarded letter, I look away from him. Because this was now embarrassing. It wasn't just me privy to my downfall at Arna's hands, the slow way she had been picking away at my heart from beyond the grave, but Ethan was here, too, because for some dumb idea I thought I should try to be like her. Do something impulsive and unpredictable. And it was biting me in the ass because there would always be one other person who knows now. Knows what a colossal loser I am and always have been, apparently.

I don't watch him read the letter. I don't want to see any of it—not the pity, not the awkwardness, not the moment he realized my parents had been right about me all along. What was I worth? Certainly not enough to protect the sanctity of a friendship. And certainly not enough for my boyfriend to only want to sleep with me. It didn't matter if it was after we broke up. She cried with me. She made a fucking voodoo doll with a shitty cut-out photo of him pinned to the head. She wasn't supposed to sleep with him.

When Ethan finally speaks, his voice is careful, pointed but shaking with what might be poorly restrained anger. "Has it ever occurred to you that maybe she was a shit friend? That maybe she liked the fact that she loved you more than you loved yourself, so she could keep you there? Under her thumb?"

"You have no idea what you're talking about," I answer before I can even think about it. The need to defend Arna is innate and unmoveable.

"All these stories you've told me. These letters—this fucking quest she's got you cavorting on. She slept with your boyfriend for Christ's sake!" Ethan's eyes widen and finally the anger gives way to pity, like he can't believe me. That I would be this pathetic.

But I am. So I stand, snatching the letter from his hand and take the thorns that now exist on me because of Arna and stab him with them, too. "What would you know about it? You've pretty much confirmed for me that you don't have any friends, and no one can even stand to be around you while you wallow in self-pity because your career is over. No one wants to tell you because you won't hear it, but get a new fucking dream, Ethan. It's done."

Ethan's nostrils flare, and it looks like he was about to stab back. To say something just as cruel, just as abhorrent, but he's a better person than me, and he doesn't. He just shakes his head and rubs his jaw. Those eyes are on me for just a moment longer before he walks right past me, and I can barely hear him before he slams the door.

"She didn't deserve you, November."

I find Ethan sitting on another chair that's, yet again, much too small for him. He's tipping back, neck craning to look at the TV hanging precariously from the palmed awning of the bar. The chairs spill out onto the street, tables weighed down under perspiring buckets of beer. Ethan doesn't have a bucket, but there's an empty bottle beside him.

I watch him tip the full one in his hand back, and my lips twitch when I realize his teeth are biting against the glass. Before reading the letter, before my world imploded and my life somehow tipped even further off its axis, I liked being here with him. A tiny beach town with colorful bars, the scent of the ocean in the air, my skin warm from the sun. And I like the way Ethan looks in a tiny town like this.

Weaving through the mismatched chairs, I drop down beside him.

He glances at me sideways for a moment before handing me the beer that was resting against his lips. Ethan's mouth in general has been invading my thoughts since I crashed into him. At first, it was because of the obviously superior jaw structure, the perfect teeth I now know were just luck. The implant was fake, but that was because his tooth was knocked out during his last World Cup. But slowly, other thoughts about his mouth started to take over.

I take the beer from him and press it to my lips tentatively, taking a tiny sip. Not out of fear or discomfort like it used to be, but because I feel guilty and awkward and embarrassed and sorry. Setting it down, I push the bottle back across the table to him.

Ethan's looking at me now, and I have no idea why or how, but his stupid plain black t-shirt makes his eyes look even more disarming.

"I'm sorry. I was embarrassed," I whisper, offering him the only apology I have. It's the truth.

"She should be embarrassed." Ethan doesn't grab the bottle but raises his hand to a man standing behind the bar, washing the same glass repeatedly, and staring up at the same soccer game Ethan was watching. "I've said it before, and I'll say it again. It's cruel, this game of hers. If there's a hell, I hope she's fucking burning in it."

"Don't," I whisper uselessly, my lips downturned. "I don't expect you to understand. She's all I have, Ethan. For years, she was it. To infinity and beyond. I can't just forget who she was to me because—"

"Had," Ethan interrupts, voice forceful. "She's all you *had*."

I tip my head, and my breath catches, because he's looking at me so intently, and those eyes look like the kind of sky that would make people think they need to stay inside, but they just make me want to stand outside in the rain. His impossibly dark brown hair is everywhere, and the muscles in his neck are tense, so I speak softly because I don't want him to run away. Not when he's offering me something I've never been given. "Had."

"Had," Ethan repeats, looking away only for a moment to grab the bottle from the bartender who's appeared beside us.

He twists the cap expertly before tossing it into an empty ashtray on the table.

"You aren't going to give me the new one?" I ask incredulously.

Ethan's already looking back at the TV and only spares me a sideways glance. "No. Penance for being a bitch."

My lips twitch, and my fingers feather uselessly against his old half-drank beer. I don't know what to say, so I stay silent and try to think about anything but Arna fucking Jake, and the way I hurt Ethan. My heart might have been cleaved in two, and I couldn't decide what was worse. But I look at Ethan, and I see the way his cheek muscle tenses and loosens, and I know.

Hurting him feels worse than anything on the planet.

I wrap my hands around his discarded beer bottle and take another sip, pressing my lips to the exact spot his were. When I'm done, I tip the bottle to the TV. "Do you know any of the players?"

"Yeah, few mates I played with. That one's having a shit fucking season." Ethan isn't looking at me, and he has this habit of that.

He looks somewhere else when he's speaking to me, but I never feel like he's ignoring me.

I know a few things with absolute certainty. I know the exact chemical breakdown of a tooth. I know how to slice and suture the soft tissue of a gum, and I know how to match a bite mark with more precision and accuracy than anyone in the world. And I know Ethan Barclay is *always* paying attention to me.

He points with his beer bottle, and I watch him roll it loosely between his fingers.

I have no idea what player he's pointing at. They've all moved on from whatever position they were in before, and I would have to squint to even try to see what the names on the back of the jerseys are. Ethan corrects me whenever I say that and calls them shirts. It's fucking annoying because half the things he says sound preposterous.

We sit in silence, Ethan watching the game, or match if you ask him, and ordering a bucket of beer now that I'm sitting here.

Usually, I don't mind to just sit and watch people. I like it. I like looking around, trying to guess what kind of dental work or facial reconstruction people have had, but I'm not now because I can't stop looking at Ethan.

"I don't think you need a new dream, Ethan. I actually know several leading orthopedic surgeons who—"

He turns his head, and he's only looking at me now, tattooed fingers twitching against the bottle. "You didn't hurt my feelings. Already got a new dream, Ten."

My lips part, and I want to say something, anything.

Because in and amongst the poisonous vines and evil flowers and my bones crumbling under Arna's lies, hope blooms. Because I think he's talking about me. I can feel it in the muscle tissue of my heart. Right in my left ventricle that's pumping all the oxygenated blood throughout my body.

I'm someone's dream. I'm his dream.

Chapter Twenty-Four

I might be Ethan's dream, but he's a bad influence. Our silver bucket is empty, and the table is littered with the empty beer bottles. I'm holding the last one, thumb picking at the already frayed label.

Ethan's eyes are a bit wild, but he hasn't looked away from me in about twenty minutes. He asked me what my favorite tooth to remove is, and he was serious. I'm telling him about the fact that my favorite tooth is actually a premolar because I think they're underrated, and even though extractions are enjoyable, I feel a bit like I'm playing surgeon, I actually prefer it when people don't need extensive dental work.

And he's looking at me like I'm endlessly fascinating.

"Your cheeks are flushed, Ten." His lips quirk to the side, and he brushes his thumb across the apple of my cheek. They felt warm before, but they feel warmer now.

I can see the outline of the number eight just under his knuckle. His number.

"That's what happens when someone gets me drunk." I know I should pull away from him, but I don't.

I find myself leaning my head to the side, that aforementioned warm cheek brushing the rest of his fingers.

"Got yourself trolleyed, I think," Ethan says, voice all low and gravelly like it is in the mornings. "Let's get out of here."

I'm about to argue with him and tell him that "trolleyed" is a ridiculous expression, but he's already standing over me, imposing as always.

He grabs my beer from my hand to drain the rest.

Two sips is all it takes, and I watch the muscles in his throat and neck move.

"That was mine," I offer, because I'm trying not to look at his mouth, the way he's grinning at me from just behind the bottle.

"More back at the flat," he answers, holding out his hand, and I realize it's my favorite one. The left, the one with all the important dates on the back of his knuckles. World Cup, Euro Cup, league championship. I didn't realize I had a favorite before, but here it is.

He has so much to be proud of, even if he can't see it, and even if I'm mean sometimes.

I stand and grip his hand in mine, and those fingers wrap around my whole hand like it's nothing. I pause and study the size difference when mine is palmed in his like this before looking up at him and smiling. "You'd be a terrible dentist, Ethan. You'd never fit your hand in anyone's mouth."

His gaze narrows on me and then sweeps over our joined hands, and he grins again. "That why your patients like you? These tiny ineffectual hands?"

"That, and I don't insist on talking to them while my fingers are in their mouths. You seem like you'd be a talker." I raise my eyebrows at him. It's a joke; he's one of the least loquacious people I've ever met.

I fall into step beside him, sandals slapping against the worn and cracked pavement.

This small road leads back to our rental, and even though Arna picked Costa Rica, I don't want anything to do with her right now. I don't want to leave. I want to stay here in this little town with Ethan for a bit longer with no letters or instructions from beyond the grave hanging over me.

Ethan doesn't let go of my hand and tugs me insistently along beside him, even though he's a solid foot taller than me, and his impossibly muscular legs take significantly longer strides. "I only talk to you. Any patient of mine would be safe."

"I doubt that very much. You'd be like a first-year dental student and accidentally stab someone the second they held a scaler in their hands. I've seen it happen countless times," I say, raising my eyebrows at him.

"Like you've never stabbed anyone." Ethan glances at me sideways, and I shrug my shoulders in response, biting at my lips.

We wander down the tiny street, more bars and restaurants that spill off the sidewalk with colorful chairs and tiny tables. Buckets full of perspiring bottles like the one we had have people surrounding them, skin tanned and glistening from a day spent on the water with bathing suit ties still around necks under loose tops. It's the kind of carefree Arna was. The kind of carefree she wanted me to be.

I could picture her here, hair twisted into a too big bun on the top of her head, wisps flying every which way, or pulled back in a fishtail braid she had been sleeping on for days. She would hold court at a table just like any of the ones we've passed, smiling coyly at the people sitting around her that she had ensnared into her circle, her mouth, and the meaning of her words hidden behind the tequila soda she would sip from.

I stare at all the people crowded around tables as we walk past, and I see them all as Arna. I wait for the ache, for my heart to simply rupture and stop like hers probably did when she crashed into that cliff. But it never comes. I trail behind Ethan, and I recognize her in everything I see, but I don't wish for her back. I don't wish to be someone else, who she wanted me to be.

I want to be who I am now. I want to be the person I am when Ethan's around, always. Everything is still there—my food behaviors still bother me, and my eating disorder remains my ever constant, ever silent but looming companion. Its fingers feather against my shoulders, ready for its claws and fingernails to pierce my skin and start steering me mechanically through my life. But those things feel further away. They're a part of me, and I acknowledge them, but that's all it is when Ethan's around.

I'm walking quicker to keep up with Ethan not only because I don't want him to drag me behind him, but because he's a part of me now, too.

We're both irritable and off-putting in entirely different ways, and if you asked anyone in the greater United Kingdom, they would tell you he's a washed-up soccer player with wasted potential and a drug record. But there's no one to ask anything about me back home, and somehow it feels the same. Somehow his regret, his despair and anger for no one but himself fit perfectly with my loneliness and exile, self-imposed or not.

I'm not paying attention, and my toe catches on the end of my sandal when Ethan takes the sharp right turn to the street that leads to our rental.

His hand is around my forearm instantly, pulling me upright, the other still wrapped around my—in his words—small and ineffectual hand. He says nothing, but his eyes linger on me, and my cheeks warm.

We're standing in the middle of the worn road, the pavement giving way to packed down sand I can feel beneath my thin sandals.

I've had these forever, an item of my wardrobe Arna took umbrage to. She said they were heinous, falling apart, and reminded her of something someone would wear on a public cruise. She once ripped them off my feet when I sat on the stone ledge that surrounded one of her family homes in Spetses. I remember her clearly, eyes narrowed on me while she held them over her head threateningly, even though she was shorter. The whole thing seemed terribly ironic now—she followed it up by telling me that she would share her sandals with me forevermore, because what else were best friends for?

We ended up sharing much more than sandals, as it turned out.

My expression must sour at the thought because Ethan's thumb presses into my forearm, and his lips turn down. "What are you thinking about?"

My gaze lands on his lips. I love them—full with that tiny scar and always telling me what he's thinking or feeling. I watch his pupils expand, gray eyes widening a fraction, too, and at the same time, we both whisper: "Arna."

She's been a ghost, my ghost, haunting me and dogging my footsteps but wrapping around me, whispering taunting words, reminders of all the love I used to have and would never have again. She isn't a cruel ghost. She just *is*. And I thought she would be forever. But now I'm looking at Ethan, and the only lights around us are the ones shining through the windows of places like the one we're staying at.

I'm looking at him, sharp cheekbones look like they could cut glass under the dim starlight, a muscle feathering in his jaw, and those full lips hiding those perfect teeth. I love it and want to run my tongue over it. I love his tattooed fingers, and I love the fading ink that winds up the corded muscles of his forearm, and I love the unmarred skin of his other arm, too. I wish I had a number just for me inked on one of his knuckles. I love how he stands so much taller over me, that his chin fits perfectly on the top of my head, and I love that he flosses the way I told him to.

He's not *washed up*, and he's not someone who wasted his potential. He didn't have a career-ending injury, and I don't mind that he snorted a line of cocaine and failed a drug test because he was sad. It makes me want to offer him the comfort he's never had. He makes me want to be less abrasive, less sharp.

I think I love him, and I wish Arna's ghost would disappear, fuck off entirely, because she was a liar, because she slept with my boyfriend, because she's gone, and Ethan's not. I wish that, I want that, but I can still feel her whisper past my ears, feel her manicured fingers tapping on my shoulders to steer me in death like she did in life. I want to let her go. I want her to go away. I want to make her go away.

I blink, and Ethan is still looking at me, my eyes prickling.

"I don't know how to let her go," I offer uselessly, like that will somehow make up for the fact I've let her steamroll everything. Every possibility, every stretch of silence or stare between us that went on too long. I would wrap her memory—her stupid letters—around me like a shield that no one, not even Ethan, could break through. "She did these...these horrible things and I think I'm mad at her, so fucking mad at her, but it was me and her for so long that I don't know how to be me without her. How to be me and anyone else."

Ethan says nothing, but his thumb is brushing over the radius bone in my forearm. He doesn't push, but I watch him roll his shoulders back, the cotton of his shirt straining. He waits for me to continue.

"I want to." And I do.

My heart hurts, and I'm heavy in a way only the person I loved with my whole soul could weigh me down.

His nostrils flare, and I feel his fingers tense around my forearm and pulse around the hand he's still holding.

Despite the fact I don't have an athletic bone in my body, our reflexes are similar. I know because we tested them one night, each seeing who could grab a falling pen quicker when we got in a debate about how quick a goalkeeper's reflexes need to be. Mine are similar from years of quick precision and small movements. His are because he's in peak physical shape and probably has more fast-twitch muscle fibers than the average human being, and that's what makes him so spectacular. But I don't see this coming.

His hands are around the back of my thighs, and he's hoisted me up, my arms hanging uselessly at my sides.

I'm face-to-face with Ethan. Close enough that I can see the stroma fibers that are full of extra collagen in his irises. They're darker than the rest of his eye.

Gray eyes are rare. Less than three percent of the population. Ethan Barclay is rare.

My thigh muscles tighten around his waist. It happens on instinct because as a human being, we're naturally afraid of falling. It's evolution. And somehow I can feel his fucking obliques through his shirt, jutting into my exposed skin, like they're the fresh end of a scalpel.

But there is no way in hell I'm going to fall because it's Ethan holding me. He's stronger than me and carrying me is nothing for him.

He's already started moving. We're maybe five-hundred meters from our rental.

I can see the gate. I can see the canopies of the flowered trees that are weighed down by too heavy branches falling over top the fence.

Ethan's steps are shockingly long, considering the fact I'm now clinging on and providing all sorts of extra dead weight. His chin rests on my shoulder, and his lips brush my ear. He says nothing, but we stop in front of the gate, and he hoists me up higher, my thighs clenching around the stacks of muscle under his shirt. One palm drops from the back of my thigh and begins to twist the combination on the lock.

"You can set me down," I whisper, staring resolutely at the building across from us.

But I don't want him to set me down. I think I could stay wrapped around him, together like this forever. He makes me want to unwrap Arna and all that she was from where she sits around my body, so our skin could finally, really and truly touch, with entirely nothing between us.

"No fucking chance, Ten. I can multitask," he says, voice brushing past my hair. A groan leaves him, and my body jostles as I feel him pulling on the lock, the metal clanking loudly through the night, interrupted only by the sound of cicadas and nocturnal birds. "Fuck."

I bring my palms up to his shoulders, the cotton of his shirt soft, and the muscles underneath firm. "Drop me, you can't remember the code. I'm excellent with numbers."

"How much lidocaine to remove a molar?" Ethan's voice is teasing and low, but it's followed by another groan of frustration and pull on the lock.

"No more than 2.0 milligrams per pound of body weight," I answer, pushing off his shoulders to try and climb down from him. "Put me down."

"No," he says, and the lock clatters against the door.

He's dropped it, and his hand is back under my thigh. But he's looking at me, and then his lips crash against mine, my back slamming into the still unopened gate. He groans into my mouth and presses himself between my thighs, palms tightening against my skin. His tongue parts my mouth, and it's just him and me now.

I hear nothing. No distant shouts from the not very faraway town, not the cicadas or the birds. Arna falls away. It all does. I want him all over me. I'm usually very aware of time, but I don't know how long we'll stay here, trading sloppy kisses, my hands roaming all over him and grabbing greedily, like two teenagers who were just left alone for the first time.

His teeth catch my lip with a small, gentle tug, and I want him more than I've ever wanted anything.

A small gasp escapes me, like I'm in pain, when he finally pulls away. His forehead drops to mine, and his breathing is heavy.

One of my hands is wrapped around the back of his neck, pulling him close to me, while the other is fisted in his hair.

His lips brush mine once more, softly, reverently, and a small noise of need comes from my throat because that's not enough.

It would never be enough. Everything else in my life pales in comparison to this. Every other touch from every other person. Every other kiss, bite, movement against my body, thrust into me—anything. They all fade away. My heart has never beat this erratically, no one else has ever sucked the air out of my lungs like this. No one has ever felt like this, pushed against me.

My breath catches because I realize we fit together perfectly. Like I'm exactly the right number of inches shorter than him, my waist and my hips, and my legs are all exactly the size they should be to fit around Ethan Barclay. My eyes prickle because maybe this lifelong war with myself has only ever been leading here. Nothing would ever feel right until I fit with him. My body has been right this whole time, but it was just waiting for him.

"I'm going to set you down. You're going to use that fucking brain of yours to open that lock in less than ten seconds; I'm going to pick you back up, attempt to carry you across that lawn without ripping these fucking clothes off of you and doing everything I've thought about doing with and to you since you crashed into my fucking life, yeah?" Ethan's voice feels like something exploding in my chest. Something good. Not a myocardial rupture that will kill you quickly—something that could cure cancer. Something that could become a certified miracle.

"I like your voice," I say, because I know Ethan doesn't mind.

He likes everything I have to say, and even when his eyes narrow and his mouth opens, because whatever I've said is out of nowhere, he asks me about it.

"Yeah?" he asks, knees bending to set me down. His hands skim up the back of my exposed thighs, over the back of my shorts, before they stop on my hips. "Rather fond of yours myself. Can't wait to hear what it sounds like when I make you scream. Alright, feet on the ground. Ten seconds to open that lock, Nov."

"I'm not really a screamer," I offer with a shrug, because it's true.

I turn and move my fingers swiftly across the dial of the lock—6093.

It's not a complicated combination to remember. Ethan is just horrifically impatient, and his fingers are much larger than the small dials. Mine are small and thin, and I have excellent dexterity. I scored high on the Manual Dexterity component of the Dental Admission Test. All the planes of that stupid bar of soap I spent months carving for practice were flat and smooth, with no noticeable errors in symmetry, and all of my angles were sharp and accurate.

"Not yet." Ethan presses his chin to my head, and his fingers start to drum on my waist. The lock clicks, and the gate creaks open without the force keeping it shut. "That was about three seconds."

Ethan hoists me up and tosses me over his shoulder, one hand securely around my waist keeping me from bouncing around, and the other is on the back of my left thigh.

The gate shuts behind us, and I reach up to slide the latch back into place.

The property is quiet, the gate sealing us in here, in our own little world. Small lights illuminate the rough stone pathway that leads to our rental. I can hear the pool, the tiny rock waterfall bubbling along the fence.

Ethan crosses the small yard, and I know that at the end of it is our tiny little house for the week. *One bed*. It didn't matter before because it's huge and there was an endless expanse of distance between us. Arna was between us. I know that when he steps off this stone path and up onto the wooden slats of the deck, there will never be distance between us again. Our lips are going to touch again, our tongues, our hands, our bodies. I don't want anything between us.

The deck comes into view, and Ethan walks up the steps. And then the sliding glass door comes next. He pulls that open in one fluid motion. I left the light dimmed when I finally followed him into town. It makes the whole room look soft somehow.

Even in the low light, I can see how dilated his pupils are. Ethan's hand moves from my thigh to my waist, and he plants me down in front of him.

Everything in the room looks soft, the edges of the tucked-in sheets on the giant bed, the teak sideboard that spans the length of the room under the paned windows that look out into the foliage.

Everything looks soft, but not him. The planes of his face are sharpened, and the cut of the exposed muscles on his forearms are harsher.

I stare at him, and he stares back. I'm acutely aware that his hands are still on my hips, and I'm flush against him.

The ridges of his abdomen press into my ribcage. All of him presses into me.

"I'm sorry for what I said," I whisper, placing my palms on his chest.

He makes a noncommittal jerk of his chin. "I meant what I said. Got a new dream. Feels like it might just be within reach right now. But before I lay you down, show you how perfect you are and how dumb whoever that loser was that slept with someone over you, you need to promise me. You're coming with me. You're moving forward with me. We can stay on this dumb quest, we can try the food, I don't care, but she doesn't run your life anymore."

"Yes." It's out of my mouth and out into the universe before I can even think better of it, and I watch as that one word sinks into Ethan's skin, into his blood and his heart and his marrow in the same way that Arna's lies sank into mine.

Before I can think of what I'm giving up, think of the fact that even though in this moment I hate her—I fucking *hate* her—I love her. I'll always love her because even though she was fucked up and flawed, there will never be anyone like her again. I don't realize it's a promise I can't keep, because at this moment, I don't care.

A smile unlike anything I've ever seen—I swear it's brighter than the sun—stretches across Ethan's face, and I wonder if this is what he used to look like all the time. "I'm going to kiss you again. All over. That okay with you?"

I barely nod, and he's guiding me back with his thighs pressed into mine until the back of my knees hit the bed, and he sits me down.

He tips his chin at me and grins. "Arms." He means for me to raise them, but his hands are snaking under my shirt, across my ribcage, and pulling it up over my head, temporarily obscuring my view of him. Which is a shame because I don't think I've ever found him more perfect than I do right now—sharp features, ragged breath, and a deep voice that's bordering a groan, and all that ink stark against his skin.

But it doesn't last long. My shirt is gone, and I watch Ethan ball it up and toss it to the far corner of the room, so I couldn't even dream about grabbing it again. His breath catches, and his eyes are roving me.

"Fuck," his voice is low, and one thumb traces my collarbone, up the column of my neck to rest under my chin where he tips my face up, like he's examining it, looking at something particularly fascinating underneath a microscope. Like I'm fascinating. "Look at you."

My brow furrows, and I glance downward. It's just a plain black bra. "You've seen me in a bathing suit. That's less fabric than this. It's no different."

"No. No, this, this is different," he says, leaning down and arms caging me in now.

He drops my chin, but I keep my head tipped back because I never want to look away from Ethan. He stares back, and his lips are just a breath away.

But I don't want to wait. I bring my lips to his, and they part for me, a groan vibrating against them.

Just like outside, we're a tangle of tongues and limbs, and he nips my lip when he pushes me back onto the bed.

I can feel every ridge of every muscle in his body as it pushes against mine, lowering us both down. He pulls my lip between his teeth again, his hands move down my ribs, and fingers deftly begin unbuttoning my shorts. He pulls away from me, and my hands dig into his shoulders, trying to bring him closer to me, because I don't think I can breathe if I'm not kissing him. He's oxygen now.

Ethan's eyes darken as I claw at him, but he's moving down my body now to rip the denim from my legs. He's kissing me, and his lips strike a match against my skin. Tiny fires start burning everywhere they touch. He tosses the shorts to the side, too, and he doesn't move from where he is, propped up between my legs. One hand pins me down, firmly pressing my hips into the mattress. He brushes his lip with his thumb, almost out of habit, and then he takes that same thumb—the one with the number eight—and drags it down the front of my underwear.

We're still staring at each other, and I don't think either of us is ever going to look anywhere again. He's still looking at me when he bends between my legs, dropping his head, one hand now splayed across my stomach, the other pushing my right thigh down into the mattress.

I want this. I want him, but I watch in a sort of abject horror as he drops his lips right where his thumb was moments ago. I already know I'm going to ruin it, and even though I'm flushed everywhere and I want Ethan, when I feel one of those hands wrap around my underwear, I speak. "Stop, stop."

Ethan goes preternaturally still, every single muscle fiber freezing. All the individual stacks of them in his back as it goes taut, staying that way suspended in time. That hand is still wrapped around my underwear, pulling them to the side, and exposing me entirely. But those gray eyes have sharpened, and they're only on my face.

My voice is small, and it quivers. "I've always had a problem with...that. It's not the actual act. It feels good. At first. It's...I can see myself, then I get in my head, and all I can think about is how I look. Then it stops being anything good at all."

Ethan nods, gently letting go of my underwear, and he presses a kiss to the inside of my thigh before climbing up my body. He drops beside me, and he doesn't cover me, press into me, or consume me like he did before.

I notice his absence on my exposed skin. If the root of a tooth had sentience and it was flayed open, I wonder if it would feel the way I feel now.

"I want to be here with you. I don't want to miss any part of this," I whisper.

"Shh." Ethan's sharp features collapse, and he grips my chin. "It's alright. We can work up to that, yeah? I personally can't fucking wait."

A hiccup escapes me, and I shake my head, wishing I could have stayed out of my own mind for once, then he speaks again.

"But I'd like you to feel good. Can I try something else? Just my hand. You don't have to look down. Just look at me, yeah?" Ethan says, pressing his lips to mine. "If you don't like it, I'll stop."

He breaks away from me, still holding my chin, and I nod.

A grin, a look of feral delight, spreads across his features, and he looks so radiant. I forget there's another hand moving its way down my body because I'm just looking at him.

I gasp when that hand pushes under the fabric covering me again. My gaze flicks down and—

"Eyes on me."

I snap my head up as his fingers start to move. I only look at him, and he only looks at me.

That hand, his fingers, move in a slow circle, while his other hand still grips my chin. My lips part and we're staring at each other as his pupils expand, dilate entirely until there's nothing of my favorite sky left. My teeth come down onto my bottom lip because those slow circles turn faster before they stop, his hand moves further down and gently, reverently, like he might break me—he pushes those two fingers inside me.

"Fuck," Ethan's words are harsh, and he looks away from me, just for a moment, gaze flicking down to where his fingers are moving, soaked with me. A groan leaves his throat, and he looks back up at me. "Do you feel good?"

"Yes," I pant, my words nothing more than a gasp, and my hands claw at his shoulders, nails digging in. My back arches, his fingers move faster, into me and pulling out of me when he presses his thumb, the number eight, his number and all that he is, down to the center of me. Nothing has ever felt like this—nothing, nothing, nothing.

My teeth bite down on his bottom lip, fingers clutching his shoulders, digging into the edges of the whirls of ink as I come entirely undone because of Ethan Barclay's hand.

His mouth is still on mine, swallowing the last of the noises I'm making when he pulls back.

I watch, lips still parted and only tiny, panting breaths coming from me because I don't think there's any oxygen left in my lungs, this room, this world—when Ethan looks at me, nothing but dark eyes and rough breathing, and brings those two tattooed fingers to his mouth. I'm still watching, body entirely alight—little fires everywhere—when he starts to taste me on them. Those fingers, the ones that were on me, inside me, are in his mouth now. I see his tongue drag down them as he slowly pulls them out, and his other hand finally drops my chin. "Can't fucking wait, Ten."

He was right. He did make me feel good. Because as it turns out, in my head isn't such a bad place to be if I'm there with him.

Chapter Twenty-Five

I couldn't get enough of Ethan Barclay. We weren't having sex, at least not in the penetrative sense of the word. But we were touching, biting, kissing, doing things to one another, and almost fucking a lot now. I wasn't stopping us, at least not on purpose.

I loved exploring him, watching him come, breath ragged and muscles taut, when it was just my hands or my mouth on him. I loved the way he learned about me, how his tongue, his teeth, his hands drew a map of everything I loved on my skin. I could have stopped and thought about it, wondering why I didn't push for it to go further when I wanted him more than I had wanted anyone in my entire life. There were condoms in the rental that he bought one night while we laughed over it in the drugstore—hanging off one another like teenagers, kissing and whispering to one another as we moved through the aisles. But I liked the bubble we were existing in, so we stayed there.

It had been three days, and Arna's letter, her latest betrayal, was still on the floor, halfway jutting out from underneath the sideboard. It mocked me, stared at me, the rest shoved into the safe, locked away where they couldn't hurt me. Gone but not forgotten. But then Ethan would smile or say something outrageous in his accent that I was learning only became even more pronounced when he was turned on, and I would forget her and all her wants for me. I was keeping my promise. Sort of. For now.

We'd barely left our rental. We would lie there on the tiny deck, his hand snaked under my bathing suit bottoms. Or mine moving over the top of his shorts in the poorly lit hallway of an equally poorly lit bar when we ventured into town in the evenings for food. His mouth had been all over me, and mine all over him. Maybe this was what Arna wanted for me—a worldwide adventure that would lead to endless orgasms from someone I was beginning to suspect was the most beautiful man in the world.

But I could practically hear her from beyond the grave—nose tipped in the air as it often was and telling me that if she hadn't slept with Jake, this never would have happened for me. Ethan never would have happened for me. It had been her plan all along. She was certainly self-important and narcissistic enough to think so. And in a way, her ghost was right. Because if it hadn't been for her, there would be none of the earth-shattering, actually scream-inducing orgasms he was giving me on a steady basis. I wouldn't know what he looks like and sounds like when he's coming, but most of all I wouldn't have gotten to see what no one else does.

That he's quietly brilliant, dry, irreverent and rude, most of the time, but also more thoughtful than anyone I have ever known. That he's restless and doesn't know where he's going, what he's supposed to do now that his once-in-a-generation talent sits unused inside of him. That in moments of uncertainty, he looks to me, wants my advice, but he's also just fine if I tell him something true, irrefutable, that he didn't know before to help distract him.

The fact that our bodies fit together just so, that he can read all of my verbal cues and the physical ones, that he knows before even I do when I'm starting to grow nervous, agitated, or anxious, and he works to correct it. The fact he's two steps ahead of me at all times, and he uses that to make me feel the way he says I deserve to feel, is just a nice bonus. And when he's asleep and the moonlight is streaming in through the glass door or the windows, I can't help but remember at the end of the day, all of it was because of her.

But I don't want Arna to have him. I want, and I wish, he was just mine, and I could untangle the two of them in my brain. To keep them in separate boxes where their edges and what they mean to me would never touch.

We're sitting at a high-top in one of the many nameless bars in this tiny town I don't ever want to leave, having just practically devoured one another in the back hallway.

My feet dangle above the rungs of the chair. It's a bit too tall for me, but I know Ethan's feet are resting on his.

His eyes are hidden behind battered Ray Bans, and as always, his fingers are rolling a sweating bottle of beer between them.

My eyes are shielded with my own sunglasses because we're sitting on the deck that actually spills onto the beach. The ocean glitters just behind Ethan, and it's funny because it makes him look iridescent, and to me, he kind of is.

But he always gives me the seat that faces the water because he knows I love it, and the closest ocean is miles and miles away from me back home.

There are a handful of letters left. And I can't imagine what secrets they hold, and when it gets brought up, I pretend I don't care. When really, there's still a part of me that's screaming and raging, that wants to tear them open and try to understand who Arna really was. Who I really was to her. I want to know her secrets, or maybe I don't, but I'm curious by nature, and I always have been. It's what made science endlessly fascinating to me. But there's something I want more. To stay here with Ethan just a little bit longer.

I must be smiling because I can see one of his eyebrows arch just above his sunglasses. "Alright?"

"Just fantasizing about bones," I answer dryly, raising my own eyebrows at him.

He likes that because he starts to grin and leans forward in his chair, muscles tightening under his shirt. But before he can answer, loud whispers punctuated with shrill giggles erupt.

My eyes flick over his shoulder, one that I sunk my teeth into just last night. My bite mark was still there, much to Ethan's enjoyment when he looked in the bathroom mirror this morning, pulling at the still red skin before looking at me and saying he would wear any mark from me with pride. But beyond the impressions my teeth left on his skin, a group of three girls, all impossibly tiny and tanned, but naturally so from time in the Central American sunlight, were smacking one another on the arm, phones out, and gesturing in our direction.

Ethan's eyes narrow, and he cranes his neck, sending them into a renewed fit of laughter, British accents becoming clearer as their whispering grows louder.

My stomach tightens, and I feel heavy because it's obvious they know who he is.

It's oddly reminiscent of when Arna would be recognized. It didn't happen often when she came to visit me. Unless you were a member of the British Monarchy, uber rich European heiresses weren't that recognizable in Toronto. But whenever I went to Greece, or anywhere else in Europe with her, this happened. I would just sit there, usually growing bored and reading on my phone or responding to case notes or requests for consults on dental identification, or matching bite marks. Those were things you could do from a distance sometimes.

I wasn't a stranger to it, not really, ending up in tabloids alongside her more times than I could count. I can picture the captions: *Arna Pavlides and friend step out in Monaco,* or *Arna Pavlides, Sebastian Pavlides, and friend.* I sort of forgot that Ethan was recognizable in his own right, and the thought of becoming a nameless friend in yet another photo of someone else makes my stomach tighten. But it's not just that. The thought of being called his friend, it seems like a gross oversimplification of the way my body fits with his. The way his mouth articulates just so to make the syllables that comprise my name. The way his tattooed fingers drum on my ribcage. The way he whispers to me and makes me laugh and likes what I have to say. I'm not Ethan Barclay's friend, and I don't want to be.

I can tell by the way his neck muscles move that he offers them a polite smile. But he turns back to me and drums his fingers on the surface of the table, and I notice his cheek twitches. I know enough to know that this *quest,* as he likes to call it, has been a reprieve for him, too. No one to recognize him, no one to judge him, no one to stare at him with obvious contempt or pity, and the preconceived notions that he blew it, gave it all up. Just the occasional narrowing of his gaze when a pain twinges in his Achilles.

For someone who says they hate everyone, he's really liked being alone with me. But we aren't going to be alone for long because the three of them are walking over to us, just a tangle of long, tanned limbs and smiles as they push one another toward Ethan.

"Pardon?" the tallest one asks, her cheeks flush beneath her sun kissed skin.

Ethan's cheek twitches, and he stops drumming his fingers.

I think he's going to take a swig of his beer, but his hand finds mine. He glances to the side where they're standing, all holding out phones expectantly.

I can see his features shift, pulling back and changing into something sharp and indifferent. I've grown used to his accent; I hardly notice it anymore, but I hear it now.

"Hello, ladies." Ethan's grinning now, but his thumb is brushing over the back of my hand and his fingers squeeze tighter.

"Are you Ethan Barclay?" the same tall one asks, bouncing back and forth on her sandaled feet.

I see a brow rise above the frame of his sunglasses, and he says nothing for a moment. "One and the same."

"Can we buy you a pint?" I notice the way her voice rises, her own accent more pronounced on the last word.

My lips pull down, and despite the pressure of Ethan's hand, I think of Arna. How I faded into the background, where I was content to be, but I wanted to be in the forefront of anything to do with Ethan.

"Ah, I'm afraid I'll have to pass." Ethan turns back to me, raising my hand, and brushing the back of it with his lips. "Cheers."

He's only looking at me now, lips still pressed firmly against my hand.

I feel the light graze of his teeth, a tiny nip at my skin. I can tell they're upset by the way they all put their heads together, giggles fading entirely, and a furtive glance or two back in my direction.

"That was rude," I offer, and I feel Ethan's lips spread into a grin against my hand.

He cranes his neck to look over his shoulder where they are, back at the bar and bent over their phones, fingers moving furiously.

"They do look a bit miffed, don't they?" He presses his lips to my hand one more time before bringing it to rest by his beer. "Can't really be bothered when I'm with you, can I?"

I feel my cheek twitch, and I want to protest because I'm sure there was a time in the not-so-distant past when he would have bothered—that there was, at one point, an Ethan who would have enjoyed their company thoroughly. Despite my inner monologue constantly raking me over the proverbial coals of my own mind, I'm not insecure. I've never been insecure in relationships. Arna always said it's because I knew who I was, deep down in my core, and that even though I also possessed what she and her therapists said was a deep-rooted sense of self-hatred because of my absentee parents, I was so assured of who I was—no partner would ever change that or make me doubt it. I've always known who I am, and I've always been okay with that.

I'm about to tell Ethan that it's okay with me if he wants to drop my hand and go over there. That he owes me nothing. But like he's privy to those thoughts, the words that my tongue is about to elicit, he takes his sunglasses off and winks.

"I'd rather be with you than anyone, Ten." Gray eyes widen a fraction, and his mouth quirks to the side. I can feel my cheeks warm and blush.

My lips part, a small smile just for him. That makes his grin even wider. "That chuff you up a bit, babe?"

I tip my head, and I'm smiling now, all big and bright the way only he can make me smile. "You've got a rather inflated sense of self-importance, no? That your attention on me should have me so pleased, so delighted?"

Ethan raises his eyebrows and takes a sip of his beer. "Yeah. That about sums up how I feel when your attention is on me. But you've got me constantly competing against bones, those depressing ass books you read at night, and whatever else goes on in that brilliant little mind."

"You know for someone who claims to want all of my attention, you have no problem saying how odd you think my hobbies are." I make a show of untangling my hand from his, plucking my fingers away, and holding them out of reach.

But my cheeks are still warm, and I arch an eyebrow at him over my own bottle of beer. It's gotten warm in the time we've been sitting here, but like most things with Ethan, things that used to bother me, don't really. Arna used to call me her little weirdo, tell me how strange everything I liked was, or when I would say something particularly disarming, she would level me with a look, somehow looking down her nose at me, even though she was a bit shorter, and tell me that I was so fucking weird. But she made it sound like a bad thing. Ethan makes it sound like it was the thing that turned the world on its axis.

"I think you're quite fascinating." Ethan drops his voice, and he leans across the worn table.

I can't help but notice the way his muscles flex and the cotton of his shirt tightens.

One hand is around the back of my neck, and he drops his forehead to mine. My breath hitches, and then his lips are on mine. It's brief, and before I have a chance to kiss him back, his perfect lips are off mine, and then they press briefly to my nose, to each of my still warm cheeks and my forehead. And then he's leaning in his chair, tipping it back on its legs, sunglasses down again to cover those gray eyes, one tattooed arm hanging over the back while he drinks the rest of his beer, eyes back on whatever sport is playing on the TV.

I think he's quite fascinating, too.

Chapter Twenty-Six

People are spread out across the sand in various stages of undress—some with wetsuits peeled back, others in nothing but bathing suits, but they're all watching the rays of the sun disappear beyond the water.

Ethan and I walk along the beach, the tide moving in and out, covering our feet with water and then leaving only sand.

I look down at my feet, sinking into the shoreline, before looking up at Ethan. My lips start to curl upward, and I'm tempted to flick sand all over him, like a small child might.

"Don't even think about it, Ten." Ethan cocks his head. "I'm faster than you. You'll be in the water before you kick sand all over me."

I smile at him and dig my foot into the sand just as he starts to pull me toward the water.

"November!"

Ethan and I stop, our joined hands stretched out between us, and my leg poised, ready to kick the wet sand up toward him, when I spot Jake maybe ten feet away, pushing to stand up with his hand raised in greeting.

"Jake," I say it far too quietly, tipping my head to study him as he jogs the short distance to stop in front of us.

I'm not sure what I feel when I look at him. A lot of things that I don't think I will ever be able to untangle.

His linen shirt hangs open, revealing an expanse of abdominal muscle that quite frankly seems pathetic in comparison to Ethan's, and his navy swim shorts rise on his thighs, the light dusting of golden hair catching in the final light of the sun.

"Nov. I thought that was you." Jake smiles at me and runs a hand through his hair.

He's clean-shaven, as usual. Sandy hair is a bit longer than he used to keep it, and his skin is bronzed from the sun.

"It's me." I raise my eyebrows. I know I should say something else, that it's nice to see him, that he looks great. Maybe even that I miss him. I used to, I think. But his presence now feels malignant, just another poisonous vine snaking along my bones. "What are you doing here?"

Jake gestures over his shoulder with his thumb. A group of his friends from business school are sitting on a piece of driftwood, a cooler overflowing with beer at their feet. I recognize them all.

He smiles at me, almost teasing. But it's not. It doesn't reach his eyes, and I think I see hurt flash there. "You never take vacation."

I swallow, and my fingers feather uselessly against the back of Ethan's hand. "Arna—"

Jake's lips turn down before he interrupts. "I was going to call you after I heard about Arna. I'm so sorry."

"But you didn't," I say pointedly.

Jake finally glances sideways at Ethan briefly, eyes dropping to our joined hands. He looks sort of like he's been slapped. When he looks back up, he does a double take. "Are you Ethan Barclay?"

"Ey." Ethan nods, his smile is so overlarge, so fake, my lips part because I can only imagine what's going to come next. He extends his hand toward Jake, and he's shaking it with too much enthusiasm when he finally speaks. "And you're the bloke who shagged her best friend, yeah?"

Jake blanches, and the golden hue of his skin pales. "Nov—"

"Arna told me," I say quietly, and I feel Ethan's grip tighten on my hand.

Jake palms his face, running his hand back and forth across his jaw. "November...you—"

"Think long and hard about your next words, yeah?" Ethan's eyes are narrowed on Jake, and his thumb presses into the back of my hand.

Jake pulls his head back before his lip curls up in distaste, the distraction over Ethan's athletic prowess and celebrity clearly gone. "Nov, can we talk?"

"I'm not sure I want to speak to you," I tell him, and it's the truth.

"Please?" Jake's voice drops an octave, the way it only does when he's truly upset. "I need to explain, I need to—"

Ethan arches an eyebrow, displeasure radiating off of him. "Don't think she really cares what you need."

"We were together for five years. You've been here for what, all of five minutes? Talk to me when you're carrying around all that shared history." Jake's nostrils flare, and he shakes his head before looking back at me, the same collapse to his features.

Ethan says nothing, but when I look at him, one eyebrow is still raised before his lips press roughly to the side of my head.

"Ah, not to worry mate, fucked the memory of you away a long time ago." He doesn't even bother looking at Jake when he says it. He's looking at me. "I'll wait just up the beach, yeah?"

His tattooed thumb grazes my cheek before he turns and claps Jake on the shoulder.

A muscle in Jake's cheek twitches, but he looks back at me and gestures toward the sand. "Can we sit?"

"I don't know, can we?" I question, voice rising and petulant.

But I turn from him and drop down to the sand. Wrapping my arms around my legs, I drop my chin and stare out at the ocean. It's beautiful, and I should take note of all the colors, the way it refracts off the surface of water. But I don't.

"How long has that been going on?" Jake settles in beside me.

I don't have to look at him to know that one leg is stretched out straight, one knee is up, and his arm is slung over it.

I don't answer, but I turn to him, lips pulling back, and all I can feel is how heavy I am, because they were both fucking liars.

"She was my best friend. My best fucking friend, Jake!" I shove at his shoulder before I can stop myself, a sob sneaking up my throat and tears already falling down my cheeks.

He moves to grab my wrists, but I pull away, holding my hands out between us. A barrier. "Don't touch me."

"I'm sorry, November. I am." Jake's voice drops, and his hand twitches, like he wants to reach out and interlace our fingers.

Our hands never fit right anyway.

"I don't care." I set my chin back down on my knees. I'm lying. I'm a liar. I do care. I care more than I can even fathom, and I feel it all the way down into the marrow of my rotten bones.

My heart hurts, and I think it breaks when I realize I know what he's going to do next.

He's going to press his fingers to his forehead before he pinches the bridge of his nose. I see it all in the periphery of my vision. Confirmation I didn't want—that the two people I thought knew me best were just liars like me at the end of the day.

"She was a fucking bitch, November!" Jake exasperates, holding his hands out, like Arna is all around us. And she probably is. I can imagine her there, pursed lips and chin tipped up in the air in displeasure. "She was a fucking bitch, and everyone knew it but you. She was a fucking cu—"

"Don't you dare." My head snaps toward him. "Don't you dare finish the rest of that sentence."

Jake scoffs, nostrils flaring as he shakes his head. "You're still going to make excuses for her? She fucked me, Nov. She begged for it. Said she just had to know what it was like, how it felt, how—"

"Stop," I whisper, my voice a sad, tiny plea. "I don't want to hear it."

"Well, I do. I want to hear *you* say it. Tell me you hate her, that knowing what you know now, you'd do things differently." It's his turn to sound pleading. Jake's eyebrows crease, and he's looking for something I'll never be able to give him. "I was ready to marry you, for Christ's sake. And you never fucking let me all the way in."

I wipe at my cheeks, the salt stinging my skin. "She's not the only one who did it, Jake."

Jake jerks his head, lips pulled back. I look at him, one final time. His teeth are nice. But they aren't Ethan's. *He* was nice. But he's not Ethan. "You won't even say it now that you know? She didn't even hesitate,

November. What was it you used to say? That you were the exception to her rule?"

I turn my head and say nothing. But I'm blinking rapidly now because I'm crying. For so many things.

"Does he know?" Jake angles his head in the general direction Ethan said he would be waiting. "That you'll always, *always* pick her? Even when she's a ghost?"

I stare ahead, continuing my vigil. I try to focus on the way the sky turns; I try to remember why the colors change the way they do, why the light refracts the way it does and how your rods and cones process it.

Jake pushes up to stand beside me, and when he does, he steps in front of me, the sides of his linen shirt lifting in the breeze. I finally look up at him. He peers down at me, the man I used to love. The boy who sort of grew up with me, too. He's in front of me, but I see a different him. Twenty-five-year-old Jake with a softer jaw and shorter hair. Twenty-five-year-old Jake who looked at me like I was so interesting, so special, so unique. His little unicorn. It's what he used to call me. But he never saw me. He never noticed the things that matter. He never traded plates with me, was too focused on what I wouldn't give him, and he never bothered to ask why.

I loved him once, in my own way. The only way I knew how, and it wasn't enough.

But that love is dead, and he and Arna stomped on its grave, and fucked in its decay.

"I hope he's a bigger man than me." Jake levels me with a look, kind of like he pities me. I would pity me, too.

"Doesn't take much." I raise my eyebrows at him, and he rolls his eyes, shaking his head before he starts down the sand, but he turns to look at me one last time.

"I am sorry, November. Whether you believe that or not. But you know who wouldn't be sorry?"

He doesn't need to say it, and he's probably right. Arna never apologized for anything a day in her life.

A hand grazes the crown of my head, before fingers twirl the hair that's fallen from my braid, curling against my neck. Ethan drops beside me, one arm pulling me into his chest. His mouth finds my temple. "You okay? He say anything to you?"

I press my cheek against Ethan's shoulder. "Nothing important."

Maybe Arna and I still have something in common after all. We're both liars.

Chapter Twenty-Seven

I can't concentrate on the journal article open on my phone because droplets of water are tracking down Ethan's tattoos.

He's wading back and forth in the small plunge pool, looking decidedly North American, with a backward Aston Martin hat on, damp curls peeking out from underneath the beak. He rolls his shoulders, and I study where the end of his tattoo pops. His deltoid muscle is taut and making it look like the swirls of ink are bleeding into his trapezius. But I know they don't. The sleeve ends abruptly where the prominent muscle tapers off.

I can tell he's restless, and that his leg might be bothering him by the way he moves back and forth, one arm now stretched across his chest. We've overstayed the booking by a night, and more letters stay unopened in that safe. I'm supposed to be moving on. We're supposed to be moving on. But I like this tiny town, and I like it even more with Ethan in it. I like this house. I like the giant stone bathtub and the outdoor shower, I like the paned windows that show the natural foliage, and I like being in the giant bed with Ethan beside me.

"I don't want to leave," I offer, and Ethan turns his head, looking at me over his shoulder.

His body follows, and there are more distracting drops of water moving down his chest, his arms, and even the sides of his neck. He wades forward in the small pool, forearms coming to rest on the deck where I'm stretched out on a chair. His skin looks golden under the midday sun, and he grins at me, reaching out to grab my foot in his hand.

"You don't want to leave?" he repeats, squeezing my foot. "I'll call the host, see if we can extend a few days, yeah?"

"I can do that from my phone, you troglodyte." I smile, and an affronted sort of look crosses his face.

Ethan runs his other hand over his jaw dusted with dark stubble that I've grown fond of running my fingers over. "Well far be it from me for trying to do something nice for you, Ten."

"Do you want to stay?" I ask hesitantly because I don't think I've ever been afraid of anything as I am of his answer.

There's a tiny part of me that wonders if Ethan is just biding his time with me, until he's ready to go back home and make a decision about his future. Surgery. Rehab. Maybe returning any of the incessant calls from his agent that he's been ignoring for about three weeks now. I would be fine. I'm always fine alone. But for the first time in my life, I don't want to be.

He cocks his head to the side and tugs my foot playfully. I watch as he reaches up and grabs the legs of my chair, startling me as he drags it closer to him where it teeters right on the edge of the plunge pool.

I grab the sides on instinct, my phone clattering to the deck beside me. It reminds me of the paddleboard, the way I was gripping the edges, waves splashing everywhere, just trying to stay afloat in a post-Arna world. I can tell he's eyeing me by the way his face tightens, even though the sunglasses shield him from me.

Ethan doesn't have a poker face, and everything he thinks and feels is written all over him. "I wouldn't let you fall, Nov," he says, words soft and careful, despite the tenor of his voice.

"I know." And I do know that, with about as much certainty as I know anything. But he didn't answer me, so I repeat myself, gripping the sides of the chair tighter just in case his answer should send me entirely adrift again. "Do you want to stay?"

"What kind of question is that? 'Course I want to stay," Ethan says sharply, wrapping both his still wet arms around my legs and dropping his chin to my left knee. "Where else would I be?"

"I don't know, having another surgery? Doing physiotherapy? Rehab?" I prod, but I wince as I say it. Because even though that might be what's best for Ethan, I don't want him to go, and I don't know if I can follow him home.

Ethan stays silent, but I swear his arms tighten around my legs, and I can feel him staring at me from behind his sunglasses. "Will you come here? Get in the water with me?"

I don't really want to get in the water because my skin feels nice in the sunlight, but I nod, and he lets go of my legs and holds a hand up. I interlace my fingers with his, and he walks in the pool beside me until I reach the stone steps. I go to step in, one foot poised to drop below the surface, but Ethan steps up, water cascading off of him and all those maddening droplets creating more distractions.

He grabs my waist, lips pressing briefly to my left hip, before he sets me down beside him on the bottom step.

My shoulders tense, the water jarring on my sun-warmed legs.

Ethan tugs on my hand, moving back into the pool and submerging the rest of his body. The lines of his tattoo look distorted under the water, and I crane my neck to see the blurred numbers across his knuckles before looking at his right hand. Entirely empty. And that makes me sad because he deserves for that arm, that hand, his mind, and his world to be filled with many more accomplishments. He deserves everything he's ever wanted and more.

I flick my gaze up to him, and I jump down from the final step, a bizarre sort of squeal escaping me when my chest hits the water because it feels fucking cold.

Both my arms raise on instinct, ripped away from Ethan's hand, and I bounce back and forth on the balls of my feet, eyes squeezing shut. But they open quickly when Ethan laughs, and it warms me from the inside out. But I don't tell him because I don't want to make him feel obligated to stay.

"You look like a frat boy with that hat," I say instead, narrowing my eyes on him.

"You don't like it?" Ethan asks through a smile. "I thought it was rather North American of me."

"It's something." I tip my head and raise my eyebrows at him.

Ethan studies me, and his lips twitch like he doesn't believe me, and he's right because I'm a liar. About lots of things. But in this instance, it's because he doesn't look like a frat boy. He might be a thirty-one-year-old man wearing a backward hat in a pool with a tattoo sleeve, but he also looks beautiful.

"You don't think I want to stay?" he questions, stepping toward me, hands moving through the water until they find my waist. He pulls me to him, and he's looking down at me, but his mouth is in a tight line, cheek muscle feathering. "Where else would I go, November?"

"Home," I whisper, my hands finding Ethan's sides. He's all hard muscle still, despite the fact that he's been consuming a steady diet of beer and whatever food I direct him toward. "You said it yourself, you were in exile. You should go home. Take the referral. Do the rehab. Have another surgery if you need it. Call your fucking agent back—"

"No." Ethan's accent sounds more pronounced. It's harsh like the word is, and suddenly I'm pressed into his chest, his arms wrapped around me, and his chin on top of my head. "I don't want to go back there. There's nothing there for me."

He smells like the sunlight, and my eyes close against his chest. I wrap my arms around his back. I can feel the sun on my own skin, and it feels nice, but Ethan's arms around me feel better. It should be shocking for me, since I don't like being touched, but I like when he touches me. "False. You can do rehab, you can—"

"What if I did it in Canada?" Ethan's voice is low, gravelly, the way I like it, and I feel myself pressing my cheek harder against his chest, like I'm trying to feel his words all the way down to my bones. "Have it on good authority that Dr. Morris, DDS has connections to excellent orthopedic surgeons."

I do. I wasn't lying when I said I knew several. I know the best orthopedic surgeon in Toronto. We did our undergraduate degrees together. But that also means they knew Arna, and I hesitate because I don't think Ethan knows how much of my life is touched by her in some way. And because I don't want him to follow me there and realize I'm not the person he thinks I am. That my life is solitary, desolate even. I take calls at all hours of the night and consult on cases for multiple law enforcement municipalities. I'm always the first to answer emergency pages when someone's knocked out a tooth, and I spend two weekends a month cleaning teeth in free, mobile public health units.

When I asked him if he wanted to stay, I meant here. Here where I can pretend to be someone else, pretend I've forgotten everything she did. But that's not the truth. It's easier here, but I know once I leave this bubble, this microcosm, I'll be back in the only world I've ever known. One I have only ever shared with one person.

He must sense my hesitation, even from where I'm pressed into his chest, because he speaks again. "Do you have room for me in your life back home?"

I pull back and tip my chin up, and he's looking down at me. I know he means every word. "What about soccer?"

He doesn't even correct me by saying "football." He just shrugs and brings his lips to my forehead. They move against my skin when he speaks. "There's a national league in North America. Even a professional team right where you live. I'm not contractually obligated to anyone right now. I could try to call in a few favors. Don't make me beg, Ten."

There are thousands of things I could say. Things I should say. I should tell Ethan that I wasn't kidding when I said I was never home, that I don't date, I've failed at it constantly because I've never had room for anyone, not in the way they wanted. I don't know how to make a life back home that looks different than that. I don't know how to make a real life with him.

Most of all I should tell him that I'm a liar. That I'll never be able to give him what he wants because there won't be a day that goes by that I don't partly belong to my dead best friend.

But I say none of that because the other parts of me are falling in love with him, and I'll keep him for as long as I can.

I look up at him, and I nod. A part of me wants to die because he smiles, and it's so fucking special. I only want to be in this moment with him—his arms wrapped around me, the sunlight baking down on us, a breeze that smells like saltwater, and a tiny waterfall bubbling just for us—but I'm not just here with him. There's a ghost whispering in my ear, my brain, my heart. Telling me there are pieces of her left for me, handwritten parts of her life, secrets she's given to no one else that are waiting to be told, sitting discarded in a locked safe.

Ethan brings his lips to mine, but I'm not really here. I'll never be with him, not one-hundred percent, because I think a part of me died with her.

Chapter Twenty-Eight

Apparently May marks the start of the rainy season, so the request to extend our booking was accepted immediately.

Ethan stretches out on the chair beside me, hat tossed to the side, and one tattooed hand holding his phone above his head. He seems content now, the earlier restlessness from him gone. The muscles in his shoulders are loose again. As loose as the muscles that span Ethan could possibly be. I'm trying again and failing to finish the journal article, but I'm reading the same sentences over and over.

It's not Ethan's body, his former restlessness that's distracting me. It's the way his face lit up, his eyes, the way it was so easy for him to say he would come home with me. I want those things. I do. But I can't focus because I'm wondering what it would be like for him and me to exist in the real world together. To exist in Toronto. I'm even fantasizing, going as far as to imagine what it would be like if he played soccer there. If he were to be there permanently. If he would live in my townhouse with me. It doesn't seem like a stretch because we've been practically living together for the last month. The thought of him getting his own place, his own space, feels weird. It doesn't seem right.

I roll to my side, abandoning the article on laser techniques for fillings. It was losing me because I'm not sure I would like that. I'd miss the sound of the small instruments, the drills. I like those tiny sounds, those tiny drills, because they made everything else in my head go quiet.

But I look at Ethan, the edges of his jaw, the ridges of his abdominal muscles, and the remnants of water droplets still scattered sparsely across his chest. He makes everything go quiet, too.

It might even be a better kind of quiet. Maybe lasers wouldn't be so bad if I always had him.

Ethan's thumb swipes across his phone, and I can see a grin start to edge across his lips. "There's a sort of public health museum like an hour away. All sorts of artifacts from days past and healthcare relics found around the island. Thought I might drive you there? We could check it out?"

My lips part, but I close them again because the backs of my eyes are burning. "Are you in the habit of researching local public health history?"

"No." Ethan mimics me and rolls to the side, tossing his phone to me. "We're staying longer, and I was looking for things that you might like."

"And you want to spend your afternoon in this museum with me? Looking at the artifacts from days past? Seems like a waste of your time."

Ethan cocks his head, one curl falling to the side. His eyes are hidden behind his sunglasses, but I can imagine what they look like. I can see it in the way he looks still, almost predatory, and his stubbled jaw is all perfect sharp angles. I know his features, the set of his jaw, his shoulders all the way down to the way he cracks his fingers the same way I know how to suture gums.

It snuck up on me. The way Ethan, and all that he is, is tattooed on my heart, and that he somehow exists in my bones the way Arna and her lies do. Usually she wins out. But today, right now, when he's looking at me like that, and I'm waiting, barely breathing, for what he's going to say because I just know that it's going to break and mend my heart all at once.

"I'd be honored for you to waste my time."

And it does.

"I'm fucking starved, Ten." Ethan's voice is practically a groan.

"You ate two hours ago," I say bluntly.

We've been at the museum for less than an hour. I was busy looking at the rusted pliers in front of me encased behind glass. According to the plaque, they were used for dental extractions in the eighteenth century.

"Professional athlete." He breaths in my ear, tattooed hands finding my hips and gripping the denim of my shorts. Ethan pulls me back against him, resting his chin on my shoulder. "What's this?"

"Pliers," I answer, my entire body taut at the feel of him pressed behind me. "Used for dental extractions way back in the day. Not entirely different from what we use now."

"Yeah?" he asks, fingers drumming against my hip bones. "You pull teeth out with these?"

"I'll pull your teeth out if you don't shut up."

Ethan laughs, a bark in my ear, but his lips brush the lobe and a shudder runs through me. His fingers stop the incessant drumming against me, and he stills. "Am I making you uncomfortable, or do you like this?"

"The second," I whisper, still staring intently at the rusted metal. "We can leave if you're hungry. I never looked at the next letter to see what food I was supposed to eat, but—"

"Screw Arna. Let's pick something else. Let me take you out on a quintessential pedestrian date. Burgers. Fries. Pints. And then I'll take you home and ravish you."

"I don't—" I murmur, back ramrod straight, and the edges of the pliers start to blur. "I don't eat that type of food."

Ethan presses into my shoulder, and his fingers tense on my hips. "Would you like to try? I'll be there. Every step of the way. I'll finish what you don't want."

"You're that hungry?" I whisper, the pliers now a rust-colored blur.

"No. I'll do whatever you need," Ethan answers baldly, honestly.

"You want to take me out on a date? A date designed for teenagers?" I want to sound dry, irreverent even. But my voice cracks, and I sound on the verge of tears. I feel Ethan nodding, somehow pulling my body even closer to him. I'm flush with all the ridges and muscles that make up Ethan Barclay. "No one wants to date me. I wouldn't want to date me. You want to date me?"

"Every day for the rest of my life. If you'll have me." His words whisper past my ear. They wrap around my body, they seep through my skin, and

I feel them trying to bloom in and amongst the lies, the ghosts, the decay. Those words are tiny, beautiful little seeds. Seeds that could take root and grow into something special, something that would belong entirely to us.

"No one wants me for that long." I breathe, scared there isn't enough of me left to go around.

"I do."

I feel one of those tiny, beautiful seeds crack open, and its root stretch down into my heart. "Oh. We can go get burgers then."

I don't like how high the burger is stacked. It's weird, and I wish I knew after all these years why things like this bother me. Have always bothered me, would maybe always bother me. Because it's too big, and my mouth is smaller than this. And then it wouldn't even be the food itself that bothers me, just the mess I'd make trying to bite into it.

That always made me uncomfortable first, the looming embarrassment. And then everything else would start.

I can see Ethan rolling the neck of his beer between his fingertips. One eye on the TV, the other on me. "Alright?"

"I don't—I don't like the way it looks. The size of it," I whisper and push back on the bright yellow chair, my thighs squeaking against the plastic. "It sounds dumb. It's always been dumb, but I—I don't want to bite into it."

Those eyes snap back to me. "You don't like the way it looks?"

"No."

Ethan's lower lip juts out, and he nods, thoughtfully taking a sip of beer before he sets down the bottle and pulls my tray toward him. He eyes the burger with a sort of shrewdness I know must also be on my face when I'm observing autopsies. "Right. Right. What can I change here, Ten?"

I shrug, biting my own lip and wanting to cry, to shrink down and be anywhere but here because I'm useless and haven't come as far as I hoped, but then Ethan snaps his fingers.

"Nov. November. Look at me." Both those eyes are on me now. "Talk to me, yeah? I can't fix it if you don't talk to me."

"It's the top bun," I whisper uselessly, tears gathering in the creases of my eyes. It's not the carb content. No. Carbs are good for you. I just know my mouth wouldn't wrap around the whole thing, and then something would spill out and embarrass me, and then I would start counting the fat, the calories.

"The top bun," Ethan repeats, my favorite tattooed hand grabbing my own and squeezing it. "It's still a burger without the top bun. Let's just get rid of it."

I hiccup, because I'm lame and still fifteen, and start to shake my head.

Ethan's already flung the top bun off and thrown it onto the ground, like he doesn't care if someone has to clean that up because he only cares about me. I watch, small little gasps escaping me while he hands me a fork and a knife. Like it's simple. So simple. They sit uselessly, lying on either side of my tray, my fingers feathering and scared to grab and use them because this isn't what he really meant when he said we should go get burgers.

Ethan's jaw twitches, and he grabs them, quickly slicing through the burger and spearing the bottom half with the fork, holding it out to me, eyes now back on the TV.

"Are you feeding me?" I ask, hiccups giving way to incredulity. No one has ever fed me before. If it weren't a physiological impossibility, I would have been certain my parents never fed me, either. I just came out of the womb, opposable thumbs ready to hold cutlery and digest solids.

His eyes swing back to me, and a grin spreads across his face. "If that's what it takes. It's still a burger if you cut it up."

"I wanted to enjoy it like it was. The way I was supposed to." I'm sad, and I'm small. Because it's true. I wanted to enjoy it. A burger with Ethan Barclay.

He tips his head, still holding the fork out. The grin waivers, and those slight lines around his eyes crease momentarily. "Someday, love. It's not today, and that's okay. Let yourself off the mat and enjoy. It's not the last time I'm going to crave fast food."

There's a promise there. Like we aren't just sitting in some American fare restaurant on the beach. Like we're sitting in a life that belongs to the both of us. Like there will be many more days like this.

I lean forward, eyes narrowing in and a small smile pulling on my lips before I stop just short of the burger.

Something lights up behind his eyes, and I know he thinks this mundane thing we're doing, him feeding me in this odd way that makes sense only to us, is me moving forward into this life that only belongs to the both of us.

But I can feel hands on my shoulders, tipped nails digging in and pulling me back as I lean forward, keeping me fully cemented into a life that used to belong to someone else, too.

I lean farther and take an overexaggerated bite, because I'm a fucking liar, and he's smiling at me like I've hung the moon.

Chapter Twenty-Nine

Ethan is many things. And I think my favorite one is how secretly playful he is. He's obstinate and rude to almost everyone but me. But right now we're sitting in the dark of our rental, knees touching as we face each other, cross-legged on the bed.

His hands are out, palms up, and he's waiting for me to try to slap them before he snatches them away. We've already tested reflexes, and ours are similar, so it's been a lot of gentle scrapes of skin and brushes of our fingers. I stare at his palms for a moment longer, wishing they were all over me instead of suspended mid-air.

I flick my eyes up, and my lungs stop working because Ethan is smiling at me. And it's not one of his usual grins. The ones that spill across his face and cause his eyes to wrinkle and show me how bright, how luminous his heart and soul are. This one is quiet. His lips aren't even parted. They're just slightly pulling upward.

And I can feel it on my skin. It's reverence, it's love, it's hope. His features aren't soft. They're sharp as always, and I think that's one of the most beautiful things about Ethan. He contains multitudes. He can look at me with those cheekbones that could cut glass, cut through connective muscle tissue—and I would know because I think they've carved his name on my heart. He can look at me with that jawline dusted with stubble and gray eyes that might seem cold, but there's hope blooming on his lips.

My own lips part, and I want to tell him. Tell him that if I had just met him before her, in another life—I could give him everything, and I would gladly lay at his altar forever—when one of those hands grips my wrist and pulls me toward him so suddenly that I crash into him. The other hand wraps around the back of my neck, and his lips are on mine—and I forget what I was going to say.

I feel the vibration of a moan in his throat against my lips, and my hands that are about to scrape and pull at the muscles of his broad shoulders stop mid-air because there's nothing rushed about this.

His mouth is soft against mine, and the fingers of that hand gripping my wrist loosen. His thumb skates over the inside. I wrap my hand around his neck and gently tug him back. He lays me down, lips never leaving mine and hands brushing all over me.

The way we're touching is different. Instead of ripping and pulling, our clothes are tugged off slowly, and I can tell his skin is burning the same way mine is. Ethan's fingers skate over every inch of me with adoration, and there is nothing hurried about it. He grips my ribcage, and I wonder briefly if he knows it's not just me he's holding—my body—but he's holding my heart. Tenderly. Reverently. He moves his lips down my body the same way.

My hands cradle his head, his mind, and his brain the way he cradles my heart. Because I love his mind, his brain. All the things that make up his thoughts. I could spend all day bathing in the words he must think without growing bored.

His grip tightens, and his teeth graze my collarbone. I've learned the way he likes to move down my body, inevitably ending between my legs, as much as he's mapped out everything that I like. But this is different. The end isn't going to be the same.

Only the thin lace of my bra and underwear, the material of his, are left between us. I can feel all of him against me, but I want—I need—more. I don't want to feel Ethan against me. I want him inside of me. I want to share everything.

He pauses, his lips gently pressing between my breasts before one quick flex of his shoulders has him hovering over me.

My hands are still tangled in his hair. His chest heaves, and his eyes are endless. I see so many possibilities in them. I can't count them, but I want them all.

"Are we…" His voice is hoarse, the way it is in the morning. Those eyes stare at me imploringly.

"Yes," I whisper, watching his pupils expand, and those words go all the way down to his soul.

Ethan grins at me, a groan escaping him, and he buries his face in my neck. I feel his lips move as he speaks. "Thank fuck I bought all those condoms, yeah?"

Laughter falls from my lips, and I press them to his temple, hands moving from his hair to traverse the muscles in his back.

One of Ethan's hands moves down to my hips, gripping it, and the other finds the back of my head, tattooed fingers knotting the strands of my hair.

Ethan murmurs into my neck again, and I think he's saying my name. Just my name. Repeating it. *November. November. November.* But he pulls back, lips brushing my jaw, and his stubble grazing me. And then I realize he's saying something else entirely.

"Nova."

He's calling me Nova, and at this moment, everything is ruined. Because only one other person has ever called me that. And all of those promises I knew I couldn't keep shatter at once.

Because my best friend is dead. And I hate her, but I love her. I'll always love her, no matter how fucked up and flawed she turned out to be. I love her, and nothing will ever be the same.

Ethan must feel me tense because he's hovering over me again, eyes roving my face, like he wonders if he's hurt me somehow. His lips move, but I speak first.

"Nova. You called me Nova."

"Yeah. It means—"

"New beginnings. Bright star. I know," I cut him off. There are multiple meanings, and none will ever be to me what it used to. None will ever be as important.

Pupils still wide and lips parted, he asks, "Then why—"

"Only Arna called me Nova," I say, and then I see it in his eyes, too. He knows that I was dishonest, that I can't let her go. That I promised him something I would never, ever be able to deliver on.

He sits up, straddling me now, and he runs a hand through his hair. I watch, unmoving and caged in by his muscular thighs, while he scrubs his jaw and then his face with his hands. "She's dead, November," he says with a slight shake of his head.

And then Ethan looks at me with something akin to pity, like he's in on some big proverbial secret that's beyond my reach, my understanding. And maybe he is.

"Please don't call me that."

It was the wrong thing to say because a derisive snort comes from him, and he's climbing off me, tugging at the ends of his hair. He rolls his shoulders, and I sit up, propped up on my elbows. He crosses the room, shadows throwing his muscles into sharper contrast, and throws open the fridge. In one motion, he's twisting the cap off of a beer with his teeth.

It doesn't seem like much, but I recoil, because I know he's doing it intentionally.

"Any other nicknames I should avoid? Places? Movies? Songs? Flowers?" Ethan asks, voice sharp and one eyebrow cocked, the bottle poised at his mouth.

"You should avoid doing that to your teeth," I say, and he shakes his head, like he can't fucking believe me.

I'm still propped up on my elbows, exposed in nothing but my bra and underwear. Usually, Ethan's eyes on my bare skin lights fire. It warms me. It buoys my heart and pumps air into my lungs. But right now, it feels like they're the frozen expanse of a lake, and I'm stuck under the ice—it's cold, sharp, and shredding when I try to breathe.

"What's the big deal?" I try, voice small, even though I know what the big deal is.

"I'm competing with a fucking ghost!" Ethan raises his voice, slamming his beer down on the counter, and I watch as liquid froths and slops over the lip of the bottle. "You said you were going to let her go. You promised me that she wouldn't run your life anymore. But what? Am I supposed to tiptoe? Have a whole list of things that are off limits for you and me? Just sit around and wait until it's easy for you to leave me too?" I stay silent and say nothing. Because there's nothing to say. I just wait. "I use a nickname that she used to call you when we're about to fuck for the first time and—"

That makes me say something because it feels like something I can latch onto. Attack. It's a mistake he's committed. Deflection, readily available. "Oh, we were about to *fuck*? Is that all it is?"

Ethan scoffs and snatches the beer again. The muscles in his forearm tense, the whirls of ink sharpening, looking like the edge of a bone saw. And they must be. Because I can feel him sawing through all my limbs right now, and they crumble, because they were only made of lies, anyway.

"No, and you fucking know it, November." Ethan's eyes are narrowed on me, and he shakes his head. His voice softens suddenly when he speaks again. "Is that what life's going to be for us? For you? Life just living in the shadow of her memory? You need to let her go, Nov."

The thought of somehow coming untethered from Arna, even from her ghost, who haunts me as much as she buoys me, holds me, is impossible.

I shake my head ever so slightly, lips parting, like I want to say something, anything, but there's nothing that comes out.

Ethan's features collapse, and that might have hurt me more than the thought of a life free of Arna.

"You want a life in her shadow? You need to let her go. She's fucking dead, November!"

"I can't!" It comes out like a guttural sob, like there's blood bubbling from my mouth because Ethan's words have stabbed me. They're breaking my heart because I don't know how to let her go. And the truth is, I don't want to. "I can't. You don't understand."

"Then make me understand!" Ethan shouts, one hand pulling on the ends of his hair, and the other still clutching the bottle.

My heart breaks because he looks beautiful, and there's nothing I can tell him that will change the inevitable. I know Ethan is about to become untethered from me. I say nothing, and I think I can hear his heart shattering, too.

"You won't even pick me over a fucking ghost, will you?" His voice is punctuated by a hollow laugh, and before I realize what's happening, Ethan's throwing open the safe in the room, and he's holding the letters in his hand. My favorite hand. The number eight mocks me as his thumb presses into the stack of paper.

"No," I whisper, finally scrambling forward and throwing myself off the bed.

Ethan's eyes narrow, and his lips pull back, and at this moment, I think he looks cruel. Deranged almost. But there isn't a mirror in front of me, and if there was, I could maybe be honest with myself, that I know I'm the cruel one.

That hand holds the letters high above his head. And Ethan Barclay stands taller than me in more ways than one, so I'm lurching forward, rising onto the balls of my feet to try and grab them back from him because I'm not ready for them to be gone. For the last part of her to be gone.

"Ethan, stop. Please. She's all I had. She's all I have," I sob, ready to practically jump to try and secure the last pieces of Arna from him.

His shoulders tense, like he was about to hold them ever higher, even farther away from me. But when those words leave my mouth, his head jerks back, and I realize what I've done. I realize that I'm wrong. His heart was never breaking or broken before. But I watch it explode in his chest and gutter out entirely behind his eyes. I imagine that's what Arna looked like when her heart exploded from blunt force trauma and the life left her.

"Really? Some dead girl who turned out to be a massive bitch is all you have? Alright November, then take her."

Ethan throws the letters at my feet.

Chapter Thirty

In my life, there are a million and one things I could have, should have, would have done differently. But sitting on the floor, clutching letters to my chest while grief spilled from me, entirely unfettered, in horrific, wet rasps, while Ethan Barclay packs to leave me, will forever be my number one regret.

I should strike a match, light it on one of the many fires Ethan's fingers, hands, lips had lit along my body and burn the letters for him. I should have ripped them up and driven to a nearby cliff to drop them from, in a grand gesture to him.

There were a million and one things I should have done.

Instead, I sit here. The letters splayed on the ground where Ethan had thrown them at my feet, where I dropped to my knees between them, still in nothing but my underwear.

I sat here while he threw his clothes in his bag, shrugged his discarded shirt back on, and thumbed through his phone, surely booking a plane ticket away from me and all my ghosts.

I sit here, palms pressing into my eyes and rolling, horrific gasps escaping me, because my best friend is dead, and I would never be the same, when I feel him drop to his knees in front of me. I want to open my eyes to look at him one last time, but I won't be able to see him through the tears that won't end. But I know he's here. My sense of the space occupied by Ethan is likely just a part of me now.

I sit here as his hand wraps around the back of my head, bringing my forehead to his lips for an all-too-brief moment. I sit here while they move, and he speaks against my skin for the last time. "Maybe in another life, yeah?"

Something that sounds like a death rattle tumbles from my lips, and I almost laugh because it's fitting. There are many things both dead and dying in my life. Arna. The bodies of people I've spent my life trying to give back to their families because my own don't want me. Teeth. Nerves and roots. Pieces of me.

But nothing hurts me more than this. Whatever this is, could have, would have, should have been. Nothing hurts more than the death of my heart when Ethan walks out the door, leaving me on the floor surrounded by letters from a fucking ghost.

I didn't stay in our tiny rental home with its paned windows, foliage, and outdoor shower. I didn't stay because there was another ghost brushing past me, pulling on me, and whispering in my ears there.

But this ghost was different from my usual repertoire.

This ghost has restless, tattooed hands. This ghost is impatient, but unlike the other one whose manicured hands dug in and tried to mechanically steer me in certain directions, this one would gently stroke my skin, encouraging me. It would place a strong, broad hand against my back to hold me up, and this ghost would whisper in my ear, too. But it didn't whisper stories of the past; it shares promises of a future I'll never have.

This ghost might be my least favorite of all.

I didn't stay, but I didn't open the letters, either. I packed them at the bottom of my suitcase. The temptation to rip them up, to shred them, and to scream and scream for all that they had cost me—all that Arna had cost me—was ever present.

But most of all I wanted to scream at myself. I think about going home—my childhood home—the one I haven't claimed since I left for boarding school. But I don't really want to be there when my parents are, which leaves such a sense of bitter irony on my lips that I almost laugh at that, too. A quick, perfunctory text disguised as one of the monthly check-ins one of us remembers to send confirms they aren't traveling.

So, I go home. I go back to my life. A life I'm entirely unfamiliar with. It's not the one before Arna died where I was blissfully ignorant and unaware, happy and content to be alone with nothing but the love of her, or the one after that was hollow, mechanical—utterly empty.

This life is entirely uncharted territory. As I open the door to my townhouse, unceremoniously kicking my suitcase across the threshold and promptly ignoring it in favor of walking around it, taking in the framed degrees, journal articles, and the framed photos that really only feature me and one other person, I realize that this home will never be the same.

Artifacts of Arna exist here. They always will because I don't have it in me to throw her in the trash, to disregard her the way she seemingly disregarded me, and I don't want to. It's what I couldn't, can't, won't ever be able to explain to Ethan. I hate her just as much as I love her. People are funny that way—we spend our whole lives hoping we won't get hurt by the people we hold in our hearts, but when they do hurt us, we still bathe in their love. We keep it all—the love, the pain—and we don't just stop loving someone because they hurt us.

But what won't ever exist here are artifacts of Ethan. I have nothing to show for our time together. No evidence. Maybe there's sand in the bottom of my suitcase, caught in the pockets of my shorts, tucked away in the soft cotton crevasses where I'll be finding it for years. Out of sight but never gone. Ethan might be like that now. Existing just underneath the surface, where I can't see him, but when I brush my fingers, my lips, my heart, my soul, past anything he's touched, I'll feel him, and I'll feel his absence grate across me.

I don't know how long I've been staring at the mantle underneath my TV. It was once one of my favorite parts of this house. A seemingly random, outcropping of exposed brick someone had once painted white. Chips of paint flaked off over the years, revealing the faded original red underneath. But I loved that. I adorned that mantle with things I loved—artifacts of my life. But I fucking hate it when I look at it now.

There's the first plaster model of teeth that I made to work on in dental school, now down the right incisor, because Arna fucking dropped it once when she was drunk; a misshapen ceramic pot I made in a class that's empty because I can't keep any plant alive for the life of me, a fossilized shark tooth I found on vacation, books. Things that are supposed to represent me. Who I am. Who, and what, fills my life. But I fucking hate it, and I want to swipe my arm across it and send it all shattering to the ground. I want to smash the glass that covers shiny, artificial smiling photos of Arna and me. Because Ethan will never exist here. Because of her. Because of me. Because I don't think I have ever really existed in this house. Not really.

The edges of my eyes water, and I wipe at them unceremoniously with the backs of my hands before turning and going up my creaky staircase to my bedroom on the top floor. I leave the suitcase—Arna's letters and anything Ethan has ever touched—toppled over by the door.

Upon closer inspection, my life might be pitifully empty when you peel back the layers of my skin, open the door to my home. But it's mine, and I do the only thing I can think of. I step back into it, and I start living it again.

My strawberries are touching my hard-boiled egg, and there's a green stem still left on one. I never forget to put that stupid divider in the container to make sure nothing touches. And I was positive I had scooped out all the stems this morning. There's a specific tool I used for it that I never forgot—

"I didn't realize you were back," a voice sounds, and a body in the same black scrubs as me, albeit a much broader one, steps into the room with the name of the dental practice also embroidered across the chest.

But instead of saying Dr. Morris like mine do, his chest reads "Dr. Stern."

I jerk upward, fingers digging into the side of my useless Tupperware. "Dr. Stern. Hi. I am that. Back."

He rolls his neck, too-long blond hair flopping everywhere and devoid of the usual elastic he keeps it pulled back with, before he grabs the remote sitting in the middle of the staff table. He smiles at me lazily. "Call me Sam. I don't call you Dr. Morris."

"Well, maybe you should." I shrug, eyes narrowed while I begin to pick the stem remnants off my strawberry.

The vague hum of the TV starts, changing ever so often as he flicks through the channels. This is wrong. All wrong because little pieces of the stem are breaking off, there are tiny seeds on my fingers now, and the whole berry is getting mushy.

"Ethan Barclay dressed for practice this morning. No word on if he will play yet. The team says he's still undergoing physical therapy for the Achilles injury that took him out last season before the failed drug test that, as you will all remember, led to him becoming an unsigned free agent in the off-season."

And then there he is. Or there's a pixelated, broadcast, sorry replica of Ethan playing on the TV in the staff room. It's been almost two months, and he's a whole different version of himself. His hair is shorter, and his face is clean-shaven. He's nodding along with something a coach is saying to him, kicking a ball up with his feet before bouncing it on his knees.

The strawberry is still sitting uselessly in my palm, red bleeding into my skin. TV Ethan is now taking off his warm-up shirt, tossing it behind him without a care in the world. Like I had seen him do with his own shirts, with my shirts.

"Not only is he sporting a new team's jersey, it looks like a new tattoo sleeve is in the works."

The strawberry rolls off my palm when I stand, shoes squeaking against the linoleum. And then I'm in front of the TV. Sam is talking to me, asking what I'm doing. My strawberry collects dust on the ground, and my egg still touches the other ones in the container. But Ethan has a new tattoo. And it's for me.

"It looks like it might be the start of a bigger piece, but it's pretty clear what's in the center. Looks like it says "Ten," but as you can see, he's still wearing the number eight. Wonder what he was up to in the off-season."

I'm in the middle of his arm. *Ten.* The alleged tenth month. November.

Ethan Barclay is playing soccer, and I'm counting seeds.

For the first time in my life, I turn my work phone off when I walk in the door of my townhome. I had turned my personal phone off, too, but the number of people who would ever use that number is realistically down to zero. The few colleagues I'm social with only have the other number. It might also be the first time I don't relish how entirely silent the house is.

I toe off my shoes and kick them off; the left one goes wayward and hits my still abandoned suitcase. It's been two months, and I've left it there, keeping a minimum two-foot radius away from it at all times when I walk down the hall, like if I were to touch it, so much as brush it accidentally, or God forbid open it, all those grains of sand, all that's left of Ethan, left of Arna, might spill out into my otherwise empty house.

But all I can see is Ethan, that TV version of him that would never be able to compare to the real thing—that fake version of him would be all I would ever get because the real version is thousands of miles away. That's the version I'll have to settle for. I'll be watching him for the rest of my life, all the while knowing that I almost had the real thing.

And there it is—nestled in and amongst my broken bones and shredded muscle and the unending, unyielding sadness—the kernel of pride that swells at the thought of him. It illuminates everything for a moment, that he's back doing what he loves, what he was born to do. Maybe that's what it means to love someone; that you can hold multiple truths, two absolutes in your heart at the same time: I love Arna, I hate Arna. I miss Ethan more than I can quantify, but I'm endlessly proud he's back where he belongs, where he's meant to be.

All those things are true, but I blink, and it's just me and my empty house again.

I'm still wearing my scrubs as I pad through the hallway, leaving the wide berth for the suitcase. My townhome is nice. I like it, I do. I just think I would like it better with Ethan in it.

My eyes flick over the mostly bare, white walls that are unburdened with no photographs, no art, no posters. It's one of those smaller, wartime homes that still retains a lot of those original features, and I always loved that. It gives it character when I don't add anything to it.

The kitchen was remodeled sometime before I bought it, and even though it's more modern with a waterfall marble island taking up the center and brushed navy cabinetry, I like it. A wine fridge sits under the island, only ever home to dry white and champagne unless Arna was visiting. She had an unusual taste for red. But there's one space for beer at the bottom, and now there's a six-pack of a random Filipino beer I pulled off the shelf at the beer store because it reminds me of Ethan.

Four cognac leather barstools are tucked into the island. Four, because that's how many can fit, not because that's ever the number of people I have here. A sliding door is just beyond the island, looking out into my small backyard. It's fenced in, which is a rarity in the city.

The door opens to a tiny deck, home to two chairs. One is mine, one was Arna's; and beyond that, a small fire table sits in the yard. Lights are strung across the fence, and their cords go every which way to hang above the yard. The whole display is kind of a fucking mess, if I'm being honest. But I love it, just like I've always loved messy, broken things; and now I wonder if that's because they remind me of me.

I bend down to retrieve one of those bottles of beer before grabbing the opener that I left sitting on the island just above the fridge. I pop up to sit on the counter, swinging my legs back and forth while I look around.

My fingertips are cold against the already-sweating bottle because I forgot to turn the air conditioner on before I left for work, so my house is too warm. But I like the way the little beads of perspiration feel against my hands. They remind me of all the times I held a bottle like this, but I drank it through a smile because Ethan was sitting next to me.

My eyes swing back and forth, and I can peek through the other doorway and see into my living room. It's a good home. A good home to share with someone. I've just never really found that I wanted to before. But I would have liked to share it with Ethan. I would have liked to share a lot of things with him. But he's not here. He's on the TV. So, I take a sip of the beer, close my eyes, and pretend.

Chapter Thirty-One

Levi Morrison. Thirty-four. Two kids.

The only man Arna cared enough about to spend more than one night with—other than Jake—and the almost love of her life.

I don't even know why I looked Levi up. But I just wanted to know what he looked like. He's beautiful, in almost the exact same way Arna was beautiful—imposing, haughty features, eyes that look like they are seeing right through you. They would have made a terrifying match, judging by his business portfolio.

Maybe I looked him up because I hadn't been sleeping.

Getting to share a bed with Ethan, in more ways than one, and now being relegated to my own empty one was a special kind of torture. If I close my eyes, I can feel it. The exact weight of him beside me, how it would cause the bed to sink down and my body to shift into his, intrinsically, like maybe we were magnets instead of it being simple physics. I like the idea that maybe there's a magnet in my heart and a matching one in his. And how sad is that? Two opposite poles, two hearts straining for one another at the opposite ends of the world.

I'm combing through pictures of Levi's wedding on social media, and judging by the date stamp, it took place about two years after he met Arna. It was a beautiful wedding, taking place on some estate somewhere in Australia. She was a beautiful bride, whoever she was.

Not as beautiful as Arna would have been.

I rub at my chest absentmindedly. It hurts me to see him married to someone else when my best friend loved him. It hurts me to think about how it must have hurt Arna. She would have pretended it didn't bother her, proceeded to tip her nose in the air and tell anyone who would listen how she was too good for him, anyway. But I would have been able to see it in her eyes, if I had known.

I don't even notice when my eyes start to burn and blur. I cry all the time now.

I cried about them both. My great lost loves. When I sobbed about Arna, it would usually devolve into anger, and that was what I preferred because when I cried about Ethan, I had no one to be mad at but myself.

But when I cried for Ethan, sobbed because I loved him and I lost him, those were the times I missed Arna the most. When I wished she was there to stroke my hair, to cook for me, to hire someone to clean my house, because God knows she wouldn't have done it herself, to make sure my meals were balanced and no nefarious behaviors were sneaking up on me. The way I missed her, my love for her, curled up in my heart right beside the places I hated her, those two feelings somehow learning to co-exist, cohabitate and just become another part of me that's torn.

"November?"

Blinking, I look away from the screen. I've been sitting in the practice office at the back of the clinic, in front of a silver iMac that's usually reserved for charting. I was going to leave, go home, but I just sat down here and started looking instead.

"Shiya, Olivia." I smile at each of them, taking off the oversized blue light glasses I sometimes wear.

The stitching over the left side of their scrubs blurs, but I know the letters stitched there say Dr. Borhani and Dr. Porter, respectively. They're best friends, younger than me but not by much, and they both graduated from the same dental school that I did.

"We're heading out, and we were going to grab a drink. We saw you were still here—did you want to join us?" Olivia smiles at me.

I can tell she means it. When you spend as much time around people's mouths as I do, you develop a keen sense for when a smile is strained. Neither of theirs are. They're both open, genuine, entirely inviting.

I study them for a moment longer, and my heart hurts, a visceral pang in my chest. They look entirely dissimilar from Arna and me. But it's like looking at a funhouse mirror version of us. The people we could have been if we weren't the people we are. They're both all soft features, happy eyes, and pillowy cheeks. Arna looked haughty, permanently pursed lips and squared-off shoulders, making her look taller than she was, and some sort of glint in her eyes at all times. They were secrets, I know now. Olivia is blonde like me, but I'm certain her hair is natural. Shiya looks more like Arna. Darker complexion and features, hair impossibly smooth.

I don't know why, but I say yes. "Sure, I'd love to. I just need to grab my stuff."

Those genuine smiles stay there—not a hint of disappointment or falter in the muscles to make me think it was all a ruse.

"We were thinking of going just across the street. Does that work?" Olivia smiles at me again as we fall into step beside one another, winding through the white, overly modern and unfortunately sterile back hallway toward the staff room.

There's a tiny hole-in-the-wall bar right across the street that's also the most popular karaoke spot in the city on Friday nights. A lot of the other dentists go here after work. It's a standing invitation I've almost always rejected. But I nodded this time.

A hand—a tiny ineffectual hand like my own—grabs my arm and my eyes flick up. I try not to look alarmed or to cringe, but Shiya stares at me imploringly. "I have actually been dying to pick your brain about something—I'd love to know about your certification process. I was on the ABFO website the other day, and the certification list seemed endless. I know you don't need to be certified to start practicing and do the work, but it just feels so daunting."

"Oh." I smile at her and nod. She's not wrong. The certification process for the American Board of Forensic Odontologists feels almost malignant it's so fucking intricate and complex. "I don't think I knew you had an interest in forensics?"

A sort of snort, but one that's so clearly of endearment and love, comes from Olivia, and she wrinkles her nose. "Please don't get her started. It's only the reason she went into dentistry. It all started when she was eight years old, and she and her brother watched a CSI re-rerun and a body was dug up in the desert."

I watch Shiya roll her eyes, all movements and gestures exaggerated. Like it's a routine between them—endless teasing of one another about their passions and dreams. I recognize it all the way down to my ruined bones—they're probably malignant, too, poisoned with lies. It's like watching Arna's lips turn down and eyes go wide when she would tell me how weird I was, that no one should be a dentist let alone aspire to be one that wants to play with bones.

But it seems to end there for these two, just a teasing display of friendship. Nothing sinister is hiding beneath the surface.

"You were so young when you passed your examinations. How'd you even find the time to complete that many cases?" She continues, holding the door to the staff room open for me.

Another voice, my favorite voice, whispers in my ear. I still just as I open my locker, certain for a moment I can feel his lips by my ear, telling me my big, brilliant brain was capable of anything, and that I should never have spent so much time living in someone's shadow.

Photos stick to the back of the matte black metal door. My sweater hangs on a hook just beyond it. Some of the photos are the same as the ones that were stuck to the cement wall back when I was in boarding school. Photos of Arna and me that stood the test of time, with new ones stuck there. I almost laugh when my eyes land on a photo of us with Jake. We're spread out across a leather couch in a basement club somewhere she took us to in Prague. I'm leaning against him, and Arna is lying across the two of us, some sort of backless dress reminiscent of a disco ball riding up her legs and her arm extended, ending in an entirely unironic peace sign.

I grab my sweater and gingerly shut the locker door. I turn, offering them a small smile; one that's not exactly painful, maybe it's just one of acceptance. "I didn't have much of a life."

That tiny hole in the wall, where everyone I work with goes, had a beer on tap that is supposed to be the Canadian equivalent of Bia Hoi. The freshest beer in the world. My newly acquired taste for beer aside, I think it was just fine. It paled in comparison to the real thing because there wasn't a beautiful boy sitting across from me in a tiny chair.

I decided to walk home after hugging Shiya and Olivia goodbye. It felt weird, stilted maybe, but only a little. We stayed for three drinks, and it was the first time I can remember not missing Arna so much in a social situation that it was like someone had hacked off my right arm with a rib saw. I missed Ethan all the same, though. I smiled, and I meant it. I think he would have liked it. Anxiety had started to gnaw at my stomach when we sat down in the peeling, red leather booth. That I might say something strange. That they might not like me, but the conversation was easy. Companionable. I've started to wonder how much of those fears were of my own making, and how many were fed by Arna because she liked me where I was.

They made me promise I would go out with them the next time everyone else did. I think I was honest when I said yes.

I meant to go home. But I started walking, and I stopped when I saw the reflection of a soccer match in the window of the beer store, where it was playing on a TV hanging above the walk-in freezer. Ethan wasn't playing, but I walked in and watched for a moment before I pulled a pack off the shelf, something that looked like he might like it.

I end up in an entirely different neighborhood.

Chapter Thirty-Two

I hold the six-pack up when Jake pulls open the door. He starts, pulling his head back. The top three buttons of his shirt are undone, and his sandy hair is mussed. It always looked like that after a long day spent running his hands through it, tugging on the ends, looking at whatever numbers were floating across his screen at work. It's probably the picture of perfect, attractive to almost anyone else on the street.

But it's boring to me because it's not unkempt, dark curls that tattooed hands have run through one too many times.

"Nov." Jake pulls the door open and steps aside. "Since when do you drink beer?"

"Recently acquired taste." I eye Jake for a moment before walking past him into the hallway that leads to his apartment.

Two bedrooms, wraparound balcony, very boring beige furniture, and in one of the most uppity neighborhoods in the city. It's almost entirely the same as when I left it two years ago. That doesn't surprise me, though. He was never much for change, thriving on routine and stability.

My feet are quiet against the floor as I move into the living room. Two cell phones sit on the coffee table, and I can see the giant desktop monitor glowing where it sits in the office, the door still open. "Did you just finish work?"

"Yeah," I hear his voice, and the door closes.

His footsteps follow mine down the hallway. I still know them, could probably pick them out of some sort of auditory lineup, but they sound all wrong to me now. I drop the six-pack on the coffee table, fishing two bottles out.

"Looks like you did, too." He tips his chin toward me. I'm still wearing my scrubs.

Jake stops short of standing too close to me, and he smiles in thanks when he takes the bottle from me. He turns, moving to the sideboard stretching across the wall where he keeps a dry bar.

"They're just a twist-off," I tell him, tentatively dropping down into the chair across from the couch. "You don't need to use your teeth or anything."

"Who would use their teeth?" He looks over his shoulder, features pulling in confusion.

The ghost of a smile pulls at the corner of my lips. "You'd be surprised."

He says nothing and drops onto the couch across from me. "I didn't think I'd ever see you again."

"Me either." I raise my eyebrows and shrug.

Jake eyes me for a moment, looking like he's rolling a question around before he finally asks it. "What happened with you two? You and Barclay…can't imagine he'd be thrilled about me even breathing the same air as you if he was still in the picture."

A dry laugh escapes me, and I lean back in the chair, grip tightening on the bottle ever so slightly. "What do you think happened?"

Jake laughs, but it's entirely humorless. "Arna Pavlides, still pulling strings from beyond the grave."

My nostrils flare, and my throat burns. "Did you hate her the whole time?"

"No, I didn't hate her, November." Jake shakes his head, lips pulling to the side before he tips the beer back. "But she had her claws in you, and she was never fucking letting go. I don't think Arna was ever happy. Not with herself. I think you made her happy, maybe not for the right reasons. But you did."

I shake my head, tipping it back and biting on the inside of my lips as my vision blurs. "What am I supposed to do now? How am I supposed to reconcile the fact that she wasn't who I thought she was when—"

"She loved you," Jake interrupts, leaning forward and setting the bottle down on the coffee table. "I know it doesn't count when I say it, not after what we did. I was a terrible person, and she was a terrible person. We can call it what it is. I saw a chance to get back at you for not loving me the way I wanted you to. I don't know what the fuck she was thinking. But she loved you. That much is true."

I scoff, a loud exhale through my nose, and close my eyes, but Jake keeps talking.

His voice is soft when he says it, words that find their way down to my heart. "You should go to London, November. He's playing again, you know?"

"I know. I saw him on TV."

Jake nods, and his voice is tentative, a fragile olive branch. "Doesn't even look like he's ever been injured."

A small smile unfurls on my lips.

"That makes you happy?" Jake asks through a laugh, pressing his fingers to the bridge of his nose.

I nod, offering him a shrug. "It does."

"You should be happy, Nov," Jake offers, looking down and worrying at the label on the bottle with his thumb. "I don't think you ever looked like that when you were talking about me."

"I don't think you ever looked like that when you were talking about me, either," I point out. It's the truth. "It was a lukewarm love, Jake."

He raises his eyebrows, lips pulling down in consideration. "I guess it was."

"I didn't come to stay for long. I just had to—I don't know. I should go." I tip back the rest of my beer before pushing up to stand.

"I mean what I said. You should be happy." Jake pauses, shoving his hands in his pockets before offering me a rueful smile. He gestures to the hallway, and we fall into step beside one another, footsteps echoing together one last time. "He's still a fucking asshole, though."

That makes me smile, too, because it's true, but Ethan is perfect just the way he is. "You're right. He's not very polite."

Jake clears his throat. "I am sorry—for hurting you."

I pause, pulling open the front door before looking back at him over my shoulder. "I don't forgive you. At least not yet."

"You don't ever have to. But if I'm ever in London, I'll look you up. Think he'd give me free tickets?"

I smile at him when he leans in the doorway. "Not a chance."

Jake's mouth pulls to the side, and he rests his head against the door-frame. He exhales, eyes soft. "You deserve a life you love, November. One that's entirely your own."

I raise my hand at him, a silent farewell, and stare for just a moment longer before turning away from him—from one of the last pieces of Arna I didn't even know she left behind.

A life that's entirely my own. It wouldn't be living if it wasn't a life with Ethan in it.

The stoop of my townhouse is empty when I get home, no box that contains all of my best friend's secrets in life and in death sitting there.

I stop right before the steps because I can see myself, wearing the same scrubs I'm still in, but I'm minus a spurt of blood today. Tipping my head, I watch that old version of me, trembling, falling to her knees, and gutturally sobbing. A whole different version of me. An entire lifetime ago.

Walking up the steps, arms crossed over my chest, I'm covering that phantom spurt of blood, like I used to do out of habit because it felt like my heart was going to fall out of my chest at any given moment. But there's no blood, and I turn the key and shoulder into the empty foyer.

What's left of Arna, that whole different version of me, my former life, the tiny bits and pieces I have of Ethan, sit in my overturned suitcase.

I tentatively uncross my arms, letting my bag drop to the worn wood floor beside me. Inhaling, I wait for it. For the screaming, visceral pain, for ribs to break apart, and my heart to fall out onto the floor.

But nothing happens. It beats just as it should. Blood into the right atrium, through to the right ventricle, and out into the pulmonary arteries of my lungs. It gets oxygenated and goes back to my heart through the pulmonary veins and into my left atrium, through to the left ventricle, and out into my body through my aorta. I think those pieces of my heart were shredded in that former life of mine. They were probably never fully functioning, anyway.

My footsteps are soft, tentative even, like a fawn on new, spindly legs. It's an apt metaphor. Because maybe that's me now, in this post-Arna, post-Ethan world. It's certainly a world I never would have imagined for myself.

I settle to the floor beside the suitcase, carefully crossing my legs under me, and it occurs to me that we live so many different lives. How many different versions of ourselves we get to be. Arna had many different lives. Ones I knew about, and those I didn't.

I unzip the suitcase.

Crumpled clothing spills from the inside, haphazardly shoved in there by me. I pick up the first thing closest to me—just a plain black tank top, the cotton soft under my fingertips. It smells like sunshine. Letting it fall to the floor, I push the heaps of clothing aside, grains of sand brushing against my skin, until I feel the letters. The edges are worn now, and I purposely run my finger along them. No cuts to be found. I push them all aside until I find the one that's labeled in dumb calligraphy that for some reason makes me want to smile, to laugh at this moment—The End.

The letter that was meant to be her grand finale. The last piece of her. I should be scared, but instead I tug the letter out of the pile and hold it to my chest as I stand. The sounds of my footsteps down my hallway are louder than they should be, reverberating against the bare walls, all the way up the stairs to the empty bed I've started to leave unmade because it's easier to see the broad shoulders and valley of muscle, the wisps of ink that taper down deltoids when I close my eyes. The house that I loved. That belonged to a different me.

The door to my backyard makes a noise, too, and it kind of reminds me of a death rattle. I pause to turn on the lights hanging above me, strewn lazily across the fence in no particular order. Arna's handywork. She gave up halfway through trying to string them together in equal distances apart and just started attaching the strings wherever she wanted, throwing some over the tree toward the end of the yard. We left it like that.

I move past our chairs—mine and hers—that sit on the deck and pad down the steps onto the grass. I can tell it's wet with dew, but I don't care and drop to the ground in front of the fire. The propane turns on with a switch, and the flames spring to life, making me blink rapidly for a moment.

I can't count how many nights I sat out here with Arna. In that old, different life. I thought I was living one particular story, and I thought I knew hers, too. But that's not the way it turned out.

My fingers tear at the envelope, carefully pulling out the letter, and I look up at the lights for a moment before I unfold it.

I knew the life she lived with me. That version of her, the person I knew. She was real, and she existed here with me. She was there and always will be, living in my bones and in the muscle tissue of my heart the way that people we love do.

I should be scared, but I'm not. Because there was a version of her that was real, and she was mine.

My greatest love,

If you're reading this, you're home. Wherever that is for you now. I hope it's still your townhouse. I hope your fridge, your heart, you—I hope they're all full. I hope our chairs are still together in the backyard, facing one another, and I hope the lights are still swinging above them, the strings all chaos and confused wires. I hope the first dental mold you ever made is still on your mantle. I hope it's still missing the incisor. I'm sorry I broke it. I don't think I ever apologized for that.

I'm sure you're wondering why, and you knew me well enough to know there wasn't usually a great, deep reason for anything I did. I'd hate to disappoint you and change things up after I die. You've always known who you are, and I'm not sure I ever really knew who I was. I was always trying different things on, and nothing ever really fit. Nothing except you. Sometimes I worry that I've kept you small, kept you reliant on me and just mine on purpose. But I liked the way it made me feel, our friendship. I was wanted, needed, valuable.

I wish I had a reason for all the things I did. The things that I kept from you, the things that I knew would hurt you. Maybe I was just chasing something you had.

I wonder if I changed anything after writing this. Not everyone spends an extensive amount of time planning for their death when they aren't dying. I had time. But if you're reading this, I guess I died without changing a thing. How terribly pedestrian of me—how human. We never do enough with the time we have.

I'm sure you and Sebastian have talked about it, whether my death was premeditated somehow. I'm not sure how it happened, but as of this moment in time, I have no plans to kill myself. It's just always been a feeling, I suppose.

My final secret. Self-fulfilling prophecy, maybe. I always knew I would die young. Maybe that's why I was so reckless. I never thought I would be around long enough for it to matter. But it did matter in the end, didn't it?

People are liars, Nova. I was a liar. But it doesn't mean they don't love.

I hope you forgive me, and I hope you learn to live without me.

If you believe anything, believe this. It was the honor of my life to be your friend, November.

To infinity and beyond,

Arna

"To infinity and beyond," I offer softly, because it's true. As much as she hurt me, as much as I think I still hate her as much as I love her, she was real. My once-in-a-lifetime friend. I don't care what the other letters say, what other lies she told and lives she lived. I don't want to know. I toss the letter down into the fire in front of me.

"Thank you," I whisper as the flame licks and furls across the letter, crawling up the side of the page and eating away at the ink and the words. "For both of my great loves. Yours and his."

I smile, thick with tears, and I can taste the salt on my lips as I look up at that messy cacophony of lights.

If I concentrate hard enough, I can hear us. My laughter and hers. Echoing across this backyard for eternity.

Chapter Thirty-Three

The Pavlides family home in Ekali is still the same. It's as stately, as imposing, as always—it was just missing the rows upon rows of towering taper candles that surrounded Arna's casket. It was missing her lifeless body, too. But I don't think this house would ever really be without Arna. She was too all-encompassing. Her ghost might live with me, live in my very bones, but I was sure she split her time evenly. There was no way the Arna I knew would ever quit haunting these halls. She loved this home. One of her favorite pastimes had been standing at the top of the central staircase, chin tipped up and shoulders rolled back as she watched the world go by below her when it was full of staff or host to Pavlides Inc. employees for an event.

A bag hangs at my side, a random one I pulled from my closet, and upon closer inspection, I realized it came from a trip I went on with Arna to Paris. It's fitting that I would be returning a part of her—her packaged up secrets—back to her home in it. The unread letters in it feel heavy, her

301

script sharing forgotten countries on the envelopes and her secrets sealed within. I follow along behind one of the members of the family staff, who brings me through winding halls where I'm sure a ghost treads, toward the office Sebastian still keeps here.

I can feel my bag pressing against my hip. Maybe her ghost knows that I'm bringing these last pieces of her back home where she belongs.

That I'm giving her up.

The woman stops abruptly, raising her fist in a polite knock against a heavy oak door. I look around, taking in the ornate marble stands that host vases worth more than some people make in a year and the ivory, brocaded walls. There are family portraits that line them, the entire Pavlides family likeness committed to oil on canvas. There's one I avoid looking at, though, but I can spot the haughty expression a mile away.

I recognize Sebastian's voice as it calls for us to come in. I'm still standing there when she swings the door open and announces me, like she's an old school butler and I'm some sort of gentleman caller. When really, I'm returning what's left of his sister to him.

The heavy door swings open, and my heart breaks a bit because Sebastian looks so much like her. But instead of Arna, with her nose perpetually tipped up and somehow looking down at people who tower over her, it's the infinitely softer sibling.

He stands from his desk, and a grin splits across his face at the sight of me. She had the same nose, once upon a time, but Arna decided hers was too big for her face when we were fifteen and came back after summer break with a new one, claiming she had a deviated septum. I liked her original nose—Sebastian's nose. It wasn't delicate by any means, but it had always been perfectly straight.

His chestnut hair—the exact same shade as hers—is pushed off his face, and he doesn't give me a chance to say anything before his arms are around me.

"Nov. You're home." Sebastian's voice is thicker than Arna's, as she never had much of an accent. But you could always hear his.

I want to tell him that I can't really be home because I don't live here, and I've never lived here, but I just hug him, pressing my face into his chest, ignoring the way the buttons on his suit press into my cheek.

He pulls away, hands gripping my shoulder, and the smile he's giving me is so happy, so big, he has no idea I have his sister's last words, whatever her final secrets were, in battered, sealed, envelopes in this bag. I can't help myself and glance sideways at his hands. Unmarred, smooth, olive skin.

I think all hands should have tattoos now.

"I'm back," I finally say.

I don't want my voice to crack, but it does. I give him a small smile and watch his eyebrows crease before he gestures to the empty chair on the other side of his desk.

"So, how was it? My sister's great quest from the beyond." Sebastian asks over his shoulder as he goes back to his tall and imposing chair that rises far beyond his shoulders. He's grinning at me, but it doesn't meet his eyes.

"Enlightening," I offer, because it's the truth, and it's all I have.

His eyebrows narrow momentarily, but then his features are as normal and composed as ever.

I drop and sit stiffly in the chair across from him. The bag feels heavier and heavier. I pull the folder out before I can change my mind, tossing it across the shiny mahogany desk toward him. And there they are, in the bottom of the bag. The last of the letters.

I pick up those from the bag, too, but much more gently. These are the last pieces of her, after all.

The stack is significantly smaller than it was when I found it in that box that was still keeping all her secrets, even in death. There are only six letters left—six countries written across the envelopes in her lilting handwriting. Six countries I'll never go with Ethan.

I hold onto the letters a moment longer, throat aching with unshed tears because those six letters might represent six places I never went with him; six sets of endless possibilities defined by the borders of a map, but they also represent the places we did go. The boundaries we lived in across four countries we existed in together. The letters are gray eyes that look like the night sky; they're tattooed hands and dry irreverence, and they're a brilliant mind that makes an even more brilliant mouth. I almost don't let them go. Because as much as they're the last pieces of Arna, they're my last pieces of Ethan, too.

I clear my throat that feels like someone has carved it up, delicately, precisely—one cut for each secret I'll never have—and I place the letters gently, reverently, on the desk before pushing them toward Sebastian.

"What's this?" he asks quietly, and his voice sounds like someone has carved him up, too.

Manicured fingertips tap against my shoulders, and I know someone has.

I finally look up at him, really look at him. I can see how he wears his grief. It's in the creases of his suit, the way it stretches tight across his shoulders.

"My lawyer drew up the necessary paperwork to sign my shares back over." My voice is soft, and I know he's not asking about the folder. His eyes are focused on the letters, on his sister's handwriting. "It turns out transferring you the money back...my lawyer says—"

"I don't want the money, November. No one wants her money back." Sebastian's voice cracks, and he raises his eyes to me.

At this moment, I'm so glad that they were entirely different people. They had the same eyes, but his are impossibly dark, shrouded with grief and unshed tears. I don't know what I would do if they were Arna's shrewd, calculating eyes staring back at me. She rarely cried, but when she did—they were always hideous, gasping sobs.

I say nothing because I'm not sure I should have given Sebastian these letters, taunting him the way she taunted me.

"That's Arna's stupid handwriting. I'd recognize it anywhere. You remember she spent that whole summer with a private calligraphy tutor?" He clears his throat, and he palms his jaw. "But I've never seen those. There was nothing in her will aside from—"

I exhale, tipping my head and taking one final look at that handwriting that she did work tirelessly to perfect—she thought it was fitting for someone of her "station." I take one look at all those secrets I was leaving behind, giving away, even though they weren't really mine to give.

Looking up at him, I finally speak. "She left me letters. She left me letters, and she left me secrets. She wanted me to go to all these different places she had been and try all these different foods and—"

Sebastian interrupts, "This feels very premeditated. Her death was an accident. In the letters—did she—are these some sort of suicide note?"

I shake my head and want to laugh because he's forgotten who his sister was. "She was dramatic, Seb. Even in death. There was no way it wouldn't have been a production."

His eyes widen, and a strangled laugh bubbles in his throat. But it's wet with unshed tears. "These don't look open."

"That's because they aren't. She left me those secrets, too, Sebastian. And I don't think I wanted to know them all. Her stipulation was that I could give it all back to you, the shares, the inheritance, but only when it was all done. But I tapped out around letter five, and as it turns out, her will wasn't all that ironclad."

I tip my chin toward the folder that contains the paperwork.

But Sebastian isn't looking at me. He's focused on the envelopes again. I can see it in his eyes now, that he's curious. He's wondering what pieces of his sister those letters might hold; what he might be able to claw back from death and keep safe on this side of life.

"I'm not sure I would read those, if I were you," I whisper, like I'm afraid her ghost might hear and tell me all the things I don't want to know anyway.

"They can't be that bad," Sebastian answers, voice half a whisper, too.

"I suppose that's all relative." I shrug, blinking rapidly because all I can think of now is what those secrets cost me. I clear my throat. "Anyway, like I said. Shares are back in the company name. Money is a bit more complicated. For that amount, I can't really gift it to you, but my lawyer said—"

"Keep it." His voice is firm, and his jaw muscle twitches as he looks at me. "She'd want you to have it. I want you to have it. Open a dental practice, and do all your work for free, I don't care. Do something that makes you happy." My lips part to argue, even though I don't really have anything to say, but Sebastian keeps talking. "She loves you, you know that right, Nov?" His eyes are imploring now, like he wants to drop to his knees and beg me to fix whatever it is his sister broke. "In life, and in death. She loves you."

"I love her too," I offer quietly, because it's true, and it always will be.

He nods, blowing air out and making his cheeks puff before he says something that breathes all the air back into me before robbing me of it. "I heard a rumor, you know?" I arch an eyebrow at him, and he continues. "Friend of mine who plays in the pro league over here said he saw a photo of you with a guy who plays over in England. He was kissing your forehead at some beachside bar in a tiny little town in Costa Rica. Says he recognized you from pictures I've posted."

My vision edges in now, and I feel the tears well on my lash line. "Sounds like quite a rumor mill churns over here in Ekali."

A snort of air flares his nostrils, and a wistful sort of smile pulls at his mouth. "She'd want you to share your life with someone."

My voice cracks, and some of the bitterness seeps out. "Really? Because it doesn't seem like she wanted to share me at all."

"Is there anything I can do? Anything to fix whatever it is she broke?" Sebastian whispers, and there's so much behind those words. They're thick with anguish, and I know he would do anything to help his sister, even after she left the Earth.

I'm crying now because the only person who can fix this is me. "Never give me those letters back, even if I beg."

I'm half-joking, but it's the truth at the end of the day. I can't choose a ghost over myself, or anyone, ever again.

His eyes crack a bit, and his lips part to say more, but there's nothing he can do for me.

"I love him," I tell him uselessly, shrugging as a gasping sob escapes me. It's the kind of crying I only ever would have done around his sister. "I love him, and I chose her over him."

"What can I do?" Sebastian's voice is strangled, and he stretches a hand out to me. I feel myself recoil slightly, but I take it anyway. "Let me help. You don't have to do everything alone, Nov."

I sit there, holding his hand, and crying for a while because I don't have an answer, for him, or for me. I just know I need Ethan. I want him, and I'll do anything to show him. My pride is long forgotten.

I finally look up at Sebastian, lashes thick with tears. I watch one escape his eyes and track down his cheek, too. "Can you do me a favor?"

Chapter Thirty-Four

I've been on the Pavlides jet before, but it was usually just with Arna.

Today, it was with Arna and Sebastian. She was so fucking nosey there was no way she wasn't there, lips pursed as she listened to every word we said.

Sebastian told me how often he thinks of her, quite similar to me, actually; that she's gone but not gone because how could someone so effervescent and bright ever really disappear? Someone so magnetic that there was no way they became fully untethered from everyone who loved them when their body stopped functioning.

He told me how her death strained his relationship because he never expected to be without his parents and his sister in this lifetime, and he asked me about Ethan, so I told him.

That he's perfect, entirely impossible to leave, entirely impossible to forget.

In the end, neither of us wanted to know all of Arna's secrets. She was complicated, an ambiguous, morally gray character from a novel brought to life, a heroine or a villain depending on the day, and she probably played both roles for longer than we ever knew.

It sounded nice, actually. The idea of her like that. No secrets. Just us and the memory of the person we loved with our whole hearts.

The stadium is huge—bigger than any sports venue I've ever been in—but the list was small to begin with. Now Sebastian and I walk alongside the team sponsorship director, Christian, but I'm barely paying attention to him.

I only care that I'm breathing the same air as Ethan Barclay. I don't even really remember what Sebastian said, something about Pavlides Inc. being interested in an advertisement package.

I'm trailing behind them, watching Sebastian nod thoughtfully with his hands casually tucked into the pants of a dove gray suit. The director is gesturing every which way, pointing at various things like concessions and alcohol endorsements.

We round the corner, and I cross my arms just for something to do when I stumble, sandal catching on the worn stone floor, and crash right into Sebastian's back; we've come out into the open concourse, and there's a giant photo of Ethan that stretches from floor to ceiling. His name and the number eight are written in giant navy block letters beside him. He's in his new jersey, his new team-issued equipment, and he's holding a soccer ball in his palm. The way his arm is outstretched, you can see his new tattoo. The one for me.

Sebastian turns around, grabbing me with steadying hands. His eyes swing to the larger-than-life poster before swinging back to me, and I watch them soften. He smiles at me before squeezing my shoulder and turning to the director. "I heard you signed Ethan Barclay. That's a pretty big get, even after the...scandal."

I'm still studying the photo of Ethan, looking at his face—hair shaved on either side and the top cropped close. His jaw still looks like it could cut out your heart, and his cheekbones are as sharp as ever. Those gray eyes, though—they look impossibly dark. He might look sullen, irritated even, to anyone who doesn't know him. But I know him. And I know he's just concentrating.

"Mhm. He's still a star. It's pretty unbelievable. He plays like he never had surgery." Christian nods thoughtfully, hands still folded demurely behind his back.

"Any chance we can see him play?" Sebastian asks, his voice the picture of casualness, and his expression giving nothing away, but his hand still grips my shoulder.

Christian clears his throat, brow furrowing as he checks his watch. It's a Patek Phillipe. I only know that because Arna wore one that belonged to her father, and she never took it off. He looks up at us and nods. "Practice should have just started. It's closed, but we can make an exception for interested investors."

Sebastian nods, one piece of chestnut hair flopping onto his forehead. He seems entirely unfazed and doesn't seem to care that we've pretended to act so interested, he's probably going to have to write some sort of check. "That'd be great. Dr. Morris is a big fan."

He winks at me, and I smile politely like it's just that. But *big fan* is a gross understatement.

I think Ethan Barclay put the stars in my sky. He certainly hung the moon, and I think he's all the oxygenated blood in my body.

Christian nods, smiling at me while he gestures to an open stairwell on our right. "I'm not surprised. He's very popular amongst fans of your...demographic. The jersey has been our number one seller amongst women aged 18-30."

"I doubt anyone is a bigger fan than Dr. Morris," Sebastian responds, his voice cool. "After you."

He turns on the heel of his polished shoe and strides toward the stairwell. Sunshine spills through the open walkway, and I squint as Sebastian and I fall into step behind him.

I think my heart might beat out of my chest—might very well fracture one of my left ribs. Ribs don't often fracture cleanly, so it would be my luck that I'd end up stabbing myself in the heart in a bid to get to Ethan.

Sebastian gestures for me to step ahead of him, follow this man down, down, down toward that impossibly bright green field. To Ethan.

But I pause and look up toward Sebastian. The sun beats down on us now, so I have to shield my eyes to see him.

"Thank you," I whisper, my voice thick and cracking. "You didn't have to commit to this so thoroughly."

Sebastian smiles down at me, eyes crinkling. "I'm probably going to have to write a check, but that's okay."

Then, we speak at the same time. A stupid saying that we each heard his sister say more times than we could probably count. "What's a million when you have a billion?"

Sebastian and I stop, two feet suspended in mid-air for a moment before we start down the steps to the field.

A smile cracks across his face, and Arna's ghost places her manicured fingers at the edges of my mouth and tugs my lips upward, too.

We stare and smile at one another before I need to wipe my eyes. Sebastian's look like they might be glistening, too.

"What a stupid fucking saying," I whisper, but it's half a wet laugh. "She was so dumb sometimes."

"She really was," Sebastian whispers in return.

We stay here for a moment longer before he clears his throat and tips his chin down toward the field.

"What are you going to say?" he asks as we fall into step beside one another again.

I look toward the field, and it's really just a mass of bodies clad in the same navy warm-up jersey with the team's crest stamped on the chest.

But I see him before I see his name or his number. Even from this far away, my heart knows it's him. I feel a tiny flower bloom up from the marrow of my bones, and I can feel my lungs open just a bit extra because we're breathing the same air again.

I know it's him. I've memorized the way his tattoos twist just so on the cords of his forearm muscles, the way his full lips pull tight when he's concentrating, and I probably know the breadth of his chest and shoulders down to the millimeter.

I watch as he pulls back his leg, the faint scar hidden beneath his equipment, and then I see his foot connect with the ball, the exact way he told me it's supposed to—not with your toes, with the inside of your foot. He doesn't flinch when it connects, and it looks so effortless that my bones crack open and flowers erupt from every single one.

"He looks happy," I whisper, even though that's not what Sebastian asked.

"So do you," he answers softly, and I turn away from watching Ethan, my eyes thick with tears that make Sebastian nothing but a designer suit wearing blur.

"Mr. Pavlides, Dr. Morris?" Christian's voice carries from where he's standing at the bottom of the stairs, by a railing just before the field, talking to someone carrying a clipboard.

His voice carries up to us, and I look back to the field. No one else has noticed or cared, but I watch when Ethan's head snaps up at the sound of my name.

And then my life must have been borrowed from a movie because he's sprinting across the field toward this side. Someone shouts his name, and I'm moving down the steps as Ethan vaults himself over the railing. I'm running now, and I don't have it in me to be embarrassed because I just want to touch him.

We collide on the second to last landing.

Ethan's arms are around me, and mine are around him, hands greedily mapping the broad muscles of his back. One of his hands finds the back of my head and presses me right into his chest above his heart.

"Barclay! Get fucking back here!" The voice snaps again, carrying all the way up to us, but I feel Ethan shaking his head against my neck where his face is now buried.

His lips move against my skin. "Not a fucking chance."

A whistle blows, and Ethan pulls away, looking down at me. I can tell my face is wet with tears, and his eyes crease, a thumb brushing my cheeks. My favorite thumb. The one that has the number that's tattooed on my heart, too.

"I was coming down there to you," I tell him, and I can taste the salt from my tears on my lips.

"No fucking way was I letting you take all those steps alone." Ethan's voice is low and strained, and my heart hurts a bit as his eyes trace my face, like he's checking if I'm real.

Both hands cup the side of my face, and he brings his lips to my forehead and then each of my cheeks before he drops them to the bridge of my nose.

"How'd you get in here?" he asks, a grin stretching across his face.

I hear footsteps behind us, and just over his shoulder, I can see a man that must be his coach and Christian storming up the stairs, but I don't care because my hands are on Ethan Barclay's chest, and he's holding my heart.

"Trickery," I say softly, looking up at him.

I can feel the tears weighing down my eyelashes, but the sunlight makes everything sparkle, and I don't care.

"Good girl," Ethan's voice is rough, and he drops to his knees, wrapping his arms around my waist.

He buries his head in my stomach, and my hands find his shoulders, fingers digging in. I never want to let go.

Sebastian clears his throat, and he comes to stop beside us on the landing, hands shoved into his pockets again. Christian seems to be whispering fervent apologies, and Ethan's coach looks like he might be suffering from a myocardial infarction.

Ethan doesn't seem like he's ever going to move, and he certainly doesn't care that his coach has barked his name again. I can feel his fingers grip me tighter, and his face push into my waist.

Sebastian speaks first, and his voice is smooth, like the scene before him isn't out of place at all, and it probably wasn't. He was used to theatrics. "Christian, if you'll accompany me back to your office, I'd be happy to start the paperwork for corporate sponsorship."

"Barclay, get off your fucking knees NOW."

Ethan turns his head, fingers drumming on my waist, his cheek now pressed into my stomach. His coach stands in a similar jersey, but it's red, with his salt and pepper eyebrows narrowed in on Ethan.

"Sorry, bit hard to control yourself when the love of your life reappears." His words are punctuated with dry laughter, but he's looking at me now, those gray eyes imploring.

The love of his life. I see a muscle twitch in his jaw, and the cords of muscle in his neck are tense. How many times has he heard me say the love of my life was dead and gone?

But all those flowers blooming through my cracked bones tell me otherwise.

"Barclay, get up, now. Windsprints. I don't care if the fucking Pope shows up. If you're not back on that field in three—"

Ethan stands, tattooed hands cupping my face now, and lips finding my forehead again. "Don't go anywhere, please?"

The last word is just for me. It's soft, full of the vulnerability I think he's only ever shown me.

"I'm not going anywhere," I tell him, leaning into his hand. "It would be impossible to leave you."

And then that hand, my favorite hand, is pointing toward Christian, who still looks decidedly put out. "Give her whatever she wants, Christian."

Ethan looks back to me, a grin stretching across his features, before he winks and starts walking backward down the stairs, like he can't bear to look away from me.

"Barclay! Walk forward. If you trip and tear your fucking Achilles again, I swear to God—"

He raises his hands, palms up in defeat, still grinning at me before turning and jogging after his coach down to the field.

Christian clears his throat, looking at me with pursed lips and poorly veiled irritation. "Bit more than a fan I see?"

"No," I shake my head truthfully. "I think I'm his biggest."

Glancing over at Sebastian, I see his features are soft in a way his sister's never could have achieved. He's smiling at me, and I want to tell him that it's because of her, without her death and her need for flair and drama, I never would have been the love of anyone's life.

"Worth every penny, November," he says softly, eyes looking misty, because he was right, and I can feel her ghost tapping excitedly on my shoulders.

Sebastian clears his throat and tips his chin back up the stairs. They turn, and I know I'm supposed to follow, but I take one more look at Ethan.

He's sprinting up and down the side of the field, and I watch his ankles carefully. I see his calf muscle strain and twitch, and I watch the way his arms pump back and forth.

I breathe in the same air that he is, and I tip my head to the side, feeling those manicured fingers for just a moment longer before they whisper by and disappear.

Chapter Thirty-Five

In the end, it wasn't even close to a million. Christian seemed decidedly less angry when Sebastian pulled out a checkbook. He smoothed it all over with the same smile I had seen his sister use countless times.

I don't know how much it cost him, and he didn't seem to mind when he folded the checkbook back into the pocket of his suit. I didn't think people still carried checkbooks, but it was something both his father and grandfather used to do.

Christian left us alone in a dark hallway, seemingly warming to me now that I was the proclaimed great love of his number one revenue stream's life.

We're beneath the stadium right outside the locker rooms because apparently Ethan requested I be delivered right to him. I usually would have scolded him, told him not to be so fucking demanding, but I didn't want to be parted from Ethan for a moment longer than necessary.

Sebastian leans against the concrete wall, eyes surveying his surroundings and hands shoved into his pockets again.

I look up at him and smile, a real smile. One with the teeth my parents randomly paid for, and I mean every second. Every single strain of the muscle. It's called the Zygomaticus major, the one that makes you smile. An absolutely horrific name when you compare it to the name of the person who makes it even possible for the muscle to function in the first place.

I tilt my chin up at him. "I'll write you a check for whatever that cost you."

Sebastian's lips pull into a rueful sort of smile, and he shakes his head. "It's good business. Advertising outside our usual market. One of the most watched teams in Europe right here."

I shake my head at him. "You don't run some sort of delivery company."

He tips his head down, hands staying tucked in the somehow still freshly pressed suit. "Nothing wrong with advertising to diverse audiences."

Sebastian smiles, staring intently at me. "It was worth it, November. I don't want—I don't want to lose you, too. She's gone, but we were friends, too. I can't think of anything I'd love more than to have you in my life." His voice is low and earnest.

Sebastian probably took all the humility genes in the womb, leaving nothing for his sister. The thought makes me smile because Arna wouldn't stoop to ask anyone for anything, but I know she's thrilled—chin tipped up and saying our budding friendship is just another thing we can add to the list of what's owed to her.

I nod and smile at him because I mean it. A new friend sounds nice. "She was my best friend. The other love of my life."

Sebastian tips his chin, like he's gesturing to everything around us, to the very thing that the stadium contains. Like slabs of concrete could ever contain all that Ethan is. "This mean I'll be seeing you more often?"

"I hope so," I answer, my words honest and bare.

He clears his throat—and there it is again—that grief, that insurmountable sadness. "I don't know what those letters say, and I don't think I want to know. But whatever it is, whatever she did...she loves you, November. I hope you can find it in your heart, to hold space for that. To one day—"

"She led me to him," I interrupt and wipe my eyes. "I'll work on it. Forgiving her."

I hear a laugh, one of triumph somewhere just beyond us and this world that we're in; and then, I can see her—nose tipped up and lips pursed, the haughty set of her features.

Sebastian's shoulders slump, and then he's hugging me, rubbing my back, and it's such a Pavlides' gesture that I'm less frozen than usual. I can feel his throat move against the side of my head. "If you're staying, I'll have your bags sent from the jet."

"She's staying."

I turn, and I can't breathe because I've seen Ethan in many states. I've seen him sour, rude, and dry. I've seen him when he's inebriated and his cheeks get softer than usual, those gray eyes just a dull, hazy sky. I've seen him when he's coming, shoulders and neck tense and eyes glazed over. That's when his eyes are an endlessly cloudy sky you would be happy to suffocate in.

But I've never seen him like this. I'm so proud of him, this version of him, that I could die right here. I can tell he's freshly showered, even though there's no wet hair curling against the nape of his neck. I just know because I know all the versions of Ethan. But he's in a suit, not unlike the color of Sebastian's; and his tattooed arms—my tattoo—are covered, but I can see my number eight on his left thumb. I can see the whirls of ink that start on the back of his right hand. There's a bag slung over his shoulder, and he looks back, holding the door open for a teammate.

Ethan shakes his head, answering whatever was said before the door opened. "Nah. More important places to be."

Gray eyes flick up, and they're on me. "Speaking of. See you, yeah? Sorry about those extra windsprints."

He's on me in a second, and he doesn't seem to care that Sebastian is standing right here.

My back is against the concrete wall, body caged in between his arms, and the cold stone against the back of my exposed legs. I didn't have it in me to care that I was only wearing frayed jean shorts and a t-shirt, and everyone else around me is in a suit; I just wanted to get here.

"We've got unfinished business, you and me." Ethan stares down at me, and even though it's not there anymore, my fingers reach up and brush his forehead, twisting an invisible lock of hair.

"We do?" I ask, eyes tracing those full lips and the tiny, white scar there.

"Yeah. Me. You. My bed. We can talk afterward if you're amenable," Ethan says, voice low.

"I'm amenable." My voice is small, but my eyes rake over him, taking in every single part of him, all the space he occupies here in this world and in my heart.

Sebastian clears his throat, and Ethan rolls his neck, glancing sideways and leveling Sebastian with a look.

"Sorry mate. Ten and I have lots to discuss. Lots of ground to cover."

Sebastian's eyebrows come together, and his gaze flicks down to Ethan's forearm, the one with the brand new tattoo that's in photographs all over the stadium. He looks back at me, lips pulling into a smile while nodding softly.

"Don't be rude," I chide, but all of the love and affection I hold in my chest for Ethan spills into my voice anyway.

"I am rude." Ethan's voice drops again, and his eyes are back on me.

If I turn my head, I could brush his hand with my lips where it's still caging me in.

I narrow my eyes at him and jerk my chin. "This is Sebastian. He made a very generous donation to your organization to get me here."

Ethan's lips crack into a grin, and he finally pushes off the wall. But not before he cups my cheek with his hand, thumb brushing over the bone.

"I can write you a check for that, yeah?" He turns and swipes a hand over his hair, maybe brushing that same invisible curl I had been playing with earlier.

Sebastian smiles politely, but not before his eyes move to me with a look that somehow borders on amused and loving at the same time. He shakes his head, holding out a hand for Ethan. "No need. I consider it an investment."

Ethan grabs his hand, shaking it before tipping his head toward me. "You get her here?"

Sebastian twists his lips to the side, and he shakes his head again. "No. She got herself here."

He turns to me and holds his arms out.

I walk into them and bury my head in his chest. We stay here, hugging until I look up at him, smile watery. "Thank you. I'll call you, we can…"

Sebastian nods, a wistful sort of smile pulling on his lips before he drops his chin to my head. "Call me. We'll get together."

I think I feel a third set of arms around us. Just for a moment.

And then they're gone.

Chapter Thirty-Six

I think I fell in love with Ethan somewhere in the middle—around the time he traded plates with me. I stopped looking at his implant and started looking at the full curve of his lips, my eyes still tracing the scar there but generally spending more time wanting to run my tongue over it. I loved him when he traded plates with me, eyes never straying far from the game he was watching on TV. I loved the way he looked, bringing a dark bottle of beer to his lips, sitting at a much-too-small table on a crowded street in Hanoi. I even loved the way he played soccer with those kids on the beach right after we met, even though I'm not particularly maternal. I liked the way his face lit up. It was all still rough, sharp edges, but his eyes looked like the night sky.

And I loved him, I loved him, I loved him in that tiny beach town where I broke both our hearts.

But I don't think I've ever loved him the way I do right now.

He's laying beside me, the arm with my tattoo propped up against the side of the round, wicker daybed we're sharing that sits on his rooftop. I can see the London skyline just beyond his profile, but somehow all those lights, those famous landmarks, they all pale in comparison to the way his cheek muscles pulse and the stubble lining his jaw looks darker under the night sky. He looks sharper, harder, with shorter hair. He's drumming his fingers against the wicker armrest.

I watch, tipping my own head as he leans his neck back against the ivory pillows that are stacked here.

The exposed brick of the rooftop is worn, and I can reach out a hand and run my fingers along it. But I think I'd rather run them along Ethan's face. Lights are strung above us, moving lightly in the breeze. Potted plants line the edges of the rooftop, and they look well cared for. I know he's not watering them, and I know how disastrously messy he is, so I'm sure a housekeeper comes up here daily to keep the towering palms vibrant and their leaves smooth and waxy.

Some sort of white, retro outdoor cooler on wheels is shoved against the wall, lined up symmetrically, and I know Ethan would have just shoved it haphazardly against a wall somewhere. A patterned, loom rug lines the whole space, and it's surprisingly soft underfoot.

I can hear some of the noises of the city, the occasional rise of a voice above the din, the lapping of water from what Ethan told me was called a basin, not a river, nearby.

But it's just us out here.

He's twirling the bottle of beer by the neck, the way I've seen him do so many times I could probably tell you in exactly what order his ligaments and muscles contract to do so. His lips part when he rolls his neck against the tower of cushions to look at me. His voice is low when he speaks, all the rough, gravelly promise from earlier gone. He sounds sad now. "What are you really doing here, November?"

My heart hurts because I hurt him, and I shift in my seat to sit up. I cross my legs, covering my knees, and the rough denim of my worn shorts feels too scratchy beneath my palms.

"I saw you on TV." I shrug, studying him. "You were playing soccer, and the commentators were talking about your new tattoo. I dropped this strawberry, and then I realized the tattoo was for me."

I reach forward and pull his arm toward me. I doubt I would be strong enough to pull Ethan to sitting, not when he's one-hundred and eighty pounds of dense muscle mass. According to a quick internet search, I learned he's unusually muscular for a soccer player. They're all lean, taut muscle, but Ethan is broader and more imposing than the usual make, apparently.

He follows as I pull him up, thumbs now whispering over the edges of the new tattoo. I trace the script, the edges of the rest of the piece, a bungalow floating above the water, and my index finger skates over his veins and across the dusting of hair to find the letters. I loop my finger over them and spell it out. The tenth month. November. Me.

"Dropped a strawberry, did you? That send you running back to me?" Ethan whispers.

He's left the bottle of beer on the arm of the bed, and his other hand has found my thigh, dropped there like this is so natural. Like we sit here in this life together casually, and we touch all the time.

"No," I shake my head. "I was wrong. I chose wrong. I didn't read the rest of the letters, except for the last one. To say goodbye. I gave them back to Sebastian. I'd choose differently this time, if you let me."

"You didn't have to give the letters back." Ethan is quiet, and I'm still holding his arm, but his fingers have wrapped gently around my wrist. "I shouldn't have given you an ultimatum. It didn't have to be me or her. There's room for both of us."

"But it was," I offer through a whisper, heavy with thick tears. "And I picked wrong. I'd pick you any day. You're not easy to leave, Ethan. You never were." He looks pensive as he blinks at me, nodding ever so slightly, like he's thinking. So I keep talking because I would throw myself onto my knees and beg for him if I needed to. "What can I do to fix this?"

Ethan's eyebrows knit, and he shakes his head, hand finally leaving my thigh and gripping my chin. "Nothing. It's fixed. You're here, love. I'm just trying to figure out if you're going to stay. I was about three days from showing up at your doorstep, anyway. I just had to see if I could do it, see if I could play again like I used to, see if I could get it all back. But it wasn't really worth anything because you weren't here. Can't have it all if I don't have you."

A wet laugh bubbles in my throat, and the tears slip past my waterline and start tracking down my cheeks. I wipe at them like a child would, one hand still clutching his arm.

"And if you aren't going to stay, then I'll come home with you, yeah?"

My eyes flick up, and I can tell he means it. If I said I was going home, he would walk away from it all. "You don't usually get a second shot at your dream, Ethan."

His smile splits, and it's so fucking radiant I could die. I don't even see the stupid tower, or the dumb bridge that's meant to be a feat of engineering just behind him. His thumb caresses my chin. "Got a new dream, Ten. I told you."

"I've never been anyone's dream," I answer.

It's kind of pathetic, but it's honest. I was never my parent's dream, and I never meant enough to anyone else. I feel childlike and small, and my shoulders curve inward a bit, but Ethan is still smiling at me.

"You're mine, yeah?"

"I love you," I say, and I think I can see his cracked up, broken heart sew itself back together behind his eyes.

"Love of my life, sweetheart." Ethan moves closer to me, and I watch his muscles tense under his shirt. It's just one of those plain black cotton ones he favors, but I want to rub my cheek across it.

One hand is still gripping my chin, and he takes the other arm from my grasp, wrapping it around my waist. I can feel the muscles pressing against my back when he hoists me up to sit on his lap.

My legs wrap around him instinctually because I think my body remembers that Ethan Barclay is its greatest friend and ally. It was made for him, and he was made for it.

A groan comes from his throat when my thighs tense slightly, and his palm splays across my back. His hips roll up slightly, and I can feel him between my legs.

"About that unfinished business, Nov…" He moves his lips to the side of my face and over my ear, perfect teeth grazing it. "I might very well die if I don't get inside you, yeah?"

I don't think I've ever whimpered in my life, and I was certainly never a screamer before I met him. But Ethan has turned me into both because I feel one rise in my throat. I feel the column of his throat move, rough with laughter, and his hips flex upward again. That makes me tip my head back because I can feel him, and it already feels like this, so I can only imagine what it will be like when it's finally just us; just our skin touching and nothing to separate our bodies that were meant for one another.

"Gotta hear you say yes, sweetheart." He bites at my neck and pushes me against him with his palm.

I should take a moment to tell him not to be so fucking full of himself, that he hasn't reduced me to some breathless, sex-addled woman who desperately wants to be fucked by him with just a few rolls of his hips—but I think he has because the word slips from my mouth anyway. "Yes."

He stills, and his teeth actually sink into my neck momentarily before he pushes me backward, a hand now cradling my head as he lays me down right in front of the pillows. My legs are still wrapped around him, and he flexes against me again with a grin because the same noise rises in my throat. Both forearms come down on either side of my head, and he's hovering over me.

I miss those wayward curls, when his unkempt hair would fall forward onto his forehead when he had been like this over top of me.

My arms are wrapped around his neck, and I never want to let him go.

"I miss your longer hair," I whisper against his lips that hover right above mine.

"I'll grow it back." Ethan groans against my neck, all his muscles seemingly tight with whatever restraint he has left because he seems seconds away from panting. "I need to fuck you now, Ten. Been a long few months with just my hand. Say yes again, one more time for me."

I bring my hand to the back of his neck and pull his lips to mine, taking the full bottom one with my teeth. I nod, the word mumbled and almost intelligible, but it's good enough for Ethan.

His hands, my favorite hands in the world, push off the bed so he's sitting back on his heels. He reaches behind his head and tears off his shirt. I don't see where it lands because seeing his skin like this again, tattoos stark against it when it's not as tanned as I'm used to seeing it, makes me want to erupt already.

My hands are scrambling to bring him closer, pulling at his back because I need to touch every single inch of his skin.

His hands move to undo my shorts with equal fervor. There's no restraint between us, and he practically rips them off my body, leaving me completely bare because he's ripped my underwear off, too. He pulls me up, breathing heavily as his hands snake under my shirt, gently pulling it up over my head before he tosses that behind him. One thumb scores down the curves of my chest, through the thin lace covering one peaked nipple. I tip my head back, lips parting.

His mouth is on me now, roving my chest, and I can feel his teeth on my ribcage, and then my hip bones, and my body sings because it recognizes the feel of him.

I can see the London skyline, but I can feel his tongue against me.

One of his hands presses my hips down, and the other grips under my thigh.

For the first time, I'm not seeing my body, I don't even care, because I'm looking at him. The way his shoulders tense, his back muscles roll, and his mouth moves against me. And then his gray eyes flick up, and he sees me looking at him, lips parted and tiny, panting breaths. I prop myself up on my elbows, so I can see him more clearly.

I feel him grin against me, and that's all it takes.

He's devouring me, and my head tips back. I'm trying not to be loud because we're in a residential area, but I can't help it because no one gives an orgasm like Ethan Barclay. I want more, and I want all the ones he has to give for the rest of my life.

I might have said it out loud because a rough laugh sounds from Ethan as his lips trail my inner thigh, kissing lightly and nipping my skin.

He pushes up to sit up between my legs, one hand still pressing me down, the other raking across his shorter hair. I watch his chest rise and fall, skin taut and unmarred by ink, because it all ends right as his deltoids tucks into his broad chest.

"More, sweetheart?" He cocks his head, grinning down at me, and I think I see lightning flash in the storms that live in his eyes. "Didn't give you enough?"

"It's never going to be enough with you," I whisper, and I'm surprised to find my eyes watering. But it's true. I love him, I love him, I love him.

The thunderstorms in those eyes clear, and suddenly I'm looking at the brightest sky I've ever seen.

His grin, all feral delight from earlier, changes. Those full lips are soft now, but they're still curving upward. I can see the scar just above his top lip on the left side, and I want to run my tongue along it the same way I want to kiss the smile he's giving me. I want the imprint of his lips on mine forever. I should sit up and do that, kiss him, tell him I love him, I love him, I love him. But I can't stop staring at him.

His hand grips my hip momentarily before his fingers release and my skin misses him already. His tattooed fingers undo his own pants, and before he kicks them off, throwing them to the side, followed by the unmistakable sound of foil and those annoyingly bright color condom wrappers always are flash between his fingers, and he tosses it down beside me on the daybed.

I arch an eyebrow at him. "Presumptuous, aren't we?"

"We are." Ethan's voice is rough, and his lips are parted. His chest is still moving up and down, but his eyes never leave mine.

We've been naked around each other before, even less than this really because I'm still in my lace bra. At this point, I would have usually wrapped a sheet around myself, gotten under any available bedding, but there is none because we're on Ethan's rooftop, so it's just us, the city lights, and the sound of our hearts in our chest. And I don't mind.

You might think being this naked, this exposed, would be something to make me shy, nervous even. Or make me revert back to the version of myself who thinks she needs to be covered up, who thinks her body isn't enough. But he's looking at me, and I feel so beautiful. I feel perfect. I feel at home.

Ethan cocks his head, and he's on his knees in front of me on the daybed. One hand finds my thigh, and his tattooed thumb strokes my skin, gently, reverently. Lovingly. We're staring at one another, and the condom is sitting right there, but I don't think either of us want to look away in case this moment somehow disappears.

"I'm not going anywhere," I whisper, because I didn't answer his question earlier.

"I'd follow you if you did," he answers honestly. I watch him roll his shoulders, before his eyes rove over me and his breathing is harsh and labored. "Nov..."

"What are you waiting for?" My voice is teasing, but there's nothing funny here.

Ethan's lips pull to the side, and he reaches down, twirling the wrapper like he does everything he holds, before he rips it open.

I'm still watching him as he rolls the condom down onto himself. Usually this is the part when I would look away. Not because I thought it was awkward or weird. Protection was just a necessary fact. But it didn't really do anything for me. But I think everything Ethan does, does something for me.

Both those hands find the underside of my knees now, and he pulls me forward ever so slightly, a knee knocking my legs open just a bit farther. My hands reach up on their own accord as he's lowering himself down over me, one arm coming to rest beside my face, the whirls of ink right beside me now. I trace them with my fingers before my hand lands to grip his shoulder, the other snaking around the back of his neck.

"Think I've been waiting for you my whole life," he says, lips brushing mine and eyes entirely focused on me.

His other hand is between us, scoring right down the center of me briefly—my back arches, and another noise that never existed in my life before him sounds from my throat when he pushes into me.

He stills for a moment, a low sound catching in his throat. My nails sink into his shoulders when his forehead presses to mine. He's suspended just for a moment in time, and I'm about to beg him to move, for anything, because I don't think I can take it for a second longer; this feeling of him inside of me—when he flexes his hips.

I arch my back and press my chest into him as my nails dig in farther. And then I know for certain that our bodies were made for one another—his body loves mine like a best friend, loves it like the way my heart loves his heart—because it's so fucking perfect.

I can see his fingers grip the pillow beside me, the cords of muscle all the way down his forearm flexing when he rolls his hips again. His breathing is rough, but so is mine; I'm all tiny panting breaths now, my fingers scrambling to grip his hair, raking down his back, across the muscles of his chest. Ethan's mouth is all over me, across my earlobe, down my throat and the column of my neck. His teeth graze my collarbone, and they find my chest again, his tongue moving over the thin lace fabric of the bra that never came off. He's moving against me, in me, and I move with him, because I was made for him.

Those tiny breaths turn louder, and I can see Ethan's eyes flash. His breath is ragged because his hand has moved between us now, and he's touching me while he's thrusting into me. I'm much too loud. His hand gripping the pillow finds its way to cover my mouth, covering the sounds, but it doesn't matter because a noise catches in his throat when my teeth graze his palm.

His teeth sink into my shoulder as he comes—my nails dig into his skin, my legs wrap tighter around his waist, my eyes never leave his, and my heart finds its way to his hands.

Chapter Thirty-Seven

I broke our hearts in a tiny town on the west coast of Costa Rica, and we sewed them back together on a rooftop in Shoreditch.

I'm on top of Ethan now, painting the lines of his tattoos with my fingertips. His hands are on my hips, fingers drumming against my skin in a much more relaxed imitation of what they were doing moments ago—gripping me and moving my hips in sync with his. He's smiling up at me, and it's a lazy grin I want to tattoo somewhere on my body.

My fingers pause on the still-raised edges of his new tattoo. "When did you get this?"

"Bout the second I got home. Kind of went on the lash and paid a stupid amount of money for the artist to do that while I was piss drunk." Ethan's fingers are still brushing my skin, and he's gripping my hips more intently now. "It's my favorite one."

I smile down at him. "Well, the rest are kind of meaningless, abstract objects, so I can understand why that would be."

He raises his eyebrows, and his grin shifts to wry. It's a joke—his biggest accomplishments are found in those whirls of ink.

"Pretty fucking sexy when you're impertinent," he says, voice low. His eyes get hazy, and his jaw tenses when they track over my collarbone, over the black lace still covering my chest.

His fingers tighten, and I feel his hips shift underneath me. "You can't seriously be ready to go again."

"I could, yeah. Professional athlete, remember? Incomparable stamina." Ethan tips his chin at me and raises his eyebrows before he sits up suddenly, wrapping his arms around my back so I don't tip over. He rests his chin on top of my head, and my face is buried in his neck. His skin is warm, previously sweat-slicked because we've been out here touching everywhere and having sex off and on almost all night. "But I'm actually fucking famished. You've worked up my appetite. I'll order us something, yeah?"

"I'm hungry too," I answer quietly, lips pressed against his skin. And I am. Fucking starving.

Ethan pulls back, peering down at me. "What would you like?"

I shrug. He knows I can never decide on food, but for the first time, I don't think it's for any sort of nefarious reason. It's because I don't think I care. "Whatever your big, tough, professional athlete muscles need to refuel is fine with me."

He cocks an eyebrow, grinning at me. "Refuel? You wanna go for round four? Break a record your first night in London?"

"I've been to London before," I tell him.

And I have. A few times with Arna and her family before her parents died, once when we were twenty-two before I started dental school, and for a conference two years ago. I know that's not what he means, whether

I've ever set foot in the city before. First night implies *many*. Multiple. A lifetime full of nights here in this city with him.

"If you're about to tell me you came here for a wild weekend with Arna when you were twenty and shagged some fucking bloke, and it was hitherto the best night of your life—"

"No," I shake my head, offering him a small smile. "The best night of my life is the night I met you."

It's not the way his eyes look when he's joking, or the way his hands feel as they pass over my shoulder blades, or the way my legs feel wrapped around him. It is all those things and more, but what really makes me say it, is the way he says Arna's name. The way her manicured fingers are noticeably absent from my shoulders, that there's no ghost whispering at me. I think my bones are regrowing new life now. Her poisonous vines are dead, and new, fresh flowers bloom in their wake.

"The night you got stuck with a drunk stranger who put the Texas Chainsaw Massacre on the TV, and you prattled on all night about how to identify human remains? That one? That's your best night?" Ethan sounds like he's joking, but I can see it in the way his smile isn't just a grin, the way it stretches across his face, and how bright those eyes look. He's happy.

"Undoubtedly the best. Ranked number one of all time," I offer, raising my eyebrows at him.

"Well, let's go for round four after we eat, and I'll top that one for you, yeah?" He presses his lips to my forehead before I feel his arms tense around me, one staying to secure me and the other wrapping around my waist as he stands. "Feet on the ground, Ten."

I unwrap my legs, hopping off Ethan, my hands never leaving his shoulders, but my eyes finally leave his. We've been horizontal all night, and I was too busy looking at him to look anywhere else when we came up here.

"Wow," I whisper, eyes tracking the London skyline, all the lights and towering buildings and everything I didn't notice, not really, because I was too busy looking at him. "You've got quite the view here."

"Paid enough for it," Ethan answers, and I feel him tap on my left knee.

I finally look away, and he's holding my underwear out for me to step into.

His thumbs trace the curve of my calves, up to my thighs before his hands land on my waist as he brings them back up. He's smiling up at me, and it's a lazy sort of grin—like we do this all the time. And I want to. I want this, this life with him.

"Big signing bonus for a returning superstar? A little birdy told me today that your jersey is the number one seller amongst women aged 18-30." I laugh, watching as he repeats the process with my discarded denim shorts.

When they're back in place, Ethan stands, towering over me, still grinning down at me when his fingers start buttoning them back up. "Heard the same rumor myself, but unfortunately for them, no space left on either of my arms for tattoos about anyone else."

"What about on your chest or your back?" I ask, my fingertips grazing where each tattoo ends on his deltoids, down his broad chest, and they find their way to his back.

Ethan shakes his head. "Chest and everything in it is all full of you, and the skin on my back is exclusively for your fingernails to rake down."

I'm not a particularly bashful person, I never have been, but my nose wrinkles, and I can feel my cheeks heat.

Ethan bends down to grab my shirt before raising my arms above my head to pull it back over me. "That chuff you up a bit, babe?"

I laugh because it sounds the same as when those girls tried to distract him, back before I broke his heart and even afterward. There's still nothing that would take him away from me. "My sense of self-importance is high enough, Ethan."

He disappears from view for a moment when the white t-shirt is pulled down over my eyes. But then he's back shirtless, and somehow, he looks more luminous than ever against the silhouette of the London skyline.

"You're right. Don't need anything making that head with that big brain any bigger." He wraps his hand around the back of my head and drops his lips to my forehead for a too-brief moment before searching the rooftop for his abandoned clothes.

Watching Ethan Barclay undress, watching him do anything really, is probably as close to a spiritual experience as I've ever had. But watching him put his clothes back on—watching how quickly those muscles that make up the entirety of him flex and tense when he pulls his shirt down; how his abdominal muscles really seem like they were painted on, but I know they're not because I've had my hands and mouth all over them; how his fingers move deftly to do up his shorts—watching him when he's coming back together after being entirely undone. This might be my favorite him.

He holds a hand out to me, and I take it; my smaller—perfect for my line of work—hand entirely engulfed by his with all his tattoos and all that they mean. He stops at the cooler pushed against the wall, free hand opening it and grabbing two bottles of beer. I watch as he pops them open on the side of the cooler, the bottlecaps falling down into a little holder.

"Thank you for not using your teeth." I arch an eyebrow as he hands one to me. The juxtaposition of Ethan's warm, oversized hand in one and the cold, sweating glass in my other hand is so at odds, but it's a feeling I want for the rest of my life.

He glances at me sideways and winks when he brings the bottle near his lips. "Never again, Ten." He tugs on my hand to follow him down the stairs, back into his too big, too empty apartment.

It's almost as beautiful here as the boy who lives in it. The worn, exposed brick walls in every room are my favorite. I always wanted one of those original, hard lofts back in Toronto. Ethan's even has a bookcase that spans an entire wall in the living room. It's sparsely populated with worn paperbacks, haphazardly stacked on top of one another in seemingly no particular order—photographs of Ethan and various teams he's played on, or championships he's won over the years, and two different soccer balls propped up on stands.

I can feel his eyes on me as I look at the shelves, bringing my own drink to my lips.

"Room for all your textbooks and accolades there, if you'd like." His voice is low again, tentative even.

I eye Ethan and smile at him, pressing the bottle to my lips for a moment before answering. "You don't have enough shelves, Barclay."

A grin spreads across his face, and he squeezes my hand. "Suppose not. I'll build you more, yeah?"

"Well, don't rush on my account. I won't be adding anything to the shelf for some time to come. I can't just pick up and start practicing here. There's a whole host of things I need to do to—"

"You're staying?" Ethan cuts me off, bringing our joined hands to his lips and kissing the back of mine before he grins against it.

I narrow my eyes at him and pretend I'm put out because he likes me when I'm ornery, even though I feel less abrasive than I ever have in my entire life. "Did you not hear me earlier? I said I would."

He's still grinning, and I feel his teeth against my hand when he speaks. "Thought maybe the sex was too good, might have scared you away. Just couldn't take that much, yeah?"

"You want to talk about having a big head?" I pluck my hand from his and raise my eyebrows at him.

I turn back toward the living room before dropping onto the worn, cognac leather sectional.

Ethan drops beside me, pulling his phone from his pocket. "We should carb up, yeah? What about..." he thumbs through his phone. "Vietnamese?"

"Do you remember—" I'm about to ask him if he remembers that trip being the moment, the place everything changed. It was when I stopped staring at his implant and started fantasizing about his lips.

"Yeah yeah, where you naffed that blond Australian. Still not a fan." Ethan's lips turn down, and he waves his hand at me, like he can wave that whole night away.

But I don't really want to. The sex wasn't good, especially in comparison to what anything was like with Ethan. But I never want to forget because it was the first night we chose to share a bed.

"You were the one who suggested it." I arch an eyebrow at him, watching as he continues to thumb across the screen of his phone through the menu.

"Because I was falling in love with you and was trying to pretend I wasn't." Ethan looks away from his phone for a moment, and I wait for him to grin, for any of the usual arrogance or dry irreverence to bleed through. But it never comes, and I think I can see his heart in his eyes.

"Well, to be honest, it wasn't very good," I whisper, reaching out and brushing my thumb across his top lip, pausing at the scar.

"Can't imagine it would have been." He presses his lips to my thumb briefly before holding up the phone. "Fancy anything in particular?"

I shake my head, hand finding his shoulder as I shift to sit closer to him on the couch. I think I'm meant for him exactly like this, too—the crooks of our bodies melding seamlessly together. "I don't care, you pick."

And I mean it. I can feel his eyes on me when I drop my head to his shoulder, tossing my legs over his. It's like we sit here, in this exact spot, in this exact apartment, all the time. Made for one another.

I watch his tattooed thumb flip through the menu, and I brush the number eight with my index finger. I think eight might be my lucky number. That I might be lucky, so unbelievably fucking lucky.

Of all the beds I've shared with Ethan, this one is my favorite. Slate gray sheets that brush against all my exposed skin and pool between my legs, too many feather pillows propped up against the exposed brick wall behind us, one floor-to-ceiling paned window open across the room, a record playing on a vintage wooden turntable in the corner, and too many open takeout containers to count.

But it's Ethan sitting beside me, shirt discarded and bare, save for a pair of sweatshorts. One leg propped up, elbow resting on it, hand holding chopsticks and twirling the noodles from the bowl that his other hand holds.

It's Ethan, and all that he is, sitting beside me here in his home, that makes it my forever favorite bed.

I was content before Arna died. Content to live my life. Content to be in my corner of the world. Cleaning and fixing teeth, spending more time with dead bodies than alive ones.

And then she died. She stopped living, stopped breathing, and she wanted me to live, really live. To go on without her.

But I'm not sure Arna even knew what it meant to be alive. Not really. Not like this.

Because this—takeout food with him in this bed that used to belong to him but now belongs to us while music plays in the background, and I can hear the sounds of the city through the open window, but they're so far away because the only thing I can really hear is his heart—I think this is living. This is life.

"Is this what life can be like?" I tip my head to the side, a small smile pulling on the corners of my mouth.

Ethan's eyes flick up, and I watch his lips turn down. There's this wild misconception because of a very factually inaccurate saying that it only takes one muscle to smile and forty-seven to frown. Neither are factual. It's actually debated, and it really depends on who you're talking to. But you're commonly looking at three main muscle groups to drop your lower lip and turn the corners of your mouth down. And even then, facial expressions are so subjective.

Even though the muscles he needs to frown have moved, I know Ethan isn't frowning. I can see it in his eyes. He's studying me, his brain is moving, and I want to know what he's thinking.

The flowers in my bones, the ones that have bloomed in the bronchi of my lungs because of him unfurl their petals, waiting to be watered by whatever is percolating behind those eyes.

But when he speaks, he's not just watering the flowers he grew. He bathes all of me in sunlight. "Our life can be whatever you want it to be, November."

How many different kinds of love are there?

How lucky am I to have had more than one great love?

Three Months Later

I have a new favorite sound. It used to be the whir of a tiny drill, or the silence in my head that would follow—when the world would go quiet.

But now it's Friday mornings. It's the noise from Ethan's game tape that carries down the hall through our cracked open door because he gets up earlier than me to watch it. It's the espresso machine, but more than that it's the swearing I can hear because he can never fit the arm into the tray. His accent is more pronounced, but his voice is still sleepy and rough because it's early morning.

It's Ethan walking down the hallway and the way he leans in the doorway and cocks his head to grin at me. It's the way his eyes linger on my shoulders, my collarbone when I sit up to accept the mug he always hands me. It's the way he wraps his hand around the back of my head to bring his lips to my forehead, and the way his tattooed thumb strokes my cheek not once but twice, before he drops back into bed beside me.

Those movements of the human body, those eyes sweeping across me, and the way his lips turn upward just for me don't make any noise. But I can hear them all. I hear all the words they whisper to me, and I feel them all the way down to my heart.

They tell me he's in love with me, and I'm in love with him.

Ethan tips his head back, another lazy smile stretching across his face. He likes watching me drink coffee in the morning. He says it's one of the only times my face looks soft, utterly content and at peace. He says he thinks I must look like this when I'm folded over someone, looking down at a particularly difficult extraction, cheeks all pillowy and eyes big behind my loupes. It's been a few months that I've been removed entirely from cavities and less than favorable root canals.

"Ready for your exam today, yeah? Baby's going to be in mouths other than mine in no time." Ethan's voice is the crescendo on the perfect symphony of noises and sounds that make up my Friday mornings now.

My licensing exam is this afternoon. I've spent the last three months studying, even though I really don't have to because I know everything that would be on the exam the same way I've mapped all of Ethan's body. I know how to draw his tattoos with my eyes closed. But it was fun to sit in the living room that belonged to both of us now, all the textbooks spread out and dental models and jaw bones in our hands while Ethan laughed and eventually grabbed one of those textbooks, the way the anatomy and procedural names sounded in his accent would make me smile. And then we would be kissing, touching, and fucking overtop of all those textbooks that cost way too much money.

I take a sip of my coffee. Ethan makes me a latte every morning because I'm trying non-fat milk now. He learned how to make them for me. I usually prefer my coffee black, but it's something my therapist suggested, and his smile while I took the first sip was the final note from the orchestra of his heart.

"It's weird, when you say it like that. The parts of my...anatomy that spend time in your mouth aren't quite the same."

The scar above his lip stretches, and it's my favorite against his sleep-worn skin in the morning. Five stitches after the last world cup from a soccer ball to the face; I've seen the video now. "Yeah yeah, you nervous?"

"No." I raise my eyebrows at him and bring the mug to my lips. It's true. I'm not nervous.

He smiles at me, and his voice is quiet when he speaks, "Little weirdo."

It sounds different, when he says it.

Sometimes we just stare at each other, like we are right now. Sometimes when we do, one of us will stick our palms out to play a game, any game really. But sometimes, we just look. That's what we're doing right now. Like neither of us can believe that we ended up here.

"Porro asked if his new girlfriend could have your number, yeah? Said she was nervous about going to the match alone on Sunday." Ethan's hand cups my knee, the picture of casual, and it is because we touch like this all the time now.

"Sure. Give him my number." I smile at him, and I mean it.

I've made friends with a lot of his teammates and their partners. It wasn't ever something I would have pictured for myself. But it fits. I started going to his games alone, and I loved that, too. But I loved it even more when he introduced me to some of them, and I stopped sitting by myself.

Ethan's smile when he found me sitting in one of the boxes with all his teammates' partners long after the game ended is one of my favorite memories. I even see some of them on other days. I waited for it, you know. For their smile not to quite reach their eyes after I told them what

I did for a living, said something off-putting and macabre or just weird in general, waited for them to not understand me, to not be seen, because I thought the only friend who ever saw me was dead and gone. But it never came. It's just been fun.

"Rest day tomorrow. How should we celebrate your big, brilliant brain?" Ethan asks and cocks his head.

His schedule varies, but he typically has a rest day on day two and day six of the week. The rest are all training, or game days, and sometimes both together. He sees a physiotherapist a few times a week to make sure he doesn't reinjure himself.

I love all days with him, but rest days are my favorite. He's shown me everything he loves about this city and his life here. He's taken me out to meet his parents. His original commentary turned out to be true. They do live in the countryside, in this big, foreboding stone house that borders being a mansion, and they are a bit uppity. But they were kind, and their smiles reached their eyes.

We've stayed in bed all day, taking the idea of rest day literally: me with a textbook propped up on my knees, napping off and on between movie marathons with Ethan beside me, typically icing his muscles. And we've done the opposite of rest, spending the days touching each other and having more sex than is probably medically recommended.

Raising my eyebrows, I pat the minimal space beside us on the bed. "Rest. There's a new documentary I want to watch on Netflix."

"Can't wait to see you get all hot and bothered over some bones." Ethan grins at me, and even though it's not a documentary about bones, not even close (it's about crocodiles), I don't correct him.

He leans in, hand leaving my knee and finding my chin. "I gotta get going. But you'll call me when you're done with your exam, yeah? You'll be brilliant, Ten."

I nod and tip my chin up, waiting for his lips to find mine. And they do. It's just a brush—but all those stacks of kindling Ethan's lips have left ready to be lit across my body, along my collarbone, down my ribcage, my hip bones, and along my thighs, ignite at once. I hope these fires burn forever. We stay like that for a moment longer before Ethan pulls away, resting his forehead against mine. His hair has started to grow back, and I can feel the brush of the curls against my own hairline.

"I should get in the shower. I need to look my best for the bars of soap I'll be carving this afternoon," I leave one tiny kiss on the faded scar before pulling back.

Ethan's eyes glint and a smile curves. He looks over my shoulder for a moment, and I know he's eyeing the clock that sits on the nightstand. "I've got time for that."

"Who says you were invited?" I raise my eyebrows and take another sip of my latte before setting it on the nightstand.

He cocks his head back. "Ten. Be serious now."

I tip my chin up at him. "I am serious. Very serious. I have a very important examination this afternoon, and I simply cannot afford to be distracted by—"

Ethan wraps one arm around my waist, throwing me over his shoulder before I even have time to shriek properly, to pull back and to throw a pillow at him like I usually do when he does things like this.

I watch the room—our room—pass by upside down until he kicks open the door to the bathroom.

Ethan drops me, hands gripping the backs of my thighs to steady me on the warm tile. He grins before a tattooed hand fists the neck of his shirt and pulls it over his head. "You're a piece of work, Ten."

This was life in this flat, with the exposed brick and too many soccer balls and my textbooks tipped over on the shelves, with the first dental mold I ever made that Arna broke sitting beside photos of Ethan and me. The past few months scattered in and amongst the pieces of our former lives, what they were before one another. This is life where I try new foods on Fridays, where Ethan holds my hands sitting across from me on therapy couches. This is life with new friends, where I care more about soccer than I care more about almost anything because Ethan is brilliant at it, and I love him. This is life where Sebastian and I reminisce about his sister because we both loved her, too.

This is life with Ethan. This is life without Arna—one whole year without her. This is life where I started to forgive her.

I step out the front door on the ground level, one hand in Ethan's. His hair is matted to his forehead, still sopping wet because he really didn't have time to join me in the shower, nor did he have time to chase me around the apartment, trying to grab my towel, to throw me down onto the bed we share and quiz me on the procedures most likely to come up on my exam and reward me with a kiss each time I answered correctly. I could have been lying; he wouldn't have had a clue, but he claimed I was far too brilliant to lower myself to that level.

He doesn't have time to linger now, but he does. Gray eyes that look exactly like the fall sky above us study me as he pulls my jacket tighter around my shoulders against the cold air. His thumb lingers against my cheek, the number eight pressing right into my skin.

This might have been the life I'd been waiting for, the only one really worth living. The one I wouldn't trade for anything.

This is life in November.

Acknowledgements

Life in November popped into my head after I was stuck on a paddle-board with no fin—and subsequently rescued by two strangers staying in an overwater bungalow.

I'm so thankful I picked the board that didn't have a proper fin, and that I was invited into said beautiful overwater bungalow so I could walk back to the resort. Otherwise, who knows if Ethan and November would ever have come to life. My partner was there too, but for the sake of the story, let's pretend I was all alone just like November was (sorry Ben).

This book is so important to me for so many reasons. November was a safe space for me to explore and unpack the ways that my eating disorder still impacts me, shapes who I am, all these years after recovery. And Ethan was a wonderful way to demonstrate those small, entirely tiny, but infinite ways you can support someone and show them you see them. It was also a mechanism for me to give life to and explore what I think is one of the worst kinds of grief in the world—the loss of a friend or the death of a friendship—and what it means to move through life with someone you always thought would be there. I meant it when I said this book was for you—anyone who has ever lost a friend. I hope you found something in these pages.

So much goes into a book behind the scenes to make it what it is, and I have endless people to thank who gave me their time and energy when I was writing this book, so here it goes.

To my editor, Krys, for your final eyes on this book and all the support you've given me, thank you always for everything you do.

To all my beta readers, Christina, Amy, Amber, Katherine, Esther and Danielle—thank you so much for your time and your energy.

Ben, thank you for always trading plates with me. I love you always, but I love you extra when you do that. You really were the inspiration for Ethan in so many ways, and I feel so lucky to have you.

Esther, I'm so thankful that our commitment to the hatred of the same things that shall not be named brought us together. Who would have known one of my virtual friendships would have become one of the most important in my life? I don't know how I would get through most days without you—but you were a special kind of supportive during the process for this one. Thank you, thank you, thank you, for the endless voice notes, for always answering when I needed to run something by you and for your enduring, endless belief in me and my writing. I don't know where I would be without you, and I can't wait for Maine 2024.

Danielle, I'm so happy Esther forced us together. She really knows what she's doing, and I don't know what I would do without you now. I'm endlessly proud of you and all that you've accomplished and have yet to, but I think I'm even more proud to call you my friend. I couldn't have done this one without you, and I mean that from the bottom of my heart. I got through so much of this because of you. So thank you, thank you, thank you. Weasels for life.

To all the friends I've loved and lost, I'll always wish you well.
And finally, to you, for reading this book.
Always,
Haley

About the Author

Haley has a penchant for messy and complex characters whose lives are as unpredictable as they would be in real life. She aims to bring that authenticity to her writing, and wants nothing more than for her readers to find a home in her characters. Haley lives in Toronto, loves horror movies with a splash of comedy, her dog, and feels most at home in the ocean. Life in November is her fourth novel.